Collingwood Fakeout

A Jack Beer Mystery

This is a work of fiction. All of the characters, organizations,
events and situations portrayed in this novel are
either figments of the author's imagination
or used in a wholly fictitious manner.

Collingwood Fakeout

A FauxPop Media production
Published by FauxPop Media
www.fauxpopmedia.com

Library and Archives Canada Cataloguing in Publication
Hundey, Rick
Collingwood Fakeout : A Jack Beer Mystery / Rick Hundey.
ISBN 978-0-9810588-2-5
I. Title.
PS8615.U53C65 2009   C813'.6   C2009-907028-6

First Edition: November 2009
Printed in Canada

0 9 8 7 6 5 4 3 2 1

For Eric, Tim and Beth

Acknowledgements

All the events and most of the characters in 'Collingwood Fake-out' are fictional, the exception being a reference to Tribute Artist, Roy Leblanc, a particularly talented entertainer whose image appears on the cover of this book. I am deeply grateful to Roy for his generosity in agreeing to let me use this photograph, taken at one of his concerts.

Thanks go to Karen Brown for providing the back cover photo.

Writing requires team-work. I remain appreciative of fellow Huron Writers' group members for their continued support. Ryan Wilkie was meticulous in the manuscript polishing process. Also, thanks go to Luise Hoffman and Cathie Brown, two reviewers whose advice is always invaluable, as is Jane Hundey's, especially with early drafts.

Music plays a big part in this novel, largely because I love tunes from the 1960's and 70's. But my knowledge of the earlier days of rock is both sketchy and biased. So, a nod of thanks is owed to Bob Robilliard, whose recall and opinions were bang on.

Another nod of thanks goes to Wiarton's Don Scott, who helped me with local geography.

Finally, I must not forget Randall Lobb and Mark Hussey who, as principals at Fauxpop.TV, are making creative pursuits possible for me and many others.

PROLOGUE

The door was unlocked.

He turned the handle, eased it open gently, and looked in.

Seeing nothing, he announced himself in a low voice, "Honey?"

Waiting. Expecting a reply.

Hearing nothing, he tried again, louder, "Honey, you here?"

Still no answer.

Uncertain, he stepped into the narrow hallway. A hum, like the drone of traffic, caught his attention. He pushed open the bathroom door on the right. The brightness of the fluorescent lights startled him at first. He flicked the off switch and the hotel suite went silent.

He finished off the hallway in three quick steps. To get it over with.

Where the space opened up, he stopped and scanned the room. Heavy curtains blocked the outside world. A pair of table lamps shed the kind of light meant to induce relaxation, failing miserably.

The bed was made up. Ten feet further stood the coffee table and couch, sitting in front of maroon curtains. Offsetting the couch's black leather cushions, an impossibly white cape took the visitor's attention and held it. Until the noise of a hallway party broke through the stillness.

"Quit fooling around." he said

Twenty seconds later, he tried again, "Honey?"

He took three more steps. And then his eyes locked in to the space between the bed and the couch. Just beyond the coffee table.

"What the hell?"

He stumbled toward the heap on the floor and dropped to two knees, pushing the low table back. He leaned over, trying to see the face. The body was on its right side, face kissing the couch's skirt, head resting on an extended right arm.

He touched the body, gently on the left shoulder, swallowing back a scream. Regaining control, he reached out to take its right wrist, acting instinctively, to feel for a pulse. But he pulled his hand back like he'd touched a live wire.

Except the shock that tingled through his body originated in his own head. He'd never before touched the skin of a corpse. But he knew right away. That's what it was – a corpse. Not a person. Not anymore.

A real person feels soft, pliant. Not waxy. Not cold.

The corpse was dressed up. Skin tight jumpsuit. Sequins and sparkles. Long fringes on the sleeves. Fully decked out for the stage, except the red sash, always worn with the costume, was wrapped around the neck.

Choked to death?

Wanting to leave but needing to confirm an identity he was already sure of, he reached around the body with one hand, took hold of the open necked shirt with the other and rolled the corpse toward him, onto its back.

For a split second he was drawn in by opaque eyes staring back at him, the upper lid of the right one half closed. Then his own eyes fell to the skin in the deep V of the jumpsuit. Blood stained the bare chest like a botched tattoo, framing the knife.

A knife that was buried to the hilt.

He watched his own hand as it reached out, covered now with sticky blood. He looked around for something to wipe it on.

He mouthed the words, "Oh my God!" at the same time someone behind him actually vocalized them.

Electricity again traveled down his spine. I know that voice, he thought. He tore his eyes from the gore and the bloodstain around the knife's entry point, just in time to glimpse the witness flashing back down the hallway and out of the room. The lighting was too poor and it happened too fast for him to make out the woman's features, if in fact it was a woman. And not a small man.

His attention returned to the corpse. To its face.

"Dear mother of God. You son of a bitch. You can't be dead."

He rose from his knees.

He wiped his hands on his own sequined thighs.

He backed away.

And then he knew. He had to get the hell out of there.

He ran.

one

AS THEY TIGHTENED THE TOURNIQUET to raise a suitable vein, I cradled her head. At the edge of my vision, I was aware of, but refused to acknowledge the hand, the practiced hand with its thumb poised on the hypodermic's plunger. And then I tried, tried really hard, but I couldn't tear my eyes from the needle.

I swallowed deeply but the dryness stayed with me. My skin felt clammy and the back of my neck tingled. I shook my head, needing to clear it.

No longer dazed, I finally forced my eyes to follow the action of the hypodermic; its plunger depressed slowly, ejecting clear fluid from the vial into the swollen vein.

With her head still resting in my left hand, I steadied her strong neck with my right. She looked into my face for a last time. Then she exhaled, a long, slow, rasping sigh. Her deflated lungs stayed that way. The life escaped from her body, like a gentle current.

I cried silent tears. Swallowing back a groan, I struggled to maintain a stone cold expression, selling a stoic demeanor to the small world around me. But I was doing a piss poor job of it. This was worse than when they had to shoot Old Yeller.

Reba was gone. And I missed her already, with an ache that started deep in my gut and spread out from there.

Reba was a good dog. A damn good dog, and now she was gone.

I just helped to kill the old girl.

Just a few short hours earlier, Reba and I had gone for our regular morning jog, heading north from the foot of Main Street in Grand Bend, on the shores of Lake Huron. Everything was fine, normal.

But by lunch time, something had gone wrong. Reba was trying to swallow but couldn't. She paced in a tight circle, head down. First clockwise, then reversing herself and going counterclockwise. Hairball, I told myself.

That's what I thought until she started to foam at the mouth because she couldn't clear the mucous clogging the air passages in her throat. But I refused to believe what my eyes were telling me.

"Clear the damn hairball, girl," I said.

At my words, I think she tried but she gagged. Violently. And reality slapped me across the face.

I rushed over and struggled to hold onto her, to stop her pacing. When she finally settled enough, I took her jaw in my palm. I held her behind the head with my other hand. Her whole body trembled. I felt it all the way up my arms, into my chest.

Reba's eyes penetrated deep inside me, begging me to make things right, breaking my heart. She needed help, more help than I could give her.

I untied her and told her to follow me and she did, but she barely made it to my truck. I lifted her into the cab because she didn't have the strength, which was so wrong.

I ran a red light getting her to Ellen, Reba's veterinarian. I opened the passenger side door and had to help her onto the ground. She staggered into the clinic behind me. I would have carried her but there was her dignity to consider. Reba was a proud dog, and with good reason.

She collapsed in the waiting room. Panting, gagging, looking at me, begging for help with doe eyes. As soon as she saw Reba, the veterinary assistant turned and broke in on another client. The doctor came out right away.

"Ellen, feel her stomach," I told her.

It was hard and distended.

She gently prodded Reba's belly, causing the poor girl to cringe. Ellen looked away for a moment.

"Aw, shit," I thought I heard her say.

"What?"

Ignoring me and noting the blue tinge to her gums and jowls, she said, "She's not getting enough air, Jack. Bring her into the back."

Reba tried to get up, but couldn't and once more, the whole situation struck me as all wrong. Reba's tough as an old root.

"Get up, girl," I called to her. Rationally, I knew she'd have difficulty. Emotionally, I wanted her to fight off whatever it was that was killing her.

It took willpower – she hadn't lost that – but she made it to her feet, and she stumbled toward me. Then she stopped, opening her jaws wide, as if trying to expel a blockage, a blockage that couldn't be moved. And there she stood, swaying, gasping.

I lifted her, all fifty five pounds of her and as I carried her through another door, I wondered out loud whether it might be poison, whether she'd be alright if we pumped her stomach.

But it wasn't poison.

"It's more serious than that," Ellen said, as I followed her into another room. Meanwhile, her assistant had me lay my dog on a padded table in the examination room where she cupped a mask over Reba's snout. Thank God, the oxygen hit brought the poor girl relief.

Once Reba came around, we moved her over to the x-ray machine. I wasn't allowed to stay. When I was called back in, Reba was getting oxygen again. She looked at me and her tail swished two or three times, hopefully.

The x-rays confirmed what Ellen already knew.

Somehow, and the vet couldn't say how, Reba had developed a torsion in her gut. Her stomach had turned completely over causing her gullet and her bowel to twist around madly. The pictures revealed a rotation that to my untrained eye exceeded 720 degrees.

I couldn't help thinking of one of the books of James Herriot, the Yorkshire veterinarian, and of the prize horse that James worried over.

"Don't these things just happen to horses?"

"No, Jack," Doctor Ellen said, "it's fairly common in dogs."

"Oh."

"You okay?"

"What are we gonna do?" Again my thoughts turned to the dilemma James Herriot faced; a newly licensed vet diagnosing a very serious condition in a valuable horse and dealing with the pompous horse expert, charged with the horse's care.

"We haven't got any choice Jack."

Like the horse, Reba had to be put down.

"Can you operate? Turn it back?"

"Reba's old, Jack. There'll be complications."

Reba had slowed up some but more telling, she was often confused. And she wasn't eating right. She was a pound dog. Maybe she was older than I wanted to believe.

"The operation will be too much for her, Jack." Ellen squeezed my forearm.

I couldn't let her suffer.

"Okay."

"What about Sheila?"

Reba is as much Sheila's dog as mine. It's bad policy to make a life and death decision about a pet without consulting the woman you love. And Reba was a lot more than a pet.

"She's in London," I said.

"How soon can she get back?"

"If I could reach her, half an hour. But she must have forgotten her cell."

"Oh."

"We can't wait, can we?"

"No."

"Do it," I said. And she did.

I left the clinic quickly, not wanting to be there any longer. I felt like crap. But I reminded myself it was lucky that I was nearby when Reba fell ill. She hadn't suffered long. But that wasn't nearly enough as consolation.

• • • • • •

It wasn't easy telling Sheila.

Reba had been with us for seven years, which made her about twelve. As I said, she was a pound orphan, earmarked because of her age and lower class pedigree for euthanasia. The minute we saw her, we knew that wasn't going to happen.

Sheila cried hard at the news, saying between sobs, "You must think I'm a baby."

"No."

"I bet you didn't cry. You never cry," she said.

She was wrong. I cry. In dark movies when the hero's sidekick dies. Or when the nightly news gets so desperately sad, I can't watch any longer. And every September, in the first steps of the Terry Fox run. Yeah I cry. It's just that when I cry usually there isn't an audience.

I looked away.

"You did cry," she said. "Didn't you?"

"You lose a dog like Reba and you don't cry a little…."

"Then you have no right to call yourself a human being," she finished my sentence.

I held her tight. And I started to feel better.

"I love you, Jack."

"Me too."

two

THE WEEK THAT FOLLOWED REBA'S death passed in a blur. I didn't feel depressed. Or sad. I forced myself to feel nothing and it got me through.

This much I remember: Sheila kept me busy serving customers at Gert's, the Grand Bend coffee shop we own jointly, and doing a half dozen jobs around the place that we'd put off for the last million years.

Gert's is located half way down The Strip, the village's Main Street, close enough to Lake Huron to hear the waves lapping even on its calmer days. Our business fights for space with a variety of bars, restaurant-bars, souvenir shops, fast food outlets and retail hangouts.

Most of the year, ours is a laid back coffee shop. There are no minimum clothing requirements. In fact, I've been toying with the idea of making bikinis mandatory for all the college coeds.

Our clientele spans all the age brackets. And in the off season, I count as my favourites the moms with their tots and the old geezers with their walkers and canes. In the busy season, my preferred customers get squeezed into the corners as the business shifts into high gear.

But Reba died in the peak of the tourist season and by the end of that first week, I just didn't feel like dealing with people whose moods were borderline euphoric. In fact, it became clear that my presence in the shop would definitely be bad for business.

That's why I spent more than a few mindless hours in my office, closing old files, throwing out useless paperwork. On the positive side, or maybe it was the hopeful side, I mailed my third 'final invoice' to an uncooperative client, an insurance company bent on denying a back injury claim. For three weeks, I followed the claimant around and never once did I catch him doing anything that caused me to doubt his pain was real. I reported my conclusion but insurance companies don't like to hear that they're wrong. So, they take their time paying. It was as if somehow I failed them.

It's one of the reasons insurance companies aren't my favourite client type. But if I held any hope of making a decent living as a private investigator in the sleepy little resort town of Grand Bend, I couldn't afford to be picky. The truth was I'd had very few new cases of late, and by very few I mean none.

But I desperately needed to work. Not for the money. Gert's customers paid the mortgage and kept me in jogging shoes.

What I needed was a filler. Something to take my mind off losing Reba. Because so far, whether I was working in my office or waiting on tables for yappy retirees in the morning, surly teenagers in the late afternoon, or the college crowd at night, none of that was doing the trick.

That's why when the filing was done, I squirreled myself away in my apartment to consider my options. Aside from drinking too much beer, my only other choice was to shift my focus from Reba to the annual triathlon in Goderich, a town forty-five minutes to the north. I could train for it and enter as a tribute to my dog, my second best running partner ever, Sheila being my best. The trouble was, I'd lost all motivation.

My apartment door screeched, interrupting my contemplations.

There are three units above Gert's Tea and Gossip House. The smallest is my office. Other than the beer fridge, it's not a very welcoming place. My apartment, unit two, is fully but badly furnished, a situation made worse by the fishing gear, golf clubs, laundry and sports stuff strewn everywhere. I like my place best when it's gathering dust. Because that means it's unoccupied. Sheila lives in the largest apartment and by far it's the homiest because of her flare for décor and because she's there. And when I'm on best behaviour, I'm there too.

Except since Reba died, I'd spent more nights in my own lumpy bed in my own dump across the hall than in Sheila's bed, with the high tech comfort features.

"You ever going to replace that thing?" Sheila asked. The door's screech rewound as she closed it.

I was lying on my broken down couch in front of my broken down TV.

She could have been talking about almost anything.

"The door?" I said.

"No. It just needs a lubricant."

"The couch?"

"No, you twerp."

"Oh, you mean the TV?"

"Yeah."

"You've got one."

"But you're not always welcome."

"I'm not?"

"What if I have a guest?"

"What kind of guest?"

"You know."

"What? The kind you don't want me to know about?"

"Hypothetically."

"I get my hands on Mr. Hypothetical, I'll throw him out the window."

She laughed.

Then, "You planning to answer my question?"

"About the TV?"

"Yes. What if I'm watching something at my place and you want to watch something else."

"Won't happen," I assured her.

"Why not?"

"Too many choices for watching nothing."

"What?"

"I guess there's always something on the idiot box. But it's nothing too. You got sitcoms that make men look like nitwits."

"Yeah, so?"

"And there're reality shows where the contestants audition and are told what to do and say."

"True."

"And I don't need to see bodies being bisected on phony cop shows."

"Me neither. But what about sports?"

"The announcers aggravate me."

"But, what if my TV breaks down too, and we have no backup and it's Monday night. And say the World Series is on."

"Monday, as in Corner Gas night?"

"Exactly."

"You got me there. Maybe I will get it fixed."

"Good, I couldn't go on without Brent."

"Could you go on without me?"

"Toss a coin."

"Run?" I suggested.

"Sure."

It was our first outing together, other than grocery shopping, since Reba passed. Usually I find running to be therapeutic. But the sky over Lake Huron was milky grey, and while flat water may be nice to photograph, it can also be uninspiring, if not downright depressing.

In consideration of my mood, Sheila never mentioned my outfit. She hates it when I run in Bermuda shorts. Thinks it's tacky. But, shorts are shorts. Besides, I like to have pockets for chewing gum and in case I find something in the sand worth keeping, like money or a fishing lure.

Earlier that year, I found a beat-up cap washed ashore, embroidered with the words, 'Never give up the ship' on its peak. Moving past the irony, I kept that hat, for the message and half hoping its owner was still alive, thinking one day he might reclaim it.

After forty minutes working our slow twitch muscles on the beach, a conjugal shower and a six pack of cold beer, while looking over the Ausable River from the comfort of padded Muskoka chairs, my emotional condition climbed up from the crawl space beneath the sub-basement all the way to the ground floor.

When we re-entered the shop to make sure our teenaged staffers hadn't run off to a beach party, I fell back to the basement level with a thud.

Mike Mackie, Sheila's brother, was seated at my favourite table beside Gert's front window. Our coffee shop doesn't discriminate. We serve anybody.

I was surprised Sheila managed a smile. About the only thing Sheila liked about her brother was his impersonation of Elvis Presley. He had the pipes and a resemblance to Elvis in the fat years. In fact, that's what I called Mike whenever he pissed me off – Fat Elvis. I called him that a lot.

I waved ambiguously to Mike, in the desperate hope he would interpret my gesture as directions to the exit sign. No such luck. Mike came over and Sheila hugged her brother the way one pitcher hugs another in the dugout after finishing seven good innings. There's no meaning in it but, it's the custom these days.

Seeing the opportunity, I reclaimed my spot by the window.

Sheila and Mike settled in at the service counter. He leaned close so that they were almost touching heads, deep in discussion. I wasn't curious, figuring I'd know before the day was out.

They broke off the tete-a-tete and Sheila came over with a friendly smile on her beautiful face. It was very suspicious. She plunked down two coffees on the table in front of me, brushed her brown curly hair off her forehead and smiled again. Something was definitely up.

Mike pulled up the rear, armed with a plate of donuts and his own pail-sized mug of coffee.

"Thanks, Babe," I said, taking my coffee and turning away from Mike a little.

"How ya doing, Jackie boy?" Mike said.

"Fine."

"That's bullshit, Mike," Sheila said about me.

"Not true," I butted back in. Though it was. I just didn't want Mike to know it.

"You're morose," she reminded me.

"Trying not to be."

"You can't help it. Because you're the biggest softie I know," she said.

Mike smiled but there was a twist to it. That's another thing Mike and the real Elvis had in common - a smirk, the kind that begged to have its owner's face punched in.

"Not me," I said, turning from Mike a little more.

"Yeah, you are," Sheila said. "A big old softie. When it comes to kids. And underdogs. And little old ladies. And war veterans, too."

"And dogs."

"And all the other four legged animals."

"Not cats."

"Not the ones who skulk around the bird feeder anyways."

"I'd like to shoot that tabby next time it comes around."

"No you wouldn't."

I smiled.

"So, what are you going to do about it?" she said.

"The cat?"

"No. Your bad mood."

Now Sheila's eyes took on a look of concern. And it was real, but that didn't eliminate my suspicions.

"How 'bout you and I enter the Goderich Triathlon?" I threw out the suggestion, even though I'd already discarded the idea, just to postpone the start of whatever plan Mike and Sheila were hatching.

"You know I don't like 'em, Jack. Besides, what was it you told me after your last triathlon, the one in Muskoka?"

"Don't know."

"It was about the running part. You said, 'running ten k after a long swim and after biking forty k is like…' "

"…pulling a hay wagon uphill."

"There was something else."

"…like running in wet cement?"

"That wasn't it."

"It's like running in someone else's body."

"What?"

"Like running in someone else's body."

"Whose?"

"Your brother's."

Mike took a breath between donuts and was about to say something rude.

Sheila broke in, "Be nice Jack."

"I'm always nice to your family." Which was only true when it came to Thomas, Sheila's father.

"Anyway, you're no good at them."

"Triathlons? I'm good at them."

"Only because you're stubborn."

"I've been training."

"You're not swimming enough and your bike's got a flat," she said. "Running well isn't going to be enough to get the job done, Jack. Besides, with Reba gone, running just makes you feel worse. You need a break. You need an escape."

"So, where am I supposed to go?

"Not you. Us."

"Oh. And where are we going?"

"Collingwood."

"What's in Collingwood? Besides Mike."

"The Annual Elvis Festival."

"You're joking."

three

SHEILA WAS RIGHT. I NEEDED to get away. And I wanted her with me, for the getaway. But the Collingwood Elvis Festival? Why not just fill my ears with well seasoned horse manure and let me off easy?

I'm a Clapton, BTO, Led Zeppelin and Bob Seger kind of guy. And Motown; the Four Tops, the Temptations, Marvin Gaye and Smokey. I want music you can thump the table to, music you can boogie around the dance floor to, music that is raw, mournful, powerful, happy, real.

I don't go in for floor shows with flashing lights and fireworks. And I'm not crazy for singers who can't sing, guys dressed like a cross between Zorro and Liberace. Guys who can't pull it off without the back up of the big choir and the orchestra, all of them wearing tuxedos and black floor length skirts. I don't go for glitz and hype.

And Sheila knew it.

But because Sheila loves Elvis music and I love Sheila, I agreed. I would go to Collingwood. And by making a big sacrifice, I acquired an edge in the horse trading department. I expected concessions for going the extra mile. I'm not a doormat.

First off, I told her, "We're not taking my truck and we're not driving your Mustang. We're riding up on the bike."

My Big Chief, a vintage Indian motorcycle restored in traditional red, was a recent acquisition, secured as compensation – Sheila calls it plunder – for the aggravation my last client put me through on the way to solving a nasty murder case, a case I was sure involved a motorcycle gang, but didn't really, except insofar as they were serious trouble-makers. So serious I nearly got Sheila killed while following the leads that took me into the biker world.

"I get to drive it?"

It was a stupid question. She had never asked to drive my bike before.

"That's not going to work. I don't fit in the sidecar," I said. The Chief wasn't designed for a tandem seating arrangement.

"And it's your bike."

"That too."

"Figures," she said.

"What's that mean?"

"Let me ask you something."

I hate it when she announces she's going to ask a question. "Does your question have anything to do with my decision not to let you drive my motorcycle?"

"I'll ask it and you figure it out."

"Okay, what's the question?"

"Why is it that it's just men you see standing at the window in the airport?" She said it with a smart ass smirk.

"Looking over the runways?"

"Yeah."

"I dunno. Why do they do that?"

"I have a theory."

"They like watching airplanes take off?" I guessed.

"No."

She stared at me, hand on hip, looking a little pissed off.

"Why then?"

"I think they're making sure everything gets done right."

I decided against asking for clarification and moved on to the next big issue, which had a lot to do with the fact I didn't want to stay with Sheila's parents in their Georgian Bay cottage. When I suggested alternatives, she pointed out that the hotels would be booked solid. And besides, she reminded me she'd already agreed to riding in the sidecar. So, I conceded we could stay with the old folks.

But I insisted we limit our social interaction with her brother and his over-sexed wife, to which Sheila replied it's important to be nice to family. So, I offered to be nice to her Dad. She was quick to point out that was no sacrifice since I liked her father.

We sawed off by agreeing I got to sit between Sheila and her father at the kitchen table, at least one place setting removed from her mother. And two from Mike and his wife, if somehow they wangled an invitation to dinner.

Finally, I insisted we get to sleep together. Sheila said I was expecting an awful lot and walked out of the room, laughing.

But I caught up to her and said, "I'm only going to this convention…"

"It's a festival."

"As I was saying, I'm only going to the goddamn thing if I get to not go to any of the performances I choose. Agreed?"

"Yes. Whatever it is you said."

"Just so you know."

She laughed again.

I was pretty sure I won that round.

• • • • • •

Sheila and I took the shore highway north from Grand Bend, stopping off for a picnic and a swim at Inverhuron. Then we cut across country, on County and township roads, preferring them over the main highways, revisiting the hamlets and crossroads that hadn't changed since my motorcycle was brand new in 1946.

I played a game in my head, betting on the number of odometer clicks between oncoming vehicles. In one stretch, we cruised through eleven miles of uninterrupted rolling highway.

I've always played these kind of games.

Like as a six year old, what time would my Mom come home from work?

When she worked.

And when I lived with her.

Later, there were other games. Like how many spitballs could I make and fling at the classroom ceiling before the teacher caught me. And how many would stick? For how long?

And there were dares and challenges. Which takes me back to the two years I spent in a foster home in Sandwich, once the settlement of choice for eighteenth century migrating Europeans. Now part of Windsor, Ontario, it was a great place for a kid to grow up. At least that's what I thought, the problem being I didn't get the full opportunity to find out just how good it might have been.

In the short time I was there, I made friends with a bookish kid three doors away. On a dare, I announced I could devise a route from my house to his, one that would get me there without touching the ground.

As my friend watched, I crawled out my bedroom window onto the flat roof over the laundry room. From there, I climbed through an old maple tree to the roof of the garage at the back of the lot. At the far end of the garage, I slid down a hydro stack to a picket fence, which bordered the back alley of the next two lots. Balancing on the fence rail, I made my way past the next two houses to an old apple tree. Crawling through, I eased from the tree onto the roof of another garage, this one belonging to my friend's dad. The drop into his yard was an easy eight feet. My friend thought I was a magician. I still smile when I think of him and my wondrous feat.

The hamlets along that country route reminded me of those days, in old Sandwich, almost thirty five years ago. Yellow brick houses, and a few of field stone, with bikes and wagons and toys on the front lawn. Big side yards with clotheslines, weighted down by billowing sheets, thick towels, blue jeans, flannel shirts and underwear. Grass longer than suburbia permits, trees with real tree forts, sandboxes tucked into a shady corner. And home-made dog houses. None of that plastic stuff. Real places lived in by real people.

The countryside and its settlements were a landscape unchanged unless you want to count the satellite dishes gathering signals from southern skies, doing irreparable damage to young minds.

We passed through Glammis, Elmwood, Crawford and Markdale where we took a detour southwest, allowing us to cruise through the rustic village of Flesherton. From there we wandered over more backroads before stopping for a break in Badjeros, the hamlet with the weird Mexican-sounding place name. The glass covered fridge in the General Store offered up iced tea for Sheila and a carton of chocolate milk for me.

As we cooled down in front of a silver fan on a long steel post, the screen door swung open and a farmer came in. His peaked hat, advertising Case tractors, was stained by decades of sweat while his green and beige checked shirt, dated by the oversized collar, looked relatively fresh. Meanwhile, his overalls were a good mate for his hat. He was a senior but his exact age was impossible to guess. Facial wrinkles have as much to do with hard work and sunshine as with age and week-old stubble muddies the signs. I wondered if this was the guy Murray MacLaughlin met the day he penned his most famous song.

We finished our drinks and I tipped my nonexistent hat to the farmer and the store clerk as I stepped toward the door, prompting slow nods, mostly with the eyes. Sheila smiled, getting a better response.

The road to Singhampton put us back on track but the sun was still high and we weren't ready to call it a day yet. So we detoured again, northwesterly this time, across pastures and old orchards and woodlots to the Niagara Escarpment where we dropped down into the Beaver Valley. County road 13 led us through Kimberley, Heathcote and Clarksburg returning us at last to the 21st century in the re-made resort town of Thornbury. Five minutes later, we pulled into the Mackie retreat near Craigleith.

"Doesn't that car belong to Fat Elvis?" I said. I could have sworn Sheila told me her brother and sister-in-law were booked into their own place. Or maybe that was just an impression she left.

"Mike needs a quiet place to relax before the competition starts," Sheila said, taking off her helmet and turning away. Likely ashamed to face me. Unless she was laughing.

"As long as Lori stays out of my way," I said, not happy about it.

Lori Mackie, Mike's wife, likes to present herself as prim and proper. But she isn't prim, although I'm not sure what that means and when it comes to propriety, she's never had me fooled.

The side door opened and out popped Sheila's entire family, Mike, parents Tom and Liz Mackie and Lori Mackie, a few paces removed from the rest of the clan. I squatted beside my bike to unstrap the luggage.

But hiding never worked with Lori. She made her way over, head slightly bowed and hands behind her back. The effect she was after was timid. The result was something else: timid and her tank top didn't go together. Putting her elbows on my bike seat, she leaned over to talk to me, showing me cleavage. It's the only way she knows to get my undivided attention. And it worked. I paid attention but I never heard a word she said.

Following an exchange of pleasantries with Sheila's parents, Mike was next in line to greet me.

"You did a nice job, fixing her up," he said, standing back with an unwarranted look of expertise on his face.

"Thanks."

"What year is it?"

"It's a '46."

"Too bad," he said.

"What's that mean?"

"Well, if it were a '53, it'd be worth something."

"It is worth something," I said.

"Still…"

"Listen to me, there were less than six hundred Chiefs made in 1953 and then they stopped. How many you think are left on the planet?"

"I dunno."

"I don't either, 'cause I don't check."

"Why?"

"I'm not prepared to rob a bank to get one."

"Oh."

"Tell you what Mike, just stick to your goddamn singing."

Sheila came over before I got around to dropping her brother with a shot to the solar plexus and led me into the cottage, and then to the smallest of three bedrooms.

"This is where we're staying?" I said.

"My room," Sheila answered.

"How many decades ago?" I studied the boy band posters on the walls. Then I said, "Crying out loud Sheila, there's only a single bed."

"And there're mats under the bed."

"For you or me?"

"We'll alternate."

"Isn't there a double bed in the second bedroom?"

"Yes."

"I'm guessing it's spoken for."

"Yep."

"Why do Lori and Fat Elvis get the good bed?"

Her answer was a meaningless shrug.

"You know she's got a devil tattooed to her left boob?"

"They're married," she said to my first question. "You want me to get one?" she asked concerning my second question.

"If we could have the double, I'd marry you," I said, although my head was still wrapped around boobs and tattoos.

"What? Just for the week?"

"Okay, it's not practical. But, this is my last concession," I said, giving the tiny bed a hard kick.

"Agreed," Sheila said. "What about the tattoo?"

"For you? Absolutely not." And I was pretty sure of my answer.

"Thanks," she said. On her way to the living room, she added, "We need to go to town, Jack."

"We just got here. I was thinking of a swim."

"You need a sports coat."

"What for?"

"But if you really want, we can go for the swim first."

Then she was out of earshot.

And I won another one.

four

APPARENTLY, THE VIP DINNER TO KICK off the Elvis festival was a dress-up affair. The blazer Sheila picked out for me went well with the beige cotton pants and loafers she snuck into our luggage. In protest, I selected the ugliest tie I could find from the rack on the back of the Mackies' bedroom door.

Sheila's parents were born to look great. And I was thankful they passed the right genes on to one of their children. Sheila wore a tight white dress, buttoned up the front and covered in sequins and glass diamonds and dangly stuff. Her long, brown curly hair was pulled back to show more of her face. The sun brought out her freckles and her make-up was perfect. Or maybe she wasn't wearing any – I never felt she needed it. And her eyes danced, possibly in reply to my reaction to the sight of her.

She looked so delicious I decided that first decent song, if they played one, I would take her for a spin on the dance floor.

In contrast, Mike made me want to barf. Decked out in one of his high collared white jumpsuits, accessorized with a white scarf and a white sash with beads. He reminded me of the Man from Glad.

Lori Mackie's dress was both subdued and seductive at the same time, if that's possible. It may have been the stilettos and the bare back that tipped the scales one way.

I didn't say anything to Sheila but I felt I'd been tricked.

The VIP dinner fit into the category of Elvis festivities which we agreed I would not have to attend. But I did, out of the goodness of my heart. It's a lucky thing she looked so good, that's all I've got to say, otherwise I was prepared to protest. As it happened, the meal was a counterbalance of another kind. That is, the food was very good - chicken and roast beef, corn on the cob, cottage style potatoes and no salads.

On the downside, I nearly started World War III with the Mackie clan, in the lull between main course and dessert and coffee.

It began when Mike, trying to annoy me, said, "Look at all these people, here to celebrate Elvis. Elvis will always be king."

Sometimes I know when to keep my mouth shut, and this was one of those times I heard my inner voice, but just because I receive sound advice doesn't mean I'll take it.

"Elvis wasn't king."

There, I said it.

The loud gasp signaled an extended silence. Mike and his mother stared daggers at me. Sheila and her dad studied their empty plates, shaking their heads. Lori's eyes darted back and forth between her husband and me. Her smile was borderline diabolical.

"What did you just say?" said Mrs. Mackie.

Realizing I put my foot in it, I said, "Don't take this wrong. I liked Elvis, especially the burns and those scarves he twirled over his head."

"It's called stage presence, Jack." Mike turned red in the face.

"And the super size bell bottoms," I said. "They were cool."

"How about the cape?" suggested Mr. Mackie. "How'd you like the cape?"

"Dad, you're not helping," Sheila said.

"Yeah," I agreed. "Combine the cape and the bells, and from a distance doesn't he remind you of a table lamp?"

Mr. Mackie spluttered back a laugh. So did Sheila.

"Elvis was really good," I added by way of fence repair, although personally I felt the adjective I attached to the word 'good' was an exaggeration.

"Get this straight, Beer," said Mike. "Elvis Presley wasn't 'really good.'"

"He wasn't?"

"No. He was the best, bar none."

Mrs. Mackie nodded like her head was going to fall off.

"The best?" I said.

"Damn right."

"Look Mike, he was before your time and I was just a baby when he was in his prime but, my take on it - Elvis was a forerunner in the field of media hype."

"You can't be serious."

"Tell me: how much music did he write?"

No one was answering so I carried on, "He was no musician either. And there were better singers."

"Like who?" scoffed Mike. "Frank Sinatra?"

Mrs. Mackie's facial expression said, "Perhaps."

"No," I said. "Wasn't he a crooner? For sure he wasn't a rocker. But if you insist on tossing Sinatra into the mix, he was overrated, too."

The scowl returned to Mrs. Mackie's face. I thought about backtracking but it isn't in my makeup.

"You don't like Frank either?" she said, near tears now.

"I thought he was great in the 'The First Deadly Sin.' Top notch," I said, in reference to the thirty year old suspense gem.

"The topic was Elvis," said Mike. "And am I hearing you right? You don't think he's the goddamn king?" It was more of a shout.

"Calm down, Mike," Sheila said. Only she was looking at me.

"Since you asked so nicely," I said. "No Mike, Elvis wasn't the king of rock and roll. He was a pretender." At this point, I recalled the trouble I'd had with the word, 'aghast' in the morning 'word scramble' and I thought how odd it was when these random thoughts come to you from out of the blue.

"A pretender!" they all said. Sheila included.

Lori's exclamation was followed by a "Holy shit!"

"What about Sam Cooke?" I suggested. "If we're talking about trail blazers, he was a good candidate for king."

"Sam freaking Cooke!" Mike was getting out of his chair, but his father held onto his forearm.

"Calm down, Mike," Sheila said again.

"Sam Cooke had a helluva a voice," I said.

Mr. Mackie agreed, "He was good - 'You Send Me,' 'Cupid.' They were great songs. And didn't he sing, 'Chain Gang'?"

"He did," I said. "But his best might have been 'Bring it on Home.' And now that we're talking about it, there's Jackie Wilson."

"Powerful range," said Mr. Mackie.

"From a different category," I said "I'd put the Isley Brothers forward as contenders." Although I didn't really believe what I was saying because most of my examples weren't popular enough to be called pioneers. By this point, I was just running at the mouth.

"The guys who sang, 'Shout'?" Sheila said.

"And 'This Old Heart of Mine'," I said.

"I love that song."

"Me too."

"Bobby Darin was good too," said Mrs. Mackie.

"Would you people stop!" Mike screamed. "He's trying to tell us Elvis Presley isn't the king! It's freaking sacrilege!"

"Mike, if he was the King, name some Elvis tunes the Beatles or the Stones covered?"

"Meaning?"

"The best of the second wave rockers celebrated the ones who came before."

"By doing their songs?"

"Exactly."

"You're talking about Buddy Holly?" said Mr. Mackie.

I smiled an answer, adding, "He was a genius."

"So what, some English bands liked him," Mike said.

"Buddy Holly wrote and sang more hits in two years than Elvis did in twenty five."

My take: had they lived even a few years longer, the debate over who was king of rock and roll would have centered on Holly and Cooke. Elvis would have been a runner-up. At best.

"Bull," Mike spit out at me. "No way Buddy frigging Holly had more hits."

"Okay, I just made that up."

"I knew you were just blowing wind. Nobody remembers Buddy Holly."

Pissed, I said, "We can do a numbers check on top ten billboard hits, if you want."

"Any time."

Kids in the school yard.

"Okay Mike," I said, "here's a question. Name me one sixties rock group named the Presleys." Although there is a debate as to the origins of the name, 'the Hollies,' that's not something Mike likely knew about.

"The whole world loves Elvis."

"Look," I said, "your hero was okay."

"Okay?"

"But Mike, listen to me."

His red face and bulging eyes suggested I had his attention. Either that or he was having a heart attack.

"What?"

"Elvis is dead. Get over it."

Mike fell back in his chair.

"Throw some water in the boy's face," I said, as I got up to stretch my legs.

I wandered away, trying to get out of range of any loose cutlery at the Mackie table. And to escape the speeches by the festival organizers and the Mayor and the rest of the blowhards. I'm convinced the first thing they teach public figures is how to mess up a punch line.

I headed south as fast my legs could carry me through the tangle of bodies on the convention floor. When I realized Sheila was dogging me, I let her catch up while scrunching down in case she was planning to swat the back of my head. But I felt nothing. Instead, she grabbed my elbow, turned me around and laughed.

Sheila has a wide repertoire of laughs. There's her self-assured snort when she's won a point with me, (she snorts a lot), there's the giggle that follows when she euchres my lone hand or when she downs her third glass of wine and there's a snicker that she doesn't think I can hear after I've done something idiotic.

Then, there's the howl that goes with a very good joke. This laugh was the howling kind.

I smiled into her face and she grabbed my lapels.

"The mouth on you," she said, shaking her head. Then she kissed me.

"I was going to apologize."

"To Mike?"

"No, to you. I know how much you like this Elvis stuff."

"It's just fun, Jack. I'm not obsessed."

"So, what about Mike?"

"He deserves it. He's insufferable. But, maybe I should stand guard at the bedroom door tonight."

"Nah, we'll hear him coming."

"What with the squeaky floors?"

"And Mikey's excess baggage."

She howled again. Then she knocked back her glass of wine, and this time she giggled.

We escaped the building and went for a walk.

Obligatory mingling was next on the agenda. And we returned just in time – the last speaker was stepping down.

"I see some old friends from last year," Sheila told me.

"I'm going to hide," I said.

While Sheila flirted with her favourite Elvis tribute artists, I found a quiet corner with a table that had been vacated by avid minglers.

My escape was short-lived.

"You're not one of the groupies," a Roy Orbison look alike said.

My eyebrows said, "What are you talking about?"

"Know how I know?"

"That I'm not an Elvis type?" I said.

"It's the haircut."

I keep my scalp somewhere between shaved and a brush-cut.

"And the outfit. I like the tie. But that blazer. God. You're either a school boy or a senior citizen." He walked around the table, hands on his hips, giving me further study. "And the look on your face. You're bored to tears. You don't want to be here."

"I'd rather be fishing."

A passable Bobby Darin and an exact replica of Wayne Newton joined Roy and all three of them sat down at my table without asking permission. Still, I decided I might enjoy the diversion so I postponed my bathroom break.

"Nice jacket," said Bobby, with perfect sarcasm.

"My girlfriend's mother's a Bobby Darin fan," I said to the double.

"Tell her thanks." I decided against clarifying that her admiration was for the original. Mine too.

"No one likes my preppy look?" I said, revisiting the insult.

"It's summer. Try linen. Light colours."

A waiter walked by and I ordered beer all around.

"Danke Schoen," said Wayne Newton.

Bobby and Roy amended my order, preferring their own brand of poison.

"What about you, Double Roy?" I asked. I couldn't bring myself to call him just plain Roy. "Why aren't you mingling with the Elvis people and the mucky mucks?"

"We're outsiders."

"Outsiders?"

"It's an Elvis festival. And we're the competition."

"The competition?"

"Historically," said Bobby.

"And still today," said Roy. "We're an act. They gave us an hour at the Galaxy Theatre."

"When?" I said, meaning to mark the date and time down in my head.

The drinks arrived.

Wayne said, "Danke Schoen."

"So, Double Roy, how's your 'Pretty Woman'? I'm a big fan and so is my girlfriend." At her brother's wedding, Sheila and I bopped, spun and swayed to Roy Orbison's signature tune, played over and over, the dance-floor overflowing and everyone singing along.

"She left me for a Fabian look-alike," Roy said, lifting his big shades and wiping his eyes. It was a tired joke that Bobby Darin guffawed at, just like I've seen the original do on rerun. This escape thing I'd pulled off was getting creepy.

"No, I was talking about the song," I said, which he took as his signal to stand and belt out a few bars, unaccompanied. He was good.

Bobby leaned over and asked if I wanted to hear his "Mack the Knife."

I told him there would only ever be one Bobby Darin and it was best to leave it that way.

The waiter dropped another beer in front of big Wayne.

"Danke Schoen," he said with a huge smile.

Roy and Bobby were starting to wear on me so I leaned around Big Wayne and tried to pick Sheila out of the crowd. But a tall woman underneath big hair, jet black – possibly a wig - and with a full torso, supported by wide hips, blocked my view. I could have reached out and touched her but decided not to. My eyes moved up from her leopard pants to the spangles on a blouse that was having trouble containing her goodies.

"Didn't you use to be on the 'Carol Burnett Show?' " I asked.

She puckered her lips at me and then looked at my drinking companions, "Did you boys hear the news?" she said.

"Hello, Penny Sue," said Roy, not taking the bait.

But not deterring her either.

"You've been bumped," she said, putting on a sad face, without a lick of sincerity behind it.

"What?"

"I said, 'you've been bumped.' Somebody convinced the organizers that there's no room for the 'three stooges' at the festival. They say you and your groupies are fomenting unrest."

"The three stooges?" I said.

"There's only one person who calls us that," said Bobby.

"That son of a bitch," said Roy.

Bobby slit his own throat with an index finger and looked at Roy who nodded his head in agreement.

"Who're they referring to, miss?"

The woman smiled at me and puckered up again.

I stood and offered my hand.

"Ms. Stanfield. Penny Sue Stanfield."

"Jack Beer," I said.

"Well, I must run," she said. "Just thought you boys might want to know."

"Danke Schoen," Big Wayne said.

I hadn't consumed enough beer to miss the fact that Ms. Stanfield hadn't answered my question.

The emergence of a conflict between the Elvis crowd and the 'anybody but Elvis' faction piqued my interest. So, I left my drinking companions alone to lament and conspire among themselves and went looking for Sheila to discover what she might know.

The Mayor, a tall silver haired fox, had Sheila backed into the dessert table. I couldn't blame the guy. She was the tastiest looking treat in the room, although the butter pecan pie looked mighty fine too.

"Hey, beautiful," I said to Sheila. I don't usually talk like that but the occasion seemed to call for it.

"Jack, this is Charles Watson, Mayor of Collingwood." Then she turned to me, with eyes that said, 'don't act out' and with lips that said, "This is Jack Beer."

We shook hands. "Good to meet you Jack," he said. "You can call me Chuck, Big Chuck Watson."

"Good meeting you, too."

He looked at me and then at Sheila. There was a question mark in his face. "You two together?" he said finally, like he couldn't quite believe it. A beautiful young woman decked out for partying and an oldish guy decked out to process tax forms.

"Sheila and me? Together? Mostly," I said.

"We're a good fit," Sheila added and she winked. I may have swooned.

I'm not good at small talk with people I don't know well. Especially when the people I don't know well are politicians. When I was Police Chief in Grand Bend I spent eight years, which by the end felt more like a life time, fending off municipal politicians. Puffed up roosters who saw it as their duty to stick their noses in my business.

It's as if politicians and police chiefs are born to clash. Or maybe it was just me. But there's one thing I do know - give a politician a drink and what do they want to 'small talk' about? Politics.

"I'm a political animal," he said, confirming my theory, yet again.

"No kidding?"

"You?"

"Me?" I said. "Just an animal."

Chuck laughed. "Tell me something..."

"Okay." Thinking I could always change my mind.

"I'm interested in how electors make their decisions."

"Why?"

"Call it field research."

"I don't follow municipal politics much anymore."

"Well, you see Jack, I'm thinking of moving up."

"Up?"

"Yeah. I may run federally next time."

"Good," I said.

"So, how do I win your vote?"

"I can't vote for you. I'm not from around here."

"Hypothetically. What factors do you consider?"

"Okay. I guess first off, I consider whether I can pronounce the guy's name. If I can't, I'm not voting for him."

"So far so good," he said laughing. Probably thinking I was joking.

"And if he talks without saying anything, he doesn't get my vote."

"Well, there you go. I'm a practical guy. So far, I get a passing grade. Anything else?"

"If he lies like a duffer recalling his last game, I'm not voting for him."

Watson looked at me, as if he'd stopped having fun. Then he said, "So tell me, who'd you vote for last election?"

"Nobody."

More VIPs showed up to talk to Chuck Watson, ending the misery for both of us. The Mayor took over social niceties because it was one of the things he was so damned good at.

"Jack, Sheila," he said, taking Sheila around the waist and pulling her closer while I pulled back on her, "I want you to meet Honey Hicks and her husband, Dwayne Curtis Hicks, last year's winner of the Collingwood Elvis Festival."

He motioned with his free hand to the guy, decked out in black like Elvis on his comeback trail, which was sometime in the late 60's. I have to admit, if I were a different gender I'd say he was a hunk.

No sooner we were through introductions and Comeback Elvis said, "I go by Collingwood Elvis, now."

"How's that?" blurted the Mayor. His arm loosened and I had Sheila to myself again.

Ignoring his Worship's state of shock, Hicks carried on, "Or, Curtis if you must." He lisped some of his words and his breath reminded me of a brewery I once toured.

I looked at Sheila and she smiled. So, I squeezed her hand. "Nice meeting you, Honey, Curtis," I said, hoping to make an exit.

Honey deftly stepped in front of me and we collided. It wasn't unpleasant and somehow she saved her drink from spilling.

"Whew," she said, downing the cocktail in a single swallow, likely not wanting to risk another close call. She smiled. And she may have batted her eyes at me. For sure, she licked her lips.

"So, Jack. Seen my show?" Collingwood Elvis wanted to know, unplugging the electricity in the air.

"Haven't had the pleasure." I smiled at Mrs. Hicks as I answered her husband. Sheila elbowed me, and when I looked at her she'd just finished rolling her eyeballs.

"What do you do for a living?" Hicks said. "You're obviously not in the entertainment business."

It's obvious? How so, I wondered.

"He's a PI," Sheila said and I wished she hadn't.

"No way. A private investigator? I thought your brother told me you two lived in Grand Bend," Honey Hicks said.

"We do," I said, wondering how it was Mike knew this good looking woman.

"Any real work for private detectives in Grand Bend," Hicks asked "or is it just something for you to brag about at fancy dinners?"

"It's for the bragging, Dwayne," I replied. I looked into his pretty face, leaving my eyes there, going for intimidation.

"It's Curtis or…"

"Right, or Collingwood Elvis."

"Got a card?' he asked, acting like he'd missed my tough guy look entirely.

I handed cards to both of them. Honey studied hers. A frown formed on her perfect face. "The cards are new," I said. "I threw out the last batch. Too plain."

"What am I looking at?" Honey wanted to know.

"What? You mean the logo?"

"Is that a big eyeball?"

"It is," I said. "An eyeball inside a magnifying glass. Only the magnifying glass is in the shape of a 'P.' Get it?"

"Oh yeah. P-eye. And you're the PI. I get it. Cool."

"I told him to keep the other cards," Sheila said. "More business-like. Less hokey." She was right but I like hokey.

"I gotta tell you, Jack. I agree with your wife," said Hicks.

"And I agree with yours, Dwayne," I said looking into Honey's big brown eyes. She smiled at me and I reciprocated, throwing a wink in, at which point Sheila dragged me off for who knows how many more stimulating encounters.

"You are such a pig," she whispered as we wormed through the suits and skimpy cocktail dresses.

"Not my fault," I said. "They're drawn to me."

"Only when they're too far into the sauce."

"So, can we go now?"

"No."

"Okay then, I have a question for you. You met the three stooges?"

"Who?"

"Roy Orbison, Bobby Darin and Wayne Newton look-alikes."

"I've seen them."

"What do you think?"

"Good resemblance. Why do you ask?"

"We had a few drinks."

"Well, what do you think of them?"

"Double Roy sounds better than any of the Elvis impersonators I've heard so far."

"You haven't heard any yet."

"Oh, right."

"And they're not impersonators."

"Pretend Elvises, then."

"Are you trying to annoy me?"

"Just in a half-assed kind of way," I said.

"So what about these guys you met?"

"Bobby's an okay guy but, I told him I'd rather listen to vinyl."

"What about Wayne Newton?"

"Only heard two words out of him all night."

"Is this what you wanted to talk about?"

"Not really. A woman named Penny Stanfield came over and told these three guys they were no longer welcome. Someone, a person with some influence apparently, convinced the organizers to cancel their act. And there were implied threats. Makes me wonder who the troublemaker was."

"You must be really bored."

"Why do you say that?"

"Gossip isn't usually your thing."

"You're right. This is beneath me."

"Is not."

"Hello," the man in the tuxedo said, extending a hand to me. I remembered him as one of the hotshots at the head table, sitting beside the Mayor's wife, a woman whose face looked like it had been slapped silly with a flour filled throw pillow and then customized with Indian ink around the eyes and fire engine red paint around the mouth.

I ignored tuxedo man's speech but caught his CV as summarized by the program moderator. Apparently, he was principal in the largest resort in the region and his seed money kick-starts the festival every year.

"Hello," said Sheila. She introduced herself and me. His name was Ted Olson and I didn't like the way he undressed Sheila.

A tall brunette sporting a pair of spectacular, and possibly artificial, conversation stoppers wormed her way into a spot beside Olson. She looked a little pouty, likely annoyed with Sheila for stealing the spotlight away.

"Hello," I smiled at the perky newcomer. "You must be Mrs. Olson?"

She shook her head and tried for demure but it didn't work. My guess was she was keen to fill the vacancy.

"I noticed you two talking with my daughter," said Olson. "Friends, are you?"

"Honey Hicks is your daughter?" Sheila said.

He nodded and smiled.

"And Dwayne's the son-in-law," I said, right away identifying the family tie. I am after all, a trained detective.

He nodded his head, showing a furrowed brow and an upside down smile that may have been meant to question my intelligence.

"How's that working out?" I said, throwing Lady Olson-in-waiting my winning smile.

But she missed it likely due to the tall dark-haired athletic specimen who caught her eye. I wanted to mention his type usually fell short in the personality department but I missed my chance. She followed the guy as he headed for an exit.

"Jury's still out," Olson said to my question about his daughter's choice in a husband. "Not that it's any of your damn business. And by the way, he prefers Curtis." I put down his rough language to the fact I lingered a tad too long on his date's departing figure. All I was doing was checking for evidence of additional enhancements.

"So, I understand Dwayne wants to be known as Collingwood Elvis. What's that all about?"

"He won the thing last year." Olson wasn't paying me much attention, being caught up in the matter of the sudden departure of his latest 'squeeze for the night.'

"The Collingwood Elvis title?"

"Right. And he figures he can cash in better with the new name."

"He plans to make it legal?"

"Yep."

"How's that going over?" I asked.

"Like a rat in the feed bin."

"Organizers don't like it?"

"Other Elvis tribute artists aren't crazy about the idea either."

"So, why's he…"

"The boy's a jackass."

A greasy drummer and a bearded keyboardist started to warm up, making further conversation difficult. Sheila smiled at Olson as we eased away.

"Well, he's a slimeball," I said.

"You just met the man."

"I know all I need to know."

"Based on what? He's filthy rich?"

"Supporting evidence but, that's not it."

"Then what is it?"

"Two or three things."

"Namely…"

"No loyalty."

"How so?"

"You don't dump on your family. Especially not with strangers," I said.

"Come on Jack, you and Olson both pegged Hicks the same."

"He's not my son-in-law."

"Well, I think Mr. Olson was disarmingly open and honest."

"Never said he was a liar."

"What else, then?"

"Pardon?"

"You said you had a few reasons for calling him a slimeball."

"Here's one," I said.

"I can hardly wait."

"I have trouble with guys who wear tuxedoes and fancy dress shirts buttoned all the way to the top."

"Yours is done up to the neck."

"But I'm wearing a tie."

"Which won't last much longer. What's the rest of your evidence?"

"You see how we shook hands?"

"I did."

"Did you really see?"

"Yes Jack. I really saw. You shook hands."

"But you didn't see how he offered his hand."

"What are you talking about?"

"Palm up. He offered me his hand palm up."

"So?"

"That's not the way sincere people shake hands."

"Sincere people?"

"Genuine people, then."

Snickering, Sheila asked, "How do sincere, genuine people shake hands?"

"Hand vertical."

"What?"

"Like this," I said, showing her. "Perpendicular to the floor. Thumb at the top. If he shows his hand, palm up, he's after something."

"What about palm down?"

"Arrogant. Or, expect a power play. Snobby women do it that way. Like they want someone to kiss their hand."

"Lots of very nice people offer their hands palm down."

"The ones who do and are also nice are gay."

"You're an idiot."

"Just watch. You'll see I'm right."

The rest of the musicians brushed by us on the way to the stage. Led by lead and bass guitarists, a portly, older man dressed in a white jump suit came through with a flourish. I was tempted to knock the pompadour rug off his head but Sheila caught my arm too late. Or too early. Depending on your point of view.

"Who's that guy? Nearly dead Elvis?" I said.

"It's Buck Ryder."

"You're joking."

"No. He's an old time country singer turned Elvis TA."

"TA?"

"Short for tribute artist."

"TA. Okay. Now what about this old guy – Ryder?"

"He's quite good."

"Babe, I have to get out of here."

"Mike's singing later."

"All the more reason."

"If you have to. How am I getting home then? With Mum and Dad?"

"If you want, you can take the Chief," I said, before I realized what I was saying.

"Okay." Sheila loves my motorcycle.

Free, but still feeling snookered, I left the convention hall and dumped my new blazer in the bike's side car. I retrieved shorts, t-shirt and running shoes from its storage compartment and changed, in the parking lot, away from the lights.

Comfortable at last, I went off in search of a proper drinking hole.

five

ALTHOUGH IT WAS STILL EARLY in the countdown to the festival, the streets were already filled with party types, ranging from toddlers all the way to octogenarians. Everyone was having fun, just not my kind of fun, not yet in any event.

I climbed into a cab and told the driver to take me some place where the Elvis droolers wouldn't find me. He dropped me under a neon cowgirl who invited me into Heart Breakers, a tavern on the edge of town. George Strait blared at me from the door-step. It wasn't 70's rock but it was music to my ears.

I opened the door and was nearly knocked on my ass by a thirtyish couple, grappling with each other on their way out in search of a bed. The bar was crowded but I found a table, maybe the one just vacated by the couple in a big rush to jump on each other's bones, ordered a couple of beers and settled in to take in the atmosphere. The patrons who weren't already coupled off seemed to be made up of large groups of men facing off against smaller groups of women, being coy about their purpose, but not so coy as to deter anyone.

Despite a smattering of cold stares, the place held promise. The ceiling was low, the room dark and cool. And within five minutes, I discovered the beer was smooth and cold, like a Muskoka lake at dawn. As sanctuaries go, Heart Breakers would do fine.

A long drink of water bumped my table as he stumbled by. I grabbed his sleeve to steady him. He gave me a sloppy smile and said, "Cigarettes." I didn't know the word had fifteen syllables.

His 19th century wild west face was narrow and serious, almost academic looking, except for his salt and pepper hair which was a rat's nest. His blue eyes were clouded and bloodshot and he was possibly twenty years older than me. Closer inspection revealed a twisted grin behind his Lanny MacDonald moustache. I smiled back but got a perplexed frown in return. Deciding whether he knew me, maybe.

Then his forehead smoothed like he'd given up on sorting me out. And abruptly, so abrupt in fact it made me jump, he straightened himself and tapped his forehead – it was almost a salute - as if he suddenly remembered what he was doing and where he was going. With a steadiness that betrayed his intoxication, he turned away from me and stepped forward smartly.

For two and a half paces.

And then he lost it.

My second attempt to catch the man was a beat late, my reaction time slowed by my own consumption. His legs tried to catch up with his head, but they lost the race. His forehead rammed the vending machine's plexi-glass front, but somehow he managed to avoid going down.

Now standing at an angle, his head taking most of his body's weight, one hand came up to relieve his forehead of the job. With his other hand he fished around in his right front pants pocket. Then he stopped and stared through the glass. "Just a goddamn minute," he bellowed. "Who the hell took all the goddamn cigarettes out of this frigging thing?"

"Pipe down, Garnet," called the barkeep.

"Bloody hell."

"It's not a cigarette machine, Garnet."

"S'not?"

"No."

"Whazzit then?"

"A candy machine."

"Since when?"

"Since fifteen years. Whenever those new smoking laws came out."

"Frigging useless politicians," said Garnet.

"Damn right," came a chorus from out of the background.

"Sh'okay, I'll go for a candy bar."

He went back to digging around for change.

"Damn," he said.

Wrong pocket. In a blink, the drunk switched hands and resumed his search. This second fishing trip bordered on the obscene. A new smile told me he'd found something unexpected.

At last, he withdrew the hand from his pocket and looked into his palm, like he'd never seen silver coins before. Trouble was, now he needed both hands and the math skill, never mind the balance, necessary to count the right change and insert the required amount into the miniscule coin slot.

Having abandoned his means of support, not counting his legs, he took to swaying, all the while aiming for the coin slot. I should have looked away. His gyrations made me queasy.

Then, for some reason, he gave up on the coin slot, and he started the arithmetic all over again, separating the coins he needed from those he didn't. When he finished, he tossed the surplus onto the floor, looked my way and winked, meaning he was ready to proceed. Except when he reached out to insert a quarter, it slipped from his fingers. His head followed the coin as it dropped and rolled under the machine.

This was too much for his ravaged equilibrium. The man pitched forward and delivered another blow to the vending machine with his head, this one much more violent than the first.

I rose from my chair to help when the bartender yelled, "You, Cue Ball."

"Me?" I asked. I felt like telling him I wasn't bald, that it's my hair style.

"Yeah, I'm talking to you. Leave the guy be. He's fine." Truth was, in this redneck bar run by the redneck barkeep and full of rednecks and a smattering of girls dressed for line dancing and other pursuits, I wasn't about to get into an argument. No more than I'd punch my favourite Led Zeppelin tune into the jukebox, assuming the old rockers had made the machine's roster. As I scanned the room, it seemed as if everyone was looking at me. I felt a small measure of appreciation as to what minorities faced a couple of generations ago, entering the domain of the white man. I stuck out, a misfit, dressed in my Bermuda shorts and an old Jimi Hendrix t-shirt.

But I couldn't just ignore the old drunk.

Shrugging an apology to the bar-keep, I made my way through a tangle of new arrivals and rolled him over. His breathing was more like a soft snore and despite the blows to his head there was a look of serenity in his face.

"Thanks, darling," he slurred. "Just something for my head."

A sympathetic waitress tossed me a towel. "Here, use this," she said.

I did, making the guy a pillow, before asking the waitress for another round and then returning to my seat, where I concentrated on ignoring the barkeep's scowl. I would have donned my Stetson, or whatever those cowboy hats are called, and tipped it down over my eyes to block out the guy, except I didn't have a Stetson, which was just another reason I felt conspicuous.

Instead, I hunched over, sipped my beer and got reflective, something I used to be good at avoiding. But that changed when Reba died. She still weighed me down. And Sheila wasn't available to distract me, being busy anticipating Elvis competitions and Elvis trivia contests and reminiscing about a man who died before she was even born.

It was the cussing I heard first, likely because the ruckus was happening practically right on top of me. A tall athletic-looking blond woman, maybe Sheila's age or younger, was letting a cowboy have it in both ears with both barrels. She was holding onto the arm of another man leaning precariously on crutches, the kind that are strapped to your forearms.

The argument seemed to end when a man, standing and waving his hand, said something like, "He's had too much. Just ignore the asshole."

The woman must have agreed because she carried on toward a pair of seats, apparently saved by her friend. But then the cowboy made another comment, which I couldn't exactly hear because he wasn't facing my way. Whatever the words were, they made the blond woman pause for a long second before releasing the grip on her companion and settling him into a chair.

She patted his arm and turned. Covering the distance between them in a blink, she roundhoused the cowboy, catching him square on the chin. The punch sent him flying backwards, landing him on my table, knocking it, my empties and me to the floor. I saved my half consumed beer from a similar fate. Priorities.

From a reclining position, I watched the woman bend over the cowboy, who was lying flat on his back beside me, rubbing his jaw.

"If I ever hear another word coming out of that hole you call a mouth," she said, "I'll serve your frigging balls on a plate to the coyotes. You got that J.D.?"

I turned my head toward them and I laughed. Not smart. But I couldn't help it. And given the look in the cowboy's eye, I knew I'd made a mistake.

The woman straightened up and flicked her fingers, dismissing the man like he was a piece of dirt caught on a fingernail. As she walked away, I watched her ass and decided it was a very nice one.

J.D. caught me checking the woman out, which seemed to annoy him as much as my laughing at his predicament had, seconds earlier. He rose from the floor and gave my table a good kick. I decided not to ask him to help me clean up. Seeing no other volunteers, I righted my table and slid the broken glass out of the way with my foot. I sat back down, took a long draw on my beer and finished it, feeling like I wanted another. But at the same time I was asking myself whether I should make my exit because sticking around might amount to the same thing as volunteering to be the next target for J.D.'s frustrations.

But the blond woman made the choice for me. Landing out of nowhere, she plunked two fresh bottles of my brand and one of her own on the table, as she sat herself down. I backed away a little. I had twenty five pounds on her but I'd already seen that she was, for damn sure, tougher than J.D. and he was three suit sizes bigger than me. If either of us ever wore one.

"Don't worry," she said, "I'm not the violent type." I took that to mean pounding the crap out of people wasn't part of her routine.

"I never suggested…"

"My name's Carrie," She pushed one of the beers my way. "Carrie Griffith."

"I'm Jack Beer. And you didn't have to," I told her, tipping the bottle her way.

"Yes I did have to, Jack. I knocked your table over."

"And me. Still, no harm. I actually kept my drink out of harm's way."

"Maybe so, but you could have been hurt. You aren't are you?"

I shook my head.

We talked for nearly half an hour. While we were exchanging niceties I didn't really pay any attention except to her green eyes and her perfect face and her full lips, which served to remind me of the fact I was drunk.

I sobered a little when she told me that Rob, the guy with the crutches, was her husband. Like it was a story she was tired of telling, she said a hit and run accident crippled Rob's legs and damaged his brain too.

Then she explained that J.D. was one of those guys who after a few dates think they own you, even when the dates were ancient history.

"What'd he do?" I asked.

"You mean, why'd I lose my cool?"

"Yeah."

"He said 'if I was ready for a real man…' Damn…If I'd had my rifle handy…." She censored her next words.

I nodded my head, to tell her I understood.

"Well, you've heard enough from me.

"I'm really sorry for messing up your table. And thanks for listening. We'll be leaving shortly. J.D. spoiled the mood, you know?"

"Too bad," I said.

She walked away. I decided not to watch her retreat this time, out of respect, or maybe it was sadness.

She helped Rob out of his chair. I smiled at her as she left and I nodded to Rob but he looked right through me. And then I was left alone in this overcrowded country and western bar. Alone except for the only other person I'd had any positive social interaction with, a drunk, lying on the floor, passed out beside the candy machine.

<u>**six**</u>

OUT OF THE CORNER OF my eye, I studied J.D. – as I said, he was a hard looking bastard – he leaned on the bar, one foot on the rail, one hand in his jean pocket, the other holding a half consumed local brand. I estimated, like Carrie, he was roughly twenty years my junior. His five o'clock shadow was painted on, it was that heavy. His John Deere hat, which was sitting on the bar, had given his face a two-toned appearance, sunburned or wind blown from the top of his nose down while his forehead was pristine white, like a baby's butt. The cowboy's powder blue denim shirt was tight and under his sleeves, his biceps looked like a couple of five-pin bowling balls. His scuffed cowboy boots had those pointy metal tips that on him looked dangerous rather than decorative.

J.D. looked right at me when, slurring his words, he said, "Since when do we serve Elvis freaks, Garth?"

He took me for an Elvis fan? I had no burns. No spangles. No jangles. No bell bottoms. Hell, hadn't he seen my Jimi Hendrix T-shirt?

Garth, the bartender, shrugged his shoulders and said nothing in my defense.

"Isn't that in your job description, Garth?" I mumbled to myself. "Stopping the big nasty morons from picking fights with the undersized patrons?"

Except Garth was saying, "Don't know how he got in, J. D. Maybe he's not here for Elvis. Maybe he's just some tourist."

"Which is bad enough," says J.D.

I readied myself. Because I knew his type, from long experience. J.D. is the kind of guy who never leaves things at a verbal level.

And just at the moment I noticed the hand that had been in his pocket had become a clenched fist, the opening bars to James Taylor's song, "You've Got a Friend" broke into our stand-off, prompting everyone to freeze. And I found myself hoping J.D. wasn't the only one who missed the irony.

The son of a bitch answered the question by taking a step in my direction.

Tensing for a pre-emptive attack, I pushed back a little from my table and was half out of my chair when a hand on my shoulder pushed me back down. And the voice belonging to the hand said, "Stay put, son."

I didn't try to identify the voice. My eyes hadn't left J.D. but the cowboy stopped inches shy of my table.

The voice sat down and joined me.

"Holy crap," I said. It was my friend, the drunk. Somehow he'd managed to get vertical and mobile. He scowled at the cowboy, the same way a father stops a three year old, hand halfway into the cookie jar.

"Back off, J.D.," he said. He sounded tired or bored, like he was familiar with the routine.

"Not your business, Garnet," said J.D. Only his voice didn't sound as cocky as it had when he and Garth were verbally abusing me.

"Wrong."

"Just planning to teach this city boy a lesson. Maybe show him the door."

I wasn't sure how he picked me as an urban type but understood his confusion about my age. From a distance and in the gloom, who can tell the difference?

"Wrong again, J.D. This young fellah isn't going anywhere. Not 'til he buys me a beer." Garnet took the bottle from my hand, knocked back a long pull and followed up with a monster of a belch. "And then," he said, "this young fellah's going to take me home, before I get drunk and make a fool of myself."

J.D. was about to laugh but he gulped it back when Garnet moved ever so slightly, as if he was about to rise from his chair. Amending his reaction, J.D. bit a lip, pointed a finger at me, pulled an imaginary trigger and backed off.

Garnet glanced my way and for a few seconds smiled with his eyes. So did I.

"Got any cigarettes?" he said.

"Don't smoke."

"Me neither," he said. "Not anymore. I seem to recall I quit. Long time ago. Tonight...." He paused, looked off and finished the thought, "Just felt an urge."

"Some urges are best ignored."

"Yeah."

"Thanks," I said.

"For?"

"For running interference."

"Helps to have a reputation, son," he said. "Not sure what I could have done had J.D. called my bluff. Looked to me like that two bit snake brought along his twin brother."

His comment baffled me.

" 'Cept he doesn't have one."

His eyes got droopy and he took to swaying in a slow circle.

"A twin brother?"

"Huh?"

"J.D. doesn't have a twin brother?"

"Right. Was just him, right?"

I put a hand on his wrist and steadied his swaying. "You alright?"

"Eyes are wonky. Sign I've had one too many. Sign I need to stop. What was the question?"

"You okay?"

"Yeah. I will be."

He took my beer again, drained it and said, "You gonna order me a beer or not? Need to come down slow-like."

I signaled the waitress. We waited for our drinks.

"James Taylor fan?" I asked, figuring him for the last coin in the jukebox.

"Sweet sound that boy makes."

"And they let you play it in here?"

"It's the reputation, son." Again with his reputation.

"How do you mean?"

"Another time. Another life. One that I got tired of."

"Oh," I said, trying to be a good listener and hoping for more.

"I got out with my sanity. But I left everything else behind, starting with the goddamn job…." His words drifted off. "Or maybe that was already gone, anyway."

Our beer arrived before he could fill in the blanks with answers that made sense. Except, he did make sense. Any job can hit a rut you can't get out of, short of cutting loose.

As he nursed his beer, Garnet drifted in and out of an upright sleep, the waking periods getting longer. While it seemed improbable, he was edging very gradually toward sober. And at the same time his long face told me he was edging more and more toward depressed. As if the two conditions were flip sides of the same coin.

I was curious. "So, what was the last straw?"

"You mean 'why'd I leave?'"

"Uh huh."

"It was the 'accident,'" he said in a way that suggested I had a good working knowledge of the local lore. "And, you can put the goddam word in quotation marks, son. Accident my ass. Hit and run's murder." He pounded the table once but once was enough. He made his point.

"Murder?"

"Granted," he said. "No one died. Although might just as well have…"

"You talking about what happened to Rob Griffith?"

He looked at me. "You know about that?" he asked, but it was more like a statement."

"Yeah, you saw the fight?"

He stared at me, like my question came from outer space.

I came at the explanation from a new direction. "A woman named Carrie, Rob Griffith's wife, told me what happened to him," I said. "Is that the hit and run you're talking about?"

"When was this?"

It was then I realized that Garnet must have been passed out at the time of the altercation between J.D. and Carrie and that later, he hadn't noticed Carrie sitting at my table. "It was tonight. Earlier."

"Carrie and Rob were here?"

"Left just before you straightened out J.D."

"First off, it'll take one hell of a lot more than our little pissing match to straighten out that particular loony tune. Second, I have a question to ask - did Carrie see me? Lying flat out cold?" The man was upset.

"It would have been hard to miss you," I said softly. He had to strain to hear me. "The candy machine is right by the front entrance."

"Damn."

"I'm sorry, Garnet," I said though I didn't know what I was sorry about.

I finished the last inch of my beer. Garnet's was still half full when he said, "Can you walk?"

"Sure," I said.

"Then, you're sober enough to drive me home."

It wasn't a valid test under section 253 of the Criminal Code of Canada, but I said, "Sure, I'll drive you. Problem is, I'm on foot."

"S'okay." He stood and I followed him outside and across the parking lot where he stopped beside an old truck.

"This'll do," he said, tossing me the keys and crawling inside. He was already asleep by the time I circled round to the driver's side, climbed in and found the ignition, making the truck jump into the curb in front of us. He woke up. "Standard transmission, son."

"You might have said something." It was pitch black and the dome light of the vintage Ford was burnt out.

"Hell boy, what did you figure the big red knob on that end of that stick beside you was? A candy apple?"

I found reverse and backed her up, releasing the clutch too fast and bunny hopping into the aisle.

"You sure you got a valid driver's license, son?"

"Can't you tell?"

"That way and hang a right," he said. I made it onto the roadway without incident not counting the car that swerved out of my way. He rhymed off the rest of my directions and promptly fell asleep again.

As we left town, I decided headlights were in order and keeping the truck a few clicks under the limit, I did my damnedest not to draw attention to myself. In five minutes we were in the quiet of the countryside. It wasn't easy recalling a drunk's verbal directions and I had to rouse him a few times but eventually I found his trailer, on a gravel township road, up the escarpment and I think, beside a gulley. Which may have had a stream, the sound of water running being a clue.

I left the lights pointing at the front of the trailer and eased Garnet out of the truck, steering him as he shuffled around his garden to the door, which he opened – it was unlocked – passed through and, promptly slammed shut, leaving me outside.

I knocked but there was no answer. I tried the door but now it was locked, which left me with a dilemma. Unless I stole Garnet's truck, which I seriously considered, I had no way of getting back to Collingwood or to the cottage. It was too far to walk, even if I knew where I was, which was also the reason I couldn't steal his truck. Or call a cab.

So, I sat on the stoop, dug out my cell and gave Sheila a call.

"You're drunk aren't you?" she said, after I remembered to say hello.

"No."

Then she laughed.

"But I'm stranded."

"Stranded?"

"Yup. Stranded."

"Stranded where?"

"Out here in the dark somewhere."

"What do you want me to do about it?"

"Maybe you could drive out and pick me up."

"Where are you again?"

"Not exactly sure.'

"As I said dear, you're drunk." She laughed again and hung up on me.

So, I went back to the truck, pulled out a blanket from behind the seat and curled up on the bench seat. It wasn't as good as a real bed but likely better than the puny mattress that was Sheila's when she was a ten year old. Assuming it was Sheila's turn for the floor mat and not mine.

seven

THE MORNING SUN FOUND A hole in the maples behind the trailer to glare at me, its heat magnified by the truck's windshield. I tried to stretch my twisted back but an instant headache, the throbbing kind, made me reconsider. I was pretty sure I was still alive and that soon, I'd be able to move.

At the precise moment I designated to straighten my body, the passenger side door flung open. My head and one of my arms, the one which fell asleep, fell out and flopped around in mid-air. My right foot was tangled in the steering wheel and the gear shift knob was making a permanent impression on my ass.

"Garnet?"

"Get the hell out of my truck, you bucket of slop," he said, sounding too damn cheerful.

Using body parts that belonged to someone else, unless it was my own corpse, I unfolded and refolded legs and arms and eventually I slid out of the cab, where after just two steps, I sat on the ground and leaned back into the certainty of the truck's right front wheel.

Garnet retreated to the trailer's low wooden porch and took a seat in a weather worn rocker. Maybe to watch. From a safe distance.

I studied him and thought he looked showered and shaven. For sure he looked smug. After a while he must have got tired of waiting for me to do something because he went inside, allowing me to get to my feet and beat a path to the far side of an ancient apple tree to relieve myself. Next, I found an aluminum lawn chair in the bed of his truck, unfolded it and sat down in time for Garnet's reappearance. He walked over, spryly I thought, and gave me a coffee along with five more minutes to regain full consciousness.

The oily brew did its work and Garnet eased me back into his truck for the drive back to the Mackie cottage. Thankfully, he spoke not a word, just whistled softly, all twenty two kilometers, a Shania tune. As bad as it sounded, at least it wasn't Elvis.

When we pulled into the driveway and stopped, he grabbed my arm, just as I opened the door to get out.

"You get me home last night?" he said.

"Yes."

He nodded his head. "See ya around."

Sheila came up from the stony beach wrapped in a beach towel. I saw Mike's wife just behind over her left shoulder. The top half of Lori's wet bathing suit was stressed to the failure point.

Sheila laughed when she saw me. Her sister-in-law looked my way briefly, gave me a weird smile and then darted into the house, covering up with a towel but not really.

Sheila gave me a quick hug. "You stink," she said.

"Your sister-in-law gives me the creeps."

"Lori? She's harmless."

"She's always giving me looks."

"Looks?"

"You know. It's like she's checking me out."

"What for?"

"You know."

"The tart," she said and laughed like she'd made a joke.

"Not a tart. Tarts are obvious."

"You know this for a fact?"

"She's sneaky seductive."

"Meaning?"

"She only does it when you're not looking."

"So, you think she's coming on to you."

"Uh huh."

"Well, Jack, it would help if you didn't spend so much time looking at her breasts."

"It's like they're talking to me."

"What? Her breasts are talking to you?"

"Not just hers."

I made a grab for Sheila and she slapped my hand away.

"I told you. Take a shower."

Hell with a shower, I was on vacation. We were at a cottage. Showers are redundant. I went for a swim, a long swim. The cold pristine water cleared the fog as I free-styled parallel to the shore until a granite finger, dropped at the end of the last ice age, ten feet below the surface pointed me in the direction home. Rejuvenated, I picked my way through the shale rubble to the shore where I found Sheila waiting for me.

"Where's my towel?"

"Get your own damn towel."

"So, what's up?"

"Besides wanting to know whether you'd drowned, I took a phone call," she said.

"Who?"

"The Mayor."

"Chuck Watson?"

"Yep."

"What's he want?"

"Wants to hire you."

"Hire me?"

"You."

"What for?"

"Needs a PI, he says."

"No shit."

"Yeah, go figure."

eight

"I'VE ALWAYS ADMIRED THIS BUILDING," said Sheila, as she climbed out of the motorcycle's side car.

"Yeah, like a castle."

The turrets and grandeur of Collingwood's town hall spoke more of civic pride than of function.

"Why's that?" Sheila said.

"Style of the day. Or maybe local government used to be a bigger deal than it is today. And maybe the politicians were respected more in the past."

"You'd have to think so. Who in their right mind would want to be a local councilor these days?"

"It is thankless," I said. "But not all the time."

We climbed steps into an entrance hall. There were marble stairs left and right and a bank of doors straight ahead. We took the doors and found ourselves up against a counter, a barrier really, apparently designed to keep the public at bay. Likely wise, especially at tax time.

"Jack Beer and his assistant Sheila Mackie to see his Worship," I said, handing a clerk my card. She was about sixty years old and she wore sunglasses with thick black sideburns hanging from the arms. An "I love Elvis" button pinned to her high-collared satin blouse was the closing argument on where she stood.

"I am not your assistant," Sheila hissed.

I smiled at the receptionist, "I know someone can take care of that facial hair."

She smiled back. It was the best imitation of an Elvis sneer I'd seen since I landed in town.

"What's that funny looking thing beside your name?" the receptionist said, studying my card. "It looks like a bug or something."

"Actually, it's a magnifying glass…" I started to say.

"Actually, it's a long story," Sheila said. "Please tell the Mayor we're here."

"I'll see if he's free."

When the receptionist left, I asked Sheila whether she thought the woman's sideburns were real. And she mumbled something about there being way too much fodder around for guys with a juvenile sense of humour.

The Mayor apparently could be found somewhere back out the doors and up one of the sets of marble stairs. Just as Sheila raised a knocking fist, I opened the door and walked in, preemptively.

His office could have accommodated two teams of three and a basketball hoop for a half court game. Trimmed with the wood of ten full grown oak trees, it was a room that no one in today's world would replicate. Too costly, even if you could find that many trees.

The Mayor rushed over to shake my hand and to smile charmingly at Sheila.

Backlit by high windows, I picked out the silhouette of a man standing near an old desk, its deep maroon patina speaking to me of days long forgotten.

It was Olson, one of the festival's financiers, the same guy who I earlier detected being full of lustful thoughts for Sheila and whose handshake, as I told Sheila, was of the suspicious variety.

The Mayor's chair, along with matching couch and guest chairs, were black leather. One was occupied by a suit, with slicked back black hair and eyes to match. I didn't like him. Based on his dress shirt, which like Olson at the opening night party was unadorned by a tie, yet buttoned to the top, suggesting who he worked for.

Turned out I was right.

On some barely perceptible signal, the suit stood and made his way to the door, Olson beside him. As he passed, I got the feeling he paid more attention to Sheila than his boss.

These goddamn Collingwood movers and shakers needed a cure for their roving eyes. Like a good kick in the pants.

Sheila's smile lingered on the departing figure and I reminded her in a low voice she didn't like short men. She reminded me that she liked me, on which point I reminded her that she just happened to be a little taller than average, making me seem short. Which I'm not.

Olson returned to his spot by the window. After re-introductions, Mayor Chuck invited us to sit. I took the couch and pinched myself to stay awake. Sheila sat close to make sure of it. The office walls were covered with the photos of mayors and councils for the last hundred and thirty years. This didn't help me with my urge to yawn.

For something to do, I asked Olson, "Who's the little guy?"

"The guy who just left?"

"Uh huh."

"He's my go-to man. Name's Peter Lake." He said it like there was nothing more to say on the subject.

"Thanks for coming by on short notice," the Mayor said, jumping in with a tone that said first of all, he was a very busy man and on top of that, it was his meeting. He took his place on the throne behind his desk.

Olson moved from the window and seated himself in a chair kitty corner from Sheila. He looked her up and down and then reversed directions. Sheila smiled at him as if he wasn't a slime-ball. I don't know how she pulls it off.

Mayor Chuck puffed himself up, rose from his chair, now that the rest of us were finally comfortable, and began pacing around the room.

"Mr. Beer," he began.

"It's Jack."

"Jack, Sheila, we have a delicate situation," the Mayor said, "involving one of the tribute artists."

"Which one?"

"Mr. Hicks," he said.

"Isn't he your son-in-law?" I said, turning to Ted Olson.

"He is," said Olson. "And the jackass has goddamn disappeared."

"Disappeared?"

"Gone missing," said the Mayor.

"Since when?" I said.

"Since last night. He missed his performance in the elimination round. But, as a past winner, we're giving Dwayne a bye."

"I thought he went by Curtis?" I said.

"Or Collingwood Elvis," said Sheila.

"Who cares," said Olson. "The point is - he's missing. Likely because he's found some groupie he hasn't gotten around to groping yet. Check the hotels, you'll find him."

"He's a womanizer?"

"And a goddamn drunk. That's the other possibility. He could be on a bender. In which case, you'll find him sitting in a gutter somewhere. That's two leads for you Mr. PI. Find the broad. Or sniff out the booze. Or do it the other way around."

"He into drugs?" I said.

"Could be shooting up opium or something more vile."

"I believe one smokes opium. And it lost its popularity when the hippies went mainstream," I told him.

"Not interested in a history lesson, Jack. Just find the dumb shit."

"That's all you've got for me?"

"Honey said the last she saw him, they were having a Coke in some old diner. He went west. She went east. Hasn't seen him since.

"What's the name of the restaurant?"

"Connie's Grill."

"That the one on Hurontario Street as you're heading south out of town?" It was a greasy spoon I'd seen in my travels and one I'd been planning to check out.

"That's it."

Next, I asked, "What have the police said?" Although my guess was the cops told everybody to wait. Guys with Dwayne's personality flaws always turn up, for money or for mothering.

But my guess was wrong. No one had called the police. "That's the thing, Jack," said the Mayor. "We don't want to bring the authorities in yet. Embarrassing for the town and the festival people."

"And I'd rather the whole world not know I have a jackass for a son-in-law," said Olson.

"When you're a jackass, it's a hard secret to keep," I said.

I told them my rates and they nodded as if to say, 'no problem.' Then I asked for a retainer of $1,600, equal to a couple day's per diem. They hemmed and hawed until Olson finally cut me a check.

nine

"YOU SHOULD HAVE GOTTEN A bigger float."

"You don't think they'd be good for it?" I said.

"You're dealing with a politician and a land developer, Jack."

"Oh yeah..." I descended the wide marble stairs doubletime, because I didn't want to get into a discussion of my business sense, or as Sheila sometimes calls it, my business incompetence.

When we reached the Chief, I handed her a helmet but she just held onto it. "How do you want to start?" she asked.

"I need to get more background. Fast."

"Why fast?"

"Be good if I didn't have to ask for more money."

Sheila rolled her eyeballs but didn't comment, maybe because she didn't feel she had to. As she folded herself into the sidecar, she said, "So, how do we get more background?"

"I need to talk to your brother."

"Michael's got nothing to do with his disappearance," Sheila said.

"Not what I was thinking. Besides which, how would you know?"

"That he's not involved?"

"Yeah."

"I know."

"How?"

"I know Mike better than anyone."

"What about his wife? Doesn't she know more?"

"Airhead."

"Your parents?"

"Okay, Dad has him pegged pretty good, too."

"What about your mother? I thought Mike was a Momma's boy."

"He is. Which is why Mom doesn't know him as well as I do."

"So what do you know?"

"Mike can be a jerk."

"And Mike's pissed off with Hicks over this name change," I said. "And over professional jealousies. Which might mean your brother was keeping an eye on the guy. Seeing who he's partying with. Collecting dirt on him. Who knows what he knows?"

"None of which would cause him to do anything stupid."

I didn't challenge the point because she was overstating her defense. I could hear it in her voice and she knew it, and knew I knew it. It was the kind of thing you let slide in a relationship out of respect. Or something bigger than that.

Besides, Mike was no more a suspect than any of the other tribute artists, or any of the Elvis detractors for that matter. It's just that he was the only Elvis pretender I knew well enough to fire nosy questions at.

So, I just said, "All the aggravation over this name change thing must be poking a hole in Mike's belly."

"So?"

"So, maybe I should poke a little deeper," I said.

"Might be fun."

"It's not just about fun," I said.

"Meaning…"

"A guy usually knows more about his enemies than his friends."

"Like what?"

"Like his habits. And his hang-outs and more important, who he hangs around with in his hang-outs."

"Okay, so we'll talk to Mike."

"But first, let's eat."

"They say food's the best thing for a hangover," Sheila said.

"I don't have a hangover."

"So, why the shades? You never wear sunglasses."

"Trying to blend in."

"Where's the sideburns?"

The big seller on the streets of Collingwood was sunglasses, with thick black Elvis burns attached, like the ones the Mayor's receptionist was wearing. Even babies in diapers were wearing them.

"Didn't want to overdo it," I said.

I kick-started the Chief but Sheila had me take a detour, deciding to lunch at the cottage without me. Likely thinking she'd prep Mike for my upcoming third degree.

I didn't care. When I got around to it, he'd tell me what I needed to know. First priority had to be my stomach, however. It was calling for a hit of carbs covered in ketchup followed by sugar injected into deep fried dough and lots of coffee to help the settling process. And I knew just where to go.

The seductive sandwich board advertising an all day hearty man breakfast for $5.99 told me Connie had the cure on her menu. The reverse side was almost as enticing – Connie's famous Irish Stew. The soup of the day was green pea.

The restaurant's layout and décor surprised me with its 1950's retro look. Whether it was planned or it was all original and Connie just did a good job with the cleaning and maintenance, an outsider couldn't be sure.

When I'm alone, I always choose a counter seat, if one's open. The servers will treat you better. It's like you're one of them. And sometimes they'll open up, tell you what you want to know. And what you need to know but didn't think to ask.

The Formica surface was spotless. I played with the Heinz bottle, snuggled up to the tall silver napkin dispenser. I thought the bottle looked too filmy and the content too runny to qualify as original product. And a true expert can always tell. Oh well, these places have to turn a profit somehow.

There were two staff, one of them, Leona, according to her name tag, reminded me of an offensive lineman I once knew. She walked by with an order of sausage, eggs, toast and fried potatoes. It smelled so good I felt like tackling her. "Be coming back this way, deah." she said, drawling like a Louisiana transplant.

"I got this one, Lee," said the other one, a full half smaller.

I looked her over. Her hair was pinned into submission and dyed beyond recognition. She was one of those paradoxical women. Somewhere between thirty and forty, slight and full of energy, and hair aside, she might be called attractive by a woman's definition. But a man would say her hips could use a plate of pasta and a cream-filled dessert twice a week, minimum. And as I said, her hair needed to be turned loose.

I stole another glance around me. Patrons half filled the room, looking relaxed, as if they were sitting at the same tables, in the same chairs they always used, like it was home. I liked the place.

"What's good?" I said.

Hand on a cocked hip and with a silly grin on her face, her flirty attitude gave me an answer I wasn't looking for. Then she laughed at her own joke. The smile which came next sold me. It was real. And it changed her face from one that said life can be hard to a face that spoke of fun and potential. I suddenly expanded my personal definition of the word 'attractive.'

"What's good?" she repeated, like it was a brand new question. "Coffee's passable," she said.

I nodded. "What else?"

"BLT. Fresh field tomatoes, ripened on the vine. Heavy on the bacon. Red onion. Great with beer if we served it."

"Make me two," I said. "With a side order of fries. Let's start with the soup."

"Done." She relayed my order through the open window to the kitchen.

"You Connie?"

"Connie was my mother. I own it now." She thrust her narrow chest at me and I read the name tag.

"Nice to know you, Maddie. Short for…"

"Madeleine. What else?"

"Name's Jack."

I gave her my card. She studied it. "I get it," she said in no time flat.

"You do?"

"Yeah. The logo. It's an eye, behind a magnifying glass. PI. Cool. Hardly need the words."

"Want to get married?" At the very least I should have kissed her.

"Huh?"

"Never mind," I said. "Hardly anybody gets it – the magnifying glass thingy."

"What's a PI want with me?" She leaned on the counter and we faced each other. Smiling like we shared something. A joke maybe, or social status.

"Were you working late yesterday afternoon?"

"Honey, I live here."

"It was about four o'clock. Maybe the dinner time regulars hadn't begun to trickle in yet."

"And?"

"And, was there an Elvis impersonator in here with his wife? Having coffee?"

"They don't like being called that," she said.

"I know."

Her smirk took on a devilish flavour.

"This 'impersonator' - you wouldn't be referring to Dwayne Hicks, would you?" she asked.

"Yes I would."

"Well, he was here and his Barbie doll wife was too."

"You know them?"

"Since they were teenagers. This used to be a hangout. But we got no TVs or video machines so we lost that crowd."

"Problem for you? I mean losing customers like that."

"More like a relief."

"How well you know them?"

"That Honey bitch is loaded," she said before pausing and then adding, "You'd think her hair-dresser might mention the Ann-Margret do is done."

"I believe she's keeping in character."

"Well, she could use a character transplant."

"So, why's she a 'bitch'?"

"I called her that?"

"Uh huh."

"I guess I did. Well, she's a snob. The kind who won't lower herself to even look at the people who clean up after her. Acts like I don't exist."

"What about Hicks?"

"As a kid, Dwayne was a dink. Likely still is."

"That all?"

"Well, they like their coffee black. But I don't know what kind of birth control they use. Or whether he secretly paints his toenails. Put it all together, I know as much about you."

"I like to think I'm not a dink."

"I notice you're dodging the toenail question." Her smirk grew some. Then she said, "Thing is, they run in different circles than me. In fact, I just have one circle and it's about the size of this room."

"Anything happen?"

"What's this all about?"

"Keep it under your hat but, no one seems to be able to locate Dwayne Hicks."

"And you were hired to keep it that way?"

I chuckled. "So, back to my question - did anything happen? A confrontation or anything?" I smiled at her.

"Well, after Hicks finished his blueberry pie and Honey took her third sip of coffee – pushing the cup away like I served her poison, he threw a fiver down and they left."

"Decent tip for coffee and a piece of pie."

"Only in percentage terms."

"That it?"

"That's it."

My soup arrived. It was hot and peppery and it made me sweat.

Maddie left me alone so that my head and body could take in the soup's healing properties. I felt like asking for a refill but my sandwiches appeared in front of me before I could get the words out. The bacon was Canadian. The tomatoes were juicy. The fries were crisp and salty. I added vinegar and ketchup, the real McCoy as it turned out, and I was a new man. I left enough to cover the bill plus a ten spot.

"Thanks, Maddie," I called across the room. She looked up from her other customers and waggled her index finger. I waited by the exit where she joined me, eliminating my personal space. I didn't mind.

"So, Jack," Maddie said, looking up, because she barely reached my shoulders, "I've been thinking about your questions."

"And?"

"And you were wondering about anything unusual. Is that right?"

"That's right."

"These kids were here."

"And?"

"And as I was saying, I don't get teenagers in here anymore. What with all these franchises, with the glossy pictures of plastic food. And their high tech crap."

"So you had some kids in here. While Dwayne and Honey Hicks were having their coffee?"

"Yeah, four of them. Three guys and a girl. Dressed like freaking bums. Baggie clothes. Chains and studs and tattoos. Hair dyed weird."

I held my tongue but couldn't help double-checking Maddie's tint. I wasn't quick enough with the cover-up.

"Asked my girl-friend to try out a new rinse," she said, like it was an apology.

"Huh?" I said, dodging the subject.

"Let's just say, it didn't work. Otherwise, never mind."

"You were saying something about the girl's weird hair."

"Yeah. It was jet black with green bangs."

"You know these kids?"

"Never seen them before."

"They here when Hicks arrived?"

"Maybe. I don't know."

"When'd they leave?"

"They followed the Hickses out the door."

"Hmm."

"Mean anything?"

"Not likely," I said. "Especially if they come back again."

"God, let's hope not."

• • • • • •

When I got to the Mackie cottage, Sheila and I decided to divide the workload. Sheila took Lori shopping because that's what her sister-in-law does best, the theory being Lori would be more inclined to open up about the comings and goings of Collingwood Elvis and the people around him if she found a new dress to her liking.

It was my job to meet with Mike.

Usually the best strategy is to be casual about these things. People open up when their guard comes down. But the trouble was - we don't hang out. And even if we were so inclined, he doesn't watch baseball and he doesn't play tennis. He doesn't jog or swim. He plays some golf but it's best if I'm not holding something called a club when I'm with the guy.

I think about Mike and Sheila and I figure the guy's adopted. But, at least Mike's good at drinking beer, possibly leaving me a mere twist cap away from his bottle of secrets.

"Sheila says you have some questions," he said, breaking the ice for me. I couldn't help notice that he wasn't very specific. Either Sheila didn't tell him much or he was being cagy. I assumed the latter.

"Let's go," I said, lugging a twelve pack and a portable radio down to the shore. Mike helped by toting the lime flavoured chips.

We sank into canvas deck chairs and I tuned into a local station that was playing Elvis non-stop, in celebration of the festival. It drove me crazy but I left the dial alone, the plan being to win Mike over. I cracked open two beers and handed him his. We clinked bottles, as if we liked each other.

"Hear about your buddy?"

Mike didn't answer but his eyes told me something. Only I wasn't sure what.

"You know," I said, "Hicks."

Mike stared at the horizon. Meanwhile I couldn't stand it anymore. I turned the goddamn radio off.

"Collingwood Elvis," I said, just to be clear, just to keep the words flowing, and to stir the pot.

"He's such an asshole." That's what he mumbled, I think, although it was hard to be sure, the way the surf slapped the rocks.

"How's that, Mike?"

"I said, 'What about him?'" he lied.

"Never showed up for the elimination round."

"That so?"

"Yep, gone missing, according to Honey and her father, anyhow."

"Hmm."

"How'd your performance go?"

"I did fine. Hicks isn't the only one they offered a pass through, you know."

"As a past winner?"

I'd just learned from my meeting with the Mayor and Ted Olson that all previously crowned 'kings' get a free ride to the big sing off or whatever they call the thing that decides the next Collingwood Elvis. Even though they were expected to sing whenever they were called upon.

"Yeah. But I did my bit anyhow. And I gave it all I had. Impresses the judges."

"Smart," I said, like I gave a shit. "So what do you think?"

"About what? My chances?"

"No. Why isn't Hicks being smart too?"

"What?"

"Why didn't Dwayne show up?"

"Who knows?"

"Conceit getting in the way, maybe? Thinks he's a slam dunk winner? Could that be it?"

"He's a slam dunk something."

"You know where he might have disappeared to?"

"Why are you asking me?"

"You know him pretty well. Thought you might have some inkling."

"Well, I don't."

From his wrinkled brow, I guessed he didn't know what an inkling was. "You're telling me you don't have any idea where the Elvis impersonators hang out when they're not impersonating?"

"Jack, if you use the word 'impersonator' again, I'm going to hit you with a rock."

"Impersonator," I said.

Mike picked up a rock. I looked at him daring him to take a whack at me. He backed down. I felt great.

"Jerk," he said, reaching into my beer case and pulling out twins. "I'm going to town." And he left without saying goodbye.

I mulled over my interview with Sheila's brother. My mulling led me to three impressions.

First, Mike already knew Hicks was missing but he wasn't prepared to admit having prior knowledge. Why not? I didn't know except there's something about acting indifferent when something happens to your worst enemy that makes you think.

Second, Mike was awfully surly.

And third, number two was my fault.

· · · · · ·

Before making my next move... actually, to help me decide my next move... I concentrated on the rest of my twelve pack.

Despite the brain lubricant, I drew nothing but blanks and so, to fill the void I turned the cheap portable radio back on and pushed one of the pre-selection buttons. The station was a local, specializing in country music.

Following a twangy tune by someone I figured was named Tammie or Loretta, the next cut caught my ear. It sounded a lot like Hootie of Blowfish fame which made no sense, not to me, not on that station.

The song was about kids growing up too fast. A tear jerker.

The disc jockey told his audience that the nice little ditty did indeed belong to Darius Rucker, Hootie's lead singer, which revelation jarred me. Not only because of Darius' defection but because I realized I was in danger of becoming a country music fan. I did my best to compose myself as I left the beach.

By the time I stowed the radio and the empties, I'd made up my mind. Firing up the Chief, I took the shore highway west, turning inland after a short distance and passing through ivy covered gates. I swerved to the right of the ledge-rock lined boulevard and took the bend to the left, then pulled into the second driveway on the right. I found the condo unit opposite the crook of the shepherd-staff street. My destination was a two storey stone job, bracketed by two other townhouses, each of unique design.

The doorbell played a gospel tune, performed by Elvis. There was just no escaping. Thankfully, before the recording rewound to repeat itself, the door opened.

"Who the hell are you?"

While Honey Hicks scowled at me, I studied her face.

Somehow, she didn't look like the same woman I met at the festival kick-off dinner and I blamed Maddie for that. Because now that I thought about it, she was right: Honey's big hair combined with the bedroom eyes did make her look like Ann-Margret. But it wasn't all good. For one thing, the beautiful smile was missing. Instead, her mouth gave her a hard, smart-ass look.

Another thing – this woman and Lori Mackie could have been sisters, not that they looked like each other. It was more like they both hired the same make-up artist, though Honey's make-up leaned a tad more toward subtle, but not so subtle that an observant guy like me would miss the signs. And those signs were telling me she was available and on the lookout. Or, maybe my imagination had run amok.

Tired of waiting for an answer out of me, Honey Hicks tried again, "I said, 'What do you want?'"

"No you didn't."

"Didn't what?"

"You didn't say, 'What do you want.' You said, 'Who the hell are you?' which is close but not the same."

"Well answer one of the goddamn questions before I close the goddamn door in your goddamn face."

Maddie was right. She was a frigging bitch.

"We met at the party, Ms. Hicks," I said.

"It's Ms. Olson-Hicks. And what party was that?"

"The festival kick-off party."

"We met?"

"Yeah. My name's Jack Beer. You flirted with me. But thinking back it might have been the booze. On your part. For my part, I was charming and that was definitely the booze."

Her forehead creases softened a little. Before I got the chance to tell her that her daddy hired me to find her husband, my new client appeared behind her, swinging the door wide open. "What the hell do you want?" he said.

"I was just starting to answer that very question," I said. "I need to hear from Honey about the time leading up to Dwayne's disappearance."

"Curtis," said Honey.

"Come on in," said Olson, like it was his condo and his decision. "Want a drink?"

"Beer?"

While his daughter found a seat, Olson went to the bar. "Corona okay?"

"Perfect."

"What do you want to know?" Honey said. Only the question came with an exasperated sigh.

Before I could answer, a flushing toilet interrupted me and the same short, wide-shouldered, dark haired suit I'd met for thirty seconds in the Mayor's office appeared from down the hall. This time he was dressed fashion magazine casual. In full light, he was handsome in a movie star kind of way, except for the fine scars near the corner of one eye.

His stare was condescending. He was trying for intimidating, too. Dealing with an inferiority complex, I decided.

I stood and extended my hand. His grip was firm. Almost vice-like. He grinned at me. I grinned back. After all, I had a couple inches on him. Something I enjoyed given the averages for my gender.

"You are…"

"Peter," he said. "Peter Lake."

"Peter Peter Lake? Named after both your father Peter and your Grandfather Peter? Must get awkward." Something about the guy released the smart ass in me.

Lake laughed and put a hand on Honey's shoulder, "Who's the comedian, Honey?" Acting like he didn't remember.

"His name's Jack Beer. He's a PI. Daddy hired him to find Curtis."

He turned to Olson, still behind the bar, "Why waste your money? He'll turn up. With a king-sized hangover."

"You're sure?" I said to the back of Lake's head.

"Yeah, I'm sure. None of this would have happened if I'd stayed with him," he said, without turning around again.

"Why would you have done that?"

"Babysit the guy? It's my job."

Olson had told me Lake worked for Hicks but I wanted to know more. "Your job being…?"

"I manage Collingwood Elvis," he said finally facing me again. "The name change was my idea."

"Managing Dwayne….that a full time job?"

"Only before and during these festivals."

"Peter has a personal service contract with me," said Olson.

"I thought he was your 'right hand man'?"

"He is."

"What's that mean?"

"None of your business," Olson told me.

Which was probably true. Still, Olson's attitude pissed me off. And Lake's attitude pissed me off even more. And don't even talk to me about Honey 'Olson-Hicks.' Problem was for the time being there was nothing I could do about it, unless I gave Olson his money back.

Giving up on the men, I returned my attention to Honey since she was the one I wanted to talk to in the first place. "So, tell me about the last time you saw your husband."

"There's not much to tell."

"What happened when you left Connie's restaurant?"

Honey Hicks looked up with a question in her face.

"I went to the restaurant," I explained, "talked to Connie's daughter."

My answer confused her for a moment and then she decided she didn't care. "Whatever."

"Where'd you two go?"

"We left the dump, spilt up. I came home. Here. Curtis was supposed to go to the Galaxy Theatre. Later, Peter and I drove over. Getting there, maybe half an hour before his performance was supposed to start. That's when we found out Curtis didn't show. We waited. Then we gave up."

"And you haven't heard a thing since?"

She shook her pretty little head, hair bouncing back and forth, lips parting a little showing me impossibly white teeth.

I was stumped for the next question to ask and I didn't like the way Olson and Lake were looking at me. Could they tell I'd been drinking?

"Lookie here, Beer," Olson said while my brain was cranking over but not catching. "I could have told you all this. In fact I already did. I'm paying you top dollar to find my son-in-law. Enough of this goddamn walking in circles. Get your freaking ass in gear."

I shrugged, giving up, and made my way to the door. Meanwhile, Peter Lake moved closer to Honey Hicks and offered a comforting hug, not that she looked like she needed it.

Olson walked me out to the porch.

"Look Jackie," he said. "Dwayne is not much more than a bag of shit. But he's Honey's bag of shit so find the S.O.B, asap.

"That's what I'm working on, Teddy," I said.

Olson did a double take at the misuse of his given name.

"And Teddy, here's a question. Who keeps shit in a bag?" It was a really dumb thing to say but at least my brain was back in gear.

ten

MRS. MACKIE AND HER DAUGHTER-IN-LAW were busy listening to Mike's rendition of Military Elvis on one of the ten million stages set up in town somewhere. Somewhere far away, I hoped.

Meanwhile, Mr. Mackie tagged along with Sheila and me for ribs and beer under one of the big festival tents. My new case reminded me of a dose of poison ivy – seriously aggravating and guaranteed to hang around for a while – but a Georgian Bay breeze moderated the temperature and injected my general outlook with champagne.

While waiting for our first rack of ribs, Sheila told me, in a way that her father couldn't hear, that her talk with Lori went nowhere. Her sister-in-law 'didn't know anything' but I wasn't sure if that was a general observation Sheila was making or a particular one.

Just as the food arrived, she asked how my afternoon went. I didn't feel like telling her it was even less productive than hers, so, I told her I wanted to concentrate on the food.

She wanted to talk about my new case anyway. "Who do you think would want to kidnap Hicks?"

"Who's talking 'kidnapping'?"

"Get real, Jack. Why'd Olson hire you? To find a guy out on a bender? I don't think so. He suspects something."

"I guess Hicks has never been gone for so long before."

"And that doesn't make you suspicious?"

Going missing is no light matter but I don't like to jump ahead of the facts so I said, "I don't see a motive. He's a tribute artist."

"Meaning?"

"They're all so harmless."

"That wins Hicks an exemption?"

"No."

"You realize that you're dodging my questions."

"Okay. I can think of a few people who might want to make the guy disappear."

"Give me a 'for instance'."

"Start with his father-in-law," I said, though I wasn't sure why.

"Didn't he hire you?" Mr. Mackie jumped in, surprising me, because he usually only comments if I ask. Maybe hearing Sheila interrogate me gave him the courage.

"Yeah, but that could be a diversion."

"Sounds like a strange strategy," he said. "What are you saying Jack?"

"I don't know. Maybe he's assuming I'll look elsewhere? Or, he's giving me phony leads to put me off the trail."

"You believe that?" he said.

"No."

"Why?"

"The theory has to be based on the idea Olson believes I can't get by a stuck door."

"And you can?" said Sheila.

"Usually."

"So?"

"So," I said, "it isn't a diversion."

"And if Olson is playing a weird trick," she said, ignoring the fact I'd changed my mind about my client's motives, "why would he?"

I answered her question, without clarifying, in part because the discussion had me confused. "He can't stand the guy," I said. "Wants to get rid of him."

"Is that motive enough?"

"For some it is."

"How about the wife?"

"Ah, yes. Honey Olson-Hicks. Though I prefer plain Honey Hicks."

"You got her pegged?" Sheila asked.

"In what sense?"

"You know what I mean, Jack."

"She's indifferent. It's like she doesn't notice he's gone."

"So, why not his wife then?"

"Maybe."

"Are you serious?"

"You asked."

"Still, do you think she did it?"

"Not yet, I said. Except if something bad happens to someone involving a criminal offense of some kind, you have to consider the bed partners as possible perpetrators.

" 'Not yet'? Isn't that a little cryptic Jack?" Mr. Mackie smiled at me. And here I thought he'd backed away from the issue.

"There's always Mike to consider," I said to him. Only I laughed when I said it, to make it sound like a joke.

Sheila shook her head, slipping a quick glimpse at her father.

"Even if Mike had the nerve, which he doesn't, why would he do such a thing?" Sheila asked.

"Why? Revenge, for starters – he doesn't think Hicks deserved to win last year. And I'll give him his due, your brother's a better singer."

"No way. Mike didn't do it." Sheila's hand found her father's forearm, and she smiled her reassurance. She's never as concerned about her mother's feelings, but over the years, I picked up on a strong father-daughter bond.

I liked the guy too but I ignored Sheila's stop signal anyways. After all, she brought the subject up in the first place. And her Dad kept digging away, even though they had to see I hadn't a clue how to answer their questions. So I said, "Why not? Revenge and anger are good motives. Mike's pissed off, along with the festival mucky mucks and all the other Elvis impersonators…"

"For the last time Jack, they're tribute artists," Sheila said for the tenth last time.

"Forgot," I apologized.

"Why's everybody pissed off at Hicks, anyway?" asked Mr. Mackie.

"He's changing his name to Collingwood Elvis," said Sheila.

"Can he do that?" Mr. Mackie wanted to know. "My goodness, that's the name of the festival and each year someone new is crowned 'Collingwood Elvis.' No wonder they're all mad."

"To answer your question, 'can he do it?' I'm not sure, but I don't see why not. The name's probably not copyrighted," I said.

"Still, it's an attack on the integrity of the festival," said Sheila.

I was holding back on a lame wisecrack, when something caught Sheila's eye, over my shoulder.

"Whew! I didn't know Sam Elliot was in town," she said.

"Who's Sam Elliot?" I said. "Some old flame?"

"No but I have to confess, Jack. If Sam Elliot were, that's one flame I wouldn't have let go out."

"Huh?"

"Sorry," she laughed. "Just fantasizing a little. The guy who just walked in looks like the actor, Sam Elliot."

"Never heard of him. I thought you had a thing for Kevin Costner."

"Who doesn't?"

"Yeah, Costner is dishy," I said.

Mr. Mackie chuckled.

Then turning to his daughter, Mr. Mackie said, "Never realized it before. But by golly, old Garnet does look an awful lot like Sam Elliot."

Sheila studied the man, trying to place him.

I finally looked over my shoulder, catching sight of the new arrival. "You know him?" I said, turning back to Sheila's father.

"Everybody around here knows Garnet Henderson."

"You're not from around here though."

"That cottage of ours has been in the family for generations, Jack. You come back year after year, you're bound to run into the Police Chief."

"He's the Chief of Police?"

"He was. Of the town department. Until he up and quit. Or was forced to quit. That was just before the OPP took over the whole kit and caboodle."

"No shit, he was Chief of Police..." I said.

"Yeah, just like you. Except Collingwood's a lot bigger than Grand Bend and Garnet lasted a lot longer than you did. He put in almost thirty years."

Ignoring the criticisms that, coming from Mr. Mackie, I doubt were intended, I looked back again to where Garnet had been standing, but he was gone. I was left with the feeling he'd walked away the minute he recognized me.

"So," I said, "Garnet left his position on his own because the Provincials were taking over and he didn't want to sign up?" Which is what happened to me in Grand Bend. "Or was he forced out?"

"It was the accident," Mr. Mackie said.

I realized I knew what was coming, so like a smart ass, I jumped the story a couple of chapters ahead. "The hit and run," I said.

"Yeah," Sheila's father said, surprise written all over his face. "It messed up his son-in-law pretty bad. His crushed legs healed more or less. But he's not right. Head injuries are an awful thing."

"Did Garnet head the investigation?"

"He did, but he didn't solve it. Which upset his daughter, I understand."

"Carrie," I said.

"How do you know these people?" Sheila asked.

"We've met."

"Why was his daughter upset with Garnet? Lots of cases don't get solved."

"She claimed to know who was driving."

"How would she know?"

"She was with him. She and her husband were cycling home. From a house party if the newspapers got it right. It was late but they had lights on their bikes."

"And Rob was run over," I said.

"She got hit too. But she was luckier. Came away with scrapes and a concussion."

"Who was it?"

"The driver?"

"Yeah, do you know?"

"Rumour has it that Dwayne Hicks was the driver."

"Holy shit," Sheila said.

"Hicks? Are you kidding me?" I said.

"Nope."

"It's a bombshell Tom, but what's it all got to do with Garnet quitting?"

"Carrie felt her father should have been able to solve the case. Hicks and his wife were drinking that night. But Hicks claimed his car was stolen. And nobody saw him drive away from the bar. Says he called a friend for a ride and the friend backed him up."

"How reliable a witness was the friend?"

"I always thought the alibi had holes. But what do I know?"

"I don't remember this," Sheila said.

"Happened after you left home. You had your own place. Everyday news gets lost over the distance. Anyhow, Carrie felt her dad would have solved the case if it weren't for his drinking. And I know for a fact he was really into the sauce at the time."

"So he quit his job or was he asked to resign?"

"I like to think he quit. And it wasn't the booze. He always drank and despite that, he still got by. I think his quitting had more to do with guilt than with questions of competence."

"Guilt over failing his daughter?"

"And disappointment in himself for not solving the most important case of his life."

"Or maybe he was just worn out," I said. "Thirty years in policing is a long time for anybody. In human years, it's a couple centuries."

eleven

AS FAMILY GATHERINGS GO, IT may have been typical. I say that even though I have no basis for comparison, unless TV sitcoms are a valid yardstick.

It was past midnight, and at that hour one's behaviour is less guarded. Mrs. Mackie, Mike and Lori were already seated at the kitchen table, looking tired after a long night of carousing. Sheila, her father and I invited ourselves to the post-party party by sitting down with them. Mike may have used a swear word. Otherwise there were unspoken greetings all around.

Settling in, munching chocolate chip cookies and drinking coffee strong enough to wake the dead, I surveyed the group. No one was in a talking mood. Mike's scowl confirmed he was indeed grumpy, likely still mad at me. I thought possibly he was mad at Lori, too. Maybe they'd had a lovers' spat. Or maybe you just stop talking at some point after the first couple years of marriage.

Mr. Mackie took a sip of coffee and turned white, suffering a gas attack from too many ribs and not enough milk of magnesia or vice versa. Ignoring her husband's discomfort, Mrs. Mackie was close to nodding off. Sheila aside, it was not a picture the Mackies would want sent out on their Christmas cards.

Bored, I spent a good ten minutes trying to detect if Sheila was wearing her bedroom eyes but I gave up when I remembered the sleeping arrangements. Instead, I passed the cookies around. Everyone took one but no one ate.

It was a silence broken, thankfully, by the opening bars to 'Badge,' a damned fine cut from Cream's 1969 Goodbye album. I let it play a second and third time. When I went for a fourth, Mrs. Mackie rose from the table, threw her coffee down the drain and stomped out of the room. A lot was happening without a word being said.

"Jack here," I said into my cell.

Sheila headed for her bedroom, likely to fantasize about boy bands, their posters taped to the surfaces around and over her bed. I headed for the back porch to get out of earshot of the rest of the Mackie clan.

"Remember me?" the caller said. "You gave me one of your cards?'

"You got my logo, first try."

The woman laughed. "Hope it's not too late."

"Nah. Always vigilant."

"Oh?"

"It doesn't say that on my card?"

"I'll check."

There was a pause.

"Nope," she said.

I laughed. "How are you, Maddie?"

"I've been thinking, Jack. Watching."

"Ear to the ground too?"

"Yeah."

"And?"

"It's not like I've found Hicks for you or anything."

"But you have something?"

"You might call it a lead." She giggled, getting into the lingo.

"I could use one of those."

"You know the three impersonators?"

"I thought we weren't supposed to use that word?"

"It's allowed as long as we're not talking about Elvis impersonators."

"So which impersonators are you talking about? The three stooges?"

"What?"

"Sorry, it's a nickname I heard used for three guys I met at a party."

"Yeah?"

I explained, "Three guys. Pop star look-alikes. A Roy Orbison, a Bobby Darin and a Wayne Newton."

"Okay. Yeah. Them."

"Somehow, Wayne doesn't belong with the other two, don't you think?"

"Exactly. Different genre. Different style."

"Wasn't Wayne always big with the older crowd?"

"The blue hair set?" She laughed. "The man doesn't say much, does he?"

"He says, 'Danke Schoen.'"

She laughed again.

"So what about these guys?"

"They were here for dinner. I overheard them talking to two non-Elvis tourists. Two young fellers dressed in fancy hiking duds. Pressed khaki shorts, matching shirts, double breast pockets with flaps, neck scarves and boots that hadn't seen much hiking. Real cuties."

"Cuties? They don't sound like your type."

"I meant to each other."

"So, what's the deal?"

"The hikers left and while I was clearing their table, the other three guys…"

"The three stooges?"

"Yeah, only it was Roy Orbison doing the talking. He says to me, 'those two city boys got a pretty good scare.' And I says, 'How so?'"

She paused, letting the airwaves go quiet. Letting the suspense build, enjoying it.

"What scared them?" I said finally.

"They were somewhere near 'Old Baldy'" she said. Old Baldy, one of the more popular features of the Niagara Escarpment, is a white dolomite skull jutting into the sky on the east side of the Beaver Valley. That's what the literature says. The cliff face looks human. Like a giant skull. But I've studied the rock prominence and all I see is a rock prominence.

"I thought you said they were armchair hikers?"

"Maybe they parked in the Conservation Authority lot up there, or they stopped at the side of the road. Who cares, Jack? They got there somehow, but that's got nothing to do with what I'm trying to tell you."

"Sorry. Finish the story."

"According to Roy, the hikers were wandering around and ended up going down an old driveway off the Bruce Trail."

"Why?"

"Why's got nothing to do with what I'm trying to tell you either, Jack."

"Sorry."

"Anyway, they were taking pictures and apparently they zeroed in on an old farmhouse. You know what I mean. One of these old, abandoned places. Rustic. Kind of thing appeals to the artistic type."

"And what happened?"

"They shouldn't have been there. It was way off the public trail."

She was really milking it.

"And, here's the thing. The place wasn't empty."

"It wasn't abandoned?"

"No. You may not know this but in some parts of this county you don't want to be caught trespassing."

"What happened?"

"There were three or four guys. Young guys. They showed up. Scared the crap out of 'em."

"Got anything more on these four guys?"

"Rapper types, according to the hikers."

"And according to Roy Orbison," I added. Maddie was passing on third hand information and I saw the Orbison clone as a big talker. Despite that, the story had the ring of truth to it.

"How'd these rappers scare the hikers?"

"They surrounded the city boys, pushed them around, beat on them a little and stole their camera. Then they told them to piss off."

"Hmm." I wasn't about to mention it but my adrenalin notched up. The hikers walked into something but maybe it wasn't what they thought it was. Sure it could have been a bunch of locals just being assholes or protecting a marijuana crop.

But maybe it was something entirely different.

And maybe this juicy tidbit was the break I'd been looking for, a break leading to a viable, concrete theory. Or, at least to a good idea.

At worst, it gave me something to think about. Or not.

"Does dead air mean you're putting two and two together, Jack?"

I hadn't come to four yet, but I said, "If the hikers were trespassing, I'd be willing to bet they weren't the only ones."

"Nope. The thugs didn't sound like landowners."

"What are the chances these young toughs were the same ones who were in your restaurant the other day? Maybe following Hicks?"

"That's why I called," she said. "I had this funny feeling."

On the one hand, it seemed like a stretch for these guys, rappers the hikers called them, to have enough of an interest in Dwayne Hicks to kidnap him. On the other hand, it's never smart to ignore coincidences.

"Thanks, Maddie," I said. "I owe you a big one."

"I can get free tomorrow night." She laughed the same laugh I heard first time we met. Then she said, "So what are you going to do with all the valuable leads I just dropped in your lap?"

"I have to find the hikers."

"Or, the rappers?"

"Priority is finding Hicks. If I find him, chances are good, the rappers will be there."

"And the hikers are the key?"

"You're in the wrong line of business, Maddie."

<u>twelve</u>

SHEILA WAS ALREADY IN BED, the only bed in the room. It shouldn't have surprised me, though I could have sworn it was my turn. Not wanting to make a fuss, I pulled the floor mat out and settled down for the night.

But Sheila had other plans.

"There's room in here for you, Babe," she said.

I can be irresistible. Either that or the boy bands got her engine warmed up for me. But it wasn't the time to ask questions. And an hour later, I forgave her for taking the bed out of turn.

• • • • • •

At breakfast the next morning, Clapton's guitar riff shattered the morning gloom and stirred the Mackie pot again. Mr. Mackie threw a tentative smile my way. Mike scowled and swore, again, under his breath. Lori was still in bed, likely dreaming about me. Mrs. Mackie stomped off to the living room, spilling her coffee on the way.

I looked at Sheila, my eyebrows making a question mark.

"Mom thinks you're being disrespectful," she said.

"Maybe I should mute my cell?"

"Naw," she said. "Why don't you turn it up. See what she does?"

"Think she'll hit me?"

"That'd be fun."

"Sheila," said her Dad. But as he left the room to join the missus, his smile widened some.

"Jack," I said, flipping open my cell.

"It's me again. They're here."

"The hikers?"

"No. The three stooges."

"They likely to stick around?"

"They just ordered breakfast."

"Hold onto them. I'm on the way." I closed my cell.

"Where you going?" said Sheila.

"The three stooges are at Connie's restaurant."

"Who?"

"Remember those three guys I met at the V.I.P. dinner? Roy Orbison, Bobby Darin...."

"Oh yeah," she said, "And Wayne Newton. The three look-a-likes. You think they're involved?"

"It's a remote possibility."

"Why remote?"

"Sure, their dislike of Elvis impersonators is intense, but...."

"But as suspects go, how serious are we talking?"

"All the talk – it seems like an act."

"Actors have been known to commit murder."

"Except in this case, their expertise doesn't seem to go beyond gossip and drinking."

"So why are you so excited?"

"I'm pretty sure they know something."

I grabbed my riding gear and pushed through the screen door.

"Put the helmet away, Jack. I'm driving." The baritone belonged to Garnet Henderson, lounging in a deck chair, boots resting on the porch rail, just outside the door.

"Where is it you think we're going?"

"Don't know but, I heard you got hired to find Dwayne Hicks. And I figured you might need somebody knows the lay of the land. Somebody can open some doors."

He was right, but there was a problem.

"The guys who hired me are skinflints," I said.

"Wasn't applying for a job," he said. "At least not one with pay."

"Then why?"

He shrugged.

I thought about it and said, "You feel like you're coming up on the eighteenth green?"

"Hell, Jack, I putted out years ago. I'm not even in the club-house anymore."

"Where are you then?"

"All I know is the buggers turfed me out. And told me not to come back."

I knew he wasn't talking about golf courses anymore.

"Let's do it." I tossed my helmet on the chair Garnet vacated and climbed into his truck.

"Where to?"

"Connie's. You know the place?"

"We gonna work together, try not asking stupid questions, Jack."

• • • • • •

The three stooges were still at Connie's, bloating up on maybe their sixth or seventh cup of coffee. There was no food left for me on the table.

They didn't ask why we were fishing in their pond, maybe because they regarded our inquiries as a chance to crack wise. And crack wise they did. Unfortunately, their serious answers were no more use to me than the wise-cracks.

For starters, they couldn't come up with a more precise location for the farmhouse than Maddie had already given me. In the second place, they didn't know where the hikers were staying.

But Maddie, who hovered nearby, was prepared to make a guess.

"Go ahead," I told her.

"I'm stereotyping here but you might check the 'Feathered Nest' bed and breakfast."

"Why?"

"Birds of a feather…"

On our way out the door, Garnet mentioned, "I know the owners of the B&B."

"How?"

"They got here and they had trouble fitting in. People were picking on them."

"Yeah, small towns usually lean toward the homophobic."

"That wasn't it."

"What then?"

"They moved here from Toronto."

I laughed,

"So, as Police Chief, you took it upon yourself to help the newcomers settle in."

"Yup."

"It work? You got the rednecks that were hassling them to back off?"

"What do you think?"

thirteen

AS HAS BEEN DONE IN so many other Ontario towns, the owners of the Feathered Nest took an architectural relic from the past and nursed it back to health. In doing so, they rescued it from conversion to apartments or worse, from the wreckers' ball. And so, their bed and breakfast and others like it, offers the rest of us the chance, if only for a short spell, to travel back in time.

Garnet was already imitating a pileated woodpecker with the help of the pitted iron knocker imbedded in the hardwood maple of the over-sized front door.

I hadn't made it onto the wraparound porch yet, stuck as I was on the sidewalk, standing between the trunks and under the umbrellas of a pair of oak giants. I looked up through the branches at the corner turret rising maybe forty feet above me, studying the sculpted stone work around the stained glass windows across the front of the house and wondering what stories lay hidden behind lace curtains.

Whether they were ruthless tycoons exploiting the land and its people or they were nation builders, I have to say the furniture makers, mill owners, lumber kings, shipping magnates and political leaders of the nineteenth century damn well knew how to build a house.

The door opened and a slight, boyish looking man appeared, beaming into Garnet's face. I caught up to them before they closed me out.

As with their outside efforts, James Marks and his partner Louis Lafontaine maintained the same kind of loyalty to authenticity in redecorating the parlour where we gathered to talk.

I wanted to give these guys an award, not only for the home they opened to visitors but for the goodies laid out for us, including the hazelnut flavoured coffee wafting my way.

Feeling pretty mellow, I picked up a magazine from the rack beside my chair. It was an older Rolling Stone, the cover of which announced the top one hundred singing voices of all time. I couldn't resist so I called a time out to scan the forty odd pages.

Meanwhile, Mark, Louis and Garnet caught up on old times.

"I'm okay with Aretha at number one," I said, upon finishing, "and John Lennon and Otis Redding are in the Top Ten. And that's good."

"Elvis in there?" Garnet wanted to know.

"Guess."

"Number two?"

"Almost as bad. He's frigging number three," I said.

"Who's two then?"

"Ray Charles."

"Interesting choice," said Garnet.

"And if you can believe this, Dylan's number seven. Shit, the guy's only got one note."

I went looking for more mistakes.

"Diana Ross in there?" James wanted to know.

I checked and told him, "No. You got a problem with that?"

He shook his head.

I returned to the job at hand.

"Stevie Winwood should be higher," I said. "And if Levon Helm's in, Richard Manual should be with him."

"Roy Orbison make the top ten?" Garnet asked.

"Nope."

"It's bogus."

I searched for more glaring omissions. "No Billy Joel. No David Crosby."

"Criminal."

"Oh man. Can you believe this? Not only did they leave Tom Johnston of the Doobies out, but Clapton didn't make it. He's not even in the top hundred."

I wanted to shoot something.

"Where the hell's John Mellencamp?" I yelled. "And Jim Cuddy? For crying out loud, I'm cancelling my subscription."

"You get this magazine?" Garnet said.

"No, but maybe James will cancel his?"

James shook his head.

"Any Canadians at all?" Garnet said. I figured he was offended at the Cuddy oversight.

"Joni Mitchell."

"Neil Young?"

"Yeah, but at 37."

"Burton Cummings?"

I flipped the pages and couldn't find his name.

"Goddamn stupid Americans," I said, tossing the magazine out of the room and into the hallway.

"And as such, maybe you can't expect them to include guys like Cummings or Cuddy," Garnet said.

"Because they're too frigging Canadian to make it through the screening process."

"And too damn good to be left out," Garnet added.

"Exactly."

"The Backstreet Boys in there?" Louis wanted to know.

I ignored the question because I didn't want to strangle my host.

"Didn't you want to talk to us?" asked James, after retrieving the magazine.

Somehow the question found a way through my disgust. "Yeah. Sorry." I said.

"Well?"

Clearing the inequities of the Rolling Stone's ranking from my head, I finally said, "We have a tip in a case we're working on. You have two lodgers that may be able to help us. Hikers."

"We know who you must be referring to but we don't like to talk about our guests, Mr. Beer," said James, the slight one.

Louis, a hefty version of James, clicked his tongue in agreement.

"We're not interested in the hikers per se," I said. "We're interested in what they know. What they saw."

"What on earth would they have seen? They only just arrived."

"What are their names?"

"Nigel and Byron."

"Last names?"

"That will be in our registry book. Why do you want to know?"

"We think Nigel and Byron may be witnesses in a case. A kidnapping."

"Gracious," said Louis. "Kidnapping. Of whom?"

I looked at Garnet. He gave me the go-ahead by nodding his head once.

"It's confidential," I said.

Our hosts moved to the edge of their Victorian loveseat.

"The information does not leave this room," I warned them.

"Oh my," our hosts said, speaking as one.

"Dwayne Curtis Hicks is missing," I said, keeping my voice low, to underline the sensitivity of the news.

"Oh, that awful man," said James, shaking his head and getting up to refill our coffee cups.

Louis now extended his forward lean, showing he could get even more discreet. "Mr. Hicks was one of the nasty men who made our lives miserable when we first came to town," he whispered behind his hand. So as not to upset James further, I guessed. "And then Chief Henderson straightened him out along with his loutish friends." It was Louis' turn to beam at my colleague, who winked at the man.

James served us from a coffee urn and then returned it to a fancy trolley sitting in front of a ten foot wide fireplace, where he stood and leaned on the mantle, showing a face that hinted at a decision.

I cued the guy with my index finger.

He turned to his partner and said, "Louis, I think it is our duty to tell them whatever it is we know."

And they did. Unfortunately, they were little more help than the three Stooges were. For one thing, the hikers had already left town. Then, they gave us two last names but they were only slightly less common than Smith and Jones. And while they couldn't recall an address, they showed us the entry in their guest registry and all that was written was the word, 'Toronto,' which narrowed the search down considerably from North America. Last, they'd paid in cash. Meaning no name confirmation and no credit card slip to be traced.

It was like they never existed.

And so we left.

Still, the Bed and Breakfast wasn't a complete dead-end. Sure, the owners' information on the hikers was sketchy, but on the plus side, Garnet and I took a pleasant trip back in time, which beat the Elvis festivities all to hell. And the scones and cream were better than anything Sheila and I offered at Gert's. But then again none of our customers would have known what to do with a scone.

"What now, Mr. PI?" Garnet said, as we left our morning break three stop signs behind us.

"I'm going to write a letter to the editor of that frigging magazine."

"Forget Rolling Stone magazine. What about Hicks?"

"Usually, when I don't know what to do, I go for a run."

"Clears the mind? Let's the relevant facts percolate to the surface?" Garnet said.

"No, just makes me feel better."

"Like you've accomplished something?"

"Yeah."

"Except don't you end up where you started?"

"I try not to think about it that way."

"When this happens to me…"

"You mean when you hit a dead end?"

"Yeah. I call it 'square one time,'" he said.

"That's about right."

"So at square one, I try some new angle."

"I'm not ready to give up my old angle yet."

"Okay. I'll drop you. Go for your run. Then meet me at the tavern."

"Which one? Heart Breakers? The country bar?"

"Yup."

"When?"

"Say two o'clock."

"Why?"

"There's someone we should talk to."

fourteen

GARNET LEFT ME AT THE end of the driveway and I hoofed it along the winding lane to the Mackie cottage where I bumped into a racing green Jaguar, the new model that crossbred sports car and sedan. It was the kind of car I would like to have become acquainted with, and there it sat, idling beside my motorcycle.

As I made my way over to investigate, Lori Mackie emerged from the passenger side. She stepped back at the sight of me, first surprised and then upset. Whether she was angry at me or the guy behind the wheel, I couldn't tell.

Not until she screamed, "Tell the bastard to go to hell, Jack." And she made an obscene gesture before running down to the beach. Although running isn't the right word to use to describe a woman in stilettos and tight jeans hot-footing it over broken shale.

I approached the car from a thirty degree angle, edging over to the driver's side window as it disappeared into the door panel to reveal Peter Lake.

"What are you doing here?" I said.

"Lori and I just went for a drive."

"Why?"

"Just sniffing around."

I looked toward the shore. Lori was sitting on a log, crying.

"Let's try again. I said, 'what in the hell are you doing here'?"

"And I answered."

"Don't piss me off, Lake."

"Is that any way to speak to your employer?"

"You didn't hire me. Olson did. I work for the man and his daughter."

"The way I see it, you work for Ted Olson, you work for me."

"You're still dodging my question."

I wanted very badly for the man to get out of his car. So I could ram my fist down his throat. Not because he'd upset Lori, but because I didn't like the self-satisfied smile on his Hollywood face, the material of his jacket or the cut of his steroid enhanced torso. In particular I didn't like his slippery tongue.

Most of all, I didn't like the fact he sat behind the wheel of a Jaguar XF.

"I'm going now, Jack. But pass on a message for me. To your sister-in-law."

"She's not my sister-in-law."

"Lori needs to learn to keep her knickers on," he said.

Now I was mad for Lori's sake.

I reached for his door handle but Peter Lake had already shifted into reverse. He looked me in the eyes as he backed away. But not before I spit on the Jag's hood. It was juvenile but it made me feel better.

As I walked to the shore, I debated on the interrogation technique I would use. Cajole the woman, trip her up with incisive probing or beat her with a stick.

There was lots of room for me on the log, so I sat down beside Lori. Which she apparently wasn't expecting because she jumped up and hissed at me, "It's none of your goddamn business, Jack" and stomped back to the cottage.

The interview was over. Good thing for her too, because there was a good sized stick on the ground right beside me.

I followed the path Lori took back to the cottage, changed into my running gear, and headed for Blue Mountain Road which, according to the map pinned to the paneling in the mud room, would eventually lead to the kind of hills that would take my mind off all the bullshit. And the map was almost right except the hills were so tough, my main concern became survival.

• • • • • •

Leaving the sunshine outside, it took thirty seconds for my eyes to adjust.

Heart Breakers was mostly empty, which explained why my eyes were drawn to the red head. But as explanations go, that one was incomplete. Shapely legs, crossed at the knee, were a good part of the rest of it. I made a study of her as I worked my way over to the bar. Too much make-up and too few garments, too tight and too scanty, hinted at what her line of work might be.

I emptied my glass before the barkeep could pocket his tip. Beer always tastes best after a workout. And it's downright medicinal following hill intervals. Before my second was poured, the door opened behind me. His lanky silhouette identified him in an instant. Then he was standing at my right shoulder.

"You're early." He carried a large, thick envelope under his arm.

"I was hoping to get a head start." I headed for an unoccupied table, figuring we needed the space if Garnet planned to share the content of the envelope.

"No, Jack. This table looks good," my partner said, sitting to the left of long legs-short skirt and patting the woman's wrist. She smiled sweetly as he called out for a round.

As I pulled up my own chair, I stole a closer look at the woman's face. She was very pretty but the creases told me she'd put in her time.

"Jack Beer," said Garnet, "say hi to Jeanie Brown."

I smiled and extended my hand, "Nice to meet you."

She straightened in her chair. Her gauzy blouse failed to hide the fact she wasn't wearing a bra. Jeanie's aqua blues tried to seduce me, like it was an automatic response, designed specifically for my gender.

"I'm spoken for," I said.

"Most of the good ones are," she said.

"Jeanie, does Corey still live with you?" Garnet wanted to know, breaking through our rehearsed connection.

"Not since he left school."

"He finish?"

"He finished grade 10. Though he didn't even deserve that."

"What is he? Twenty?"

"Seems like he should be, all the grief he's caused me. No, he just turned eighteen."

"Corey on his own?"

"He lives out there somewhere." There was a catch in her voice.

"He leave or you kick him out?" Garnet asked.

"He left.... though I should have kicked him out. Frigging music of his. Crimester music. Rap or hip-hop. Head banger stuff."

"Not sure it can be all those things at the same time," I said.

"Whatever the hell they call it now, it's noise and it made me crazy."

Jeanie saw my head going in agreement.

She smiled again. It was some kind of smile.

A sudden ray of sunshine hit Garnet in the face, or maybe it was the sight of the woman walking over to our table that brought him to a stop.

I used the break in the conversation to whisper into Jeanie's ear, "I have this theory."

"What theory is that, sweetie?"

"I don't believe the ash trees were knocked off by the emerald ash borer."

"No?"

"No. I believe it was rap music killed 'em off."

"Worth checking into," said Jeannie.

Her smile broadened into a laugh. I turned to see what the intruder wanted.

"Why Garnet Henderson, I thought that was your truck in the parking lot," we heard her say.

"It surely is," he said.

"You old dog, you still hiding from me?"

"Can't be done," he answered.

The woman's voice sounded familiar but I got no clues from the shadow she formed against the light of the still closing entrance door.

Dark again, I refocused until I was able to recognize the leopard tights.

"Jack, this is Penny Sue Stanfield," he said.

"We've met."

"You two teaming up?" she asked, talking to me but looking at Garnet.

"We're giving it a try," I said.

"Your new partner tell you about him and me?" Penny Sue said.

"Penny." Garnet's voice was a warning.

The woman shrugged, turned her attention to Jeannie Brown and said, "How's that boy of yours, hon'?"

"Corey's fine." Which even Penny Sue Stanfield could see was a lie.

"Sometimes I can't believe he's the same sweet little baby I helped deliver."

"You a nurse?" I said.

"Used to be," she answered. And then to Jeanie Brown, "Whatever happened to that poor child?"

"I'm sure you'll tell me, Penny Sue. If only for my own good."

"Well, he can't be all bad. If only he used the sense God gave him…"

"Meaning what?"

"The company he's keeping."

"I know the kind of person he hangs with." The cockiness and fun in Jeannie Brown's voice was gone and the emotional timbre I picked up earlier was back.

"What do you think he and that TA might have been talking about?" Penny Sue asked.

It disturbed me that I'd reached the point that the festival insider code, its acronyms and short forms, meant something to me. I wondered which Elvis tribute artist she might be referring to.

"Get to the point, Penny," Jeanie told her.

"No point dear. Just thought it was curious, Corey and his pals deep in discussion with an Elvis TA. Never would have thought they'd have anything in common to talk about."

"Where was this?" I asked.

"The park with the cenotaph."

Penny Sue Stanfield made a big production out of getting ready to leave, but first she leaned over and said directly to me, "You know who he looked like?"

"Who?"

"The tribute artist."

"No, who'd he look like?"

"Mike Mackie."

"Mike?"

I didn't believe it. There were likely a half dozen reasons for Mike to meet with a bunch of underachieving wannabe rappers, but I couldn't think of one that would look any good on him.

"Yes, Mike Mackie." She paused and then said, "Oh, that's right. You two know each other. You were with him at the festival opening bash. Is he a relative or something?"

"Not quite," I said.

And then she was gone.

"That bitch has a screw loose," said Jeanie.

"No," said Garnet.

"Then she's pissed at you over something, Garnet," I said.

He stayed quiet and still, until I nudged him with my foot. "What is it you wanted to ask Jeanie?"

He turned to our table companion and told her gently, "There's a possibility Corey's getting into something."

"Something to do with what Penny Sue said?"

"That's hard to say until one of us talks to Mike Mackie."

"Okay. So there's trouble. Are you sure he's involved?"

"It's just an educated guess."

"How bad?" Jeannie Brown wanted to know.

"Bad enough."

"Can you fix it?"

"Don't know," Garnet said.

He looked at me. "We'll do our best," I said.

"Sometimes Corey's not too swift," the woman said about her son. "If he's in trouble, it's because he happened to be there, not because he started it. Mostly, he's a bystander. It wouldn't have been his idea. He's a wrong time, wrong place kind of kid."

"I know. Look, on the subject of 'wrong places,' " Garnet said, "do you have any idea where he might be? Some kind of hangout?"

Jeanie played with her beer mug, glossy red nails tapping out a tune I didn't recognize.

"There's a place. It's near Duncan Lake."

Garnet turned to me, "Duncan Lake's just north of Old Baldy."

"Near the place the hikers ran into difficulty?"

"Yep."

"Just curious," I said, "was there a Young Baldy?"

Garnet stared at me, shook his head and turned his sleepy gaze back to Jeanie Brown without answering my question. "Have you been there?" he asked Jeannie Brown.

"Yeah, once. Couple years ago. I drove out with Linda Martin," she said. "We wanted to break up a pot party. Before the cops beat us to it."

"Corey still hang with Linda's kid?"

"I wish. Drew Martin's a good boy. He's gone to college in Kitchener."

"Got any names?" Garnet said.

"There's Jeremy."

"Jeremy Linkletter?"

"Yeah. The little prick."

"I knew him as a kid. Played hockey on a team I coached. Not too big but tough. Wiry build. Good player."

"What'd you think of him?" I said.

"Smart mouth. Worse though, I couldn't get him to stop using his stick like it was a weapon."

I turned to Jeannie. "Tell us about the hangout."

"It's an old farmhouse. It was boarded up once, but that didn't keep the kids out. And there's a barn. It's a long way from the road, but once you know where it is, it isn't hard to find."

"Could you take us there?" I said.

"Do I have to?"

"You'd rather not know if Corey's involved?"

Jeanie Brown nodded her head.

"I've got some maps," said Garnet, opening the thick manila envelope he brought with him.

Shuffling through the worn topographic sheets, he picked one and opened it on the table. We all leaned in to take in the details; lakes, streams, roads, contours, even buildings and vegetation cover. Jeanie moved me out of the light and got still closer. Eventually, she stabbed a spot with the red nail at the end of her index finger.

"Thought so," said Garnet.

"You know that property?"

He nodded his head and said, "You ready to roll?"

"Let's do it." Then, meaning to thank Jeanie, I saw her eyes mist over. Instead, I said, "We'll keep Corey out of it." Figuring a half-assed promise was worth more than a worthless thank you.

"Got a picture of your son?" Garnet asked.

She dug into a tiny beaded purse. "This was before the weird hair and the piercings."

Garnet placed a large hand on her shoulder and left it there while she covered his fingers with her cheek. On our way out, Garnet paid for Jeanie's drink and another round.

fifteen

"HOW DO YOU KNOW ABOUT this place?" I said.

We were driving Garnet's Ford pick-up after having dropped my motorcycle at the cottage.

"The old farmhouse we're heading for is notorious," he said. "Or least it used to be. Through the years, it's been a hang-out and a place for bush parties. We raided it more than a few times. Usually backing up the OPP. "

"It would have been their jurisdiction."

"Yeah, but there were as many town kids as country kids who used the place."

"Major headache?"

"It wasn't as bad as I'm making it sound. We usually didn't lay charges. Just confiscated the booze and dope and made the kids call their parents to come pick them up. And roughed up anyone who talked back."

"Best thing to do," I said.

"We were a lot tougher on the assaults that sometimes happened out there."

"Best thing to do," I said, again. "I'm thinking it doesn't sound like a very good place for a party, let alone a hideout. Too well known."

"You're right. But things have changed. It's been a few years. Ever since the kids figured out the cops had the property on their radar, they smartened up. Now they wait for the next farm kid to let it slip that the parents are away and they all show up for a bush party."

"I don't see these rapper kids as part of that crowd. They must have been fringe."

"They're fringe all right."

"Yeah, but as Jeanie said, their little subculture used the place in the past."

"And maybe lately too," said Garnet.

"Because the rappers realize the hangout's off the screen by now. Smart."

"I know Corey and some of his friends. Other than the Linkletter kid, smart isn't the word I would apply."

"Of course, this could be another dead-end."

"Oh well. Nice day for a drive."

Garnet punched in on an old rock station just in time for one of John Lennon's masterpieces. We went quiet, bobbing along to 'Starting Over,' taking in the scenery and letting the Beatles' best singer do his thing.

John finished and I looked over at Garnet.

"What do you call that part where the song stops and if you don't know better, you think it's over. But you do know, so you wait and then wham, the band powers up again. Usually the drummer hits the skins. Makes you turn up the volume and you want to punch the air."

"Like Alice Cooper. In that song 'I Feel So Strong,'" he said

I smiled, "It's called, 'Hello, Hooray,' I think. Amazing what a full symphony orchestra will do for you. "

"Don't know why I mentioned that. He was such a frigging weirdo."

I sorted through the catalogue of songs in my head and came up with another one. "Remember that song by Glenn Frey," I said.

"After he went solo?"

"Yeah."

"Which one."

"'True Love.' Great dance tune. Almost has a Motown sound to it. It's got one of those pauses. Signal to freeze on the dance floor. Until the song cranks up again and then you spin your partner, or do a half turn. Maybe you dip."

"You like to dance?"

"Sheila does."

He laughed and so did I.

"So, you like Glen Frey. What did you think of the Eagles?" he asked.

"Great. Never like to see the good ones split up. But I have to say, those other guys did some really good stuff solo too."

"I'm glad they got back together."

We covered a few more clicks while the Doobies, another group that should have stayed together, sang about a China Doll.

When the song ended, I turned down the volume again and said, "What about Blue Rodeo's cover of 'To Love Somebody'?"

"You're right. It's got one, too."

"So, what do you call it?" I said.

"The pause before they crank it up again?"

"Yeah. There must be a word for it."

"Songwriters must call it something."

"'Badge' has one."

"'Badge'?"

"Clapton. Opening riff's programmed into my cell," I said.

"Didn't know the title. It's a good one, too," he said.

We thought about it some more while Stevie Wonder sang the praises of Duke Ellington.

"Maybe they call it a 'time-out'?" Garnet tried.

"That doesn't sound right to me."

"Me either."

"How about a 'fakeout'?" I said, liking it soon as I said it, maybe because 'fakeout' is a sports term. Or maybe I liked the word because it reminded me of my work – someone is always throwing false leads at me, going for the big 'fakeout,' all the while believing I'm too dense to catch on.

"Yeah," Garnet said. "First time you hear it, you figure the song's over. But the band tricked you. There's more. It's just a fakeout."

"Notice sometimes the DJ doesn't even know?"

"Most of 'em are just too young."

"Some of my favourite songs have a fakeout."

"Have fakeouts fallen out of favour?"

"Hard to know," I said. "Don't listen all that much to anything done after 1978. Unless it's Blue Rodeo. A few others."

"You that old?"

"I was a kid for some of the best '70s stuff. But, you have to agree, it was music you could lose yourself in."

"You needed to lose yourself?"

"Sometimes."

Garnet turned down a song by the early Beach Boys.

"I just decided something," I said.

"What?"

"First chance I get, I'm going to fill a CD with all time best fakeout tunes."

"You know how to do that?"

"Do what? Scorch a CD?"

"I think you 'burn' them.'"

"That so?"

"Yep."

"Well anyhow, one of the teenagers who works at the coffee shop does it for me, when things are slow."

"Have her 'scorch' me a copy."

"Done."

Garnet took the Simcoe-Grey County line dead south and then Grey Road 19 west until it turned into gravel after a couple of concessions. We jogged left, right, left again, right and up, down and backwards for all I could tell. I was thoroughly lost, which was not a concern. Garnet knew exactly what he was doing.

The farther we went, the rougher the land and the prettier the scenery got. Rail and stone fencelines separated us from 'crops' of thigh high grasses and broken apple trees. Good country for bluebirds and indigo buntings, making me think we should stop and find a quiet spot, a spot where we could blend in and see what comes along. Garnet smiled like he knew what I was thinking.

"Get this bullshit out of the way Jack, and we'll come back. We'll do some hiking. I'll show you around."

At the twenty five minute mark, Garnet pulled over. We were nowhere, which I discovered was a peaceful place. He pointed through the windshield glass. I followed a line out from his long index finger over a bumpy field that climbed sharply to a tree line and from there to a building barely visible through the foliage.

"We going in naked?" he said.

"Got a problem with that?"

"No, for this, I prefer it."

"Likelihood is they aren't armed. It's not Toronto," he said.

"That said, I suggest we go in quietly. Come at it from the back side."

"Agreed."

We scrambled over a destroyed stone fence and angled across the old pasture dodging the boulders left by the last glacier, toward the treeline, a football field away. Except instead of breaking through to the lane, we turned right and for cover, we used a low rubble fence, overgrown with junk trees and grapevines, in case anyone was watching from the farmhouse for unexpected guests.

Our screen ended a full pitching wedge from the house, provided the golfer was Tiger Woods. We crouched behind a tangle of raspberry bushes and considered the scene beyond. The building was more eyesore than the subject of artistic study that the Toronto hikers found it to be. Asphalt shingle siding turns ugly long before a structure falls over. The sagging roof suggested gravity was due to finish the house off sometime within the decade. I figured the outbuildings had more character, but that didn't make them habitable.

I raised binoculars for a closer view and saw no evidence of human activity, no boots by the door, no garbage bags on the porch, no lace curtains and no apple pie on the kitchen sill. I passed my glasses to Garnet.

"Damn," he said. "Looks deserted."

"We'll check it out anyway."

"Right," he said. "I'll go left. You go right. We meet at the back of the house."

Five minutes later, we were leaning against the back porch, comparing notes. There were tire tracks which could have been yesterday's or last month's. There was no way to tell and Gil Grissom wasn't around to ask. The empty beer and liquor bottles lying in the matted grass were also impossible to date, but peering between the boards someone tacked on the windows, I thought the abandoned milk cartons and candy wrappers scattered around the living room looked, "contemporaneous."

"You sound like one of those anthropologists."

"Someone's been here," I said, translating. "Recently."

"Gotcha."

The back door opened easily, not counting the screeching sound that sent the mice packing. I propped the door open for light. Porcupines had gnawed at every piece of exposed wood and the floor droppings indicated a variety of vermin shared the lodgings.

There were three doors leading from the kitchen, two open, one closed. The first showed us a hallway that would have led to the front door and another opened into a dining room. We left the closed door for later consideration.

Garnet entered the hallway, which eventually took him to a parlour on the right. I took the open door, which took me left through a jumble of musty smelling, broken furniture. We found nothing, not counting each other, having returned to our starting point. As the main floor contained no clues as to the whereabouts of Dwayne Hicks, we were left with only two investigative paths, if you could count the closed kitchen door and a staircase at the front of the house as investigative paths.

I jiggled the closed kitchen door and figured two things: one, the door led to the cellar and two, it hung by one last hinge and three rusted set screws. I finished the job with a side kick I'd seen Jackie Chan use in the movies. I wasn't being paid enough not to have fun. The door screeched and tipped over before sliding, at an angle, down the stairs. But before even taking the first step of my descent, two quick thuds brought me up short.

We looked up at the ceiling.

"That was no raccoon," I said.

I turned around and charged down the hall and up the stairs at the front of the house, Garnet right behind me. Why we were in such a rush to dive head first into the unknown I can't answer. We were unarmed and we had no idea what the thumping was. I suppose adrenalin affects judgment. Besides, I'm tougher than shoe leather. Garnet was old school too. But, we were also aware that sometimes knowing we can take care of ourselves guarantees nothing. Common sense finally slowed me down when I reached the landing.

A six paned window let the sunshine in. My trained investigator's eye suggested three bedrooms. There were four doors, two wide open and two shut tight, one of which we discovered hid a closet full of empty shelves. The last door had to be the third bedroom.

It was locked up tight. Another clue.

Despite what you see on TV, it hurts like a bitch smashing through a padlocked door. I hoped for an easier way.

"Anybody home?" I called.

"Get me the fuck out of here, you fucking shithead!"

"You think someone's in there?" I said.

"Possibly."

"You think it's him?"

"Whoever it is, he sure is rude."

"Let's leave him," I said.

"Okay with me."

"No, we better not." And then to the door, I said, "That you Dwayne?"

"Who the fuck you think it is?"

"You alone?" I wanted to know.

"No, the Queen Mother's with me."

"Don't shit me around, Dwayne. The Queen Mum died a few years ago."

"Not funny!"

"Yeah, it is."

"Quit screwing the dog and get me out of here, you son of a bitch."

"He makes it hard to want to effect much of a rescue," said Garnet.

"Don't go away," I called through the door. "We're going to find a pry bar. Or dynamite. Or something."

A broad axe, a pitch fork, three shovels and a dozen tools I couldn't identify, together with a collection of mismatched lumber, formed a small mountain in a dark corner of the barn. I chose the broad axe and left the pitch fork behind because I didn't want the temptation when I came face to face again with Dwayne.

I rejoined Garnet on the landing in front of the locked door.

"You didn't get in yet?" I said.

Garnet stared at a point above my head, which I decided meant 'no.'

The door was solid but we had all day, except it only took three or four good whacks. We crossed the threshold in what might be called a flourish and I may have said, "Ta dah."

The room was gloomy, being mostly boarded up, like the downstairs.

We brought Hicks out onto the landing where the light was better. He looked healthy, aside from his colouring. It was pasty and blotchy. I'd have suggested a blood pressure check if I cared a lick for him.

Once he finished threatening to kill the sons of bitches who kidnapped him, he started into ordering Garnet and me to find the bastards and then screamed like a little girl demanding 'some goddamn food to eat.'

"Shut your hole," I told him, tired of being yelled at.

"Who the hell you think you're telling to shut up?"

"You are Dwayne Curtis Hicks, are you not?"

"Damn right."

"You're an Elvis impersonator."

That's when he took a swing at me. He missed because he was no fighter.

"Fuck you, you son of a bitch," he said.

"Settle down, Dwayne."

"I'm not a goddamned impersonator. I'm the real deal."

I wanted to hit him and it wasn't just the attitude. My violent urges had as much to do with the Elvis sneer that was plastered on his baby face.

"What's that?" I said. "A new jingle? The 'real deal.' Buy your used vehicle from me, 'Collingwood Elvis' and I will guarantee you the 'real deal.' It's got a ring to it, no?"

"Shut up," he said.

"You lose your voice, you could get a sales job anywhere."

"Fuck you," he said again, because he didn't have much of a vocabulary. In any event, that's when I really did hit him. Not too hard. Just a cuff at the back of the head. It worked. It shut him up, for a short while.

As we took the easy route back to the township road, along the overgrown laneway, a white panel van turned in. Hoping to catch the bad guys, I pushed Collingwood Elvis into a patch of thorns and dived in behind him. Garnet was already hiding by the time I reacted.

The van bounced through the potholes, coming too fast, suggestive of an inexperienced driver. Because he was concentrating so hard on maintaining control, he had no chance of seeing us even though we were huddled together in the overgrown ditch, three feet from the nearest tire rut. The van braked as it pulled up beside the house. A young guy, dressed in sloppy jeans and basketball jersey got out the driver's side and a tiny whiff of a girl decked out from head to toe in black, despite the summer heat, emerged from the passenger side.

"You know them?" I said to Garnet.

He had a Polaroid out and he was studying it. "I think it's Corey Brown."

"Shit, he's in deep."

"Maybe not. Let's talk to him."

"Do I get a say?" said Hicks.

"No," we said in chorus.

"Wait here," I told him.

"Not a chance. I'm coming with you."

"Your call," I said. "Just stay out of the way."

By the time we arrived at the back door of the house, the shouting had already started.

"Do you think they've discovered that 'Elvis has left the building?'" I said, edging up to a boarded over window and peaking into the kitchen. The prison keeps were discussing the problem and the discussion seemed frantic.

Not knowing what else to do, the rapper kids turned to leave by way of the back door, where Garnet and I had planned a reception. Except still looking through my peak hole, I saw Hicks enter the scene swinging an old board at Corey Brown's head. Luckily Corey brought a shoulder up in time to deflect the blow. Still the board broke in half.

Garnet was already on the way in as I rose from my knees. The fracas was pretty well all over by the time I got there. Corey Brown sat on the floor, rocking back and forth, rubbing his neck and shoulder. On the opposite side of the room, Hicks was curled up on his side, holding his stomach and looking like he needed to puke. Garnet stood over him, fists still clenched.

The girl looked bewildered but that didn't last.

"You fucking bastard," she screamed, as she spat at Hicks, whaling and kicking at him like a crazy person. She was a tiny thing. So by silent agreement, Garnet and I decided to be spectators for a while, only making sure her mammoth black boots, part of the uniform of her tribe, found no vital points.

It was when she snarled, 'We should never have showed up. We were going to turn you loose, you dumb prick,' that I stopped the girl, wrapping her up from behind in a bear hug.

Picking her up and moving her away from Hicks, I sat her down on the cleanest of three paint-bare press back kitchen chairs. But I still held her tightly by the arms. Because she didn't seem inclined to stay where I put her.

Her feet barely touched the floor. There were big holes in the black fish net stockings she wore under tight black denim shorts, though I guessed the rips were part of her look and not damage from the fight. Underneath the black mascara and the maroon lipstick and looking past the paper clips, the spikes and the tap washers and whatever the hardware represented, I saw the face of a girl who was once someone's pretty little daughter.

She breathed in great heaves that wracked her thin chest and she looked like she wanted to cry, but she was fighting the urge and winning. Meanwhile, Garnet checked on Corey. Neither one of us bothered with Hicks since his mouth had resumed running in overdrive, which meant he was still healthy enough.

"What's your name?" I said to the girl.

"You a cop?" she asked.

"Used to be."

"That case, I ain't talking."

"Yeah, you are," I said, "and you can start by telling me your name."

"Then what? You have me arrested?"

"Then we figure out if you deserve our help."

"Get stuffed."

"Her name's Chelsea." It was Corey talking.

I looked at Garnet who was feeling the tender spot on Corey's shoulder. He mouthed the words, 'He's okay.'

"Thanks," I told the boy and turning to the girl, I asked, "Was that true, Chelsea?"

"What?"

"The reason you came here? To let this shit-head go?"

"Shove it up your ass," she hissed.

"It's true." Corey butted in again.

"Shut the fuck up, Corey," she told him.

"Why not tell us?"

"Tell you what?"

"It was your idea, wasn't it, Chelsea?" I said.

She tried to make a rude gesture but it was hard the way I was pinning her arms.

Garnet grabbed Corey's wrist. I could tell it hurt.

"Speak boy," he said.

"That hurts, man."

"She wanted to let him go?"

"Yeah," he said, squirming ineffectually to escape Garnet's grip. "We came here to let the asshole go."

"Is that what you wanted too, Corey?" Garnet said.

"He wants nothing to do with the jerk-offs he hangs with." Chelsea joined the discussion, obviously watching out for Corey's best interests.

"That right, Corey?" Garnet said.

He hesitated, thinking I guess. "These guys…"

"These guys," I interrupted him, "they push you around. They make you run errands. You don't do what they tell you, they threaten to cut your balls off. Hell, I'm thinking they even tell you it's time to take a shit. Am I right, Corey?"

The boy looked away.

"So, why the fuck do you do it, Corey?" Chelsea screamed.

"You two got something going?" I asked her.

"What the fuck you talking about?"

"You a couple?"

"Screw you."

I looked at Corey and he nodded his head.

"Two things, son. Find some new friends, starting now. And two," I said, letting go the girl's arms and standing over her, "see if you can't hold on to this one. You could use a positive influence in your life."

"Fuck you," she said, kicking me in the shin.

I smiled and she shot out a fat tongue with a stainless steel stud poking out of it.

"So, what are you going to do with us?" Corey said.

"Why don't you go home and play some video games?"

The kids looked at each other like they'd just won a new car.

"No fucking way," Hicks shouted, as Chelsea led Corey toward the door.

"Not your call, Hicks," I said.

"I want these two druggies arrested and I want him," and he paused to point at Garnet, "I want him charged with assault."

"Assault?" I said.

"Yes, assault. He came in here and punched me in the gut."

"I didn't see that but I did see you strike Corey Brown with a weapon."

"It was a board."

"Same thing," I said. Then calling to Corey, catching him before he left, "You want to press charges against the mouth here?"

He stopped, turned and shook his head.

Then I told him to go buy his girlfriend something nice. She told me to do something unnatural to myself again and then they were gone and we were stuck with Hicks.

We knocked five off the drive back to town but it still seemed like it took a week and a half, what with all the whining and yelling.

As we turned into the resort complex where he lives, Hicks told Garnet to pull over to the curb. He wanted to talk. According to the kidnappee's story, he left his wife outside the restaurant and then he set off on the ten block or so walk to the theatre where he was scheduled to make an appearance. But four or five guys jumped him before he got there. He didn't see any faces. 'Not with a fucking burlap bag tied over my fucking head.' But he could see they wore basketball shoes and baggy pants. His captors tied him up, put him on the floor of a van and drove off. Eventually they stopped and threw him in the boarded up bedroom with a week's supply of water and a lot less food. His only furniture was an air mattress and 'a freaking piss pot to piss in.'

Hence the name, I told him.

"Don't be a wise ass, Jack," he said.

"It comes naturally, Dwayne."

"The name's …"

"I know. Curtis or Collingwood Elvis. It's just that I prefer Dwayne."

"You listen up asshole. You better think hard over who you're dealing with."

"Okay."

"And another thing…"

"There's more?"

"If you knew what you were doing, you wouldn't have let those two punks go."

"You never saw your kidnappers," I said. "We've decided it wasn't Corey or Chelsea."

"Based on what?"

"Hair style for one thing. Chelsea's hair had no green in it." I recalled the description Maddie had given me.

"So, how'd they know where I was?"

"Maybe they heard something. I don't know. The point is Dwayne, they were planning to cut you loose."

"You don't know that."

"Shut up."

"At the very least, you should have found out who the ring leaders were."

"Shut up, Dwayne." The guy was right but I knew I could find the rappers, whenever I wanted to…if I needed to. Handling it my way, Corey and Chelsea could truthfully say they never gave anybody's name up.

Hicks got the last word in, demanding we take him to the police but I told him my job was to find him and to keep everything on the QT. So, we finished delivering the sorry pain-in-the-ass Elvis impersonator to the condo he shared with Honey. When she opened the door, I thought she looked more annoyed than relieved, although I may have been projecting.

I told her to phone her dad. And I told Hicks, now that he was no longer my responsibility, to call the police, if he felt like it. Otherwise he was not to talk to either Garnet or me, ever again. And then we left.

"We planning on doing anything about the kidnappers?" Garnet asked, not taking his eyes off the road.

"I wasn't paid to do anything other than find that moron."

"You're really good at not answering questions."

"Thanks," I said.

"So?"

Garnet was good at not letting other people off the hook.

"Okay, here's what I'm thinking. We've got two problems. First of all, I saddled myself with an obligation to protect Sheila's brother's fat ass. If Penny Lou Stanfield is right, Mike broke some serious laws. Do I make him fess up to his part in the kidnapping? Do I cover it up? Do I punch him silly because it will teach him a lesson while at the same time making me feel better?"

"Her name's Penny Sue."

"Right. There some history there?"

"Some."

"Seems like you've got some history with just about everybody around here."

"It's not always an advantage."

"Penny Sue being a case in point?"

"Maybe. What's the second problem?"

"If the shit hits the fan, how do we keep Corey Brown out of the spray?"

"You have to talk that way?"

"What do you mean?"

"Never mind."

"What do you think?" I said.

"We can keep Corey out of it."

"How? Just keep him away from the bad influences?"

"You got any other ideas?"

"It's what I'd do," I said.

"Good, I'll take care of it."

"Okay."

"You're forgetting something, Jack."

"What?"

"To hell with what you were paid to do. Can we let these punks get away with kidnapping?"

"I'm prepared to hold my nose if it means Jeanie's kid gets a second chance."

"And Mike Mackie?"

"Grown-ups don't deserve that kind of break. But, I can't have it both ways."

Garnet stared at the road ahead. After a while, he said, "Jack, there's something else."

"What?"

"You've got Sheila to think about. And if she's important to you, you gotta give her a say."

"I know."

sixteen

FOR REASONS I CAN'T EXPLAIN, I didn't take Garnet's advice. Even though it is a damn good idea to keep your spouse – and after nearly a decade Sheila qualified as such – informed, especially on the big issues.

Of course, Sheila would say my suspicion that her brother had committed a serious crime was influenced by my negative feelings about him. And it wouldn't have mattered a damn that Sheila doesn't like Mike either. It's the job of a sister to defend her siblings and when it comes to family, Sheila is not good separating evidence and feelings.

So the question came down to this: what was the point of talking about it?

The point might have been found in the queasiness in my gut telling me Sheila clearly needed to know and I clearly needed to convince her to face certain realities.

Then I was bounced back again by another brain flicker: what was I doing in Collingwood in the first place? Answer: I was on vacation, with Sheila. And that was something I didn't want to spoil with family breaking news because, griping aside, I was having fun. The music was of the foot stomping and slow swaying varieties. The crowds were mellow. The food and beer flowed. I loved the party atmosphere. Most of all, Sheila and I were together, having a blast not running our coffee shop. And we were well into the process of laying Reba to rest in the appropriate vault of the memory bank. So my zipped lip policy also had something to do with selfishness.

Personal biases, ulterior motives and human weakness aside, one big problem remained: if anyone started scratching around, Mike Mackie was 'anyone's' prime suspect in the kidnapping of Dwayne Hicks. My Hail Mary hope was the whole thing would blow over. If only I were Roman Catholic.

On the morning of the second last day of the festival, a Saturday, Sheila and I ate a half dozen pancakes between us. We would have had more but Sheila said she was finished after one.

Then, at Sheila's insistence, I lugged all the starch and syrup I'd consumed out to the antique car parade, where we argued over which one we'd want parked in our driveway. At first, we leaned heavily toward a 1956 Lincoln Continental, two door sedan, classier and even rarer than the 1956 Thunderbird, a model with similar lines. A Studebaker Silver Hawk looked good too. In the end, we picked a gold '67 Firebird convertible on the grounds we wouldn't be afraid to let it get rained on.

That settled, we strolled up the town's main street sidewalk, shoulder to shoulder with the Elvis wannabes, the retro bobby soxers, the little kids in fancy jumpsuits and the seniors of both genders under gigantic black pompadours, everyone basking in the glory of a perfect July day and grooving to the echoes of Elvis tunes from the band-stands at almost every intersection.

We gave our feet a rest under a tent and smiled at the antics of a talentless but enthusiastic barely-pre-death Elvis. He outlasted us and we moved on to 'check out the shops.'

By mid afternoon, the summer sun on cement and asphalt turned a gorgeous day into a scorcher. Add to that, I needed a break - a restaurant or a bar - the goals being air conditioning and sustenance, like maybe a barbecued horse. I figured we'd have no trouble ordering food at that time of the day but, despite finding a table, the place we picked was still busy with a late lunch crowd.

"Cold beer would be nice," said Sheila.

"More like three or four," said Garnet, appearing out of nowhere and sitting down. He nodded to Sheila with a cockeyed smile under his Lanny MacDonald growth.

She smiled back, obviously thinking of the movie star Garnet reminded her of, yet again.

For some reason, Garnet's arrival prompted Sheila to bring up the kidnapping case. I countered Garnet's strange looks with barely perceptible head wags until he figured out I'd not discussed Mike's troubles with Sheila. Revealing disgust, his hairline dropped as his forehead folded inward and his eyes retreated. And, at last I saw a clear resemblance to the actor.

"How many times has the waitress gone by our table?" I said, trying to shift the agenda.

"Enough for at least a head nod," Sheila said.

"Or a smile?" said Garnet.

"Which we ain't getting." I looked around for help. There was none until finally, the young woman in uniform with the perfect make-up who'd been passing us by found a place for us on her busy schedule.

"Sorry, I didn't see you," she said.

I laughed and Garnet shook his head.

"Just bring me a damn beer," Sheila said.

The waitress gave Sheila her best impression of superiority. Sheila just grinned back.

After losing the staring contest, the waitress turned to me. "What would you like?"

"Bring me," I said, studying the menu and then looking up, "another waiter."

"I beg your pardon?"

"Another waiter."

"Pardon?"

"Another server," I said. "Clear enough?"

"What?"

"Get us someone whose service style doesn't involve insulting the customer's intelligence."

"I did no such thing."

"Look, the fact I left my tie on the dresser does not mean you get to mistreat us."

"I did no such…"

"Yeah, I know, 'you did no such thing.' Except you know damn well there is no way you did not see us. You practically tripped over us. Here's the thing: No one at this table missed the message behind your words."

"I'm not following. What message was I supposed to be sending?"

"You hold your customers, the ones you judge unworthy in any event, you hold them in disdain. You saw us. And you lied about it. It's your way of telling us we're really not important."

"You're crazy."

"That's closer to the truth than saying you didn't see us."

"I'm going to get the manager."

"Do it."

The server left in a huff.

"I was kind of hard on her," I said.

"She exceeded my tolerance scale, too," Sheila said.

"I prefer the bitchy kind to the phonies," I said. "They usually have good reason for their mood."

"Do you think the manager's going to show?" said Sheila.

"Yeah," said Garnet, as he pulled out a chair for the Mayor.

"Buy you three a beer?" he said.

"We've been hoping," I said.

The Mayor turned and signaled and two pitchers of draught appeared out of thin air.

"Wow," I said. "The power of higher office.'

"Not really."

"Yeah, really," I said.

"No Jack," said Garnet. "Chuck owns the place."

"Oh."

"Was Brianne acting up?"

I smiled.

"She's my sister's kid. I'll talk to her. In the meantime, there's something I want to ask you, Jack."

"Go ahead."

"Are you still on the clock?"

"No. Olson used up my retainer."

"Too bad."

"Why? What's wrong?"

"Well, so far, nothing. You found Hicks. And we were able to keep things quiet. And although there are rumours flying all over the place, no one really knows for sure that Hicks was kidnapped. The cops are asking questions but, I can handle that."

"So, what's the problem?"

"Hicks is yapping," he said.

"I can believe it."

"Yeah, but it's more than the usual drivel."

"What's it about?"

"He says he knows who was behind the kidnapping. He says it was one of his competitors. And he's gonna get him."

"What's he mean by that?"

"He wants to beat the crap out of him."

"He got the balls?"

"His friends do."

"People like Peter Lake?"

"Maybe." My opinion of the Mayor climbed a notch. Maybe he wasn't in Ted Olson's hip pocket after all.

"What do you want me to do?"

"Talk to him. The town doesn't need the negative publicity."

"Feuding tribute artists? You don't see the marketing potential?" I said.

"Will you help me out or not, Jack?"

"Sure thing, Mayor. Except I doubt he'll listen to me."

"Tell him your investigation of the kidnapping shows no connection to any of the other TAs."

"So, he'll see there's no point to all his tough talk?"

"Yeah. What do you think? Will you do it?"

"Okay. Where is he?"

"He's somewhere around."

"I don't feel like forming a search party again, Chuck," I said.

"He's not going to try anything right now. Too much going on. Wait 'til tomorrow. Or Monday. Somewhere along the line, you'll bump into him."

"After the sing off?"

"It's not called a 'sing off' Jack. But, yeah, he'll be too busy to do anything about his threat before that."

The Mayor left and after drinking a lot more than a third of a share of the beer, so did Garnet. When we realized the Mayor was no longer available to arrange my horse on a platter, Sheila and I called it a day too.

That night we cooked hotdogs over a campfire on the shore.

Sheila looked beautiful through the glow of the jumping flames. She smiled at me, like she knew what I was thinking.

We moved to our deck chairs to chow down, our feet cooling in the shallows.

In the middle of her second dog, she said, "When are you going to see Hicks?"

"Don't know. You heard Chuck. He won't be hard to find."

"Well, while you're straightening Hicks out, see if you can find Peter Lake."

"And?"

"Get the jerk to leave Lori alone."

"You know about that?"

"Unlike men, women talk to each other."

"Men talk."

"About baseball."

"And hockey."

"And fishing."

"And golf."

"Exactly," she said. "So, you'll do it?"

"Of course, but I have to tell you I don't understand all this sleeping around."

"It's only because these poor guys don't have someone like me," she said.

"That can't be it."

She flicked cold water at me.

"What don't you understand?" she said.

"Lori and Peter Lake. Look at the guy. He's a self-centered hotshot with a mean streak. She's got to see that."

"Yeah, but she's brainless. And that's why I want you to see him. To tell him to back off. What else can't you understand?"

"I can't understand Honey Hicks and Lake."

"Really? Honey and Peter Lake?"

"Yup. I see the signs," I said, though I was really just guessing based on the flirting games I'd seen them play.

"Didn't know about that one."

I decided not to be smug and watched her think on it.

"Maybe it's just not a very big pond," she said.

"Then there's Dwayne. He spends more time in other people's beds than his own."

"Including Lori's."

"Yikes."

"But that affair's all in the past now."

"She tell you that too?"

"She did."

"You believe her?"

"I believe her about the affair."

"But not that it's past tense?"

"She cheats on her husband, telling lies about it is automatic."

"So your sister-in-law has scruples? She only likes to be seen as cheating with one man at a time?"

"Something like that."

Then her furrowed brow told me she had more to say.

"That was nasty of me," she said.

"No it wasn't. They're acting like alley cats."

"I need to give Lori the benefit of the doubt. She says it's over with Hicks and Lake, then it's over."

"Until it's proven otherwise."

"Yes."

"Who does Mike have the hots for?" I asked.

"He's not a member of the girls' team."

"So, it's my job to find out."

"Yup."

"I don't think I want to know."

seventeen

FOR THE LAST NIGHT OF Festival week, we had two choices. One – relaxing over barbecued steak, cottage potatoes and cold beer, consumed while the setting sun played out its magic over the softening northern skies of Nottawasaga Bay. Or two – sitting in a hot, crowded arena listening to Sheila's brother and the other finalists stretch their vocal chords in search of notes only Elvis could hit, on his best nights.

We had a vote and somehow, Sheila won a majority.

Despite the kidnapping, Dwayne Hicks did a commendable job in the role of Collingwood Elvis. In fact, he did a better job than Mike this time, according to Sheila and if she knew, then Mike knew it too, even if he lied to everyone else about it. Regardless of his take on the scoring, he was bound to be in a sour mood. Not wanting to be around for the blow-up, Sheila and I left, planning an early night. The vote on that one was unanimous.

Sheila and I gave sleeping together in her childhood bed the old college try but after I elbowed her in the eye, I was back on the floor, tossing and turning hour after hour.

The digital clock beside my head told me it was a few ticks past four in the morning. I listened to Sheila softly snoring, a sound that comforts me. Usually. But now, because I couldn't find a comfortable position, her night-time noises made me slightly homicidal.

Still, I knew my insomnia had to do with more than a lumpy mat and Sheila's crooning. Nagging questions clogged the plumbing in my head and I was all out of Drano.

Ironically, there was no good reason for the back up in my neural pipes, since technically, my job was done. Sure I promised the Mayor I would chat with Hicks to settle down his testosterone, but that was no big deal.

I realized the problem was Sheila's brother, the son of a bitch. He was costing me a good night's sleep. And he didn't even know it. He also didn't know I kept returning to the words that strange woman, Penny Sue Stanfield, said, which brought up the question - what if she was right? What if Mike was the CEO in Hicks' kidnapping? Would street punks have thought that one up on their own?

Of course, I didn't give a damn about the answers if the Elvis that Stanfield saw wasn't Sheila's brother. But if Mike was that guy, that Elvis, then I had to face the poser that was bugging me for three days. Do I talk to Sheila about her stupid ass brother or do I carry on in the hope that I can figure things out and save her some grief?

I wasn't getting any answers staring at the black ceiling and I wasn't getting any sleepier. So I pulled on my shorts and a hooded sweat, collected my quilt, and snuck outside, following the sound of lapping waves and finding a Muskoka chair.

Last night's coals had enough life to catch some new kindling. I wrapped myself up to fight off the early morning dew, made a pillow out of part of the quilt and put my head back, to take in the show. And it was good one. The glassy surface of Nottawasaga Bay was ink black while over my shoulder, before a three quarter moon, somersaulting clouds presented a succession of canvases in yellow, white and charcoal. When the wispy clouds moved on, the moon painted the Bay satin grey to the horizon.

My jangled contemplations eased and eventually, I dozed, until the eastern sky warmed my face.

Half awake now, I heard Sheila pass behind me left to right and then she crossed in front of me, wrapped in her short terry cloth bath-robe. Like she wanted to be sure she got my attention. She smiled, her tangled hair covering one eye, and then she turned her back to me and walked away, her flip-flops slapping the soles of her feet, stopping only when the water licked at her ankles.

Without warning but granting my wish, she threw her water shoes at my head, shucked her robe and ran full tilt into the water.

It was a powerful invitation. So, I threw off my quilt and my clothes and ran after her, wondering how the hell she managed to dodge all the pointy edged rocks. I dove too soon and scraped bottom. Within ten strokes, she was within reach.

"You forgot something," I said, grabbing her left foot.

"It's a tradition," she replied, kicking loose.

"I like this tradition."

"Besides, my bathing suit was damp. I hate putting on a wet bathing suit."

I caught her again and pulled her close.

"Neighbours tolerate skinny dipping, Jack," she said, "but that's as liberal as they're prepared to go."

"Neighbours can't be up yet," I said.

She kissed my cheek, pushed me away with her hands and feet and swam back to shore, where she picked her way through the stones to her bath-robe. I watched it all, stamping the scene onto a memory card.

I caught up to her as she neared the cottage. She shivered and I pulled the quilt around both of us. As we lifted feet in unison to mount the stairs, the screen swung open. Lori held out my cell. I took it. She went back inside, in a snit.

"It's Garnet," the caller said.

"It's early, man." I took hold of Sheila's arm and pulled her close. For some reason – maybe something in his voice - I wanted her with me.

"I've already sat on this news a couple hours."

"What's happened?"

"I heard from an old friend, guy named Bronson. Used to be my second in command. He joined the OPP after the town force folded up its tent. They made him a sergeant." His long explanation seemed a lot like a delaying tactic.

"This Bronson called you?"

"Yeah. A courtesy. He knows I was helping you find Hicks."

"I thought the cops were kept in the dark on our little adventure."

"Just the Provincial guys were out of the loop."

"Bronson's Provincial now," I said.

"They sign his checks..."

"But he can't get used to the change?"

"You could say he has trouble assimilating."

"Let's hear it."

"The guy's dead."

"Who?"

"Hicks."

"What's going on, Jack?" Sheila asked.

"Dwayne Hicks is dead." I told her.

Sheila's jaw dropped.

"He's dead?" she said.

I nodded my head and she stared at the ground. Then I said to Garnet, "We just saw him. Performing. He finished his set maybe half an hour, forty minutes before midnight."

"None of that makes him any less dead, Jack."

"Murdered?"

"That's what Bronson says."

"Shit."

"Might have been safer to leave him with the rappers."

"Unless they did it," I said.

"You believe that?"

"I don't know enough to believe anything, pardner."

"Me either, Jack."

"Details?"

"He wouldn't say anything more. C.I.B. takes over in these cases."

"Criminal Investigations Branch? Don't the local guys get a crack first?"

"There're local detective constables but they follow the protocols and don't stick their necks out."

"Which means they call in the big guns?

"Yup."

"Why'd your friend Bronson tell us?"

"You answered it. He's a friend. Officially, he has to say it's just information. No role for us."

"Of course."

"You talk to Sheila about her brother yet?"

"No."

"She needs to know."

"I know, I'll tell her. Somehow. Then, you and I need to talk."

"You tell that woman of yours to take care."

Sheila took my hand and walked me to the park style bench under a silver lace-strangled arbor and pulled me down with her. It was a perfect spot for everything except passing along bad news.

"Tell me what, Jack?" she said. "What else does Garnet want me to know?"

I took a deep breath and the story spilled out. But I downplayed Penny Sue Stanfield's comments and my suspicion that the rappers and Mike were in cahoots on the kidnapping. And I didn't mention the link that the cops were bound to draw between Hicks' kidnapping and his murder. I just wasn't prepared to come completely clean until I had the chance to confront Mike. Besides, Sheila was smart enough to add up the columns on her own.

"What do you want to do?" I said.

"I can't believe Mike had anything to do with any of this."

"I never said he did."

"Not in so many words."

"Let's just say for now, it doesn't make much sense." I paused and then said, "You know where we have to start."

"Talking to Mike."

"That's my thinking."

We retreated to the cottage and put on fresh clothes. Then together, we knocked on Mike and Lori's door.

"Mike," Sheila said, a little shrilly, "I need you out here."

He came to the door and opened it quarter way. "I'm busy," he said, holding onto the door knob with his right hand.

I noticed his left. It hung loosely near his crotch, shaking like a sick puppy left out in the cold.

"This can't wait," I said. "It's about Dwayne Hicks."

He looked at the floor. "Not your business, Jack."

"Mike, get your goddamn ass out here where we can talk," Sheila said, ready to pull him out of his bedroom by the gonads.

But she didn't have to. Mike swung his door open the rest of the way. Except as it turned out, it wasn't because he agreed to talk. Concentrating on ignoring us, he stepped out, forcing us to give him room. We brushed shoulders and he walked down the hall, through the kitchen and into the washroom. Following a flush, he emerged and acted surprised that we were still hanging around, the two of us leaning back on the kitchen counter, arms folded. He weaved past and exited through the screen door.

We chased him onto the porch and down the steps. I caught him from behind, by the shoulder.

"You're kind of grouchy, aren't you Mike?" I said.

"Get stuffed."

"Not a morning person?"

"What do you want?"

"Curtis Hicks is dead," said Sheila.

I didn't like his reaction. The sideways glance that escaped in the split second before he forced out a look of shock, told me most of what I didn't want to know. I waited. Twice he opened his mouth as if he were ready to talk. Then he clammed back up.

"How'd you know?" I said.

He did a double take at my question. "How'd I know what?"

First he tries walking away. Now he treats me like I'm a moron. "That Hicks is dead. How'd you know that, Mike?"

"What are you talking about?" he said.

"He knew?" said Sheila, shifting my way and taking hold of my wrist. Tears were in her eyes.

"Yeah, he knew."

I turned on Mike, my face in his. Despite the morning breath, I encroached further into his personal space and repeated my question, "How'd you find out?"

"About his murder?" His clarifying question missed the mark.

Sheila caught him up again. "We never said he was murdered, Mike." There was a hitch in her voice.

"I just assumed…"

"No more ducking and dodging, Mike," she said.

"You're both talking crazy."

Fear took over from phony shock, and the replacement emotion struck me as real. He turned and walked away from us, again.

"Damn it, tell us," Sheila said to his back. And then softening, "We'll help you."

He quickened his pace and I caught his sleeve. Standing in a triangle, Mike looked everywhere but at us, maybe hoping a miracle would emerge from the trees and airlift him to a place where problems were no more. Giving up on that, he let go a big sigh.

"It's time," I said.

"I found him," he said. Only it came out like a sob.

"You mean you found Hicks' body?"

His head nodded.

"Oh, Mike," Sheila groaned.

"Where?" I said.

"In a hotel."

"In town?"

He nodded his head.

"The one with the convention hall?"

Another head nod.

"What was he doing there, Mike? Honey's condo's only a few miles away."

"I don't know."

"What were you doing there?"

"It's hard to explain."

"Real soon, it's gonna get a lot harder," I said.

"Yeah. I know."

"So, you found him."

We took his silence as a "Yes."

"And then you called the police?" Sheila said.

"No. I left." It was an answer that I could have predicted.

"No way, Mike. You didn't," she said.

More silence.

"When was the last time you had the fluid levels checked?" I asked.

"Huh?"

"Your brain. It's gotta be down a least a quart."

"I panicked."

"In the worst way. Why'd you go there in the first place?" I said. It was the all important question he'd already sidetracked once.

"Doesn't matter. All that matters is I had nothing to do with his murder."

"Yeah, it does matter. You were there and you left. This wasn't a fender scratch in a parking lot. You left the scene of a murder. It matters, Mike. And you damn well know it."

He was caught between denial and the real world. "What am I gonna do?" is what he said next.

Sheila looked sadly at her brother.

I wasn't feeling much sympathy. I poked him in the chest. "You say you had nothing to do with his death Mike but, tell me this: what do you know about a little band of teenaged thugs I keep hearing about? Country kids acting like city rappers. Why were you hanging with these guys Mike?"

"Those little pricks. Maybe they killed him."

"The kidnapping was your idea, wasn't it?" I said, now that Mike verified Penny Sue's assertion he was the rappers' Elvis contact.

"What?" My quick change in direction confused him.

"The kidnapping. Tell me about it."

"You're way out of line."

"Mike, listen hard. I have a witness who…"

"Okay, okay. I talked to those kids but I'm telling you - it wasn't my idea."

"Yes it was. And logic says there's a thread attached to your sorry ass that ties right back to Hicks' murder."

He shook his head at the ground.

"Mike, tell us."

"I'm telling you there's no connection between the kidnapping and the murder. In fact, I wasn't in on the kidnapping."

"Convince me," I said.

"I tried to talk them out of it. I told them the snatch was off."

"It was your idea?" Sheila said.

"Sure it was his idea," I said. "He was jealous of Dwayne Hicks."

"Shut the hell up, Jack."

"Over Lori's affair with him?" Sheila said. "I thought that was history."

"I can't get by it."

"And that's not all. You had a shopping list of motives," I said, "didn't you, Mike? After the cheating, there was the name change. He beat you out for last year's crown. The prospect he was going to put you in your place again this year didn't sit well either. Kidnapping seemed like a good idea."

"No. No."

"You're saying you never talked about it?"

"I was never serious. I was mad at Hicks."

"And Lori," I added.

"Yeah, but I was drunk. I say stuff I shouldn't when I drink. I was just mouthing off."

"Who'd you mouth off to Mike? Those rapper kids?" Sheila asked. "They went along?"

"No."

"Why no?"

"Because I changed my mind. I wasn't really going to do it in the first place."

Sheila looked at the sky and wiped a palm across her forehead, fighting back tears.

"But the rappers did it anyway," I jumped back in.

"Yes."

"Why?"

"So the little fuckers could blackmail me."

"You pay them anything?"

"Just a few hundred."

"If that's true…"

"It is true!"

"If it's true, then you may be the stupidest jackass outside of reality TV."

"Can you guys help me?"

The screen door squeaked open and swung back with a sharp smack. Lori stood on the porch, the door bouncing its way back to serenity.

"What's with all the shouting?" she said, but the attitude she'd assumed lately was gone. I thought she sounded nervous.

"Where's Mum and Dad?" Sheila hissed at her brother.

"They left. Pancake breakfast."

"Good," she said, and then turning to her sister-in-law, "Bad news, Lori."

Lori's face showed nothing. Then she turned to go back in, like she was running away.

"Wait, Lori. This is something you need to hear." There was a tone in Sheila's voice that made her stop. The slump in Lori's shoulders could have been seen from across the bay.

Sheila called again. As Lori turned, she straightened and her fists clenched. She mouthed an expletive and walked towards us.

"No, Lori! Stop," Mike said. Then to me, "There's more. I have to tell you something else. Lori can't find out."

"No secrets, Mike," I said.

"No," he screamed and he took off down the driveway.

"Tell Lori what's going on," I shouted at Sheila, over my shoulder.

Before he reached the main road, I grabbed Mike Mackie by the shoulders. We fell into the ditch. Well, that's not quite accurate. I guess I threw him into the ditch. And then when he tried to get up, I buried my fist in his belly, releasing the tension that had built up in my shoulders.

As he rocked in and out of the fetal position, I kneaded the back of my neck, thinking yoga might help my aching back. Or, maybe a decent mattress.

"Shake it off, Mike," I said.

But the guy was spent, panting like an old man at the top of a flight of stairs. For the sake of his ticker, I hoped his exhaustion was more emotional than physical.

"You didn't have to hit me so hard," he gasped.

"Hell, I pulled the punch."

"Asshole."

"Enough with the bullshit. Talk."

"Give me a minute."

I decided not to. "What is it you don't want Lori to hear?"

"I said, 'Give me a minute,' you bastard."

"Oh alright," I said, trying to get more comfortable, sitting in the ditch beside him, waiting and waiting some more, until impatience won the contest. "You want to tell me before the World Series gets underway?"

"I got a phone call, last night."

"What about?"

"Someone told me to come to the hotel."

"Where Hicks was killed?"

He nodded his head.

"What time was this?"

"Past midnight. Maybe 12:30. I don't know."

"So who was it?" I said.

"You can't tell Lori."

"Mike, don't make me hit you again."

"It was Honey."

"Honey Hicks?"

"Yes."

"Don't tell me. You're screwing around with her." It seemed like a safe bet.

"I thought it was over months ago."

"Maybe it was."

"So why's she call me?" he said.

"I don't know. But it wasn't for what you had in mind."

"Don't tell Lori."

"Least of your worries," I told him.

I nudged and pushed and shoved Mike back to the cottage where I told him to go to his room and stay there until I said he could come out. Lori followed in behind.

Sheila and I headed for the water, to get away from the impending explosion.

"What have we got here, Jack?"

"It's not good Babe."

"How bad?"

"Well, it's widely known that Mike hated Hicks. Didn't feel he deserved his Collingwood Elvis crown last year. And he was pissed about Dwayne's decision to change his name."

"So was everyone else involved in the festival."

"But everyone else hasn't slept with the victim's wife."

Sheila grimaced. "Tell me you're not serious."

"I can't do that."

"Mike and Honey Hicks? Is that what he didn't want Lori to hear?"

"I guess, although the way Lori screws around, why's he so worried?"

"Head in the sand?" Sheila said.

"If you say so."

"This is real bad, Jack."

"Yup."

"And Mike probably left his prints at the scene," she said.

"I'd say all over the place."

"I don't believe this."

"And then there's the kidnapping."

"What about it? That Mike may have planned it?"

"Yes."

"Or might have done it?"

"Yes."

"Could this get any worse?"

"Only if he actually killed the guy."

Sheila stared at the horizon. I let the crap sink in. Then I asked her what Lori had to say.

"I don't think she loves Mike," she said.

It was not the answer I expected.

"She was surprised, upset that Hicks has been murdered."

"But?"

"But, she just shook her head when I told her about the trouble Mike was in. Like she didn't really care that much."

"Did you learn anything else?"

"Yes. And it was a zinger."

"A good zinger?"

"The bad kind."

"What?"

"Lori had a confession, too. She's been messing around with Hicks."

"Crap. I thought she told you that was all over."

"It was. But they started up again."

"Which may explain why Lake was hassling Lori." I was thinking of my confrontation in the driveway, when I spit on his Jag.

"What do you mean?"

"Lake doesn't like it when his little slut goes to bed with another guy. Especially when the other guy is Dwayne Hicks."

"Lake's treatment of Lori is hardly the issue now."

"Does Mike know about Lori and Hicks?"

"Lori doesn't think so."

"Of course, that may not matter. The police will say he did know. That'd be my position if I were the investigating officer," I said. "Look at it this way: it was already a strong motive when the affair was in the past. Now we find out Lori and Hicks have been sneaking around again. And he has the hots for Honey? How many strikes against him now, you figure?"

"What are we going to do?"

"Take him down to the station before the cops catch up with him. And get him a lawyer."

"No. I mean after that."

"Poke around."

"Do you believe he did it?" Sheila's question was full of faint hope.

"Let's go with the premise he didn't."

"But, everything points to Mike."

"And there's probably more he hasn't told us."

"Shit."

"But you know, there's just so damn much crap stacked up against him.... it's ridiculous."

"So?"

"You'd think even a nitwit like your brother would have tried to cover his tracks. Or, come up with a reasonable story."

"You think he might be innocent?"

I thought about my answer and decided to tell the truth.

"Not really."

The truth was I didn't know what to think.

eighteen

WE TOOK MIKE TO THE police station and presented him as a material witness and an upstanding citizen, but who also wouldn't answer questions until his lawyer arrived.

The game plan was to bring in a damned good criminal lawyer, a guy by the name of Hughie Morrison. Hughie is my best friend, from way back, starting with college football and professional baseball dreams. Then, there were police cadet days together, a stint as City of London beat cops and finally, teammates in the Grand Bend police force.

After we turned in our uniforms, Hughie took to fancy suits and lawyering and I took to sale-rack jeans and detecting. Today we're business associates. Whenever he needs an investigator, he calls me first. Unless it's got anything to do with fraud involving the use of technology. Computers and I don't get along very well.

Hughie's 'yes' was automatic when I asked him to represent Sheila's dumb brother. In the meantime until he could get there, I called a local expert in compiling billable hours, an all-purpose lawyer Garnet recommended. Sheila stayed with Mike to make sure he didn't blab prematurely.

I left Mike's car keys with Sheila, which left me stranded. I contemplated whether to go back to the cottage, until I recalled Lori sitting at the kitchen table, catatonic or close to it. Besides, Mr. and Mrs. Mackie were likely back from breakfast, not getting answers from Lori, and wondering where the hell everybody else got to.

Without thinking much more about it, I walked from the cop shop to the town's main street and pointed myself downhill to Highway 26, hugging the bay. After thirty boring seconds, I broke into a jog, heading for Sunset Park. After thirty seconds more, an old Ford truck cut me off.

"What're you running from?"

"A big pile of crap."

"Just stopped by the police station."

"Lawyer there yet?"

"Yeah. But Sheila says Bronson won't be talking to Mike until Boroski and his people arrive."

"Not a good sign," I said. Boroski was the regional big-shot with the Ontario Provincial Police. If Mike was regarded as a run of the mill witness, he'd let the local boys take his statement.

"I need a coffee."

"I was just thinking the same thing."

"You're heading the wrong way for Connie's"

"Felt like I needed the run first."

"Run later."

I climbed into Garnet's truck. He smelled of stale beer.

We sat at the counter and Maddie rushed over with her coffee pot, like she was responding to an emergency. Garnet drank half of his cup, black and piping hot, in one swallow. He smiled at Maddie and she smiled back, like they found comfort in a familiar routine.

A big order appeared at the kitchen window. Maddie made her delivery and passed the time with the trucker types that belonged to three hungry man breakfasts. I scanned the rest of the room. It was nearly full of locals. And it was full of chatter too, more chatter than normal, was my guess.

Maddie came back and refilled our cups.

"They know?" I said.

"Well, yeah," Maddie answered, in a voice spilling over with sarcasm. Garnet's sideways look also told me my observation was idiotic. I've lived in small town Ontario for most of my adult life and it still surprises me how fast news travels.

I looked around again. "Well, clearly crime is good for business."

"That's cynical," Maddie said, smiling.

"Any of the busybodies got a theory that makes any sense?"

"Table six thinks it was a Johnny Cash fan." Maddie nodded her head in the general direction of the table she'd just served. One of the diners, a half ton train wreck who may have been an escapee from Folsom Prison, gave Maddie a near toothless grin and winked.

She winked back and then returned her attention to me, "What do you think, Mr. Private Detective?"

"I don't have a better idea."

"Jack," she whispered, leaning close, "the word is that Mike Mackie was there."

"Shit," I said.

"Sorry. He's your Sheila's brother isn't he?"

"Who told you about Mike?"

"Table four. Bonnie." A stout woman, wearing a tight bun, waggled her fingers our way.

"How'd she know?"

"Bonnie's daughter-in-law changes beds at the hotel. Reception desk saw him coming and going."

"Who told the daughter-in-law who told Bonnie. I get it. Shit."

"Maybe it wasn't him," she said.

"This can't be good, image wise," I said, to take us into new territory, "you know, for the town."

"Are you serious?" she said. Garnet gave me another one of his looks and I felt like an idiot all over again.

"What is it with you two?" I said. "The Mayor's been trying to keep a lid on all this trouble."

"That was before anybody got killed. Hell, Jack, we've got a new spin now. This puts us on the map," Maddie said.

"Well, what about the festival?" I said. "The murder's got to keep people away."

"You never worked in a marketing department, did you?"

"No."

"Me either, but I know what brings people in here. It's called gossip and the juicier the better. Hell, it blows advertising on the cable channel out of the water."

Clapton rang out before I fully digested Maddie's lesson in marketing.

"Jack Beer."

"It's Chuck," the Mayor announced like there were no other Chucks in the world.

Thinking I'd let the man down, I said, "I never got the chance to talk to Hicks."

"Would that have made any difference?"

"Maybe," I said.

"No matter. That's not what I'm calling about."

"What's up?"

"Can you come to my office?"

"For…"

"A meeting."

"With?"

"The OPP. Regional Commander Leonard Boroski …"

"Ah, crap."

"I see you know the man."

"I know him. He never goes anywhere alone. Who else is there?"

"Sergeant Bronson. The big fellah said, 'no.' I insisted."

I'd already gathered that Bronson's underlying loyalties were still with Garnet. Which was why the two of them had been exchanging phone calls. And now the old rivalries between the defunct municipal force and the OPP were bubbling to the surface in the Mayor's office. If gunfire broke out, maybe no one would notice the anomosity Leonard Boroski and I felt for each other. Or maybe not.

"Anyone else?" I asked.

"Not yet. But two detectives are due here any minute. A woman named Jennifer Rowland and a guy named Derek Smith."

"What's it about?"

"Bronson told them about the kidnapping and the rescue."

"Boroski come down off the ceiling yet?" My recollection was the man did not like being the last to know.

"Bronson's taking a lot of flak."

"Why exactly am I required?"

"To round out the kidnapping story."

"We'll be there."

"Just you Jack."

"What?"

"Boroski doesn't like Garnet."

"He doesn't like me much either. But somehow I get an invitation?"

We said our goodbyes to Maddie and I left my card at a couple tables in case anyone saw anything, or had any new theories.

"I got a hangover, Jack," Garnet said as we pulled into the municipal lot behind the town hall.

"So?"

"So, it shortens my fuse."

"Boroski?"

"Boroski."

"What happens when you blow your gasket?"

"Depends."

"You won't kill anyone will you?"

"No guarantees."

"Let's do it, then," I said.

Inspector Leonard Boroski looked mightily pissed off at the sight of me.

Added to the fact he was already mightily annoyed with the world that no one told him about Collingwood Elvis' kidnapping and rescue, and it was a sure bet a fireworks display was the last item on the agenda. Or maybe the first.

I scanned the room and realized the Mayor was angry too, I guess because I brought Garnet to a meeting he was specifically not invited to.

The two detective constables, Rowland and Smith, acted appropriately indignant whenever Boroski happened to look their way. Otherwise, they grinned like they were looking forward to a good show.

I kicked things off by telling Bronson, the detective constables, and Mayor Watson how the Hicks rescue went down. I make it a policy not to talk to Boroski unless absolutely necessary. I never mentioned Mike's part in the kidnapping because that would be disloyal. Besides, whether or not he was involved in anything criminal was just hearsay. And I never mentioned the rappers either, covering up for Corey Brown and his girlfriend Chelsea. But also because I didn't feel like it.

Boroski and his detectives didn't quite believe our version of events, so they poked and prodded. We provided a few additional details but generally we kept Mike's name out of it, and the kids too. As far as anyone at the meeting was concerned, we found Hicks in the old farmhouse all by his lonesome, not counting the neighbourhood vermin. And Hicks was no longer around to contradict us.

Boroski was frustrated but I didn't care.

As we left I told Garnet I thought the meeting went well, particularly since he'd refrained from killing anyone by the name of Leonard Boroski.

"No worries," he said.

"You've calmed down in your old age?"

"I just look old."

"You don't feel old?"

"Not so much."

"Still, you kept your mouth shut…"

"Okay, I'm old."

We laughed.

Then Garnet said, "You see why I told this bloody hick town to get stuffed?"

His tone made me glance over. Garnet looked more upset than pissed off. "It wasn't just Boroski's presence that ticked you off," I suggested.

"No."

"What then?"

"You don't want to hear."

"Try me."

"You got baggage, son?"

"Like regrets?" I said. "Not anymore. You?"

"I quit for a lot of reasons. Corporate policy bullshit was one of the bigger ones. Even before they took over completely, the OPP mucky mucks had begun cutting the small town forces out and giving all the real police work to the ass kissers in their own outfit."

"Then to save money, the Town finally got around to disbanding the local force?"

"Yep. But that was after I already left."

"I know the story, man."

"I was screwed up. But even if I wasn't, and if I'd stuck it out, I'd have been given a title. And that's all. Except for a fancy OPP uniform."

"Still," I said, "mostly they're good cops."

"Yeah. Too many kids, though. The kind who have all the paper skills and computer back-up. But no street experience. And no local knowledge."

"Like Smith and Rowland," I said, but I regretted my words. It was too early to judge, so as an afterthought I said, "They're not all like Boroski."

"But Boroski and his ilk poison any pool they dip their feet in."

I didn't argue, remembering that Sheila was once OPP and she was good at fighting off the poison. And yet eventually, it got to her too, changed her outlook. She quit before she gave the job a real chance, making me wonder what the Provincials were left with in the younger ranks.

"There was no real on-the-job training," Garnet said, almost to himself. "Way too little of it in any event. Despite that, the young bucks transferred in and figured they could tell the locals, guys with real experience, what to do. Brass brainwashed them."

"So, you packed it in before they took over and really pissed you off."

"It was bull, Jack."

"I know you could have handled Boroski. He wasn't the only reason."

"Already told you there were a lot of reasons."

"For instance..."

"You know this story, too. You work your butt off to put a case together on a piece of garbage. Then some judge, with socialist leanings, jumps on a mistake the poor street cop makes, the bad guy walks and gets to thumb his nose at you."

"Been there, pardner."

"Or, a jury goes stupid and decides one of the good old boys was just being playful when he gets a young girl liquored up and then without her permission knocks her up."

"You're on a bit of a roll here, man."

"You interested in the whole story or the Readers' Digest version?"

"You decide," I said. "I know what you're saying. After a while the job makes you want to kick somebody's teeth in."

"Tried that."

I couldn't tell if he was making a joke or not.

"Then there was that 'last straw,'" he said. "You know the one they always talk about. The one that finally breaks your back."

"Carrie."

"Yeah. She got mad at me. And still is. Even if it gets better between us, the anger won't disappear. Not completely. Best I can hope for is a truce."

I waited.

"I embarrass her." His eyes misted over.

I still didn't know what to say. But I gave it a shot, "Just tell her …"

But he broke into the platitude others have tried on me, "No, I understand her point, Jack. She just doesn't like having a goddamn drunk for a father."

"You can change," I said.

"I notice you like to knock it back too, son."

"Yeah, but I don't have your issues."

"Exactly. I screwed up. And Carrie knows it, too."

"It's not black and white."

"She doesn't see any of the grey."

"Maybe she sees the picture more clearly than you think."

"Jack, think about it. She thinks, believes, hell, she knows her father, the goddamn Chief of goddamn Police should have been able to find out what went wrong. Figure out who was behind the wheel of the car that ran over Rob's legs and turned him into a lost soul."

"You have to stand back from it."

"I have, Jack. The perspective doesn't improve any. You know, the doctors weren't sure how badly hurt Carrie was. A bad concussion can last a life time."

"True."

"Shit, man. All this crap falls on my family and I couldn't pin the rap on anybody."

"No one solves them all. What about the OPP?"

"What about them?"

"Was Boroski involved?" By my calculations, at the time, the guy was top dog in Huron County, my home field, which left me wondering how they knew each other and where the animosity came from.

Then he explained. "Yeah, Boroski showed up. The big brass loaned him to Grey-Simcoe to lead the investigation. It happened outside of town. Technically, it wasn't even my case."

"But he found nothing?"

"He didn't."

"No surprise."

"They did what they do best," he said.

"Which is?"

"Going through the motions."

"Still, he thoroughly documented the process, I'm guessing."

"Exactly."

"So, nada."

"He pissed me off. But I blame myself."

I waited for more.

"It broke my heart, Jack. Carrie was hurt. Rob was in intensive care. I was scared for both of them. Turned out with good reason, in Rob's case.

"But when Carrie got better, I tried, I really tried. With no real help from Boroski."

"I'm thinking he told you to stay the hell out of it."

"He did."

"You ignored him."

"I did."

"So?"

"So, my problem – one of them anyways - I didn't get started soon enough. I was so damned worried about my little girl. By the time I put the investigation into high gear, the trail was cold. Witnesses had been 'talked to.' And Boroski didn't even know he was being stonewalled."

"Witnesses were told to lie?"

"You got it."

"You got proof?"

"Not really. But I know, you know?"

"Yeah, I do."

"So the investigation…it just dried up. And sometime after, I can't remember when exactly, Carrie just stopped talking to me. And Rob, well Rob he just can't."

"He never talked about it?"

"I don't think he knows who the hell I am."

"It's a shitty story, Garnet."

"'Course I made things a whole lot worse when I let the drinking take over. And then I resigned my job. I guess you could say I've been a perfect jackass going on five years now."

We finished our drive to the Mackie cottage in silence.

Garnet pulled up and offered his hand. I'm no therapist but I may have done him some good. I gripped his hand firmly, held onto it, nodded my head, let go and got out.

A new kind of tension slapped me in the face the minute I opened the screen door.

Mr. Mackie met me first, whispering a greeting and informing me that Mrs. Mackie was lying down. A man who one day ago lived the care free life of a healthy middle-aged retiree, the next day showed me a face full of strain and worry. It made me want to hunt Sheila's brother down and whack him with a cedar post.

Sheila came out of her mother's bedroom, also in whispering mode.

I took her outside for a walk during which I learned that Mike and Lori left to fill a vacancy in a downtown hotel, but not the one where the murder took place. Which meant that from now on, we got the big bed in Mike's old room, but the joy surrounding that fact was something I decided to keep to myself. At least until Sheila found a more celebratory mood.

I also learned that Mike was told by Boroski's sycophants not to leave town.

I brought Sheila up to speed from my end, noting that progress-wise, we were nowhere near the speed limit.

Despite the comfort of a queen-sized bed, I lay wide awake that night, caught up in the knowledge that Sheila's family would never be the same again.

nineteen

THE ATMOSPHERE AT THE MACKIE cottage had not improved any overnight. In fact, if the look Mrs. Mackie gave me was any kind of barometer, the mood was lower than rock bottom. I should have stuck around to help Sheila comfort her parents but I'm a terrible comforter. Besides, I had to leave, and Sheila knew it, partly to escape but mostly to poke away at the lies and misdirection blocking access to the heart of the murder case.

I'm not bad at 'poking away' since it requires no strategy, no game plan. You just stick your nose out and wait for someone to break it, or try to anyway. As PI techniques go, it's a beauty.

Because 'poking away' is more fun when done with a friend, I found myself retracing the route I took the night I drove a semi-comatose Garnet Henderson home from the Heart Breakers tavern. I had to rely on my impeded wits that night, which felt like a year ago. Thinking back now, all I remembered were roads poorly marked, a sky dark and overcast, and a landscape alternately full of black trees and the blacker spaces between. It was a night empty of buildings or the lights that mark them.

But somehow today, with the help of a sixth sense and three or four flips of a loonie, I found the plot where Garnet parked his trailer. Mark it down to luck and the advantages of daylight and sobriety.

The ravine was the first hint I was getting very close and then I rumbled over a township culvert that seemed even more familiar. After passing through an opening in a screen of junk trees, I dismounted beside Garnet's

Ford pick-up and parked the Chief in the canopy of his black walnut.

If finding his home was relatively easy, finding the man himself was more of a guessing game. I turned the three porch steps into one and rattled the trailer's flimsy front door. It wasn't locked, so I stuck my head inside. The bright window over the kitchen sink and a splash of greenery beyond, invited me inside. A combination sitting/dining room lay to the right. And opposite, a five foot hallway led to the head, a bedroom and closets. I guessed the couch in the sitting area was the pull-out kind. The trailer space was tight and the fixings were old but well cared for. The floors and counter tops were clean. Spotless, in fact. I could have lived there. Sheila couldn't.

I called Garnet's name. My voice sounded hollow. I called again. And again, I got no reply, not even the flush of a toilet bowl.

On a tiny kitchen shelf, tucked in between the stove and a bench seat filled with loose plaid cushions, was a radio and a cell phone, the latter of which suggested Garnet wasn't far away. I decided against intruding further.

Outside, I did a quick tour of the property. The bush behind the trailer was thick with second growth. A trail disappeared in the trees a hundred feet in. My shouts again went unanswered, not counting the screech of a wood duck, suggestive of the presence of an upland marsh somewhere through the trees.

Giving up, I retreated to the shade of the walnut, dragging a lawn chair with me, and there I dozed, off and on, for thirty minutes, or longer, until I began to wonder if something was wrong. Then, I heard the crunch of tire on gravel behind me.

"Morning, Jack," he said.

I kept the fact he made my heart jump a gear as a personal secret.

"Beautiful day," I said.

He lifted a leg over his seat and parked his bicycle, a five speed, at least thirty years old, its frame and fenders traditional Raleigh green. Apples, which like the bike, would be on the green side, gave shape to his sun-faded leather saddle bags.

I smiled both at him and at the realization that while Garnet was stretching his legs, I was missing my morning run, again.

"There're not ready yet," I said, referring to the apples.

"I like them baked."

"With a pork chop?"

"Or ice cream."

He untied his loot and asked, "You drop by to see me? Or, you just looking for a place to hide?"

"Something like that."

"Don't feel bad," he said, detecting something in my mood. "No way to know someone was planning to off the man."

He emptied his saddle bags into a bushel basket sitting on the porch.

"I haven't reached the same conclusion," I said.

"What's your thinking?"

"First mistake, I didn't track down the kidnappers."

"We talked that one through. It was the right play," he said, pointing a finger at me to reinforce the point.

"Two, I failed to intervene with Hicks when the Mayor told me the dumb shit was heading for trouble."

"Who the hell could know that the trouble was the deadly kind, Jack?"

"It's not working. But thanks anyway."

"So."

"So?"

"So," he said. "I guess you're here because you decided to follow-up the kidnapper angle. See if there're any links to the murder."

"Things are more complicated than you know."

"Throw in the fact the OPP won't want us sticking our noses in it, I'm not sure why we should bother."

To save time, we split up. Garnet knew people so he would ring doorbells. I would poke away downtown and around the lakeshore. The first one to score a hit calls the other. Detecting methodology 101.

It took me just under an hour to scout out the commercial district. After finding nothing of interest, I checked the school yards, the local convenience store parking lots and the municipal parks, common meeting places for young people. The Elvis crowds were gone but there were a few locals out and about.

It was behind the museum/refurbished rail station a block up from the shore highway, where things seemed quiet, that I found them, five in total. Four guys in Converse basketball shoes and baggy clothes. Two head scarves, two baseball caps. None of the rapper wannabes was Corey Brown, something to be thankful for. The fifth 'gangstah' was a female, trying her best not to look like one of her gender. Body size – she was taller and thicker - told me she was not Chelsea. Another plus to add to my list of accomplishments.

The gang had a skinny, shaggy kid surrounded. I guessed the long-hair was barely into his teens. Age is hard to judge in the young. He hugged a guitar case, whether to protect himself or the guitar inside, I couldn't tell. The guys were slapping and punching at their captive while the girl did her best to get her share of kicks in with black work boots. Although I believe there's another name for the footwear style.

There was an audience of two. That one held onto a second guitar case and the other, drumsticks, were clues that they were the victim's friends. Their wide eyes and pale faces told me they were scared, either for their friend or themselves or both. They hadn't found the courage to intervene. But at least they hadn't run off.

Closing in on them, my mind rewound to events long ago, to a time I was the spectator, the kid watching, the one who was too small to be the bully and too timid, too out of place to step up, to be the hero. Jackie Beer, one of the invisible kids. Under the rules of adolescence, invisible kids don't right wrongs even when they're happening right under their noses.

As soon as they saw me, the rappers backed off. All but one. I ignored the bravado, stupid though it was, and shoved the guy back a pace or two, not easy given my weight disadvantage.

I asked guitar boy if he was alright. He nodded his head and sniffled back tears of relief. I told his friends to take him home and to buy him a Coke on the way, stuffing a ten in the drummer's shirt pocket.

I sized up the overgrown kid. He followed some kind of weird dress code, marked by baggy denim shorts, with the crotch flapping around at knee level. A sleeveless basketball shirt revealed arms over-spilling with meaningless tattoos. His beard was trimmed to follow the jaw line, but it was more fuzz than anything else. And he wore a baseball cap, its peak signaling a left turn. A tangle of gold chains around his neck, also tattooed, weighed his head down and pulled his shoulders forward.

The fact I spotted him thirty pounds gave him the courage to spit on the asphalt in front of me as I stepped toward him. He eyed me with an odd mix of indifference and disdain.

Maybe because they saw I was alone, the three clones re-materialized from a recess in the train station wall. The girl was hanging back, leaning into a fifth wannabe rapper, a guy I hadn't previously noticed.

I glared into the faces of each of the returnees, daring them to respond to my challenge. Blank stares were all I got in return. The guy with the girl hanging all over him, the one I figured was in charge of directing mayhem, wore sunglasses and a smart-ass look that, I'd say if I had to guess, he probably practiced in front of the mirror. The big kid in chains, the one I first encountered, stepped aside and sunglasses took over.

"Have to pay more for the extra long tongues?" I said, looking at their loosely tied basketball shoes.

They may not have understood the question but sunglasses said, "Sup, crackah?"

"That English?" I asked him.

"Yo, homie," he said, gesturing my way with his thumbs.

"Homie?" I mimicked his voice. "As in homo sapien?"

"List'n up. Dawg got mouth," sunglasses said. I think he was trying for menacing.

"I'm all ears."

"Chew wan,' ol' man?"

"You class president?" I asked.

"Wha?"

"You the captain of this formidable army?" I said.

"Wha?"

Whether it was his appearance or the strange way he talked, 'sunglasses' was starting to bore me.

"What's your name?" I said, snatching his shades and throwing them, backhanded, at the brick wall five feet away.

I ducked his swing, helped him complete his turn, took him by the belt and shirt collar from behind and marched him around to the front side of the museum double time, to the grassy area surrounding the cenotaph, a more public space. I sent him sprawling into a patch of geraniums beside a park bench. All accomplished before his friends managed to drop their bad ass poses.

My prisoner jumped up, wiped the dirt from his face and called me an effing bastard. But I know scared when I see it.

"You Jeremy?" I said, making a guess based on Jeannie Brown's comments and Garnet's physical description. I poked him hard in the sternum with my index finger. "As in Jeremy Linkletter. Wasn't there a game show host...?"

"Asshole.

"That a 'yes'?"

"Wha' you want, crackah?" he said, still trying for tough.

Behind me, I sensed the wannabe rappers finally rejoined us. Not wanting to give them any time to think, I took Jeremy down to the ground again and then with a fistful of his boxer shorts, I lifted him up and deposited him on the park bench. I stepped to the side nonchalantly and faced the rest of my foes. But my words were for the head junior rapper boy, sitting on the bench I stood beside.

"Three things Jer," I said. "One – I better not see you hassling anybody again."

"Wha' chew talkin' 'bout, suckah?"

"The young guys with the guitars. Back off."

The sneers on the faces of the gang brought me little hope.

"Two, Jerry" I said, now looking at the gang members in turn, "you can send your playmates home. I think I heard the school bell ring..."

"They ain't goin' nowhere, pig," he said, But he didn't sound too sure about it.

"Number three. Jer," I said, this time bending over and looking into Jeremy's eyes from a distance of six inches, "stop calling me names, or I'll make you eat the shorts that are this minute jammed up your sorry ass."

Jeremy tried to stare back. I knew from the sweat on his forehead he wanted to be anywhere but in that beautiful park staring into the face of a grown-up acting like he didn't give a shit. Or maybe all he needed was to adjust himself, because he was doing a lot of squirming around.

Having delivered my threats, I straightened and faced Jeremy's rapper bad boys again and I noticed they'd spread out a little. Then on some kind of signal, two of them went into what I'm sure they felt was an effective fighting stance. In my peripheral vision, the biggest one, the guy I'd already confronted and who I now figured must have been the designated muscle for the group, showed a blade.

I sighed and waited for the first move.

But it never happened.

Garnet appeared out of nowhere.

"Thought you were knocking on doors."

"Thought you were going to call me," he said.

"I got busy."

"I see you found pretty well the whole bunch of 'em."

The kid with the knife made a jabbing motion nowhere near me. Disgusted whether with the feeble effort or the fact he had a knife, Garnet, moving like a big cat, knocked the kid's baseball cap off with his one hand and squeezed his wrist with the other, until he dropped the weapon.

"Pick up your hat, Tony," he said, putting him down by bending his arm into an awkward position. "And go home before I decide to pound some sense into you." Garnet picked the knife off the ground and pocketed it.

Tony put his baseball cap back on. Not embarrassed, like he was used to being manhandled by old men.

"You ain't nobody 'round here," he said, which I figured took a lot of nerve.

"That so, son?"

"Yeah, I hear you was Chief of Po-lice. 'Til yo' got yo' sorry ass fired."

Garret jerked a shoulder like he was about to drive Tony but then he stopped, breathed out and relaxed his muscles, a fraction. Maybe he saw the stop sign in my look, or maybe he found the control that comes from years of police training. No matter. Because the kid was smart enough to recognize his choices, opting to forgo pain and blood.

"S'go," Tony said.

"Homie!" Jeremy shouted. "They just two."

"Believe me Jer, it's a whole lot better if your buddies go home," I said.

I'm not the discerning type, but in my view it's a waste of time to look too hard for underlying reasons or to consider things like 'disenfranchisement' and 'social dislocation' when asking the 'why' and 'what went wrong' questions. Sure, Jeremy, Tony and their lemmings have always been ignored by the adults in their lives. Hell, for all I knew, Jeremy's old man used him as a punching bag. And it was a safe bet they all flunked out of school, so they aren't good at anything. It's obvious too that they were brought up on television and Fruit Loops and that they'd been into drugs since before the first appearance of armpit hair. Yeah, their lives sucked but so what? All the excuses are bogus. And everybody except the do-gooders knows it.

In fact, I think even they know but still they go around telling anyone who will listen that these bullies, these thugs in training, are misunderstood. Give me a break. We understand. And so do the kids, both the bullies and the bullied. There are no goddamned extenuating circumstances to understand. Straight up – these misfits know what they're doing day in and day out. They know doing drugs and stealing and beating up defenseless kids is wrong. These punks have working brains. So, they damn well know better.

They know, but they misbehave anyway. Because acting like a criminal is cool. Shoplifting from the guy who puts in fourteen hour days behind the convenience store counter is okay because the franchisee calls it a cost of doing business. Besides which it pays for the drugs. And it's also cool to pick on the kid who's got a hobby, who uses his brain, who explores a talent, who does something useful, or fun. Hell, picking on him is their sport. And it's how they deal with feelings of inadequacy, except that's just another lame excuse.

Jeremy Linkletter was smart enough to know it's wrong to deface property, to steal handbags and to beat up good kids. But that didn't deter him because the fact it was wrong is one of the reasons he does it.

So again, I have to ask how the hell do frigging 'sociological factors' make assault or theft excusable? Well, they aren't.

If there's no excuse, what do you do?

Nothing?

No, you throw empathy and sympathy and any of the other pathies out the window and you give 'em some of their own. You drive some of their own goddamn crap down their goddamn throats. And then maybe you can make a small start in straightening these punks out. Some of them.

The question I asked myself as I looked into Jeremy's pathetic face was this - would I bother with him, at all, for even an hour or, a minute, on the remote chance there was something to be salvaged? That he was one of the few who could straighten out?

I watched his gang leave, blocking out the threats and the cussing. That left the three of us.

"Jeanie's kid wasn't with 'em," I said to Garnet, gesturing with my head at the departing gang members.

"Nope."

"'Cause that boy's out now. We don't take no losers," offered Jeremy. I smacked him even though the first part of his comment pleased me.

Garnet, on the same page, mentioned that Jeanie Brown would be happy to learn her son had quit the gang.

"I'm going to tell you something, Jeremy," I said, "and I want you to listen carefully."

He didn't answer but his look told me he was defeated.

"You and Corey Brown. How far you go back?"

Again no answer.

"Here's the thing, Jeremy. It doesn't matter one shit to me what your past connections with Corey Brown may have been. He wants nothing to do with you anymore. So, this is from me and from Garnet - from now on, you will have nothing to do with him."

"Fuck off."

"You know Chelsea?"

"Nice piece of ass."

I slapped him hard enough to cause blood.

On one level, it didn't make me feel good. But on another, showing my violent side was satisfying. Besides, it had to be done. "You will not go near Chelsea again. Ever," I said, my face inches from his.

He cowered.

"In fact, if I hear she so much as stubbed her toe and you were in the same county, I will hunt you down, Jeremy Linkletter." I remade my fist and ground it into the soft skin under his jaw.

"Leave me alone," he said.

There was something pathetic about how he said it. And now I felt like a real shit. Still, I needed straight answers. "You drink coffee, kid?" I said.

He told me to get stuffed only less impolitely this time, which I took for a 'yes.'

Garnet went one way, Jeremy and I the other, toward my parking spot. I invited the kid to settle into my side car. He looked at the tight space for a minute until I pointed out that the seating plan in a '46 Indian Chief didn't contemplate a passenger behind the driver. Besides, I'd have felt vulnerable considering the nature of our recent social interaction. Eventually he climbed in and we went for a spin. By the time we pulled into Connie's Grill, Garnet's truck had already cooled down.

"You take the scenic route?" he said, as I nudged Jeremy into the booth and slid in beside him. Garnet sat opposite.

"Something like that," I said.

There isn't a teenaged boy alive who isn't fascinated by motorcycles. Besides, Jeremy needed a break after being roughed up by two grown-ups.

"What are you having, Jeremy?" Garnet asked.

He studied the menu front and back.

"And no, Maddie doesn't serve beer. Which makes me wonder what I'm doing here." Garnet gave me the evil eye.

"Chocolate milkshake," the kid said.

Garnet ordered the shake and our coffees and I mentioned the strawberry-rhubarb pie sitting under glass. Combine all the sweet stuff with the free motorcycle ride and I figured I had Jeremy Linkletter primed to confess to every crime dating back to the disappearance of Jimmy Hoffa. Except he wasn't old enough to take that fall. So I narrowed things down to murder in Collingwood.

"Who cares?" was his first response. "Some guy's fucking dead. Nothin' to do with me."

My contemplations about the kid and confessions were now filed in the wishful thinking folder.

"You don't watch the news?" I said.

He looked at me like I had a screw loose.

"So, the name Dwayne Hicks doesn't mean anything to you?" I said.

"He the dead guy?"

"He's also the guy Mr. Henderson and I recently rescued from an old farmhouse. Where he was being held captive."

Jeremy did the arithmetic and a look of guilt passed over his face. "Yeah, well, you didn't do a very good job, seeing's how you rescued the man like yesterday and you turn around next day and he's already dead."

"We never said when the murder took place, Jeremy."

As his eyes darted around the tabletop, Maddie came by as if on cue to pour fresh coffee. I winked at her. She smiled and gave me the once over, like she wanted to take the afternoon off. Still the actor.

"Have a look at this guy, Maddie," I said, putting an arm around the kid. "Is he one of the punks who followed Dwayne Hicks out of the coffee shop just before he disappeared?"

She made a big production out of studying our prisoner. "Yes," she said, index finger on chin and head cocked to one side. "This person of interest was said punk." She laughed at her use of cop shop talk.

So did Garnet and I.

"Details?"

"You want details?" Maddie said. "Okay. He was here, along with four others. I remember because they shorted me. I always remember customers who rip me off." Then she left to take an order.

Of course as court evidence goes, Maddie's testimony would register in just a notch above meaningless. An Elvis tribute artist, soon to be murder victim, and a bunch of teenagers left a restaurant at roughly the same time? So what?

Here's the so what – the goal was to make Jeremy nervous. And his face told me I was on to a winning strategy. I scored another point when I said, "Guess whose fingerprints we found all over the place at the farmhouse, Jeremy."

"What farmhouse?"

"You know what farmhouse. The farmhouse where Dwayne Hicks was being held captive."

He stared into his milkshake.

"Go ahead and guess," I said.

He shrugged his shoulders but without anywhere close to the same 'who cares' conviction he'd showed us earlier. Still, as with Maddie's observations: fingerprints - so what? The old farm's been a well known hangout for years. Who can say how old the prints were. Even if I'd taken any in the first place.

All of which was irrelevant.

We were already 99.9% certain Jeremy and his friends were the same gang who'd kidnapped Hicks and who'd been blackmailing Sheila's brother. What was relevant was establishing whether he was involved in Hicks' ultimate demise, something I needed to do, even though the smart money said Jeremy and his gang weren't the perpetrators. I didn't see them as far enough down that road or smart enough either. Besides, you have to consider the obvious. These rapper kids are hard to miss and no one mentioned seeing any of them in the hotel on the night of the murder. No, I pegged Jeremy's gang as innocent. Relatively.

Still as I said, I had to be sure. My tendency to jump to conclusions may have already factored into Hicks' death.

"Start talking to us Jeremy," I said.

"Okay," he said.

"Okay what? You know what I'm talking about here, Jeremy?"

"Yeah, we grabbed the Elvis freak. And we took him to a place we know."

"The old farm, near Old Baldy."

"Whatever."

"Then what?"

"Then we shook down another Elvis shithead."

"Mike Mackie?"

"You know him?"

"As a shithead? Yeah, I know him," I acknowledged.

"So we made a couple hundred."

"Not a very big score even for rookie blackmailers."

"We were working out a bigger deal."

"A ransom demand?"

"Guess so."

"Didn't get around to it?"

"Yeah. Because next thing you know, fucker got loose."

"He did, with our help. Already told you that, Jeremy."

"So that makes you a hero?"

"What happened next, Jeremy?"

"What do you mean?"

"You found him again, didn't you?"

"Who?"

"Hicks, the guy you kidnapped. You found him and you killed him."

"Why the fuck would we do that?"

"To keep him quiet." Which, considering the victim, I regarded as a worthy motive. "To stop him from fingering you as his kidnappers."

"No fucking need to keep the dude quiet. He never saw us. We followed him and we took him down from behind."

"He didn't turn around?"

"We bagged his head." I was beginning to question my assessment of the kid's expertise.

"How'd you get him out to the farm? You steal a car?"

"You don't steal no freaking car."

"You boost it?

"Ain't no damn baby chair."

"So what do you call it?"

"You jack the car, man."

"You jack a car, Jeremy?"

"Nah. We used Brit's car."

"Your girlfriend?"

He shrugged.

"She owns a car?"

"Her father's got three. She has one of 'em, a van, all the time."

"A white one?" I wondered if it was the old Ford panel van Corey and Chelsea used.

"It's a cheap mini van."

"Dodge?"

"I guess."

"So?"

"So what?"

"So you stuffed Hicks in the van and you took him to a remote location. And there, you boarded him up in the farmhouse. You left him food. And then you went out to check on him?"

"We went out a couple times. Last time we were there, he wasn't any more."

"And then you hunted him down?" I said, getting back on theme but now, fully convinced that Jeremy Linkletter and his rapper friends were not murderers.

"No we didn't. We said, 'what the fuck' and we forgot about it."

"I'm not convinced, are you Garnet?" I decided I wasn't done scaring some sense into the kid.

"Nope," Garnet said, shooting an evil eye his way.

"All we did was the kidnapping."

"That's all you did?"

"Yeah."

"If that's all you did, you expect maybe a free pass. Or at worst, a 'good talking to'?"

"Ain't no big deal."

Garnet shook his head.

I didn't know what to think either. Kids play too many computer games. Consequences and repercussions get skimmed over. And then one day it's too late. They never get a chance to start living in the real world. It's like their brains were still under construction and then there was an electricians' strike.

Still, speaking of consequences, I wasn't clear on the fall out from turning Jeremy in to the authorities. That was the right move, but was it the smart move? Jeremy's testimony would implicate Sheila's brother in the snatch and de facto further implicate him in the murder investigation.

And once that happened, maybe they wouldn't look at the case the same anymore. They'd start to ease up. And then next thing you know, the cops would pull their resources off the table, just when I needed them looking for the real killer. Of course I was proceeding on the assumption, or the prayer, that Mike Mackie wasn't the real killer.

I hemmed and hawed and eventually, I let Jeremy go, telling him to smarten the hell up. Garnet told me I was dead wrong to spring the kid loose. I told him he might be dead right. But we didn't let our disagreement interfere with the next step. We left Connie's in search of a real watering hole, but not before inviting Maddie to join us so we could properly thank her for helping us out. She nearly took her apron off. But in the next second, better judgment prevailed.

twenty

LIQUID LUNCHES FOG THE BRAIN. So I left Garnet with most of our second full pitcher to drown an emerging case of the blues. Sheila's brother and I needed to have another talk. I reached him on his cell, told him where to meet me.

"No. Not at the cottage," he said. "Mom hates me."

"I hate you, the three stooges hate you, your goldfish hates you, your wife hates you, but your mother doesn't hate you. She's just mad at you."

"Well, Dad has that disappointed look on his face."

"At least he doesn't hate your guts. Not like your goldfish and me."

"Doesn't matter what you say, I'm not going out there."

"Look Mike, I've got zero patience for the 'poor me routine.' And in case you didn't notice, I'm trying to pull your ass out of the firing line. And no one's paying me to do it."

"No one's asking you."

"Sheila is, you dumb shit."

There was a long silence on the other end of the line. "What can I do for you?" he said after a while, like he was the one doing the goddamn favours.

"Meet me down at the shore, in front of the cottage. We'll hide behind the cedars where your Mom can't find you and come after you with a switch."

"I don't know…"

"Mike, this isn't going to go away without your active help. Be there by three o'clock."

Pissed off, I made a sandwich and took my picnic and a six pack to the water.

At the appointed hour, I heard his car drive up. I felt like hiding in the cedars and jumping out at him. Instead, I just called out.

"I don't want to be here, Jack," he said.

"Makes two of us," I said.

"I'm not talking unless you stop with the wisecracks."

"I'm not like this with anybody else."

He swore at me and sat in the other Muskoka chair but before I could offer him a beer and ask my first question, Sheila turned up, carrying a cheap collapsible chair from Canadian Tire. When she set up, she bent over and kissed me, saying, "You've already had a few."

I showed her there were still two soldiers standing at attention waiting to be uncapped. Sheila gave me the kind of look I didn't get too often, the kind with a serious message in it. I looked right back at her, my eyes saying that I had everything under control.

Mike broke up the staring contest by saying, "I'm leaving Lori."

"What?" Sheila barked.

It was like the guy was working his way through a lifetime's worth of major crises in single week.

"At least you didn't kill her," I said.

Now both siblings stared at me.

"Get a sense of humour," I said.

"You're splitting up?" Sheila said.

"Uh huh."

"No way."

For my part, I didn't care other than the fact my interview plans just got thrown out the window.

"Yeah," he said.

"Why?"

"Lot of reasons."

"Name one." Sheila didn't like what she was hearing. Maybe as far as she was concerned, Lori and Mike were meant for each other, despite all the cheating. And as long as they had each other, Mike stayed out of her hair, and her parents' hair. Never mind my hair.

"She's bored. I'm bored."

"Jack bores me, Mike. We're still together."

"Leave my name out of this," I warned her.

"Come on, Mike," she said, "you know marriage is not always fun and games."

"It isn't?" I said.

"Thought you wanted to be left out of it."

"She told me to talk to my GP about Viagra," Mike said.

Because Sheila turned beet red, I came to the rescue, "You need Viagra?" Mike was younger than me. Chronologically.

"For her I do."

"Your wife's a looker," I said. "Never mind perpetually horny." Unless it was an act.

"She's a ball buster," he said.

"Well," I said, "you think you two can hold the marital warfare to a minimum until this trouble you landed in clears up?"

"I just don't know what to say," Sheila said as she packed up her chair, and left me to interrogate her brother without her. In no time flat, I wished she'd stayed because I saw from Mike's answers I'd get nothing out of the guy I didn't already know and because I wondered if she might have done better.

The noise of Mike's tire treads on gravel was Sheila's green light to rejoin me. I finished the rest of my beer. She didn't comment, even though restraint isn't one of her strengths. The hot sun combined with my alcoholic consumption to produce a head pounder. I suggested a swim. It wasn't as exhilarating as our last dip, although Sheila's skin tight Speedo kept the memory fresh.

Drying off and looking out over the aqua green waters, she said, "I blame Lori."

"Only because Mike's your brother." I decided not to remind her of Mike's cheating ways.

"She better keep her hands off you." The warning came with a laugh, a harsh laugh, which told me two things. First, she was having a hard time with the crap her brother kept throwing her way. Second, she had doubts about my sexual appeal.

"I'll do my best to fend her off."

"So if it wasn't Mike, who did it?" she said.

"Who said it wasn't Mike?"

"Me."

"Okay. But you're not so sure now?"

"I've been stupid," she said.

"No. He's family."

"He's different now."

"You mean from when he was a kid. We all are."

"No. Mike was a good guy. In college and right after, we got along great."

"Then he met Lori?"

"Relationships shouldn't change you that much."

"It's the Elvis thing?" I said.

"Just like Hicks, it changed him."

"Fame, even the obscure kind, is addictive. Makes you act like a nitwit."

"Got any other theories?" she asked.

"That's too strong a word."

"What about the punks who were blackmailing Mike?"

"Ever notice how guilty people try to avoid saying things that incriminate them?"

"That so?"

"Yeah and here's the thing: these rapper kids admit to their crimes freely. Like it's proof of something."

"And what – murder isn't one of the crimes they're confessing to?"

"Exactly."

"Maybe they're putting you off the trail by confessing to lesser crimes."

"These rapper kids aren't nearly devious enough to divert a trained investigator's probings."

"Or yours either."

"Funny."

"What exactly are you getting at?"

"Look at these kids," I said. "They commit crimes, but the reasons come from the last TV show they watched. They nab Hicks and then after we spring Hicks, they lose interest in the venture. I don't think it occurred to them to kill the guy, Sheila. They just went back to their lives on the street."

"If the kidnappers are too obvious to be suspects, what's that say about my brother?"

"I know. He's even more obvious."

"They're going to arrest him aren't they?"

"Eventually."

"Damn."

"We're on it, Babe."

"So, who else is there? Another tribute artist?"

"Doubtful. But can't be discounted."

"Well, do you have any ideas at all?"

"We're both former cops."

"And?"

"You have a murder victim. What do the odds tell you?"

"The victim knew the killer."

"Intimately."

"His wife?"

"She's one candidate. But I was using the word in its wider meaning."

"Who then?"

"Gut feeling tells me to check into the manager, Peter Lake."

"Why? Not the hand shake thing."

"No, Olson was the guy with the iffy handshake."

"Some other sign then?"

I ignored her snickering as she posed the question. "You know how some people won't look you in the eye?"

"What? You're saying he wouldn't look at you?"

"The opposite. He looked right at me, like he was assessing me, deciding how to peg me, how to deal with me."

"Why would he have to deal with you?"

"He's hiding something. It may not have anything to do with Hicks' murder but…"

"I remember a judge who said, you can't tell a bad guy by looking at him," Sheila said.

"You can if you look close enough."

"Okay, you can look close. Maybe I can check on some of the other Elvis impersonators."

"I thought they were tribute artists."

Sheila smiled, which is something she had done too little of since Mike starting acting like a bonehead. Except then the smile became a frown. "What about Garnet?" she said, "Is he still working with us?"

"Garnet's slipped into one of his funks. Maybe I can get him to reverse the process if I ask him to see if Honey has an alibi."

"My take; she's a light weight." Sheila paused before adding, "Unless she's Lake's teammate."

"It's a possibility," I agreed.

"Give any thought to her father?"

"I'll see what I can learn about Ted Olson while I'm checking into Lake."

twenty one

IT WAS TOO LATE TO pay a visit to the Olson Enterprises offices, my logical starting point for investigating Peter Lake, so I went back to Heart Breakers to look for Garnet. He wasn't there.

I tried his cell but it went to message.

I tried Connie's and Maddie hadn't seen him.

Which left his trailer. It was a beautiful drive, especially on a vintage motorcycle, but his truck wasn't there so I left a note on his door, not bothering to knock.

As I kickstarted the Chief, I remembered one last possibility.

I wound my way back to the County Road and took it down the Beaver Valley, slowly, enjoying the scenery, turning east just short of a hamlet called Clarksburg. In a few clicks, I found a name on a dark brown mail box that told me I'd arrived.

Tucked into a corner of an abandoned orchard, the house looked like a larger version of the mail box. I dismounted near a gnarly survivor of the nineteenth century and plucked what looked like a Northern Spy from one of its overburdened branches. Four weeks short of ripe, it was sour but it took away the lingering taste of beer. A fifteen year old Plymouth Acclaim sat in the drive, the powder blue paint flaking off its hood and roof after too many years in the sun.

The door opened before I reached it.

"Hello," I said to the pretty blond woman, stepping out onto the porch.

"Well, Jack Beer." There was a teasing tone in her voice.

"Win any bar fights lately?"

Carrie Griffith laughed. It was a great laugh, but I sensed she didn't get to use it often.

"What are you doing here, Jack?" she said.

"Looking for Garnet."

Her pleasant smile faded away. "Why here?"

"You're his daughter."

"Estranged daughter."

"So, you haven't seen him?"

"I didn't say that."

"So, he was here."

She nodded and frowned, like she'd rather not talk about it.

"When?"

"He left an hour ago."

"How was he?"

"Drunk. Wouldn't have found the nerve to drop by otherwise."

"It wasn't his fault." I wasn't referring to his drunken state and I believe she knew it.

"Never said it was."

"But?"

"But," she said, looking off in the distance, "if he'd been on top of things, if he was sober, he might have found enough evidence," already contradicting herself, assigning blame for the failure of the hit and run investigation, an accident that marked her life.

"You sure Hicks was the driver?"

"It was his car."

"Well, he's dead now," I said.

"Which means the job's half done."

"What do you mean, 'half done'?"

"Think about it, Jack." She turned and closed the door behind her, which I took as a hint to leave.

I did. I left. And I thought about it and what I thought was I'd have to ask Garnet what the hell his daughter was talking about, because I didn't like the answer I came to.

Early the next morning, as I adjusted one of Mr. Mackie's ties around the neck of a wrinkled dress shirt, I recalled what I knew of Peter Lake's job description; Collingwood Elvis' manager and some sort of business advisor to Ted Olson. Meaning what? Baby sitter? Was he a marketing guy, a financier, a development expeditor? Or was he just a gopher?

"What's with the tie?" said Sheila, as I hung my sports coat over the back of a kitchen chair and sat down for breakfast. Her parents looked up though I wish they hadn't. Their hang-dog looks depressed me.

"May need to impress."

"Takes more than a tie, Jack," she said.

"I've got some questions. Receptionist might be more forthcoming if she thinks she's talking to a real suit."

"Not your best disguise."

"Scrap the tie?" I said.

"Throw it out," said Mrs. Mackie. "I've been trying to get Thomas to toss that old rag for years."

As I left the room, I slipped the tie into Mr. Mackie's dressing gown pocket, deciding it was his call.

Surrounded by ledge rock, walkways, fish pond and greenery, the building that housed Olson Enterprises looked more like a high end clubhouse than a business office. The soft chairs of the waiting room and the sports magazines displayed on side tables invited me to sit and put my feet up. But I resisted the temptation and made my way to the receptionist.

She was made up to look like she just stepped off a catwalk though I suspected that she was barely out of her teens. Ms. Cosmopolitan Cover Girl greeted me with a manufactured smile. I manufactured my own.

"Jack Beer to see Peter Lake please, Courtney," I said, reading her nameplate.

"You have an appointment?" She checked her book for my name when she knew damn well it wasn't there. Trying to save me from embarrassment, I suppose. Sheila would have told her that in my case, her kindness was entirely unnecessary.

"Will you just give him this?" I said, handing her my card.

"What's that thingy?" she said, giving my card careful scrutiny.

"My trademark," I explained, although that might have been the wrong word because I hadn't bothered to have the 'thingy' protected from copyright infringement. Hughie said he didn't see the necessity. And Sheila agreed.

"But what is it?"

I explained the 'P' shaped magnifying glass and the big eye.

"I know a graphic designer," she said.

"Courtney, just give the card to Lake," I said.

"He's not here."

"He's not here?"

"Nope."

"Darn."

"Sorry."

I tried to look needy.

"Mr. Maxwell's in though."

"Who's he?"

"Mr. Lake's assistant."

"Peter Lake has an assistant?"

"Why, yes."

"But isn't that Lake's job? Isn't he the chief assistant?"

"Executive Assistant, yes."

"So, in other words, the Executive Assistant has an assistant?"

"Yes."

"Does the executive assistant's assistant have an assistant?"

"We're advertising for one," she said.

"You're joking," I said.

"Weren't you?" Her smile looked a lot better.

"Okay, I'll see Mr. Maxwell, then."

Courtney talked to someone on the intercom, telling him my name and profession. Then she led me down a long hallway, her long legs and tight skirt making for a more pleasant trip than if she thought I was smart enough to find my own way.

Harry Maxwell had a chubby face and shaggy hair - I think it's called a mullet - with unfashionably long sideburns. Or maybe they were fashionable. I never know these things. He stood and walked around the desk. Physique wise, he was a taller and larger version of Peter Lake. Body building buddies, I figured.

Looking into his face, I caught unfocused eyes and a big smile, like it was a job requirement at Olson Enterprises. I extended a hand and the bastard crushed it but he let go before I had to kick him in the shins.

I gave the guy a second look. Despite Sheila's scoffing, some cops - the ones with a couple decades or more of experience - are good at reading other people; their faces, posture, their voices. The story Harry Maxwell's face told me was of a man with a façade. He was out of place in the corporate world. He had none of the slickness of his boss and he never even tried to hide the look of disdain in his eyes. Like he didn't like private detectives, maybe because we aren't much different from cops.

I fell into a stuffed leather armchair and made like I planned to camp there for a while. Harry circled his desk again where he sat down, erect and vigilant. I took a few minutes to admire the fancy doodads and other artistic stuff scattered around the room. Everybody associated with Olson had the fancy trappings. The resort development business must pay good money.

I wanted to ask about something that reminded me of a female body part, sitting on the coffee table in front of me, but decided I didn't want to sound like a hick. Instead, I explained that I was investigating the murder of Peter's boss. Maxwell noted that Ted Olson, not Dwayne Hicks, was Peter Lake's boss. I waved the distinction away like it was a bothersome fruit fly. I would have liked to have asked where Lake was at the time of the murder but I didn't want to give away that particular interest too early, so I asked a bunch of general questions having to do with the presence, or not, of suspicious characters in the lives of Mr. and Mrs. Hicks, fully expecting to learn nothing useful. And I was right about that.

Then I got to the important stuff.

"How long you known Lake?" I said.

"We go way back," he said.

"How far?"

"We knew each other in high school. Then I didn't see him for a few years."

"Where'd you do your time?" I threw at him.

He laughed, only it was the snorting kind.

"You go to college?" I said, carrying on as if I hadn't just suggested he was an ex-con.

He nodded his head, like the conversation bored him. But his squinting eyes told me he wasn't entirely emotionless.

"Then what?"

"Then two years ago, Peter hired me."

"As?"

"As a trouble shooter. I deal with problems. Make them go away."

"Hey," I said. "That's my job description."

He shrugged, still feigning boredom.

"So, what's he do?"

"Lake? Corporate management."

"Kind of vague."

"He finds investors. Buys properties. Steers our development plans through the approvals process."

"Greases palms?"

"Figuratively," he said.

"What's a guy need to land a job like that?"

"Education?"

It was my turn to nod my head as if I didn't care.

"Financial, business training. MBA looks good on your CV."

"He has an MBA? Where?"

"University of Western Ontario. Ivey School."

"Experience?"

"Investment analyst. Mortgage broker. Banking. Land development. Peter's the kind of guy the headhunters hunt for."

"Impressive. And he's so young. How old is he?"

"What's all this got to do with anything?" he said. I noticed his right hand formed into a fist.

"Racking up the billable hours," I lied.

"Rack them up somewhere else," he said.

Getting to my feet, I smiled and shot Harry between the eyes with my index finger. On my way out, I winked at Courtney and she rolled her eyeballs. Her smile was getting cuter all the time.

I rode the Chief over to Connie's, blew Maddie a kiss, ordered a coffee at the counter, dug my cell out and got a number from Information. But it wasn't quite the right number. These days it hardly ever is. As a result, I bounced from one robotic voice to another and another until I wanted to shoot the person who invented the computer.

Finally, I punched 'zero' on my phone pad, which landed me with an operator with a real voice, although it was hard to tell at first. I explained that I was returning a phone call from the Dean of the Business School and she promised to put me right through. Jackpot, I got another real voice. My spirits soared.

Although the voice didn't belong to the dean, it did in fact belong to a deanette, a secretary three or four spots down the line from the big kazooey. Using my helpless voice, I told her I had a question concerning my student records and she said I had the wrong number, but she promised to find the right one.

I redialed.

Meanwhile, Maddie returned, leaned her elbows on the counter and shot me a smile, the kind that's real and, after my visit to Olson Enterprises, reassuring. I pursed my lips at her again and she brought her hands up to steady her heart.

Someone picked up and I said, "My name is Peter Lake."

Maddie inched a little closer, sensing a conspiracy in the works.

The man on the other end told me his name.

I said, "I want to order a copy of my transcript, Mr. Johnston."

I covered the mouthpiece and winked at Maddie. "They're looking it up."

"Won't you have to prove who you are?" Connie said. "Like maybe giving him your mother's maiden name?"

"I don't think so. Not for what I'm after," I said.

I sipped my coffee, enjoying the fact I'd just brought a nugget of suspense into Maddie's life. The clerk came back on the line.

"How's that? You've lost my records?" I said.

He corrected me. Although I was already fully aware I was incorrect.

"Oh, now you're saying you have no such record," I said.

Mr. Johnston was beginning to sound suspicious, so I went on the offensive. "You leave me no choice, Mr. Johnston. I am already on my way to your office and I promise you we will straighten this out." Then I broke the connection.

"Weren't you kind of rude?"

"Was I?"

"He's just doing his job," Connie said.

"I didn't like his tone. Losing my records. It's inexcusable."

"You going down there?"

"Where?"

"I don't know."

"No, I'm not going anywhere."

Connie studied my face for a full minute. It rattled me a little. Then she said, "I get it."

"I knew you would."

"Peter Lake, the guy you were pretending to be…"

"Yes?"

"He's the same Peter Lake who works for Ted Olson?"

"That's right."

"The guy who has the hots for Honey Hicks?"

"Really?" I said, pleased to have her confirm the suspicions I'd expressed earlier to Sheila.

"Yes, really."

"Are no secrets safe?"

"There's not much about this town I don't know."

"Hrmph."

I hoped for an explanation and she granted my wish.

"My second cousin works at the Nottawasaga Inn, out Cookstown way." She winked. "Popular place for business meetings, if you know what I mean."

I did know what she meant and for the tenth time at least, I contemplated putting her on the payroll. If I had a payroll.

"So, Lake's a phony?" she said, switching back to my phone game.

"Universities don't usually lose student transcripts."

"What's he up to?"

"He's after something."

"Other than Honey Hicks, what?"

"Don't know but maybe he's planning to get it through Honey Hicks."

So far, I knew Peter Lake was an imposter, a guy who got his job under false pretenses. And he was a womanizer, which is a trait he shares in common with a few million other jackasses. But I needed to learn a whole lot more, such as the answer to Maddie's question - what was Lake's game? And what's his game have to do with the death of Collingwood Elvis?

It was square one time again. I made a brainstorming appointment with Sheila at the lakeshore in front of the cottage.

"Maybe I should goggle the guy," I told her, after I brought her up to speed.

"What?"

"What?"

"Did you say…"

"I said I should goggle Peter Lake."

"Yeah well, maybe you should let me 'goggle' the guy. Let's go up to the house and do that," Sheila said, laughing all the way.

With Sheila's expert help, I discovered that there are a lot of Peter Lakes in the world. Either that or the man has multiple personality disorder. Sheila said it was the former. She found Peter Lake musicians, Peter Lake artists, Peter Lake professors and a Peter Lake radio personality as well as a heritage potato farmer from Prince Edward Island named Peter Lake, all floating around on the web.

And then there were a handful of paltry entries about a businessman with Olson Enterprises, named Peter Lake, our Peter Lake, an expert presenter at a conference of municipal planners and politicians and an executive board member of some development organization. The web search didn't tell us anything more. Sheila clicked the mouse and the screen returned to its Lake Huron sunset.

"Considering he's supposed to be such a business hotshot, does it strike you as odd there's nothing on our suspect that goes back more than a couple years?" I said.

Instead of answering my question, she said, "Does this mean Lake's your number one suspect?"

"It does."

"Based on?"

"Based on the fact he's up to something."

"I'm convinced," she said, the words coming with a snicker.

"Look babe, this isn't just about a guy who made up his own CV."

"No?"

"What if Peter Lake isn't Peter Lake?"

"Who is he?"

"I don't know."

"So what's that tell us?"

"Nothing for certain. But it's getting easier to guess."

"Peter Lake is a new creation?"

"Brand new entity."

"As of two years ago."

"Before he came to Collingwood, Peter Lake was someone else."

"Who?"

"Be fun to find out," I said.

But for that, I'd need help. Professional police help. In the meantime, there was evidence to collect and poking around to do.

twenty two

SHEILA TOSSED ME A TIE, with red and yellow flowers on a dark background.

"What's this?"

"I'm tired of seeing you in my dad's stuff."

"Where'd you get it?" I said.

"It's not a big mystery, Jack."

"Meaning?"

"There are these places all over the country. They're called clothing stores. Some of them are just for men. They sell dress shirts and sweaters, and suits and pants with creases."

Sheila can get carried away with the sarcasm. She thinks I don't get it, but I do. She just doesn't realize being obtuse is how I dodge unpleasant activities, like shopping. And rather than explain something she'd find unfathomable, I picked up the tie and put it on, even though, in my opinion, it didn't go with my blazer and my grey shirt. But it did match the jeans, the kind with a crease.

She smiled her approval. Then she pulled a black dress out of a big, yellow, crinkly shopping bag. I watched her remove her shorts and t-shirt and slip into her new outfit. It was short, drawing attention to her long tanned, athletic legs. And it was snug, drawing my attention back up again. It was a dress that cleared the mind of everything else.

My approval may have been obvious.

"Later," she said.

It was going to be hard to concentrate if I bumped into any clues at the funeral.

I'm not a big fan of funerals but Sheila and I decided to go to Dwayne's because we felt there was a good chance the characters involved in the Collingwood Elvis intrigue would have ringside seats.

We rode with Mike and Lori. Neither of them wanted to go to the ceremony on the grounds that Mike never liked the man and Lori liked him too much, never mind they weren't talking to each other. But Sheila thought it was a good idea for her brother and sister-in-law to make an appearance, as some kind of 'a statement of innocence,' is how she put it. My thought was that Mike's presence might cause a scene, which was another good reason to make them go.

Upon arriving, Mike and Lori eased away from us, choosing the other side of the sanctuary. Sheila and I sat at the back of the church where we could observe while simultaneously trying for inconspicuous, easy for me, hard for Sheila in her new black dress.

The program, handed us by an usher whose smile suggested he was supposed to be at the church around the corner where a wedding was underway, revealed that the dearly departed had three brothers and a sister along with a gaggle of nieces and nephews. I saw a family resemblance in a number of the faces. Further observation indicated that Dwayne Hicks had enough friends and relatives to fill the left side of the church sanctuary, although funerals don't have seating plans. It just seemed to be working out that way.

Somehow, Peter Lake got elected from the thinner ranks of the Olson side of the church to do the eulogy. His words may have been inspiring and I'd guess they were touching too. The tears were my clue. I had no other way of knowing, since I didn't pay any attention. I did, however, listen to the gospel hymn performed by an Elvis look-alike named Roy Leblanc, best voice I'd heard since I landed in Collingwood.

The crowd fell off by two thirds by the time we got to the cemetery. Among the notables hanging in there were five or six Elvis types, the Mayor and his wife and various festival mucky mucks. After Honey Hicks turned her back on the grave, signaling it was okay for the rest of us to migrate to the post funeral gathering, I pulled Sheila toward the car, Mike and Lori following.

The three stooges were leaving too, walking shoulder to shoulder. The Bobby Darin clone left the pack and sidled over. "No one's gonna miss that son of a bitch," he told me, keeping his voice low.

"Not counting the whores he bedded," Roy Orbison threw in, louder and within earshot of Sheila's sister-in-law. Their Wayne Newton companion smirked.

"Good to see you again," I said.

"Danke schoen," he answered, which prompted their sudden departure.

As we drove off, Sheila looked back and remarked on our weak suspect base, to which Lori added, "why don't you check out that scuzzy Roy Orbison twerpy copycat, Jack?"

I closed down the debate by saying, "Hey, I wonder whether the guy had anything to do with the demise of Elvis, the first."

She told me to screw off.

Then she had a giggling fit.

The wake was held in the recreation centre, which was more like a fancy lounge, in the middle of the Olson condominium complex. As was typical of such events, the gathering had taken on a party atmosphere. Great finger food and copious quantities of booze jump-started old jokes, older pick-up lines and impolite laughter. If people died more often, the world would be a happier place.

The guests who skipped the burial ceremony got a headstart on the drinking and Garnet was into it big time too, if his glassy eyes and stupid grin weren't lying to me. He waved a lazy hand our way and I felt a sense of relief that I found him again. More important, his mood looked like it had an oil change since our last confab at the Heart Breakers, where he left the clear impression he was settling in for the long haul.

As I chatted with him, it occurred to me that his sunny attitude had something to do with Penny Sue Stanfield snuggling up beside him, which was a perplexing thought.

Needing to move on, I mouthed the words, "catch you later," to which he saluted, reminding me of the first time we met. Taking Sheila's hand, I shouldered through the mourners in search of Peter Lake. As we neared the new widow, Harry Maxwell stepped in front of us. More accurately, he managed somehow to skirt around me and step in front of Sheila.

"Kind of out of your league, isn't she, Beer?" Maxwell took Sheila's other hand, the one I wasn't holding, and from his six foot six height looked down at her, not even pretending to hold his dirty mind in check. Olson Enterprise's assistant assistant had been drinking, though maybe not as much as Garnet.

Sheila stepped back. She doesn't intimidate easily, but when I filled the space Sheila vacated, I understood that wasn't it at all. The guy's Right Guard had left his post.

"You going to introduce me to this sweet little thing?" he said, still holding onto her hand and craning around me, his eyes wandering over Sheila's topography, lingering.

He pissed me off. "Let go of the hand," I said.

He did, but he took his time about it.

"Now, take your goddamn eyes off my girlfriend's dress."

"Girlfriend? You're not just a pity date, Beer?"

"Let's go, Jack," Sheila said, pulling me away from the obnoxious giant.

My eyes stayed on him and his took their own sweet time leaving Sheila's body. When he finally decided to look my way, he mouthed an expletive. I mouthed a worse one.

"Strange guy," Sheila whispered in my ear.

"Very."

"What would you have done to him if he hadn't let go of my hand?"

"I hadn't thought that far ahead yet."

"Guy that big, you need a plan."

"Or a grenade."

"Who is he?"

"I think he's a cross between Elton John and Goldberg," I said, answering the question, 'what is he' instead.

"Goldberg?"

"Former WCW Champion."

"What?"

"Never mind."

"This Goldberg was a wrestler?" she said, trying to get my weird imagery.

"Think of Hulk Hogan."

"Oh, I get it. You mean he's like a cross between Elton John and Hulk Hogan."

"Yeah."

"Why didn't you say that in the first place?"

"I always thought Goldberg had better stage presence."

"Well, I can see the Elton John part in him. The hairstyle. The pug nose. The round glasses."

"Exactly."

"Except the glasses should be bigger," she said, "with red butterfly wings flying off the frames."

"I'll tell him you said so."

"But you know, I haven't seen him with his shirt off. Do you think he shaves his chest, like those wrestlers?"

"Wouldn't doubt it."

"How do you know him?"

"Assistant to Peter Lake."

"That all?

"There's more to the story."

"How far are you into the book?"

"Just enough to know he's in it."

"But he's not the main character?"

"Not likely."

"Still, he looks dangerous."

"I figured that out in Chapter One."

After escaping from Maxwell, I spied Lake between bobbing heads, stationed in front of a memorial shrine of rotating slideshow, photo albums, awards, medals and trophies. My suspect stood straight and steady beside

Honey Olson-Hicks, a comforting arm wrapped possessively around her shoulder, helping the poor, doe eyed widow deflect words of sympathy.

Most of the curiosity seekers, I was certain, hardly knew the dead guy. When the crowd thinned a little, Sheila and I jockeyed forward, pausing on the way to convey my sympathies to Ted Olson, to which he said something like 'what a jackass.' My take was he was referring to his departed son-in-law. Sheila thought there was an equal chance he was talking about me.

Honey Hicks looked immaculate, while at the same time, I sensed she was nearing complete exhaustion, whether from grief or late night parties, I couldn't tell.

Sheila touched her on the wrist. "I'm Sheila. We met at the VIP banquet."

"We did?"

"You want to take a break?" Sheila said, ignoring the slight.

"Like what?"

"Fresh air. Let's get away for ten minutes."

"Okay," she said, sounding more relieved than grateful. "I'm not good at these frigging things."

"No one is," Sheila said.

They turned to leave, two very attractive women, one outwardly vulnerable, playing to an audience, but hiding a side that was all about self and the other confident in every way, a woman without ulterior motives. Except for helping me decide how to pigeon-hole these people. I watched the two of them walk away. Tied on the physical, decency gave Sheila the scoring edge.

Brains was another of Sheila's strong suits and her slick maneuver left me alone with my suspect. I smiled, he smiled back, each of us, resisting the temptation to punch the other in the face.

"You got a ghost writer?" I said to Peter Lake.

"What?"

"The eulogy. Or you write it yourself?"

"Why are you such an ass?"

"It's not something I give a lot of thought to," I said.

"My man Harry, says you were in the office looking for me."

"I was. And now I found you."

"You came across as nosy, he says. Prying into my background."

"Just curious."

"Why?"

"I'm looking into the murder."

"For whom?"

"For me, that's whom."

"So?"

His face sported a smirk and his hands went out to the side, palms up, just as the preacher's had at the graveside, before he invited us to pray.

"So, what year was it you graduated?" I said.

Lake's nostrils flared.

"Ivey School of Business wasn't it?" I said.

"Why don't you tell me what you want, Beer."

"Okay. Here's a question. What's going on between you and Honey Hicks?"

"What's that supposed to mean?"

"Beautiful woman. Rich. And now a widow. What more could you ask for?"

"So, that's your angle." Lake laughed but it was forced.

"One of 'em."

"You know the difference between an investor and a speculator?" Lake asked me.

The question was out of left field but I played along. "Why don't you enlighten me."

"I'm an investor. My return's practically a lock."

"Uh huh."

"And you, Jack Beer, Private Detective, and general pain in the ass, you are a speculator. And in my world, speculators always get burned."

"Speculation's just the first stage in the investigative process, Lake."

"You're boring me."

"Here's a question your assistant dodged. Present company excepted, did he have any enemies?"

"Hicks?"

"You know any other recent murder victims?"

"Enemies?"

"Yeah. You were his manager. Anybody have it in for him?"

"Lot of people disliked him. He was a jerk."

"Lot of jerks in the world."

"Be good if we could kill 'em all?"

"I'm no philosopher," I said.

A waiter, dressed in a tuxedo-like jacket wormed his way by. Lake plunked an empty champagne glass on his tray and took another. As the penguin continued on his way, I excused myself and followed, trying hard to look desperately thirsty. When an inebriate grabbed the waiter's attention, I snatched Lake's glass and slipped it into my jacket pocket, so quickly, so smoothly, even Perry Mason would have missed it.

Seeing as there were no other hot suspects who needed to be annoyed, I lined up at the bar for five minutes and collected three free Coronas, thinking Sheila might want one, if I could find her. By the time I did – actually she found me - another five minutes later, I was down to the last bottle, hers, and I contemplated drinking it, too.

"What'd you learn, Mr. PI?" she said, creeping up behind me and breathing into my ear, her hands resting on my waist.

After I made her repeat the question, twice, I confessed, "Peter Lake doesn't like me. He called me a pain in the ass."

"Hard to fathom."

"I know."

"What else?"

"We talked about investing."

"Investing in what?"

"He was talking about widows, I do believe."

"And you?"

"I don't know what I was talking about."

She giggled, a sign she was on drink three, at least. For her sake, I took a long swallow from the bottle I'd been saving for her.

"What about you?" I said. "Honey say anything interesting?"

"Garnet's been 'badgering her.'"

"'Badgering'?"

"Her word."

"Really? About the murder?"

"That and an old case."

"The hit and run."

"Yup."

"Let's find our elusive partner," I said.

But we didn't.

Finally saying something other than 'Danke Shoen', Wayne Newton's double told us that Garnet Henderson left the funeral reception with Penny Sue Stanfield hanging on his arm.

twenty three

EARLY THAT EVENING, SHEILA'S PARENTS announced they were leaving the cottage for their home in London to get away from all the stress, according to Mrs. Mackie.

"That's a shame," I said, trying my best to sound like I meant it, and failing badly.

Sheila shot me a look.

Mr. Mackie chuckled and winked at me. What a great guy. Mike's troubles weighed on him but he still managed to find a way to smile. I nearly asked if he could send the Missus home and stay on for a while. Instead, I helped the Mackies load the car and we wished them safe journey.

In a moment of panic, I wondered whether Sheila would feel obligated to inform Mike and Lori of the freed up space. They were booked into one of the Town's chains, I hoped in separate rooms, as a deterrent against double homicide.

"Over my dead body," she told me when I mentioned my fears.

"We have so much in common," I said.

Feeling like a new man, I lit the barbecue and started grilling sweet potato slices seasoned with paprika, cumin and oregano, adding a big salmon fillet to the fire after twenty minutes. I would have thrown on buttered carrots wrapped in foil but Sheila vetoed the idea. Too much orange. Apparently, women have trouble digesting food that offends the visual palate. I fixed the problem by making a fresh green salad. But I left the tomatoes out, for fear of the colour clash. For dessert, I unfroze butter tarts and served us two scoops each of vanilla ice cream. No wonder the woman loves me.

Later we took the late evening chill off in front of the woodstove. And when the fuel ran low, Sheila slipped a Dusty Springfield disc into the CD player, a sure sign she remembered the promise she'd made while I was busy watching her squeeze into her funeral outfit.

Next morning, I left a phone message with Garnet asking why he'd disappeared on me again.

While I worked on what to do next, Sheila phoned one of the Collingwood Elvis Festival organizers to get the full roster of tribute artists registered to perform. She spent the morning on the web, searching the names. For the sake of thoroughness, she passed the same roster on to an OPP friend she calls 'data girl,' the idea being the two would compare their findings and ID any candidates for the position of Elvis impersonator murderer.

With my stolen champagne glass wrapped in tissue and tucked into my back pack, I biked over to the town police station where Sergeant Bronson agreed to run any prints through the RCMP's Automated Fingerprint Identification System. "But only because Garnet's an old friend," Bronson said. "You two are still working together?"

"Yes," I said. At least I thought so.

I just wasn't too sure what my partner'd been up to lately. Either he was a loose cannon taking my investigation in directions I wouldn't have agreed with, or he and Penny Sue Stanfield holed up somewhere, drinking to excess.

"Could take a few days," Bronson said.

"Can you put a rush on it?"

"I'm sticking my neck out on this one, pal."

Running prints for me was not something the district commander would have approved, given the sway Leonard Boroski held over the entire detachment. Still I needed answers. "Aren't you coming up for retirement?" I said.

"What are you implying? Because I'm closing in on my ninety factor, that I don't give a shit about getting reamed out by my boss and his boss and maybe his boss over doing you a favour?"

"Do you?"

"I'll put a rush on it," he said.

Getting the fingerprint processing underway was an important step. At least that was the hope. Problem was I couldn't think of anything else as important to do and I still couldn't find Garnet.

So I returned to the cottage and sat down to prepare reports detailing everything I knew on all the suspects. Ten minutes later, including eight or nine minutes of writer's block, I was done and I invited Sheila for a run on a stretch of the Bruce Trail I'd heard was comparatively easy on the knees. She was tied up on the computer, leaving me to run about twenty kilometers on my own. Returning home two and a half hours later, dinner was not waiting for me on the table.

"You expect me to cook while you're out having fun and I'm working my tail off?" she said.

"There's a cozy little restaurant in town," I said. "I hear the food's great and jeans are permitted."

While I was in the shower, Garnet Henderson showed up.

When I came out for air, he and Sheila were sharing a pot of coffee. She seemed to be enjoying herself and as I sat down to join them, it felt like I was butting in.

Garnet's thick grey hair had been trimmed, though it still covered the top third of his ears and brushed at his collar. His jeans were new and his beige cotton shirt was freshly pressed. I hate string ties, but it fit nicely with the moustache and the lanky build.

I poured myself a coffee while Sheila rose from her chair to search for munchies.

"How are you?" I asked him.

"Sober."

"How long?"

"A few hours. For me, sobriety's a transitory condition."

Thinking back to his recent funk and then his flip flop regarding Penny Sue Stanfield, I told him, "I like you better sober."

"You and the rest of the world."

"I hear you've been getting in Honey Hicks' face."

"You got a problem with it, son?"

"She's not on my 'A' list for the husband's murder."

"She's sleazy, Jack. She just hides it better than the rest of us."

"Anything come of it?" I asked him.

"She's rattled."

"How do you know?"

"She sicced her lap dog on me."

"You mean Lake or Maxwell?"

"Wasn't Lake. Don't know this guy Maxwell."

I described the giant whose head looked like a British rock star and whose body was carved out of ironwood. Garnet said it sounded like the same mutant who tried to scare him off in the parking lot at Heart Breakers.

"What'd he do?" I asked.

"Pointed a shotgun at my crotch."

"Yikes."

"Then he says to stay away from Honey Olson-Hicks."

"That it?"

"Pretty much. Then I left."

"Intact?"

"Yes." He winked at Sheila.

"One has to guard against such threats," she said and we all laughed.

"Damn right there."

"You see what he drove?" I said.

"SUV."

"Plate?"

"He kept his lights off. Not sure it would have made any difference anyhow, partner. I was more than halfway to lights out myself."

I thought about whether to say what was on my mind and decided to stay quiet. But my decision only lasted until we exchanged looks that spoke of unfinished business between us.

"Spit it out, boy," he said.

"If we're going to work together," I said, trying to be tactful, "we've got to agree on strategy. In advance. Or we split up and go it alone."

"We back on the topic of Honey Olson-Hicks?"

"Yeah."

"My interest in the woman goes way back."

"I heard."

"So, you know that angle ain't any of your goddamn business."

"I can make it my business."

Garnet shifted his body forward, like he was keeping his temper in check.

"If you want help that is," I added, calming things down.

"Let you know."

"So we done with the pissing match?" I said.

He nodded his head, signaling me that I may have had a valid point, or that he'd think about it, anyway. I nodded too, sending a similar signal. I went to the fridge and opened a beer. Garnet thought about it and took a pass.

"You two finished making up?" Sheila asked, plunking a bag of chips and a jar of dry roasted nuts in front of us.

Garnet smiled at her. She reciprocated and I thought for a minute she was going to kiss the guy. For some reason, I told him he reminded her of Sam Elliot, the actor. Like it was an acceptable explanation for her flirting.

"Been known to use that to advantage," he said.

"I'll bet," Sheila said.

"Don't be leaving me alone with this girl, son," Garnet said.

"I'd appreciate if you two turned the heat down in my presence."

They laughed because they thought I was joking. And I'm pretty sure I was.

Sheila and I cancelled our dinner date and Garnet joined us for burgers. Later, over cognac, I revisited the connection between Honey Olson-Hicks and the old hit and run case. Sheila and I already knew that Garnet and Carrie blamed Dwayne for messing up Carrie's husband. At least that's what we thought.

"Yeah, that was one of the theories," he said.

"But not yours?" Sheila said.

"Used to be my thinking. It was his truck. He and Honey were engaged. Daddy Olson spent big bucks covering up for the future son-in-law."

"But?"

"But, Carrie – she wasn't hurt nearly as bad you have to remember – she always said a woman was driving."

"Honey?"

"Honey."

"You think so now, too?"

"I think they were together," he said. "Hicks drank too much. So, I'd say Honey was the likely driver that time of night. But it makes no difference, the truck ran down two young people out for a late evening bicycle ride. Hicks and Honey were both there. They both ran. They're both guilty."

"Carrie sees it that way, too," I said.

"You been talking to her?"

"Just briefly."

"Me too."

"How's it going for you and Carrie?"

"I think I should only see her when I'm sober."

I knew very little about the old case, but I couldn't stop myself from poking my stick some more into the cold embers. "Olson's never liked Dwayne Hicks, has he?" I said.

"Honey's the only person ever saw anything worthwhile in that piece of rancid dog meat," Garnet said.

"So, why does Ted Olson cover up a crime Hicks committed?"

"Exactly."

"He'd go to the wall for his little girl though," I said.

"Wouldn't anybody?"

"Pressuring the widow isn't going to get you anywhere."

"And I told you already, this is my business."

"Meaning?"

"I'll keep my business and yours in separate pockets."

"Unless there is a connection?"

"Gotta protect my interests."

That night after Garnet left for home, sitting side by side in front of the warmth of the wood stove, Sheila asked a question I'd been avoiding.

"Jack," she said. Her voice had a tremor that made me look into her face.

"Just say it," I said.

"Is there any possibility Garnet was involved in Hicks' death?"

"I look at Garnet the way you look at Mike," I said.

"I don't follow."

"For the time being, I choose not to consider the possibility." But I looked away when I said it.

"Okay."

Of course my answer wasn't entirely accurate. I turned her face my way, again, when I realized I had another take on the puzzle. "Maybe it's not the same. What you feel about Mike, that's blind faith."

"What about you? How do you feel about Mike?"

"I'll go to the wall for the dumb ass."

"For me?"

"For you."

"What about you and your opinion on Garnet. It's not blind faith too?"

"No."

"So, if it's not because you feel a loyalty for the man, what is it?"

"It's just not in him to commit premeditated murder."

"He can't find enough evidence and so…"

"And so, his code won't let him take care of it any other way." I finished her sentence. "And that's one of the things that's been eating at him for the last five years."

"What about Carrie?"

"Innocent too."

"How can you be so sure? You hardly know her," she said.

"Okay, for Garnet's sake, I'm going with the blind faith angle on the woman."

"What a mess."

twenty four

ONE THING I DON'T MISS about my police days is the phone call that thumps me hard in the chest in the middle of the night. When I went private the calls stopped, for the most part. It's a numbers thing. Six years ago as Grand Bend Chief, I 'served and protected' about three thousand year-rounders.

Multiply that number by ten in the summer when the tourists showed up. On any night in the high season, it was like betting on a full house that someone would get drunk, have an accident and/or get beat up and feel the urge to give me a wake up call. On weekends, it was a royal flush guarantee.

These days hardly anyone breaks into my beauty sleep, because I seldom carry more than three clients at a time and because sometimes I have none. That's why Clapton's guitar riff nearly knocked my heart over the fence.

"Who the hell is it?" I yelled at my phone.

There was no answer.

"What?" I yelled again.

"Push the green button, Jack," Sheila said.

"I did," I lied.

"Harder then."

"Hello," I said, again. "Who's there?"

"That you, Jack?"

"It's three effing o'clock in the effing morning, Garnet," I pointed out reasonably.

"They caught me."

"Who?"

"Who do you think?"

I thought back to my last conversation with Sheila about murder suspects and friends. And I said, slowly, "You were caught for…"

"DUI," he said, which cleared up the what for.

But there was more I wanted to know about the who. "One of the old boys nab you?" I asked, thinking of the cops who signed up with the OPP when the municipal force disbanded.

"They know better," he said. "You coming or not?"

"I'm on the way."

The Ontario Provincial Police Station is tucked away on one of Collingwood's side streets, sharing a building with the fire department. It doesn't take an inside observer, or outside ones either, very long to discover there is friction between the old town cop transfers and the new provincial arrivals. Melding the two was a lot like throwing a bunch of Israelis and Palestinians into a locked room and expecting a book of love poems out of them. Something had to give and it was a safe bet the style of the local cop had changed forever.

Of course the fault went both ways. The brass didn't trust the former town cops with anything major. And the local boys ignored protocols they thought were stupid, which explains why Bronson wasn't on the Hicks case and why he was helping me. It also might explain why Garnet got himself arrested.

I found him sitting on a bench in the station's entranceway. As a courtesy to a former officer, he damn well should have been allowed to wait in the back somewhere, out of sight of the general public. It didn't matter if it was the middle of the frigging night and no one was around. At least they hadn't thrown him into a cell. I sat beside him and waited.

"Sheila with you?" is what he said first.

"She's in bed. Where I ought to be."

"How do you plan to get my truck back?"

"Can't you drive it?"

Garnet gave me a look which made me question my sanity.

"Sorry, my brain's still asleep."

"It's alright, Jack. Thanks for coming."

An officer came out. He weighed in at about two fifty and it was a familiar two fifty. "His truck's out back," Officer Muscles said, like he'd been reading our minds, or eavesdropping. "You got a sober driver, you can take it away now. Otherwise, he can have it back in the morning. He'll get a notice in a few days concerning the court date."

"You the guy who nicked Garnet?"

"Yeah."

"Smith, right? We met in the Mayor's office. You and a woman cop named Rowland are Boroski's lapdogs."

"Watch the mouth."

"I thought you were a detective. What the hell you doing, pulling traffic patrol? You get demoted?"

"Fill-in duty. Not that it's any of your goddamn business." It was a plausible answer, but I didn't buy it. My take – someone was out to get Garnet. And maybe me as well.

"Well, Smitty, let me tell you something," I said, looking up from the bench. "The man's been drinking. He's not an idiot. You have something to say concerning Mr. Henderson, or his truck or frigging court appearances, talk to him, not me. Got it, Smitty?"

"It's Detective Constable Smith. Or Officer Smith is acceptable, too," he said, looking hard at me. "Got it, big mouth?"

I turned away, fifty times more disgusted than the situation warranted. "Let's go, Garnet." I took his arm and we turned to leave.

"What's your name?" the policeman said to my back.

We kept walking.

"Are you Jack Beer?"

I stopped and looked back at the guy.

"Cut the games, Smith. You know damn well who I am. I already told you when we first met. And I'm also damn sure your boss gave you my personal bio. But I don't care if you want to act ignorant. Because look, I'm too tired and too pissed off to care."

"And why would that be?"

"Why am I pissed off? I'll tell you why. I'm no fan of 'by the book' bullshit."

"Meaning?"

"You couldn't cut the guy some slack?"

"Maybe you haven't heard of our 'no tolerance' policy."

"So, impound his vehicle. Yell at him. Call him names. Threaten to shoot him. Any of that. But you didn't have to charge him. He's a retired member."

"I know his background."

"He was entitled to better."

"You think so, Beer?"

"I do. And that's why I'm pissed off."

"Get his truck before nine, Beer. Or we add another day to the impound fee."

I told Garnet it was time to go.

But Constable Smith wasn't finished. "And one more thing. Report to the duty officer when you come back tomorrow, Beer."

I turned.

"Captain Boroski wants a word with you."

"Piss off, Smith."

"You're sleeping it off at the cottage, Garnet," I said, stuffing him into my sidecar. It was a tight fit.

"What's got your underwear in a knot, son? You weren't the one got himself arrested."

I didn't answer because I couldn't decide what annoyed me more – the cops arresting Garnet or Boroski ordering me to appear. Like I had nothing better to do. At the least, I should have told Garnet I wasn't mad at him. But I didn't, which may have been a good thing, because he needed straightening out.

The cold night air sobered Garnet up and it calmed me down. In fact, I mellowed to the point I considered a starlit ride along the shore highway, but I chose sleep, thinking it was best to be rested for my meeting in four hours with Leonard Boroski. If I hoped to keep my cool, which was a long shot.

• • • • • •

Headaches that are not the result of a hangover are uncalled for. A bowl of shredded wheat covered in nuts and dried fruit, strong coffee and three aspirins reduced the pounding in my head to a vague and foggy unease. As happened earlier that morning, I figured I could count on the cool morning air in my face, from my seat on the Big Chief, to provide remedy – to finish the job of clearing the cobwebs.

I left Garnet to sleep off his binge, relying on Sheila's good judgment not to crawl into bed with him. My day plan was to move Garnet's truck to a public parking lot for later retrieval and then to see what Leonard Boroski wanted with me. Part A went down like a snap. It was half past eight when I walked through the front door of the police station and I learned Part B had to be deferred. Captain Hotshot hadn't arrived yet, the clerk told me through the little wicket window. She returned to her desk.

"He's the one who wanted the goddamn meeting!" I yelled through the window, but no one even bothered to look up. Needing to calm my violent urges, I nipped over to Connie's Grill. Bless her heart, at least Maddie was on duty.

"It true they picked up Garnet for drunk driving?" she said, as I groaned my way onto a counter stool.

"Holy crap Maddie, that was only a couple hours ago."

"It was more than that."

"The point is how the hell'd you find out already?"

"Smart ass cop named Smith dropped in as he was coming off shift. Bragging to his smart ass partner, Jennifer something or other."

"Derek Smith and Jennifer Rowland," I said, "and you heard right."

"Shame," she said.

"Slow night and Smith, the SOB, was looking for a reason to screw with somebody's life. Either that or they were targeting the man."

"They're not all like Smith. Anybody else wouldn't have had the heart."

"The cold heart."

"Exactly."

I sipped my coffee.

"I heard them mention your name, Jack."

"Smith and this Jennifer cop?"

"Yeah."

"Well, I gave Smith a hard time last night when I was at the station collecting Garnet."

"It was something else."

"What."

"They called you a loose cannon."

"That makes sense, too," I said.

"What do you mean?"

"I have a meeting with the District Commander. I'm guessing I've stepped on his toes somehow."

As I walked into the detachment office for the second time in the last sixty minutes, I reminded myself of my plan. Boiled down, it had to do with hearing the OPP Commander out, keeping my cool and picking up any stray clues.

His royal pain in the fat ass was in, the duty officer told me, but the son of a bitch made me wait, five long minutes, just to be sure I was fully aware of the man's great importance.

A different constable came out to collect me. "You Jack Beer?" he said. Just like Smith, this guy knew damn well who I was, but was pretending otherwise.

I steamed into the office Boroski commandeered for the meeting – his usual lair is in Orillia – and stopped in front of his desk.

"What the fuck is it you want, Boroski?"

He stood up and started yelling at me on a wide range of topics; investigating a murder without his permission, interviewing suspects without his permission, digging up leads without his permission, annoying respected local citizens without his permission. There were a lot of other things I did without his permission but I stopped listening at agenda item four. When he ran out of breath, I turned to leave.

"Beer, where the hell you think you're going?"

"Haven't had my morning swim," I said. On my way out the door I knocked Boroski's cap off the coat tree.

I went straight to the shore and shucked my wallet, shoes and shirt and dove in. My swim was more therapeutic than a session with a shrink, not that I have any first hand knowledge on that score. Afterwards, I found Garnet and Sheila at the kitchen table, both looking fresh and clean. Nothing suspicious about that. They read the 'I-am-annoyed signs' in my face and didn't ask 'how my morning went.' So we avoided each other for most of the morning.

Sheila laid out a lunch spread that included deviled eggs, black forest ham, ten varieties of cheese, veggies and fresh crusty buns. My kind of feast. We took our plates out to the porch.

"How'd the meeting go?" Sheila said, when I signaled my mood improvement by ripping off a third of my sandwich in one bite and sighing contentedly.

"Better than expected," I said after choking down my first swallow.

"You had a fight with him."

"With who?" Garnet asked, though he was there when Smith gave me the invitation.

"For the last twenty years, Leonard Boroski and Jack have feuded. Professional differences," Sheila explained, making it sound civilized.

"He's a jackass," I clarified.

"He is," said Sheila.

"And yet he keeps getting promoted."

Thinking of the last time we butted heads, Boroski was only the top gun for Huron County. Now, they had bumped him a couple of rungs so he could make a mess of things all over southern Ontario. Ask me, it just didn't make sense.

"What'd he want?" Garnet asked.

"He told me to stay the hell out of his business."

"You tell him to go to hell?" he said.

"I threw his hat on the floor."

"Very mature," Garnet said, beating Sheila to the point.

"About your arrest last night," I started to say.

"It was a message," he said.

"You going to back off?"

Garnet's grin said, "Game on."

twenty five

THE GAME MAY HAVE BEEN on but for that day and the next, I whiffed at everything thrown my way. Then on the afternoon of the third day someone threw me a screwball, easier to read than a knuckleball, as junk pitches go. But only marginally.

The sun was at least an hour from its August debut. I was wide awake and had been for hours. When you can't sleep, waiting for morning takes forever. I'm one of those people who sleeps like a baby when the Tigers are winning and the coffee's fresh, and when the crooks follow the script.

I concede the coffee's been good, thanks to Maddie over at Connie's Grill, but that wasn't enough to offset the facts the Tigers were in a tailspin and the crooks weren't falling into line. Come to think of it, I still wasn't sure who the villains were. Sure, there was a bad smell coming from Peter Lake and his assistant but I needed verification that their foul scent was the one my nose was supposed to follow, the one leading to Collingwood Elvis' murderer.

Because I couldn't get ahead on the pitch count, the rhythms of my life were off kilter. I was wasting time, I wasn't sleeping, I was missing my early morning run on the sands of Lake Huron and Sheila hadn't often joined me when I did find the time to put some miles in. I was distracted, out of sync.

On top of all that, I missed Reba. Maybe Sheila did, too.

As I lay there, trying not to think about my dog and wondering whether my clues were really clues and not just useless fuss, I vowed to get up and put my running gear on as soon as the sky morphed from black to blue-grey. Except by the time that happened, I fell back to sleep, only to be shocked into consciousness by my cell phone. Unbelievably, Eric Clapton was starting to bug me. Crap. My life needed straightening out. Badly.

"What?"

"Is that Jack Beer?"

"Yeah."

"Did I wake you up?"

"Yeah."

"It's the middle of the morning."

"Not for me."

"I need to talk to you."

"My mother always told me not to talk to strangers."

"You don't recognize my voice?"

The woman laughed.

My brain stirred. "Penny?"

"I go by Penny Sue. Although it says Peggy Sue on my birth certificate."

"Your parents were Buddy Holly fans?"

The song, after which she was named, came out in the mid '50s, making her younger than I guessed.

"That's right."

"Now, you want to talk about pioneers, about the king of…"

"Shut up."

"What?"

"Elvis is the only king," she said.

"I'm only saying if he'd lived…"

"I changed my name for a reason, Jack."

"Look Penny Sue, you called me. I'm guessing the reason wasn't to pick a fight over music history."

"Sorry. It's just that people need to show more respect."

Elvis people are so close minded. "What did you want to talk about?" I said.

"The murder."

"What about it?"

"Not on the phone."

"Where?"

"Can you come to my house?"

An historical plaque by the front door told me that Penny Sue Stanfield's house was almost a hundred and fifty years old and that it was lived in by some famous guy who nobody's heard of. Judging by the neighbourhood, I figured the yellow bricked storey and a half was a very early farmhouse that soon found itself surrounded by the rapidly expanding town, a process that was completed about a hundred and twenty years ago.

The door opened and Penny Sue stepped aside to let me pass. Without the make-up and the gaudy outfit, she was passable attractive, even if she had a seven or eight year head start on me. I turned, waiting in the foyer for instructions. She winked, walked by me and I followed her generous hips into the living room, where I staggered and collapsed into the nearest chair. I was that blown away.

"Holy crap. It's a frigging museum."

"Remarkable, isn't it?"

Once over the initial shock, I rose from my chair and toured the rest of the room. Call it a shrine. On the high ceilinged wall opposite, a portrait of the 'king' from his early days looked down on me, flanked by shiny black records in expensive frames and beside them, the companion album covers. The table below Elvis displayed a half dozen studio photographs, all autographed. Elsewhere; movie posters, Elvis dolls, serving trays, books, concert posters, magazine covers, collector plates and figurines. All celebrating that a god named Elvis once walked the earth.

I stopped at a glass display cabinet, filled with Elvis spoons, pendants, buttons, ticket stubs and rings. On a shelf of its own, a letter to Miss Stanfield, signed by Elvis and dated January 12, 1964 stood in clear protective plastic on a silver stand. Beside it was a business envelope showing as its return address, Graceland, Highway 51 South, Memphis, Tennessee.

"He wrote that letter to me when I was nine years old." Penny Sue's face was all aglow.

"I thought he lived on Elvis Presley Avenue," I said, not sure where I heard that.

"Elvis Presley Boulevard," Penny Sue corrected me. "They changed the name in 1972."

"Been there?"

"To Graceland? Of course."

In the background, Springsteen sang about living in the past. The irony flew right over Penny Sue's head. She flicked the radio off before he finished and I resented her for it.

"Want to see the rest?" she said.

"The rest?"

"There's more," she said. "The really good stuff's in the safe."

"This is enough." I sat down again, but my eyes weren't done taking it in. On the table beside me, surrounding a lamp decorated with scenes from Elvis' movies, a dozen or so bottles invited inspection. I picked one up.

"Careful," she warned me.

"'Burning Love Hot Sauce'?" I said, reading the label and laughing. "Containing 'hunks' no doubt."

"It's good stuff. Or, so I'm told."

"It's a steak sauce?"

"Yeah. 'All Shook Up Hot Sauce' is supposed to be good, too."

"You haven't tried any of this, have you?"

"Can't bring myself to do it."

"Affects the value if you break the seal?"

"It's not about the money, Jack."

"Well, I have to hand it to you. The collection's amazing."

She scanned her room, her face full of pride, and obsession.

Getting down to it, I opened the meeting with a direct question, not having a gavel handy, "What couldn't you tell me over the phone?"

"Let's have coffee first."

I stifled a sigh and smiled instead, nodding my agreement. She poured and I took a carrot muffin. Meanwhile, I glanced at a framed photograph of a memorial stone. There was a swimming pool in the background.

"I took that shot," she said.

"Where's his grave?"

"Graceland."

"Really, buried in his own backyard."

"Not just Elvis. His mother and father. And his grandmother on his father's side."

"What about his favourite hamster?"

She may not have heard me.

"And," she said, with a dramatic pause, "there's a marker to commemorate his twin brother."

"He had a twin?"

She looked at me, her face showing the disgust she felt at the depth of my ignorance.

"Was he a singer too?"

Apparently it was another dumb question.

"He was stillborn," she said. "Named Jesse."

"No shit. So that means he never went platinum?"

Penny Sue stared at me until I told her I was sorry and I was. It was a dumb thing to say. She forgave me by nodding her head, slowly, once.

"Imagine if there'd been two of 'em," I said. A shiver travelled down my spine and it wasn't from the thrill of it.

"Yes, it is wonderful to imagine."

"What about Elvis? What was he when he died? Forty something?"

"Forty two."

"Pretty young but then again, he was a druggie," I said.

The daggers in her eyes came out again. Her fists clenched and unclenched.

"He did overdose, didn't he?" I continued. "Isn't that what did him in?"

"Elvis didn't commit suicide."

"Never said he did."

"And he wasn't addicted."

"But didn't he take a Mullagany stew of pharmaceuticals every day? I heard he was convinced there was a drug for every ailment from insomnia to hangnails."

"He had too many doctors."

"I've seen it before. Pills to get you high. Pills to make you sleep. Pills to wake you up. Add to that obesity and a suspect heart, wasn't it just a matter of time?"

"You think you know so much?" Penny Sue was still staring right through me.

"Well, what do you know?" I said.

"What do you care?"

"Just interested."

She calmed a little. Then almost in a whisper, she said, "There's a theory he died of anaphylactic shock."

"Allergic reaction?"

"Maybe to the pills with codeine."

"And this theory says he didn't know he was allergic?"

"I think he knew."

"But you also think he didn't kill himself."

"No."

I thought about what she was implying. Then it occurred to me, "Not another conspiracy theory," I said.

"He had enemies," she said.

I shifted the focus by taking a bite out of my carrot muffin. It was so good I finished it off right away and asked if I could taste another variety. The pumpkin and raisin muffin was even better. I made a mental note to ask for the recipe. We like to offer variety at Gert's.

"What's the story with you and Garnet?" I said but, don't ask why I was moving us even further from the main purpose of my visit.

"The story?"

"Yeah, there's something going on with you two."

"You don't know what you're talking about."

"I know. And I knew from the first time you barged into a conversation I was having with Garnet and Jeannie Brown at that country bar."

"It was the Heart Breakers Tavern. And I didn't barge in."

"Okay then. Put it this way: as first encounters go, it was pretty easy to tell there was a history. Then, I saw you two acting friendly at the funeral."

Penny Sue took on the attitude of a school girl.

"We go back a ways," she said.

"How far?"

"Years, maybe a decade."

"After his wife died?"

"Long after."

"He took it hard?"

"I guess," she said. "If you ask me, he was too good for her in the first place."

"I didn't ask you."

"You asked about us."

"Okay, you're right. So, how was it between you two? What ... ten years ago?"

"We didn't live together or anything but we were a couple."

"Past tense?"

"He broke it off."

"Now what?"

"What do you mean, 'Now what?'"

"You getting back together?"

"I don't know. We keep trying. At least, I do."

Penny Sue's eyes blanked out, like a switch was turned to off. I suddenly felt like I'd been prying, which reminded me to finally get the hell to the point. So I did. "You said you had something for me on the murder," I said, waking her up.

"What?" she said.

"The murder. You know, the demise of Dwayne Hicks, aka Collingwood Elvis."

"Don't call him that."

"It upsets you?"

"Hicks didn't care about Elvis. He only cared about himself. He had no business taking his name."

"You didn't like the man."

"He was a goddamned prick."

"Doesn't make murder okay," I said.

"Of course not."

"So what is it? What is it you need to get off your chest."

That's when she threw me the screwball. "I was there," she said.

"You were there? You saw it happen?"

"No. I never saw it happen."

"What then?"

"I saw Mike coming out of the room."

"What did you say?"

"I saw Mike."

"Coming out of Hicks' room?"

"Yes. But first I saw him in the room. He was just getting up. You know, like he'd been leaning over the body." She stopped, eyes wide open. I couldn't tell what the look meant.

"And?"

"He looked scared."

There was already enough evidence to place Mike at the scene, including Mike's own statement, but eyewitness testimony would be golden to the other team.

"Anything else?" I said.

"I saw Dwayne."

"What do you mean?"

"He was still alive."

"I'm not following," I said.

"Just before I went out for ice."

She was telling me the story ass-backward. Just to be sure, I said, "Before you saw Mike?"

"Yes."

"What was Hicks doing?"

"I saw him unlocking the door to his room."

"And you saw Mike after that?"

"Yes, on my way back."

Her statements bowled me over and, like her narrative, my questions followed no particular order.

"How much time before you saw Mike, in the room, leaning over the body?"

"Ten, maybe twenty minutes."

"It takes that long to get ice?"

"Couldn't find it at first. It's a long hallway. And I saw some people I know."

"You told the police?"

"Not yet."

"Why not?"

"I know you and Garnet are working to prove Mike didn't do it."

"So, you're willing to lie."

"I'm willing not to come forward. Is that a lie?"

"It's pretty close, Penny Sue. What did Garnet say?" I was guessing she confided in the man, considering her dogged pursuit.

"I didn't tell him."

"How's that?"

"I didn't tell him."

"Why?"

"I thought he would go to the police with it."

I nearly told her Garnet would have been right but, I held off. Instead, I asked her, "If you aren't planning to report this, why tell me?"

She wasn't saying.

"Sharing the burden?" I tried.

"Maybe."

"I have to tell you, this doesn't help."

"But, I don't believe Mike did it. The thing is - he wasn't the only one there that night." I couldn't tell whether she was stringing a line. But, something was off with the whole conversation.

"Are you telling me you saw someone else leaving the room?"

"No, but there were others in the hallways, in the lobby, in the restaurant. It's a hangout for the festival crowd."

"So who was there that night?"

"The Mayor. Mr. Olson. A half dozen other tribute artists. Those other impersonators."

"Roy Orbison and …"

"Yeah, them."

"What about Peter Lake or Harry Maxwell?"

"I don't know the second name but I'd be willing to bet Peter Lake was there."

"But you didn't see him?"

"No."

"Anybody else?"

"If Peter was there, so was Honey Hicks."

"You don't even know for sure if Peter was there."

She conceded the point.

"Penny Sue, I have to ask you something. What were you doing there?" It was a question I should have asked earlier.

"Where?"

"In that hotel, on that floor, outside that room."

"I was staying there, down the hall, four doors away."

"You were staying there?"

"Yes."

"Why, when you live right here, in town?"

"I always stay in the Mariner Motor Hotel during the festival. I like being where the parties are."

"Can anyone vouch for you?" I said.

"Garnet can, I guess."

"Garnet? He was staying with you?"

"Yeah, but as I said, he doesn't know about any of this. And I'd appreciate if you kept things that way."

I left Penny Sue Stanfield's house wondering why the hell Garnet didn't tell me he was there the night of the murder.

twenty six

THANKS TO PENNY SUE STANFIELD, I was making progress but only if you want to call having fifty new questions to write down in my case file, progress.

Mike was at the cottage when I got back, sitting on the porch step, probably uninvited, certainly unwanted. I walked by, doing my best to ignore him. But unprompted, he followed me inside where he annoyed me by opening his mouth and what came out was an apology.

"Sorry, I was a jerk," were his exact words.

I thought about it, not whether he was a jerk. Even Sheila admits that. No, it was the apology itself that had me thinking. What was behind it? The last time he apologized, it was for not staying in touch, not being brotherly enough, even though he isn't my brother. Then, what's he do - he touched me for a loan and being a sucker, I lent him a wad. It took just shy of a year to repay me, without the promised interest. This was before he hit the jackpot with Lori, his wife. Real estate agents in Toronto make good money.

The time before that, he apologized over some other insult, I can't remember what. But Mike's real motive was, as usual, about something else entirely, like getting a nasty collection agency off his back. Gambling debts.

This time, I figured his latest apology wasn't about money, although I half hoped it was, because if it was about money I knew how to get rid of the hangdog look that made me want to bring up Penny Sue's muffins. Whatever he was preparing to grovel about, I didn't want to know. So, I told him not to apologize, hoping without hope to break the pattern.

"I'm in trouble, Jack," were his next words.

"We already know that," I said.

Sheila came into the kitchen, having overheard his opening whine.

"Thank God you're here. He needs someone to wipe away the sniffles," I told her, heading for the front room. "You seen the latest 'Sports Illustrated' around here?"

"Quick screwing around, Jack," Sheila said, catching me by the arm. "Let him talk."

"Thanks," Mike said, from under bowed head and slumped shoulders.

Stuck, I said, "What the hell is it then?"

"Hughie says they're coming to arrest me."

"When?" Sheila said.

He didn't answer, going into a rant instead, "I went to the cops, just like you told me to, Jack. Now look what's happening."

"Better you went to them first because, if you hadn't, guaranteed, they'd have come looking for you."

"Well, looks like it doesn't matter a damn I went to them and told them everything I knew. How I found the body. I told them about Honey's phone call, how she asked me to come and see her and I told them what time the call was. I told them where the body was. I described it, the body, and all the blood. And I admitted I ran from the scene. I was scared. Not that they give a shit about normal human reactions."

"Hughie say why there're arresting you now?" Sheila asked.

"Goddamn Hughie Morrison! A lot of good your buddy, the super lawyer, did me, Jack. I thought you said he could keep me out of jail. I should fire the bastard."

"Not a lot a guy can do," I said, "what with you leaving little piles of crap all over the scene of the crime."

"Jack," Sheila said. "Mike's upset. You're not helping."

She took her brother's hand and looked into his sorry face. "What's happened?"

"They found a hole in my story."

"Just one?" I said.

"What hole?" Sheila asked.

"Honey denied she called me."

I thought about the fact I wasn't surprised, although not being surprised at the news didn't mean I knew what it meant. Other than the possibility was growing that someone, for example Peter Lake with Honey's help, was conspiring to make Mike look bad.

"According to the hotel room phone records," Mike continued, "there were no outgoing calls."

"So, she was definitely staying there," I said, mostly to myself.

"Yeah. She must have used her cell phone."

Sheila let go of her brother's hand and leaned back against the kitchen counter, arms folded, forehead creased. Her body language told me to take over the questioning.

"Cops have that phone?" I said, although chances were she used a throw away or a pay phone, if in fact she was conspiring against Mike.

"I don't know," he said. "Why?"

"Cell records can be checked, too."

"She phoned from somewhere, goddamn it."

"Anything else?"

"What do you mean?"

"Did Hughie tell you anything else?" I asked.

"There're witnesses."

Had the cops interviewed Penny Sue, I wondered. "Witnesses to what? Did someone see you stabbing the guy?"

"Jack!" Sheila shot. "He didn't do it."

"Just testing," I said, moving fast to my next question, "Tell us about the witnesses."

"People saw me going through the lobby. Taking the elevator."

"Who?"

"The desk clerk. Some of the other guys."

"You mean other Elvis types?"

"Yeah. Tribute Artists."

"What did you do with Lori?"

"Do with her?"

"You were with her, weren't you?"

"Who says?" he said, reminding me of their marital strife.

"You planning to answer my question?"

"Yeah, we met up after my performance."

"And?"

"And what?"

"Okay. Let me spell it out for you. You're married. You were sneaking off to cheat on your wife. Presumably you gave Lori some excuse, left her somewhere."

"Yeah."

"Yeah what? Where'd you leave her?"

"In the bar."

"Alone?"

"No, with friends."

"And then you went up to the room, looking for Honey. What then?"

"What?"

"Did you see Lori again? Can she vouch for your movements? Can she say how long you were gone for. What was it, Mike? Two or three minutes at the murder scene?"

"Lori was gone when I got back to the bar."

"Can anyone else vouch for you? Come on Mike. Think. Is there no one who can back up your story?"

"Not really."

"Okay, let's move on. Who else?"

"What?

"Who else?"

"Who else saw me?"

"Yeah."

"It's not about 'who else.' It's about 'what else'."

"'What else?' As in 'what else do they have on you'?" I said.

He looked up, begging for sympathy and I wanted to smack him in the frigging head and throw him through the screen door.

"You gonna tell us or not?" I said, shouting because it was impossible not to.

"A fingerprint."

"In the room?" I said, not too alarmed. He'd already admitted he was there.

"Make that fingerprints," he said,

"Not just in the room? Where else Mike?"

"On the knife."

"On the murder weapon? Are you serious? You actually handled the knife?"

"I must have. They found two or three."

"And you didn't think this was important enough to tell Hughie? Or me? Son of a bitch, Mike. What were you thinking?"

"I don't remember touching it," he whined.

"Why don't you just sign a confession? Get it over with."

I thought he might cry but I didn't care.

"It's a miracle you aren't already in custody," I said.

"When I went to the police, I thought that was it. I thought it would all blow over. Now they're telling Hughie they've got all kinds of evidence. But I don't know what the hell anybody's talking about."

"What did Hughie tell you to do?"

"Turn myself in."

"Then what the hell are you doing here?"

Before he could say something else stupid, the back door flew open. Must have been ten of them, Detective Constable Derek Smith leading the way. When I saw his face, I wanted to smack someone across the head all over again.

Two uniforms, directed by Detective Rowland, pulled Mike out of his chair and threw him against the fridge knocking snapshots, grocery lists, and a year's worth of reminders to the floor, along with their magnets. Smith told Sheila and me to put our hands where he could see them. She complied and so did I, showing him a pair of birds.

The uniformed officers cuffed Mike. Then two back-up cops, with hands on holstered weapons, ordered us to lean forward on the kitchen table, making it safe apparently, for Smith and Rowland to frisk Sheila and me.

Smith spent more time on Sheila than necessary. Involuntarily, the right side of my body tensed.

"Ever been tasered?" my groper asked.

"Let it go, Jack," Sheila said. "I'm fine."

"Clean," Rowland said about me.

Smith nodded his agreement. Sheila and I straightened up and turned. Mike gave his sister one last pathetic look and then the uniforms hustled him out the door, which must have been the signal for Captain Boroski to enter.

"The coast is clear, Boroski," I said.

Not getting my inference about his personal bravery, Boroski pointed a finger, "What did I tell you, Beer?"

"Remind me. I wasn't listening."

"What was it? A lousy three days ago? What the fuck did I tell you?"

"I already told you. I don't know."

"I'll tell your girlfriend, then. She's a whole lot brighter than you are. I would know, since she used to work for me."

"Did I ever mention you're the reason I quit policing, Leonard?" she said.

Boroski's face flushed.

"Check that," Sheila said. "You were nowhere near that important." Bless her heart forever.

Tossing aside her digs, he got right in her face, "Remind Jack sweet cheeks, to keep his dumb ass the hell out of my business. Will you do that for me, sweet cheeks?"

"What did you say, Boroski? I wasn't listening," she said.

"Boroski, you need to know something," I said. "I'm going up the line on this."

"What the fuck you talking about?"

"Harassing citizens who just happen to be bystanders. Overkill on the arrest."

"Overkill? What's that supposed to mean?"

"You wanted to arrest Mike? Fine. Call me. I would have brought him in. Mike's no troublemaker," I snarled. "There was no goddamn reason to break in, wreck the door, rough up private citizens."

He had to know I was bluffing. The arrest went relatively smoothly but in all the time I'd known him, Boroski never was able to muster up that little thing called self-confidence, unless he was absolutely sure of the ground he was standing on. And so, he didn't know if I'd file a complaint. Not for sure.

And if there was any gratification for me that day, it was in the way Boroski looked, a little unsure of himself and as well, a little like he wanted to ram a pole up my backside, plant me in a field and use me as a tackling dummy. But I knew damn well he wouldn't.

I told him to get the hell out.

• • • • • •

As Sheila and I repaired the back door, I said, "I'll tell you something about your brother."

"Do I need to hear this?"

"The guy couldn't hit a curve ball if I told him it was coming."

"I know."

"I mean look at the screw-ups."

"I know."

"First he drops empty threats all around town about his chief rival, right after which he drinks himself goofy with a bunch of young punks.'

"Do we need to go back that far?"

"Then, he starts running at the mouth about his plans to kidnap Hicks, over an Elvis contest that wasn't going his way, for crying out loud."

"You think all this hasn't already occurred to me, Jack?"

"Then, when the people he's conspiring with follow through with the kidnapping, he tries to fix things himself except, these punks are slicker than he is, which, by the way, isn't very slick at all. And so what happens, he succumbs to their blackmail scheme."

"I've heard it all before."

"Your brother got scammed by a bunch of teenagers."

"I know, Jack," she let out a sigh. "Sometimes I wonder if we're related."

"Then he happens upon a crime scene, and instead of being smart about finding a dead man and calling 911, he turns tail."

"Do you think Boroski knows about Mike's part in the kidnapping?"

I recalled the interrogation I faced in front of Boroski and the mayor. "Garnet and I never said anything about Mike's role. And let's pray the rappers don't mention their short partnership with Mike when the cops get around to grilling them."

"If Honey lied about the phone call, would she tell the cops about Mike and the kidnapping?"

"I'm guessing she would if she knew he was involved."

"Let's hope it never comes out."

"It doesn't really matter, Babe. Your brother left enough clues at the murder scene, even an idiot like Boroski would have fingered him for the murder."

"I know. Mike was stupid and he panicked."

"Stupidity is the foundation for 99 percent of all crime."

"He didn't do it, Jack."

"No, I don't think he did."

"You don't?"

"No, because I've noticed percentage-wise, there are just as many idiots walking around who aren't criminals."

"Meaning?"

"You can be your own worst enemy even if you are innocent."

"No doubts then about Mike?"

"Not anymore."

"Good. So, how bad is this?"

"He's in it up to the eyeballs."

"But he was duped."

"And not just by the rapper boys, which, if it comes out, may turn out to be the most damaging thing. He's the adult. He started the ball rolling."

"Who else duped him?"

"Whoever made the phone call."

"You don't think it was Honey?"

"It could have been."

"Why?"

"To trick Mike into going up to that room."

"Why?"

"Maybe she was doing someone else a favour."

"Meaning?"

"Meaning I've got some thinking to do."

"Mike needs a lot help."

"He does."

"You still volunteering?"

"I guess."

"I love you, Jack."

"You don't even like the guy, Sheila."

"Yeah, but…"

"I know."

"What are you going to do?"

"Pin the killing on the real murderer."

twenty seven

I PHONED HUGHIE, WHO WAS already enroute, and told him he needed to start working up an argument for bail. Then I phoned Garnet, who suggested we meet later at Connie's for a strategy session. I never mentioned the news I'd picked up from his girlfriend, because I didn't know what Penny Sue's description of the comings and goings in Hicks' hotel room meant yet. Sheila didn't call her parents, thinking it would be better to wait until Mike made bail, assuming Hughie had the appropriate tricks up his sleeve. We left it to Mike as to whether he should contact his wife. My thought was he should consider Canada Post. There was nothing else obvious to do but we both felt a strong need to do something.

As a way to fill her particular void, Sheila returned to her research on the internet.

I didn't have any busy work to occupy my time. Two months ago, I would have thrown sticks in the lake for Reba to bring back to me. Instead, I made bacon and eggs while I contemplated the fact that history and patterns always repeat themselves. But I don't carry a history book around with me. I don't have to, because my gut keeps track and that's where I turn when the clues aren't jumping up and slapping me in the face. And my gut was telling me the murder didn't have anything to do with climate change or global recession. Or with outsiders. And although it pissed off the wider Elvis world, Hicks' decision to change his name to Collingwood Elvis had nothing to do with his demise. Despite all the noise Hicks' self-proclaimed title caused, it just wasn't the murdering kind of annoyance.

No, the murder of Dwayne Curtis Hicks was a local matter and the answers were likely staring me in the face. I just needed to look at the facts in a new way, maybe by squinting my eyes a little.

Except, as Sheila is prone to remind me, my fielding percentage is not exactly a thousand, whether my approach is analytical or instinctual. Which is why I supported Sheila in her research into the background of the rest of the tribute artists who attended the Collingwood Elvis Festival, even though I expected the results to be negative. Which is not cynical. It was just my gut talking.

"It's always good to have one's instincts confirmed," I told Sheila, speculating from her demeanor that cyberspace was really a vacuum when it came to solving crimes.

"Come again," she said.

"Find anything?" I said. There was no need to come out and say I expected nothing useful from her keyboard efforts.

Putting the results in their most favourable light, Sheila discovered a smattering of connections among the Elvis clones and imitators, although none of the links could have been called suspicious. For example, Elvis impersonators go to the same festivals, mostly in the United States, year after year. It's like the professional golfers' tour or the Formula One circuit. They all show up. And they all know one another, at the least well enough to wave at each other.

Between festivals, most of them return to their day jobs. The rest, a very small number, actually make a living at pretending to be a dead guy named Elvis Presley by singing at clubs, weddings, conventions and private parties, even funerals.

Rounding out her report, Sheila found that about half the Elvis tribute artists had long-term connections to the Collingwood festival including our murder victim and the cops' main suspect. In fact through the years, Dwayne Hicks and Mike Mackie, while highly competitive rivals, grew close, even friendly according to various sources, especially in the early days. But the relationship soured.

Hicks was also closely linked with a 65 year old singer, a retired teacher named Bobby Harper. It struck us both as odd that Harper taught Hicks

Grade 10 math. I told Sheila I doubted Harper was holding a grudge because Dwayne skipped his detention.

"My thoughts exactly."

"Anything else?" I said.

"Like Hicks, a few of them are big drinkers. And fewer still do drugs."

"Based on?"

"Web gossip and a scattering of police reports."

"The shared bad habits – you're thinking that's all coincidental."

"That's how it looks."

"You done?"

"Not quite. Dwayne and Honey went on vacation to the Bahamas last March, same time as another impersonator and his wife. I talked to the wife and her reaction was 'so what?'"

"Meaning the Bahamas is a big place?"

"Exactly."

"So?"

"Any links between the other Elvis impersonators and Hicks are tenuous," Sheila said. "Or at best, they are links shared in common."

"You're saying, 'the foxes look alike and most of them didn't raid the chicken coop'." I said.

"I'm saying, it was likely a coyote."

"Dead end."

"Yeah, dead end," she said.

"Some dead ends are useful."

"We now know where not to look?"

"True."

"What else?"

"Your findings...."

"There were no findings."

"Your non-findings then. They support my theory," I said.

"Meaning?

"The murder was personal."

"Aren't most of them?"

We biked over to Connie's, too late to beat the lunch crowd, but Garnet had already claimed a booth. We sat across from him. While Sheila brought him up to speed on her research, I had an argument in my head how best to raise a delicate question with my recently acquired partner in PI-ing.

"So, neither data girl nor Sheila hit the jackpot," he said.

"Reminds me of my last ten poker games," I said.

"What now?"

I got right to the point. "Now, we clear a funny odor that won't just go away."

"This odor have something to do with me, son?" I couldn't read any emotion in his voice or his face, which wasn't necessarily a good thing.

"Garnet," I said, holding his gaze, "why didn't you tell me you were there that night."

"Which night?" said Sheila.

"He knows which night."

I left him no room to back out.

Thank God, he didn't get mad. In fact, if I thought it were possible, I'd say he looked ashamed. Even when they're found out, most cops and former cops don't like admitting to failure or weakness, and Garnet is no different. At least that's what I thought.

"I didn't see anything," he said, which wasn't nearly enough to wipe the slate.

"But you were there."

"The night Hicks was killed?" asked Sheila. "Garnet was at the hotel?"

"Yeah," said Garnet.

"You could have told me," I said.

"I didn't want to talk about it."

"Talk about what?" Sheila said.

"That he went there to meet someone," I answered.

"Who?" she asked.

"Penny Sue."

"How'd you know?" Garnet said.

"She told me."

"Well, she's one of the things I didn't want to talk about."

"Yeah?"

"The other was - I was drunk."

He paused and I waited. Then I poked a stick in his wound. "What happened?"

"Nothing. Penny Sue invited me up to her room. I gave in and I went. You may not know it son, but that crazy woman's got a wild side." Garnet looked at his place mat. He blushed. And so did Sheila. Maybe I should have blushed too but it didn't seem like much to be all embarrassed about.

"So what's the problem talking about this?"

"It's over between us. I took advantage of her feelings for me."

"But you already said you were drunk."

"I was. But that's no goddamn excuse."

I waited again. But I didn't need to poke him again.

"Thinking back on it, man," he said, "I just don't remember having all that much to drink."

"Meaning?"

"I was there. And I wasn't there."

"You blacked out?"

"I did. Early on."

"How early?"

"Shortly after dinner."

"Time?"

"Maybe nine or a little later."

"And?"

"We started partying. And then I remember we were getting ready to go see the finalists perform. But…"

"But?"

"But, I never made it. Next thing I remember, Penny Sue was waking me up."

"In the morning?"

"Just after midnight. She wanted to party some more."

"Spare us the details."

"I shouldn't have been there."

"Garnet," said Sheila softly, "we saw how you and Penny Sue were, together at the funeral."

"I'd been drinking then, too."

"Oh."

"It's over. But that woman refuses to believe it."

"Maybe, you're not so sure it's over either," said Sheila.

"Not something I care to think on."

Having dispersed the odor, as much as possible, we brought Garnet up to speed on the arrest, laughed over Boroski's brutish behaviour, and despaired over all the unanswered questions. In the middle of our debate over the next step, Bronson pulled up a chair.

"What's shaking, Sergeant?" I said.

"About that champagne glass, Jack?" he said.

"Yeah?"

"Jackpot."

"Hot diggity," I said.

"You don't get out much, do you boy?" Bronson laughed.

"Precisely what kind of jackpot we talking about here?"

"May be more like a bullseye," he said. Turning to Garnet and Sheila, he explained, "Jack had a hunch and I ran some prints for him."

"What'd you find?" I said.

"Peter Lake's name isn't Peter Lake. At least it never used to be."

"Who is he?"

"A missing person, named Peter Wilcox."

"What do we know about this guy?" Garnet asked.

"I did some checking for you. Petty crime, one charge of auto theft. Then he was caught passing bad checks. Of course, I don't have much on the years before he turned eighteen. Young offenders get a pass, as you know."

"When was his last arrest?"

The Chief checked his notes. "He was twenty two. Six years ago."

"Then he turned straight?" Sheila said.

"Or, he got better at it." I said.

"At what?"

"Crime. Otherwise why change the name?"

"I've got a possibility," Bronson said. "He has a wife."

"Interesting," I said. "And?"

"She's petitioning to have him declared dead."

"Insurance scam?"

"Maybe."

"What?" said Garnet. "We're saying the wife's a partner in the scheme?"

"That's one way to work it," I said. Then, turning to Bronson, "You got all this information from the Mounties' data base?"

"Some phone calls too."

"Do others know we're onto Lake's identity switch?"

"Anybody on the system can connect the dots same way I did."

"But no one else has to be told anything yet, am I right?"

"Someone will notice I checked the file. That stuff is recorded. But that may take a few days. I should tell the detective who's lead on the missing person case."

"Can't you wait?"

"Why am I waiting," he said, "if someone happens to ask?"

"You're following some leads first. You've got your own issues with Lake."

"I can wait," Bronson agreed.

"Thanks," I said.

"Just so we're clear, Beer, I can't guarantee anything. Don't be surprised if Lake gets a visit from the Toronto PD or the York Regionals before you finish whatever it is you're planning to do. We're all linked together, data-wise."

"Okay. In the meantime, no one tips him off we're on to him."

"When the time comes, do we tell Boroski?" Garnet asked.

"Let's leave that to the discretion of the big city boys," Bronson suggested, dropping a copy of the police report, tying Lake's fingerprint to Peter Wilcox, on the table as he left. I stuffed it in my backpack, which has enough pockets, compartments and zippers to double as a briefcase.

Over coffee and rhubarb pie, we debated the meaning of Bronson's information, except Sheila didn't have any pie. For sure, Bronson's news about Peter Lake/Peter Wilcox was juicy, but Sheila spoiled the celebration by pointing out his shady past and his name change fell miles short of proving he murdered Dwayne Hicks.

"Maybe," she also said, "all it proves is we stumbled onto an opportunist whose interest in Honey Hicks gained speed after somebody else murdered the woman's husband."

"My take is the guy had a big agenda," I said, "with a comprehensive set of goals."

"Which include murder?" Garnet said.

"If it advances the agenda."

"It's all speculation," Sheila said.

"The question is," Garnet added, "what do we do with this new information?"

"Won't get us anywhere," I said, "but it'd be fun to go over to Olson Enterprises and give Ted and Honey a more complete resume on the company's 'right hand man.'"

"That's just it," Sheila said. "We'd out a scam artist. But does that get us any closer to pinning Hicks' murderer down?"

"So, we confront Lake. Make him squirm. See what spills out of his mouth."

"Can't."

Sheila and I looked at Garnet, expecting an explanation.

"Why can't we?" Sheila said.

"Can't spook the man," he said.

"Meaning?" I said.

"We know he's dirty. We just don't know what kind the dirt is."

"He could run."

"Yup."

In the end, we were left with only one option. Before anything else, we needed to find out more about Peter Lake-Wilcox.

twenty eight

AS IT TURNED OUT, THERE was no electronic shortcut to tracking down the life history of the real Peter Lake. Sheila and her friend, the data girl, used all their search engines to come up with a number of Peter Wilcox hits but none of them was a bulleye. Which left me no other choice.

I needed to find someone or a few someones who knew the man before his identity switch. From there, I planned to use old fashioned street pounding, tree shaking and cage rattling to expose the real dirt on Lake.

Finding the first someone was the easy part. Bronson gave me an address for Lake's former wife. With a bit of luck, I'd talk to her before the police got around to asking any questions concerning a husband who was no longer 'completely missing.'

Newmarket was an hour and a half from Collingwood on the Big Chief.

Jody Wilcox agreed to meet with me at a little Chinese restaurant in the town's historic downtown district. Apparently, meeting at her place of residence was out of the question because, "I've been changing my back room into an art studio and the rest of the house is a bloody mess," she said.

That may have been true, but my guess was that she didn't want me nosing around, looking for evidence of a man in her life. Her reasoning: the presence of a replacement live-in wouldn't look good before a decision came down on the insurance payout for one 'dead' Peter Lake-Wilcox. I suppose there was even a longshot Lake would be there but, I had my doubts. After all, she was meeting with me.

While parking the Chief in front of the restaurant, an attractive woman sitting in a window seat caught my attention. I made a bet with myself it was Jody Wilcox, a bet I knew I'd won when she raised her eyes with a look that said she was expecting someone.

"Ms. Wilcox?"

The redhead was well put together but with a wholesome look about her; freckled forehead and cheeks, blond eyebrows and lashes too, suggesting an aversion to makeup.

Green eyes met mine. "Mr. Beer?" she said, flashing a winning smile and extending her hand.

There was dried paint staining the crevices around fingernails that had never met a manicurist, elevating my opinion of her still another notch.

"I prefer Jody," she said.

"Jack for me." I sat across from her, dropping my helmet on the chair beside me.

"Nice motorcycle," she said. "What is it?"

So I told her. That she was sincerely interested blew the rest of my preconceived notions out of the water.

"As I told you, I'm an investigator and I'm looking into your husband's disappearance." There was a grain of truth to my statement.

"You're with the police?"

"The police are aware of my inquiries," I said, this statement being closer than my last to an outright lie.

"The insurance company hired you then?" She didn't ask for my credentials, which was fine by me.

It was a fair question. My answer wasn't, but that wasn't my concern. "My client prefers to remain anonymous," is all I said.

"So, I'm guessing you're here because the insurance company doesn't believe me."

"I never said that."

"Well, I don't care about the money. I'd rather have Peter back."

Either Jody Wilcox was Lake's partner in insurance fraud and she was putting on a hell of a good act or she was a straight shooter. I paused to think about that but I didn't get very far, not after the waiter arrived and put on his best impatient act, in a restaurant half empty. What is it with these guys?

Jody Wilcox asked me to decide. Without looking at the menu, I ordered egg rolls, honey garlic spareribs, mushroom fried rice and something with greens, chicken and almonds. And two bottles of Kokanee.

"Okay?" I said, but the waiter was already gone before Jody could amend our lunch order.

"Kokanee?"

"Beer."

"Oh. Is it your favourite?"

"My favourite's a Mexican brand which isn't usually carried in Chinese restaurants."

"So Kokanee's your favourite Canadian beer?"

"Actually, I picked Kokanee because they made my favourite hat."

"What?"

"It's denim, soft, lightweight. I wear it to keep the sun out of my eyes when I run, and to absorb the sweat."

"Oh."

"Actually, I lied. My favourite hat is my Detroit Tigers baseball cap. Mark 'The Bird' Fidrych gave it to me."

"I've heard of him. Didn't he die?"

"He did, unfairly young."

"Do you wear your Tigers hat or just hang it on the wall. Maybe over your bed?" She smiled, mocking me a little. I didn't care.

"I save it for fishing."

"For fishing?"

"Or if I have a date."

"So this isn't a date," she said.

"Not if I don't have my Tigers hat on."

"You're a funny man."

"Will you sign an affidavit to that effect?"

Our beer arrived, breaking into my routine.

"You wanted to talk about Peter?" she asked, ignoring the glass provided and downing a good third of her beer. If I wasn't spoken for, I'd have fallen in love.

I didn't know where to go next, so I asked a stupid question, "How much was the insurance for?"

She never asked how it was I didn't know that, or the logical follow-up, whether indeed I worked for the insurer. Instead she answered my question, "He was the one covered for half a million."

Something in her answer puzzled me. "Half a million?"

"Yes."

Then I took a guess, "But you weren't insured."

"No."

Logic says the easier scam for Peter would have been to insure the wife to the hilt and then to knock her off.

"Is there a reason?"

"We were both going to get the same coverage but the medical exam uncovered a problem."

"Meaning?"

"I have a heart condition. The premium was going to be ridiculous. Peter wanted me to get the insurance anyway but I said no."

Her pursed lips and furrowed brow told me there was more to come.

"He wasn't the type to get angry," she said.

"But this time?"

"Yeah, my decision made him mad but, I stuck to my guns."

She finished her beer while I chewed over her answers in my head.

She looked at me. The worry lines that formed looked real. "Do you have any new information? Is that why you wanted to see me?"

"I don't want to give you false hope," I said, beginning to feel more like a fraud than her 'missing' husband.

She brushed my warning away with a subtle finger wave.

"Did you bring a picture of Peter?"

"Yes," she said, digging into her purse.

It took an effort, but I managed to control my reaction, to hide my surprise. The photograph showed a man with a heavy beard and I wasn't at all sure that Wilcox and Lake were one and the same.

Covering up my doubts, I said, "Did your husband always have a beard?"

"From the day we met. But that's not Peter at his best. It's the last photo I have of him. He'd put on weight lately. Do you think he was depressed?"

"You'd know better than I." I studied the picture, especially around the eyes. Take away the hair and the heavier jowls and I finally saw the likeness. "Can I have this?"

"It's a double."

The food arrived and we dug in. It tasted good after nearly two hours on a motorcycle under the summer sun.

"What can you tell me about your husband?" I said, after I cleaned off my plate for the first time.

"What do you want to know?" She was still working on her first helping.

"Family?" I said, taking the rest of the spare-ribs and most of the rice.

"Just like me, Peter was an orphan."

"Step-parents?"

"Neither of us. But in my case, I was already in my late teens when Mum and Dad died in a car accident. I'd already moved out."

"Still, that had to be rough."

"I was an only child, too." Her eyes filled and she regained control by looking out on the street.

"What about Peter," I asked.

"His parents were killed in a fire. He and his brother were only twelve, I think."

"His brother?"

"His twin brother. Peter never talked about him. I don't even know his name. Peter referred to him as BJ."

The interview wasn't going as I expected. Jody Wilcox was not the cagy schemer I expected her to be. Nothing she said sounded made up.

Before I could think up my next question, Jody had one for me.

"Why are you asking about his family?"

"I'm just trying to track down anyone who might have seen him around the time of his disappearance. The most likely someone would be a family member, a friend or a work colleague."

"You could try his foster parents. They used to call him at Christmas and Thanksgiving." She dug into her purse and came up with a small red covered phone book. I wrote the names and number down.

"What about his brother?" I asked.

"There was never any contact. At least none I knew of." She paused and I knew she was struggling with a question. "Do you think Peter may be alive?" Her eyes teared up again.

"I don't know." My lies were wearing thin on me.

"I always wondered about amnesia. You know from an accident. Head injuries can cause amnesia."

"That's true. But I understand it's rare."

"Still, I'm glad you're trying."

"It's been hard?" I said.

"Yeah, but Peter's friend has been there for me. He's been helping with the paperwork."

"You mean for the insurance claim?"

"Yes."

"He live in town?"

"No, but I see him on weekends."

"Lives out of town then?" I said, casting the same lure out again.

"Yes." She paused again and her hands trembled. "It's been so long, Mr. Beer. And I began to think there was no chance Peter would ever be found."

"What are you getting at, Jody? You have feelings for this guy, Peter's friend?"

"Yes, I do." She wiped her eyes with her sweatshirt sleeve.

"What's his name?"

"Harry."

I nearly said his last name but I caught myself in time and I didn't ask, because I didn't have to, not even to verify.

"Maybe you should talk to him." She wrote down his name and phone number.

"Jody," I said, staring at the paper she handed me.

"Yes."

"I want to tell you something. And it's important."

"What?"

"You seem like a good person. A decent person, who's had some hard luck."

She waited for me to say my piece.

"Sometimes good people, especially those who've faced tragedy, are too trusting."

"Of Harry?"

"Just be careful."

I changed my mind about not leaving my card. I took one out of my shirt pocket, handed it to her and told her to call if I could help with anything. She thanked me. I shook her hand and left, still believing there was an insurance scam in play but, now seriously concerned about how it would go down.

twenty nine

THANKS TO JODY WILCOX, I had a clearer picture of Peter Lake and his good buddy Harry: schemers who I was sure were willing to go to extremes to get what they wanted, the kind of guys who don't make good overnight guests. And Harry Maxwell's visits with Jody Wilcox went well beyond drinking tea and eating crumpets.

However, I still wasn't as sure as I needed to be that murder was one of the tools in Peter and Harry's box of tricks. Before I could accuse anyone of anything, I needed more, a lot more.

After his wife, logically, the next name on the interview list was also a Wilcox - BJ, the brother. Except I didn't know where to find him. Moving further down the list, the foster parents jumped out at me next. And for them, I did have a phone number, from Jody Wilcox.

A feeble voice picked up at the other end.

"Is that Mrs. O'Connor?"

"Yes," she said.

I introduced myself and mentioned I was acquainted with Peter Wilcox. The line went quiet, right when I was expecting a reaction of some kind.

"Are you still there, Mrs. O'Connor?"

"That's a name I haven't heard in quite some time."

"I got your name from Peter's wife," I volunteered, even though the woman didn't seem curious about how I found her.

"How is Jody? Such a lovely girl."

"Fine."

"Now what's this about Peter?"

"I have some questions. Are you free for a chat this afternoon? Perhaps I could take you and Mr. O'Connor out for coffee."

"Mr. O'Connor has passed," she said.

"I'm sorry."

"It was just seven weeks ago. I'm afraid I'm still getting over it," she said.

"Clearly this is not a good time."

"No. No," she said.

I waited.

Finally she said, "What did you say your name was?"

"Jack Beer."

"And you wanted to buy me a coffee?"

"And a cookie."

"Chocolate chip?" She giggled a little.

I liked the woman. "Any kind you want."

"I don't really know you but, you're friends with Jody?"

I couldn't bring myself to tell another lie not after misleading Jody Wilcox for two hours and change. "No, I just met her."

"Still, she did give you my name and phone number."

"We can just talk on the phone," I said, thinking again, there are too many trusting people in the world. Or maybe there aren't enough.

"No, an outing would be nice. Betty, my daughter, she's been staying with me, but she had to leave. She's been so supportive but, she lives in Calgary. She wants me to move out there, to live with her but you know, Mr. Beer, I just can't leave. This is my home."

I checked my watch. Jody and I finished our lunch meeting at about two o'clock. I mentioned that Markham, a burgeoning suburb of Toronto, was less than thirty minutes away depending on traffic and Mrs. O'Connor said fine, adding that the cookie wouldn't likely spoil her appetite for dinner.

The O'Connor's street was a throwback to the 1950s, or maybe the early 60s. Deep lots, small bungalows and ranches, in beige and brown and grey. Houses with six and a half foot basements, barely enough head clearance for a rec room. Roof drains that an owner could clean out with a stepladder. It was a neighborhood at human scale.

I pulled my bike onto one of two concrete strips, bracketing trimmed grass. No one makes driveways like that anymore, too much effort.

Wind chimes welcomed my arrival and the doorbell made an old fashioned ding-dong sound. Mrs. O'Connor took a few minutes. The door opened and I was met by a ninety pound grandmother leaning on a walker and peeking around the door as she shuffled for position.

I smiled into her beaming face. "I'm so pleased to meet you, Mrs. O'Connor." I pegged her at about eighty but her swollen knuckles told me arthritis may have aged her prematurely.

"Likewise, Mr. Beer," she said in her bird voice.

She looked to my right, out at my bike. "Oh my," she said. "That's lovely but I'm afraid I couldn't."

"I wasn't thinking," I said. "We need to get a cab."

"I have a car, Mr. Beer. I can't drive it but I left the insurance on it for when Betty visits. Or for gentleman callers." She giggled wonderfully again and fished her keys out of a beaded purse.

"Ready?" I said.

She nodded with a sweet smile. "I have my sweater," she said, patting the bag on the seat of her walker. "And my house key." She jangled the chain around her neck.

We left the walker behind and she took my arm as we made our way down from the low porch and into her car. I jockeyed my bike out of the way and we were off on our date.

Mrs. O'Connor wanted to go to the local Tim Horton's. I told her about my own coffee shop and made her promise not to tell anyone of my patronage of the country's biggest chain. We spent a pleasant half hour talking about Mr. O'Connor, her only child Betty, her son-in-law and her three grandchildren. I told her about Sheila and about Reba. She was a gentle, loving soul and I wanted to adopt her as my own grandmother.

Halfway through our first refill, I said, "Mrs. O'Connor, you know that Peter Wilcox has been missing for over two years?"

"Yes, Jody told me but I don't know much."

"You don't keep in touch with Jody Wilcox, do you?"

"Why would you say that?"

"She never mentioned Mr. O'Connor's passing."

"No, other than immediate family and close friends, I just never told anyone. I found it too difficult."

"Jody's a good person," I said.

"I always felt so. But our connection was through Peter."

"Did he live with you long?"

"Not really but Bob, my husband, and I made a point of staying in touch with everyone we fostered."

"Peter too?"

"He was standoffish. After he left us we called him regularly but it became clear he wasn't keen. So, we called less often after a while.

"Then he got married. We weren't invited which I understand since we didn't have him with us that long. After that we tried but he never returned our calls so Jody kept me in the news. And then one day he answered and he told me not to call Jody anymore."

"Exactly how long was Peter with you?"

"A year and a half, "she said, then redundantly, "eighteen hard months."

" 'Hard months'?"

"We fostered nearly a dozen children over the years," she said. "He was our last one."

"You stopped because of Peter?"

"No, we stopped because we were getting too old for it."

"Still, I get the sense Peter wasn't like the rest?"

"Many of them were unhappy, some had problems. We did our best and I think we made a difference."

"I know you did," I said, having had first hand experience with the system. And I pegged Mrs. O'Connor as one of the gems. "But do you feel you helped Peter?"

"Peter was a troubled boy."

"How troubled?"

"He was smart, maybe too smart for his own good. He made friends easily but none of them lasted. He treated them badly."

"Kids end up in foster homes for a reason."

"Yes, losing your parents is a terrible thing."

"That's one way," I said. "I understand it was a house fire?"

"Yes, it was. Peter and his brother barely escaped."

"Cause?"

"Of the fire? I don't know."

"So while he lived with you, I gather he acted out?"

"Not openly but, he stole things."

"From you?"

"And others."

"What else?"

"He scared us."

"How?"

"My Betty's first two were five and fourteen months when she came for a visit from Calgary. We were a few months into our second year with Peter."

"What happened?"

"The youngest tumbled down the basement stairs and …"

"And Peter was looking after the grandchildren at the time," I finished the thought.

"How would you have known that?"

I shrugged.

"I was just about to say," she said, "he was in the house and so were the grands. Betty and I were in the backyard when we heard Jamie crying."

"What? He pushed the little guy?"

"The oldest child, Lisa, said he did."

"Was the boy hurt?"

"No. The stairs are carpeted and toddlers are mostly indestructible."

"What happened next?"

"Well, that was it. My Robert was more concerned than I was. He phoned the agency and told them they had to take Peter. I agreed but, you know," she said, full of regret, "I was never sure he actually did it. It could have been an accident. He said it was. Maybe my granddaughter made a mistake. She was so young."

"You and your husband did the right thing, Mrs. O'Connor."

"Did we?"

I smiled my answer.

"But my heart went out to young Peter."

"How old was he?"

"Almost sixteen."

I sat back. There were other questions but I asked myself how useful the answers would be. Mrs. O'Connor was the type who would give a serial killer the benefit of the doubt. On our way out the door, I stopped at the counter and bought a dozen cookies.

Back at the house, I helped Mrs. O'Connor up the front steps. She invited me in, I sensed because she wanted our visit to go on, and I did go in but just to be sure she was comfortably settled. She thanked me for 'our date' and for working so hard to find Peter. I said 'you're welcome' to the first half of her thank you and swallowed back my reply on the second half.

As I left, I dropped the cookies on a coffee table.

"Oh my, aren't you kind?"

"Jody Wilcox doesn't live so far away. She'd like to hear from you, I'm pretty sure," I said.

"Maybe I'll call."

"One last thing, Mrs. O'Connor."

"What is it?"

"Was there a particular case worker, a teacher, a friend, someone who would remember Peter outside the home?"

"His social worker was a man named Bruce Weaver."

"Do you have a number?"

"No, he's retired now. Lives nearby I believe. I see him in the grocery store in any event."

I patted Mrs. O'Connor on the wrist and I left.

Weaver was in the book and his house was indeed nearby. No one answered the door but around back, I found a tall, lean bald headed man with a neatly trimmed beard, working a vegetable patch. He didn't look old enough to be retired.

"Good crop?"

"Pretty good," he said, removing a gardener's glove to shake my hand. "You are?"

I introduced myself and told him what I wanted without saying much.

He gazed over the rows of sprouting onions, carrots and radishes. I joined him in admiring the crop.

"So you want to talk about Peter Wilcox?" he said, repeating my request, like the subject was distasteful to him.

"That's right."

He bent over and pulled a radish. Wiping it off, he bit into the little root, turned and said, "That goes back some. What about him?"

"Two years ago, he disappeared."

"Really? So, what's your role in all this?"

"I found him."

"Okay. But that's not what I asked you."

"You're right. My role? It's hard to explain. I'm a private investigator," I said, giving him a card. "But no one's paying me."

"No one's paying you to do what?"

I decided I could come clean with the guy, because if you can't trust a gardener…. I took a deep breath and told him, "I need to find out whether Peter Wilcox killed a man by the name of Dwayne Hicks."

"Isn't that something the police would be doing?"

"They're investigating the murder, yes."

"So what is it? You don't feel they're up to the job?"

"They believe my girlfriend's brother did it."

"And you and your girlfriend believe otherwise."

"Peter looks more likely."

"What if you're wrong and the police are right?"

"I'm not all that crazy about the girlfriend's brother."

Weaver laughed. "What's your poison?" he said.

"Beer."

"Good," he said, "because that's all I've got." He motioned to a pair of wicker arm chairs in the shade of a mountain ash. I swept off the almost-red berries the squirrels dropped, sat and waited while he opened a small Styrofoam chest and retrieved two aluminum cans. I took a long pull on my drink.

"Nice yard," I said.

"Soothes a troubled soul."

"You don't seem troubled."

"I suppose I'm not anymore. Used to be though."

"Over kids like Peter?"

"Uh huh."

"So, what was his story?"

"The boy had a lot of issues. And I had a lot of doubts."

"Why?"

"He was always in trouble. Fighting, drinking underage and stealing. You know the story."

"Some kids get smart and straighten themselves out."

"And, for a while I thought Peter was going to be one of them, the kid who beat the odds. When he got older, I heard he found work, a better class of friends. Yeah, it seemed like he'd straightened himself out."

"Sounds like you followed his progress even after he left the agency's care."

"Yeah, I did. Unofficially."

"Why?"

"He wasn't typical. You know, with some kids you can predict their career path. One kid likes cars. He becomes a mechanic and settles down. Another kid likes cars. He becomes a car thief."

"And you didn't know which way Peter was heading?"

"Had my suspicions and I was curious. He was more complicated than most. His goals were money and the lifestyle that goes with it. I was pretty sure he'd get there, too. Either as a corporate ladder climber or as a fraudster. In either case, it helps to have sociopathic tendencies."

"And you think he's a sociopath?"

"I never saw evidence of a conscience." Weaver's eyes went out of focus before he picked up the story, "Then he got married. I retired, lost track and stopped thinking about him. End of story."

I waited.

"Or maybe it isn't the end of it. Now you say he disappeared?"

"Yeah and I'd like to pin him down before he pulls another Houdini."

"You making any headway?"

"I'm beginning to get a better sense what he's up to."

"It's likely not good."

"Nope," I said.

"And you want to know?"

"His story, Bruce."

"Right. His story."

"The highlights."

"Okay," he said, softly and looking skyward. "I first met Peter when he was a young teenager. His parents had just died in a fire."

"I heard about that and I've been wondering - was it arson?"

"Why would you ask that?"

"That's what I do. I ask questions."

"Your question has a leaning."

"Meaning 'what caused the fire' is less judgmental?"

"Something like that."

"You and I already know a lot about Peter."

"So, you're suspicious of anything bad that happens near him?"

"I guess I am."

Weaver sipped his beer and his gaze returned to the clouds, through the sagging branches. Without shifting his eyes my way for even a second, he said, "I spent my whole working life giving kids the benefit of the doubt. Giving them second chances. Coming down hard only as a last resort. But with Peter..."

He didn't finish the thought because he didn't need to.

"I don't know anything about the fire," he said, "but I knew about Peter. You couldn't trust the boy. Even at thirteen or fourteen, he lied, he stole, he cheated. He was spiteful. Thinking back, I have to admit he came across as innocent. The kid was never at fault. It was always someone else. The way he saw it."

"What about when he was no longer a kid?"

"After we passed him off on society?"

"Yeah, then."

"Everything looked okay, from a distance. I did hear he was caught passing phony cheques and he sold some roofing contracts."

"They were bogus, too?"

"Well, I'm not sure there were any convictions. And I hoped the fault lay with the people he was associating with."

"But you didn't really believe that."

"No, I didn't."

"So, what about his brother?"

"Brian was a mean sucker too, but he was straightforward about it. If Brian didn't like you, he'd let you know, like with a fist to your face. Gave Peter more than one beating. Brian was so big for his age."

"Weren't they twins?"

"Fraternal. One big, one small. Two very angry boys."

"You said Brian was big for his age. As in the past tense?"

"Yeah, he died."

"How?"

"Found beaten to death in an alley behind his group home."

"They find the killer?"

"Could have been anybody."

"Including Peter?"

He answered by taking a long pull on his beer.

"Tell me, Bruce," I said. "Did their parents leave much of an estate?"

"There was money. Not a huge amount."

"Still, it would have been a lot more if you didn't have to share it."

"The thought did occur to me."

.

thirty

GARNET LEANED ON HIS TAILGATE as Sheila and I walked over.

"Still spinning wheels, son?"

"More than David Clayton Thomas," I answered.

"He on the Rolling Stone all time list?" Garnet said.

I leaned beside him as I studied the ground. Sheila poked me in the side, wanting to know what we were talking about.

"Former lead singer with Blood, Sweat and Tears," I said to her.

"Who?"

"You've heard the song 'Spinning Wheel'?" Garnet asked. "Get it? Jack's spinning wheels."

Sheila nodded her head, still a little unsure about the musical reference.

"Came out in 1969 I think," I said.

"The song?" said Sheila.

"Uh huh."

"When I was minus nine years old."

I did a double take over her comment. It was hard to imagine there was time she wasn't part of the world I lived in. She winked at me, bringing me back to Garnet's question, from introspection over the meaning of life.

I was ninety-nine percent sure when I offered an answer. "No," I said. "Can you believe it? He didn't make the cut."

"We should write a letter," Garnet said.

"Please. Do we have to keep talking about that stupid Rolling Stone magazine article?" Sheila asked. "You guys are so weird."

"We should pound some sense into the editors' heads," I said to Garnet.

"Where's their head office?"

"Don't we have more pressing business?" Sheila suggested. But then she paused, like something really important popped into her head. And it did. "Am I safe to assume the Righteous Brothers were both included in this stupid list."

Like me, Sheila's a retro fan of early rock and she's particularly partial to the big ballads by Bill Medley and Bobby Hatfield.

"No," I said.

"What the hell?" she said.

"Now you know what I've been talking about."

Garnet looked at us, shook his head and laughed.

"Let's do it,' he said, rushing ahead to hold the building's front door open for us.

"Cage rattling time," I said, leading the way into the building.

When you run out of logical steps to take in an investigation, you toss some bait into the pond and see what bites, and you hope the wheels stop spinning. Or slow down at least.

"You again."

"How are you, Courtney?"

The receptionist wore something tight and fashionable, with a low scooped neck. She was still cat-walk beautiful but I nearly told her to do up her buttons, she was showing that many ribs.

Sheila looked at me and then she looked at Courtney. "Are there any women in this town you haven't met?"

"This one wasn't very impressed," I confessed.

"Are any of them?"

"I haven't met one," offered Garnet.

Courtney cleared her throat, not used to being left out. "Did you want something?"

I smiled. "Yes, please. We're here to see Mr. Olson." I gave her my card. "In case you lost the first one."

She looked at my card, buying time.

"We know he's here by the way, in case you've got standing orders to lie to unscheduled visitors."

Her new look was supposed to convince me I was 'so wrong.'

"If you want to get his attention," I said, "tell him his empire is at risk."

"Did you say, 'his empire is at risk'?"

Tiring of the subtle approach, Garnet butted in, "Where the hell's his goddamn office?"

Courtney's eyes darted for an instant to the hallway on her left.

Sheila and I followed Garnet at a trot. He arrived at the door that said, 'T. Olson, President' and he opened it because he was nearly as good as I am at reading clues.

Garnet and Sheila went in first and stepped to the side. I entered next and gave Olson a head nod, nothing more. Instead of explaining the intrusion, I wandered about, hands in pockets, nonchalant-like, letting the suspense build, making the man nervous, checking the place out.

Speaking of which, the décor was trendy, white and black, with shades of grey. Full of expensive looking useless fluff. All of it coordinating nicely with Olson's silver hair and his black outfit.

Olson's furrowed brow asked a question and I ignored it.

Instead, I looked at the man and smiled, jangling, staying cool, making sure I had his attention. Making him wonder, question and in no time flat, it worked.

"Jack, what the fuck do you think you're doing?"

I took the police report out of my backpack and placed it under Olson's nose. Sheila closed the door behind me, expecting fireworks perhaps.

"What is it?" he said.

"Read it."

He did and upon finishing said, "Who's Peter Wilcox?"

"A.k.a. Peter Lake."

"It doesn't say that here."

"Not in so many words," I admitted. "But Peter Lake's fingerprints match very nicely with those belonging to Peter Wilcox."

Olson looked like he'd been slapped silly.

"What?"

I repeated my explanation.

"Who is he?" he said. "Who is this Wilcox?"

"A guy with a criminal past. A guy who disappeared long enough for his wife to start the paperwork to have him declared dead, the idea being to collect the life insurance."

"Where'd the police get Lake's fingerprint?"

"They didn't. I did."

"Why'd you do that?"

"Because he's a phony. He doesn't have an MBA, Teddy, at least not from the Ivey School of Business at the University of Western Ontario."

"What?" Olson's confusion worsened. On top of that, his new skin colour told me he wasn't used to bad news.

"Your Executive Assistant has a history of fraud," I said. "And I'd bet the farm he's after your money."

"How?"

"How's he going to get it? Accounting trickery maybe."

"Or maybe he's going after it through Honey," Sheila said.

Olson's mouth gaped open, like a ten year old carp, hooked and tossed onto the shore. "I don't understand," he said.

"Ted," I said. "Think carefully about what we're saying. This isn't something we'd make up. Your right hand man, Peter Lake, is a fraud and a con artist, and likely much worse."

Our words were just starting to hit home when Olson's door opened and Peter Lake walked in. "What kind of horseshit are these people shoveling, Ted?" he said.

"Does the name Peter Wilcox mean anything to you?" Ted Olson asked, his shock now fading.

The man froze. He had the look of a dog caught sneaking food off the kitchen table. But, unlike the dog, Lake wasn't sneaking off. He planned to ride it out, likely by using bravado and bullshit in equal measure.

"That was my name," he said. "Once."

"Running from a shady past, Peter?" I said.

"More like starting fresh."

"They're saying you committed fraud and that you collected insurance money on your own staged death," Olson said, overstating my case, but I wasn't about to argue the finer points.

Lake's face was red, whether with anger or panic, I wasn't sure.

"Not true," he said. "This change of identity looks bad Ted, but appearances are deceiving."

Ignoring the look of rage on Ted Olson's face, Lake continued to counter attack. "Yes, I disappeared. And yes, I took on a new identity but I was running from a lot of things. My wife for one thing. If there's an insurance scam, that's all her doing. She was just taking advantage of the fact I disappeared. If she petitioned to have me ruled dead, I never saw a penny of any settlement."

"What about your MBA?" I said.

"I doctored up my resume. So what? Happens every day," he said.

"Not in my company," said Olson.

"Let's talk in private," Lake said.

"No."

"I can explain."

"Get out."

Lake hesitated for a minute and then he turned to go. Garnet was at the door with his hand out.

"What the hell do you want?"

"Key."

"Fuck off." Lake pointed a finger at Garnet. Big mistake.

In a flash, Garnet took the finger, bent it and his wrist back. Lake dropped to one knee, reached into his pants pocket with his free hand and handed over a set of office keys. Garnet let Lake go.

"Wouldn't he have a company credit card, Mr. Olson?" Sheila asked.

Olson nodded his head. Garnet put his hand out again.

Cooperating this time, Lake gave Sheila his wallet and she fished out the plastic. Garnet let Lake loose but he raised a long ropy arm to the door jam, blocking the way. "Anything else?" he asked.

"Company car," Olson said.

"The Jaguar's mine," he said.

"Not according to the ownership papers it's not."

Lake handed over his car keys and then after checking first with a raised eyebrow, Garnet lowered his arm to let the man out of the room.

Olson paged the front desk. Courtney arrived, flushed and looking worried. Olson ordered her to ask their auditors to come down to check over the books. Then after telling her to get the police on the line, he turned to us, "Is there anything else I should do?"

"Whether Lake has been stealing from you or he was planning a big score," I said, "is not my main concern."

"No?"

"The police have Sheila's brother in custody for the murder of your son-in-law. They're not looking hard at anybody else."

"And you think Hicks' killing might have been Lake's workmanship?"

"I think he's a lot better candidate than Mike Mackie." I decided not to mention his daughter had slept with Mike or anything else that may have incriminated Sheila's brother.

"On what basis?"

"I'm guessing you knew Lake was taking a serious run at Honey. And now with Hicks out of the way...."

"I suspected something was up between those two, almost from the day I hired him."

"Now that you know where we're coming from, do you know where Lake was on the night Hicks was killed?"

Olson thought about it and then said, "No. I told Lake to manage Dwayne Hicks. Something I did for my daughter's sake. I never paid much attention to that part of Peter's job, or to Hicks, or his 'career' for that matter. I suppose all I can say is given what was going on with the festival, it's pretty damned likely that Lake and my son-in-law were together sometime that night."

"I'm thinking Honey knows more than she's been saying," I said.

"Ask her again," he said. "But first give me a chance to call and tell her about Lake. It might prompt a change in attitude."

Lake and Harry Maxwell were waiting for us beside the company's Jag in the parking lot. I wondered if he had a spare set of keys, although it's not something I cared that much about.

Sheila was already in the sidecar when they made their move.

Maxwell charged into Garnet and drove him backward into the tailgate of his truck. It had to hurt but not so much it stopped him from driving an elbow into the younger man's shoulder.

I took Maxwell's attack on Garnet as a pretty good indication I was in Lake's sights. Ready for him, I sidestepped and dodged his haymaker, the result putting him off balance and allowing me to move in. And I did, kicking his knee, causing him to buckle and sending him to the pavement. Before he could scramble to his feet, I kicked him again, this time in the face. Unfortunately, I was wearing Sauconies. Jogging shoes do a lot less damage than sturdy leathers.

With Lake on the ground, I turned toward the other scrap in time to see Maxwell backing off. Garnet held a baseball bat over his head and Sheila was out of the sidecar, holding a small tire iron. Maxwell had a grip on his right arm and a grimace on his face. I'm not sure who hit him or whether they both did, not that it mattered. What mattered was who won.

Taking a tally, I counted serious bruises and face loss for the bad guys, and a little bit of fun for the good guys. Now all we had to worry about was the rematch.

Garnet drove off to bring his cop friend Bronson up to speed and to review the possibility of having Lake and Maxwell charged with assault, which was one way to put our suspects in the cops' crosshairs.

I dropped Sheila at the cottage to do more research into the life history of Peter Wilcox, for the time period after he left Social Services, and for anything she could find on Harold Maxwell.

Following Sheila's suggestion that looking over her shoulder was no help, I left the cottage and headed out to see Honey Hicks. Despite Daddy's intervention, Honey's answers were just as evasive as they'd always been.

"Yes, the room was booked in Curtis' name," she said, when I asked whether she was planning to spend the night at the hotel with the victim. I couldn't have called her answer a smooth misdirection.

"But, you didn't use it?"

"No, but I saw him there."

"When?"

"Earlier."

"Time?"

"After dinner."

"You can't be more exact?"

"We were partying."

"You and Peter?"

She blushed. Shame or fear for the implications, I couldn't tell.

"Was your husband planning to meet someone other than you?" I said.

"It's possible."

"Any idea who?"

"Could have been a fan. Or…"

"Who else?"

"Maybe your sister-in-law, Lori Mackie."

"So, at the time of his death…"

"What time was it again?"

"At roughly 11:30 or midnight, where were you?"

"I was either at a party or with Peter Lake."

"Lake? I thought you planned to be with your husband?"

"I never said that."

"So, had Peter Lake booked a room?"

"I think so."

"You think so?"

"I was drinking."

"I can check."

"Are we done?" Honey asked.

I thought about it. And then I said, "Why'd you call Mike Mackie?"

"I didn't."

"No?"

"That lying son of a bitch told the cops I invited him to my room."

"I believe him."

"Why would I call him? He's a loser."

"You've dropped your panties for worse types."

"Go to hell."

"You didn't answer my question. Did you call him?"

"Christ man, think about it."

"What?"

"Why would I invite the guy to that room?"

I knew what she was talking about. "The particular room being the one Dwayne booked."

"How smart would that be?"

The answer helped me understand why the cops were uninterested in Honey as a suspect. On the surface, there seemed to be no good reason for Honey to make such a call.

Except digging deeper, I came up with another possibility the cops weren't thinking about: Peter Lake killed her husband and she knew it. Maybe she even pushed Lake to do it. And Mike would make an easy fall guy. Problem was, I had none of that important stuff you need called evidence to confirm my theory.

"Are we done?" she said.

"Yes, we're done."

"Good. Would you do me a favour?"

It perturbed me. The woman was abrasive and condescending. And getting straight answers from her was impossible. On top of all that, she wants a favour.

"Penny Sue Stanfield came to the funeral," she said, not getting directly to the favour.

"I saw her."

"She's a pest."

"And?"

"And she asked if she could have Curtis' belt buckle."

"His what?"

"An Elvis type buckle. For her memorabilia collection."

"You're not serious."

"It's just an imitation but it's a big honking thing. And it looks real."

"So, what's the favour?"

"I said yes, she could have it. But she keeps phoning."

"So, give it to her."

"I thought maybe you could give it to Garnet Henderson. I've seen you with him. And Penny Sue was with him at the funeral."

I sighed, took the buckle, tucked it in my knapsack and left.

thirty one

AFTER AN EARLY DINNER OF leftover cold cuts and crusty buns, I disconnected my sidecar to take a summer evening cruise, telling Sheila I'd stop by at Garnet's trailer to compare notes, following which I'd check out the back country between Owen Sound and Wiarton.

I approached Garnet's concession road without any intention of asking him to serve as Honey's delivery man. Besides, Penny Sue is the type that shows up whether you're looking for her or not. I'd get the Elvis belt buckle to her myself.

I found Garnet sitting in an old wooden rocker, on his tiny front porch, surrounded by half a dozen empties. He tossed me a full one. I twisted off the cap and sat on the step.

One beer turned into two and then another, at which point, I asked Garnet to take the belt buckle off my hands, after having decided a half hour earlier to take care of it myself. He reminded me he was trying to break Penny Sue's spell.

It was very likely around the time of my fifth that I told Garnet of an important lesson I learned a week after I met Sheila.

"What lesson was that, son?"

"Love doesn't come knocking very often."

"Point?"

"When it does, you damn well open the door."

"And if I don't?"

"It may not knock again."

"Noted," he said.

"So..."

"So, Jack, why don't you take the goddamn belt buckle to the old girl your own self?"

Then he laughed. And so did I.

Finding my way back to the bottom of the Beaver Valley, I turned the Big Chief away from home, pausing first to watch the Beaver River ripple under the highway. Then I cruised by a golf course, revving my bike for the benefit of a Sunday hacker addressing the ball on the seventeenth tee. And thinking I was nearly old enough to take up the game more seriously than once a week.

I took the Epping Road but turned before I reached Meaford, cutting cross country to Owen Sound by way of Walters Falls. Once through the city, I headed north on Grey County Road 1. Anxious to leave the creeping expansion of resort and retirement development behind me, I pushed the old Indian and prayed there were no speed traps. Somewhere north of East Linton the landscape became pasture and woodlot again.

At the hamlet of Kemble, I came to a stop sign and a decision point. A right goes to the lakeshore but the road looked rough and I wasn't looking for paint chips. Left was a scenic, twisting drive to the main highway, but it was a road I was familiar with. According to the map, straight on would take me through Kemble Mountain Conservation Area and then via the Colpoys Bay road to Wiarton. The unexplored road ahead was an invitation I couldn't refuse.

I rumbled through farm fields and approached a stretch that climbed hard and bent to the right, cutting a swath into the limestone. Downgearing, on my right and through breaks in the trees, I took in the vista across the flats that sloped to the blue waters of the sound.

The sun slipped out of sight behind the escarpment on my left. Like magic, the scenery combined with the echo of the Indian's 74 cubic inch V-twin to erase the strain of the past few days, clearing my mind of clutter.

The road banked against the bend. Small jolts up my spine marked the pavement cracks. Beside me, the narrow shoulder gave puny protection against miscalculation.

I sensed it before it filled the mirror on my left handlebar.

The black SUV pulled out as if to pass but on a blind curve, there's no way that was the real plan. And so with no more than a bad feeling in my gut, I gave the Chief a shot of gas but my reaction was one beat off. It might have been the surprise. Or maybe it was the beer. Whatever the explanation, the SUV was beside me and edging into my path before I could take the right kind of evasive action, before I could get the hell out of the way.

The passenger window came down.

I chanced a look inside. The bent-over driver was small and his face was black. Two eye holes flared at me, white rings around dark centres. His passenger was a lot bigger. And like the driver, his head was also covered in a balaclava. The big man's right hand came through the window. It held a pistol.

I swerved. His first shot missed.

I braked hard.

But my maneuvers only bought me seconds of thinking time.

The bastards were beside me, again. And the one with the gun was taking aim, again. I calculated the odds.

Or, maybe I'm just rationalizing my decision after the fact.

No matter. The way I saw it or see it now, I don't know which it is, the chances were better than three to one the next bullet would hit me if I continued playing peek-a-boo with the shooter. But, if I hit the shoulder and jumped, my chances of being hit were closer to fifty-fifty. That was my thinking.

Stack those odds up against the ninety percent certainty that careening through a thick forest in a hundred metre drop, give or take, will kill even a healthy specimen like me, and you have to question my reasoning skills. Except having a gun pointed at you by a crazy man makes you forget everything you ever knew about arithmetic.

So, I left the pavement.

The slope was slipperier and the gravel was spongier than I expected. Before I could jump off my bike and over the guide wire, I went into a skid.

I heard another gunshot and I felt a sharp kick in my back, followed by a burning sensation. My bike hit something solid. A guide post. Momentum catapulted me into the twilight. Floating above the cliff, I looked down through a hundred mean looking tree trunks. I didn't float for long, not in real time anyway. In fright time, I could have had a shave and a haircut while I parted nitrogen and oxygen molecules in the first leg of my trip to the escarpment floor.

Luckily, the route wasn't as elevator vertical as it appeared to be from above.

My rate of speed was slowed first by a tough old bush, which thankfully was winning its war against gravity. Then, after body checking a maple with my left shoulder and hip, I took to spinning my way through the sharp, dead branches of a patch of cedars.

After which I was in free fall again until a thousand year old dwarf cedar interrupted my descent a quarter of the way from the bottom.

Caught up there and dazed, I tried to take inventory. The skin on my left forearm looked like bacon strips. My neck and my head hurt like hell. My left side ached. But my back killed me worse, right in the middle, under my back-pack. Like I'd been whacked with a sledge hammer. I felt dizzy too, which I hoped, at the time, had more to do with hanging upside down under twisted legs than with injury. Turned out to be a false hope.

The fresh spring spurting out of the rocks a scary ten metres below told me to grab hold of something solid and to right myself. I watched the fingers of my right hand encircle the cedar trunk, praying the little tree was strong enough. It was. I tested my left hand by reaching for a slab of limestone. It hurt and it bled, but it wasn't broken.

Upright at last, my head and feet properly oriented, I looked up and saw nothing but the trees and shadows through which I catapulted. The shooter and his driver would not have been able to spot me without risking their own necks. I finished unjamming my legs and decided on a route to the bottom. Ignoring the throbbing in my back and fighting back nausea, I called on every brain cell still functioning to concentrate on each handhold, each foothold. And I descended.

It felt like it was a week later when I reached level ground. Using a deadfall for support, I dug into my pockets for my cell phone. I didn't find it whether because of the return of the dizzying sensations or because I lost the damned thing, I couldn't guess.

I do know that the jackhammer in my head picked up the beat. So I abandoned the search for my cell and eased myself to a grassy patch.

First time I woke up it was pitch black. My brain felt like it'd been left out overnight in January and my throat was suffering through the worst drought since the dust bowl. I coughed to clear the tightness. But there was no relief and in the darkness, suffering disorientation and the effects of head trauma, I gave up and slipped away again.

My next memory was of flies, house flies, deer flies, horse flies and others I'd never met before, all buzzing around, driving me nuts. I opened my eyes to interrupt the meal they were making of the dried blood on my head and forearm. That there were no maggots yet was encouraging.

The sun beat down on my back. I'd moved, in the night, from my grassy bed to the rubble at the base of the cliff without knowing when or how I did that. I tried to call out but my parched tongue was glued to the bottom of my mouth. I remember rising up on one elbow and then bringing myself to a kneeling position.

I blinked the fuzziness away and wobbled to gain my feet. Sensations I knew too well sent me reeling back to earth again. I counted to a hundred, breathing deeply.

Standing again more or less, I still couldn't tell if the ground was moving or it was me. But at least I knew up from down. And I needed to go up, to get back to the road and my bike and to look for help. Except, I wasn't sure I could do that. I had trouble taking two steps, one after the other. How was I supposed to climb a near vertical football field?

Passing out repeatedly and losing time told me my injuries were serious. So, I forced my eyes to search my surroundings again. The angle of the sun told me it was already mid afternoon. Nearly a day had passed.

Then like a gift from the gods, a camera flashed a picture from a stony spillway, twenty feet away. Only it wasn't a camera. The silver metal casing of my cell phone reflected the sky high sun back at me. I prayed the little thing was in better shape than me. Carefully, I picked it up and flipped it open. Thank God, it came to life.

I speed dialed Sheila.

You out drinking with Garnet again?" she said, only there was a strain in her voice.

"Wish that were all, Babe."

"You okay, Jack?"

"I jumped off a cliff last night."

"Why?"

"Trying to avoid getting shot," I said. I touched a gooey spot under the backpack in the middle of my back. "But I don't think I succeeded."

"Where are you?"

"Look for the Chief on the east side of the road."

"Which road?"

"I remember leaving Owen Sound for Wiarton."

"And when we find the Chief?"

"Look down."

That's when I lost it again.

thirty two

MY VISION WAS BLURRED, LEAVING me in a haze, like in the thick forest, an hour before dawn. Still, through the gauzy curtain, I picked out a few clues, starting with the miniature TV, suspended in mid-air by the Canadarm. Fluorescent tubes winked down at me from behind grainy plexiglass. The walls were a nondescript pastel. And I lay, high off the floor, in a three quarter reclining position, on my back in a bed, a hospital bed.

Which meant I wasn't dead.

Despite the distant drum solo, I squeezed my eyes tight and opened them wide to kickstart my brain. But my brain never said much. I didn't remember how I got there, although I knew what I was doing there. The pain told me.

I tried the eyes 'shut tight and open wide' trick again and butterflies in my stomach stirred another memory. I was falling. And I remembered a black SUV.

I've always believed in premonitions and it occurred to me one of them played a big role in postponing my death by maybe a few decades. The way the SUV drove up my backside didn't strike me as everyday behaviour. But that wasn't the premonition. Despite the tinted windows and the facemasks, a sixth sense, my premonition, told me who the driver and his passenger were. And more important what they were planning to do to me.

So, that made my reactions quicker than they might have been and compensated for the loss of judgment that results from too much beer. I was quick enough, just barely, to dodge a headshot. But according to the hospital emergency doctor, not quick enough to dodge a bullet in the back.

After that, survival had less to do with my actions and reactions than with shit luck. Medically speaking, I'd won the 50/50 draw on the same night the house sold out. The obstacles I bumped into during my race with gravity hurt a lot but they slowed my descent. In the end, a gnarly thousand year old cedar turned my trip down the Niagara Escarpment into the equivalent of a twenty footer. And the big silver plated Elvis belt buckle I'd stowed in my backpack for Penny Sue Stanfield deflected the bullet just enough to keep me out of a wheel chair. Or a coffin.

Still for some reason, I didn't feel like a winner.

"How are you?" Sheila said, from a chair by the window.

"Doctor says 'I got horseshoes up my ass,'" I answered, recalling a faraway conversation with someone in a white coat.

"He did not."

"He's a she."

"The doctor?"

"Yup."

"Good looking?"

"I think she's going to ask me out."

"She say concussions make you delusionary?"

"She didn't say I had a concussion. She told me, 'your head's gonna be really sore' for a few days."

"Huh. 'Sore' is medical terminology?"

"Pretty sure it is."

"I looked at your chart. Says, first degree concussion."

"Don't know who wrote that. I choose to believe my doctor."

"Head hurts?"

" 'Sore' is the correct term."

"What about the back?"

"Bad bruise. And a small hole."

"A hole?"

"More like a crease. Bullet didn't penetrate anything vital."

"Lucky."

"I know."

"Jack…"

"What?"

"I thought I'd lost you."

"Yeah. I was a little worried."

"Don't do that to me again."

"Okay."

"Jack…"

"There's something else?"

"They brought Garnet in."

"What?"

"When you called me, first thing I did I tried to reach Garnet and there was no answer. So, I phoned Carrie. She went to his trailer."

"And…"

"She called the ambulance."

"Shot?"

Sheila wiped a tear away.

"He gonna make it?"

"Don't think so Jack."

Thinking back now to the day I rejoined the conscious world, I can't say what hurt more. My head, my back or the news about Garnet Henderson. As I gradually recovered, the physical pain eased.

· · · · · ·

I was sitting up in bed, watching the Tigers beat up on the Indians. At least I think I got that right. It was hard to tell from a TV screen that could have substituted for the face of a small kitchen clock.

Between innings, Sheila said, "You know who it is, don't you?"

"Who who is?"

She smiled at my imitation of a barn owl. "You know what I'm talking about, Jack. You know who took a shot at you and who ran you off the road."

"Have a look at my medical chart, Sheila."

"I know; concussion, headaches, possible memory loss."

"There you go."

"We have to tell the police."

It wasn't rational but Sheila's comment about involving the police triggered a response in me. I sat up and swung my legs over the side of the bed. It hurt but I refused to wince.

"Where you think you're going?" she said.

"I'm going to find him."

"Lake?"

"Yeah."

"How did you know it was him?"

"I saw him."

"Did Lake take Garnet out?"

"Stands to reason he did."

"Okay."

"And while I'm at it, I'm going after that big sucker he hangs with."

"Harry Maxwell?"

"And maybe I'm going to set a young widow straight, too."

"Just remember Jack. It was poking a stick in that hornet's nest that landed you in here."

"I'll be careful."

"Yes you will. I'm planning to make sure of it."

"How?"

"I'm coming with you."

Neither of which was true. Sheila didn't come with me. In fact, I never went anywhere, unless you want to count the floor. That's where I ended up, on the floor, unconscious, all caused by a dizzy spell. It must have been the sudden movement.

When my doctor heard about my fall, she threatened to beat the crap out of me. Only she said it in medical terms.

It was three more days before I was able to sit up straight in bed without tipping over. And it was still three more days before I could walk down the hall, unaided.

Sheila saw me every day, and on most of those days I saw her. At least I think I did.

There were lots of visitors – and most of them were real - with get well cards and chocolates, and books, which I was too wonky to read.

The cops interviewed me, maybe once, maybe ten times. Only they didn't bring me anything, other than questions, which I answered without telling them anything, which ticked Sheila off.

In between visits from Sheila, there were long periods of fog and confusion, during which my mother appeared. Only she wasn't there to comfort me. No, she was going through my pants' pockets, looking for money. After my mother left, a killer named Pastor Bob Coulter spoke to me, from behind steel bars. I think I told him that no one gave a shit about him, not anymore. And from the jail cell beside him, his murderous daughter spoke to me in seductive tones. I may have succumbed to her advances.

In the chaos of my mind there were kinder images, too. Sheila and I danced to the sounds of Motown, under the palms of a moonlit Caribbean sky. Sometimes I'd wake up and she'd be lying on the edge of the bed, on her side, looking at me. That felt real. For sure I did succumb.

My friend Tiny Cole, a former biker hood, turned gang informant/police agent showed his hairy mug, too. He told me something like, 'get the fuck out of bed. There's assholes out there getting away with murder.' Only Tiny lived in Ottawa. And I hadn't seen him in months.

Sheila's parents sent flowers. I could tell because they smelled up the whole damn room and geraniums are Liz Mackie's favourites.

Hughie Morrison made multiple appearances. Once he came in wearing his football uniform, all hepped up, like he was preparing for a big game. Another time he showed in his fishing jacket, the one with so many pockets he could never find his car keys when it was past time to go. Last time he came by, he wore his Bay Street suit and he had a file folder tucked under his arm and he told me Mike was awarded bail.

Speaking of Mike, he and Lori paid their respects, but in separate visits. Mike seemed bored, which made two of us. When he left, his wife came in. Lori leaned over and showed me her cleavage. Though whether her breasts were of the real world at the time, I didn't know. When I mentioned Lori's visit to Sheila, she said I was probably nuts.

At the end of the week, the visits, even the weird ones eased up. Then, Sheila and Hughie arrived in tandem. Sheila came through the door first lugging a suitcase, with Hughie right behind, looking sheepish.

"Running off together?" I asked.

"Thinking of it," Sheila said.

"Her feet get awful cold, buddy," I said.

"I'll make her wear socks."

"What's with the suitcase?"

"Jeans. Your best t-shirt. Runners."

"Mine?"

No one bothered to answer my dumb question.

"Hughie brought his truck," Sheila said.

"For the Chief?"

"They tell me you should be able to fix it," Hughie said.

"We going back to the cottage?"

Sheila answered, "No Jack. We're going home, to Grand Bend. I need to get back. And you need to get better."

"What about Lake?"

"We'll talk about that later."

Sheila's face told me the discussion was over. She wiped a hand across her eyes and sniffled. There was no argument left in me.

thirty three

THE NURSES WOULDN'T LET ME walk out of the hospital.

But they let Hughie wheel me out in a chair, while Sheila walked on one side to prevent tomfoolery and a nurse followed behind. Using the wheelchair didn't make any sense. They weren't letting me keep the chair, so, obviously they were fine with me walking away on my own once I was off the property.

I guess, that way, they could claim I was perfectly fit when I was released. And if I fell over again on my ass, or on my head, it was because I tripped over my own shoelaces. They could say it was my own damn fault, not the concussion that laid me up for a week. Making me use the wheelchair - it's like they had no confidence in my recovery, or in their diagnosis. But before the nurse had a chance to give her side of the story, Sheila told me if I would 'just shut up,' she'd buy me a six pack for the drive home. So I shut up.

Hughie left us when we reached Sheila's Mustang. I watched him drive off, heading for Grand Bend with the Big Chief tied down in the back of his pick-up.

Instead of tailing Hughie, Sheila chauffeured me around the block and parked beside the hospital's longterm care wing, where Garnet was being kept. I kept quiet for the short trip, adhering to Sheila's instructions, which gave me a chance to think about family, as a concept. My direct experience is sketchy. I knew none of my grandparents. Had no siblings. My parents disappeared from my life before I was old enough to fully appreciate the difference between having a family and being alone.

Although I wasn't completely abandoned as a child, which might have been better, because the truth was, through the years, my mother made her appearances. And she still does, even now. They're hit and miss, though. When she turns up it's usually because she's in trouble. Or she needs money. And she creates a crisis which I solve or I don't, and then she's gone again.

As far as I know, my father's still alive. At least, I haven't heard otherwise. So, I suppose he's out there, somewhere.

Two years ago, Sheila and her family experienced the loss of her grandparents, on her mother's side. They died within weeks of each other. But watching Sheila cope never prepared me, not for a minute. Not for dealing with what happened to Garnet.

When Garnet was shot and hospitalized, they said, "He might never wake up. If he does, he won't be the same." The words numbed me.

I cared but I didn't know how to act, what to do. I'd never had to deal with loss before this. Maybe because there wasn't much to lose for so much of my life.

And it sure felt like I lost Garnet. He was breathing and his heart kept pumping but he wasn't there. Garnet was gone, no more.

I thought about his impact on me. Here was a man I knew for just a few short days. But we clicked like we'd always known one another. We were natural together, open, honest. I'd come to regard Garnet as family, like a wise older brother. Losing him was like losing Hughie, or Tiny.

Losing Sheila was not something I allowed myself to think about.

I didn't know what to say or do, not when it came to dealing with his condition, with his future or, with his end.

One thing I did know. I had to see Carrie, to tell her straight up that, "Someone will pay."

But first I made that same promise to the man lying in a hospital bed, crowded in by machinery and pinned down with wires and tubes all over his frigging body. I gave him my message, out loud, just in case my words reached him. Even though the doctors said there was no comprehension. It cost me nothing to roll the dice.

After leaving Garnet immobile like he was frozen, connected to the equipment that barely kept him going, Sheila and I took the ten minute drive from Collingwood to Clarksburg. Carrie opened the door and broke down the minute she saw us standing there, heads down. In life, some people get knocked down hard. And they toughen up. No sooner are they back on their feet and fate takes another swing at them. And they're flat on their backs again, broken worse, maybe forever.

The rest of us don't know their kind of pain. Sure we hit a few bumps along the way. But most of us have health, friends or family, jobs, hobbies. We carry on, without thinking about the 'what ifs.' Oblivious or indifferent. Because the rest of us believe everything eventually turns out right, not giving a second thought for the lives we leave in our wake.

Carrie wasn't one of 'the rest of us'.

"How are you Jack?" she asked.

"I'm good."

"What about you?" Sheila said, touching one of the forearms Carrie folded across her heaving chest.

"I'm okay," she lied.

"Rob?"

"The same."

"Is Garnet going to stay where he is?" I said.

"The hospital? I don't know. I'm trying to find out what kind of financial support we can get. Move him somewhere nicer."

It occurred to me that people in grief shouldn't have to worry about bureaucracy.

After a short silence, I said, "At least you and your Dad resolved your differences before…"

"Well, Jack," Carrie said, "my motives weren't exactly pure." We waited for the explanation she needed to give. "I agreed to see him," she said, "after I learned he was investigating Honey Hicks. I wanted to know how that was going. I pushed him to go after her hard."

We waited some more.

"I hoped …. I wanted her to be involved in the Hicks murder." She nodded her head once, to underline the point.

"Because?"

"Because if she were and if she were caught, she'd be punished for it. And that would count as something for..."

"For what she did to Rob?" I finished the thought.

"Yeah."

And now her father was in a coma. And she was beating herself up over it, as if she was to blame, even in a small way. And to make matters worse, Honey Hicks was going to walk away clean from a fucking mess, for the second time in her twenty five year life.

"I'm not dropping this."

"Okay."

"You need anything," I said, "call."

After our awkward meeting with Carrie on her front porch, Sheila took me into the rolling uplands above the escarpment, on roads I'd traveled while visiting Garnet at his trailer. A gravel concession road led us to an abandoned orchard. She pulled onto an overgrown ditch crossing and we got out. Following a stone and cedar rail fence line, we picked a high spot, folded over a patch of grass under an ancient maple and sat on our improvised cushion to watch the sun sink on the other side of the Beaver Valley.

They say a view cures everything. You look over a patchwork of pasture, orchard and cropped field, separated by tree lines, fences and winding roads. And in the valley, through thin spots in the trees, you catch a glimpse of water jumping over rocks. It can take your breath away. And it's as if you own something, something others don't have, a place here, on the planet. It's just a view but it's all yours. And it helps make things right. Most things.

Sheila leaned into me and she cried. And we said a prayer for Garnet and one for Carrie and Rob. And for Penny Sue. And the prayers sealed the promise I made at Garnet's bedside.

When the last of the sky's fiery pillows turned to deep purple and then to charcoal and Venus made its appearance, I kissed Sheila's forehead and we got to our feet and watched where the sun had been, not wanting to leave. But we did.

Back in the car, we sat some more, Sheila's keys in her lap.

"You never did say how you managed to find me," I said, not looking at her.

"At the bottom of the cliff?"

"It was pretty rugged."

"It was," she said. "A highway post was broken off and the gravel had deep skid marks. The Chief was dangling on its side, just over the edge, caught up in the fence cable."

"Easy to miss."

"We did once. But then on the way back down, Dad noticed the sawed off post."

"Your dad?"

"I called him when you didn't come home that night, and he came."

"He drove up from London? Just like that?"

"I needed him."

"And you'll always be his little girl."

"Thank God."

I thought about how to repay Mr. Mackie and wondered if he liked fishing. "So," I said, "he saw the broken fence post, telling you where I went over."

"That's right."

"And then?"

"We called emergency. But no way was I waiting. Mike and I found a way to the bottom. We had to zig and zag. Dad stayed by the bike at the top. Kind of a beacon for Mike and me."

"Wasn't it dark?" I said, still not fully grasping that I'd skipped most of a whole day after my fall.

"It was getting there. There was still an after glow, higher up. As we descended, the shadows got deeper. I was afraid we wouldn't find you."

"What about the Fire Department?"

"Dad was waiting for them, too."

"Couldn't have been easy for Mike. It had to be a rough climb down."

"It wasn't easy, but he stuck with it."

"Maybe I'll stop calling him 'Fat Elvis'?"

"You could."

"Unless he ticks me off."

"There's always an exception to the rule."

"How'd you get me up?"

"You were there, Jack."

"Yes and no. Mostly no. "

"Getting you to the ambulance was easier. No need to go up the way you came down. Emergency Services arrived and decided, with the help of the Fire Department, to take you out through the flats to the township road a few hundred metres to the south."

"Huh."

"You don't remember any of this?"

"Vaguely. The parts I remember are like a movie."

"Like it wasn't happening to you?"

"I know I saw your face. I think you were shouting at me."

"I thought you were going out on me. Forever."

"I remember the ambulance ride."

"It's behind us now," she said.

I looked at Venus, our most beautiful planet.

"It's over," she said again.

"The game's going into extra innings, Babe."

"Not yet, Jack. Not until you're ready."

thirty four

I'VE HAD MORE THAN MY share of concussions. It's a lifestyle thing.

Winter jogging is one way to acquire one. I now come to a full stop before I change direction on ice. Meeting a 250 pound fullback jaw on shoulderpad on the one yard line is another way. So is squaring off against a steroid juicer with the temper of a spoiled toddler.

But I never expected to get one from jumping off a cliff. And on a scale from one to ten, my latest brain injury hit an eight where a ten means you don't wake up.

Still, by September, the double vision and dizzy spells had cleared up; the headaches too, although bright lights bothered me. I'd reached something I call near-full recovery.

Sheila and I were back to running most mornings on the damp, packed sand at the edge of the lapping waves. After work, when the temperature agreed, we swam and dried off by watching the sun set over Lake Huron.

One night, Sheila treated me to take-out pizza from the bucket seats of her Mustang. Sitting in the parking lot at the end of Main Street, Grand Bend, I ate two slices for every one of Sheila's, not that there was a race or anything. I felt good, washing the salty flavour away with Coke, taking in the grandeur and feeling the butterflies … night was falling and the lake was full of wild energy. A storm was on the way.

Sheila broke the spell. "I liked Garnet a lot, Jack," is how she started out.

"He's not dead."

She ignored my clarification.

"He was smart and fun," she said.

"He was."

"And damned handsome."

I laughed, recalling the flirting.

"But he was damaged," she added.

"I know. First he loses his wife. Then the hit and run."

"So, he drank."

"Too much."

"Understatement."

"Yeah. It did get out of hand."

"Jack," she said.

"What?" I asked, though I had a suspicion about what was coming next.

"You aren't damaged."

I looked at her.

"Scratch that," she said. "You are damaged. But you've always been good at damage control."

"We're still talking about the drinking."

"Yeah. The drinking."

"Mine?"

"Yes."

"I wasn't drunk when they tried to kill me. My reactions were good."

"Maybe."

"But?"

"They could have been better."

"Point taken."

Busy season for the coffee shop and the rest of Main Street was over a good three weeks now. Our bank accounts were flush, no thanks to my one man detective agency. But I wasn't looking for new work. And Hughie sent no clients my way, not that I would have taken them. It's not that I wasn't fit enough, I just wasn't ready. Because I needed to tie off the loose ends in the Collingwood Elvis case. No, that's not quite right. I needed to strangle those loose ends, the sons of bitches, before starting on something new.

In the weeks since we returned to the Bend, a few issues were resolved in our favour. The sudden disappearance of Peter Lake and Harry Maxwell convinced the cops to consider more seriously the option that one or both of these guys were linked to the demise of Dwayne Curtis Hicks. Statements by Ted Olson also may have helped shift suspicion in that direction. Long and short of it, the charge of murder against Mike Mackie was now on the backburner and it looked like it would stay there. The job Garnet and I set out to do was done.

The cops also asked me whether the attacks on Garnet and me were connected to our murder investigation. And by way of corollary, whether they were the work of Peter and Harry. But I continued to play dumb, for dumb reasons.

For my work in ferreting out Peter Lake, fraud artist, Ted Olson sent me a check, half of which I forwarded to Garnet's daughter to hold for Garnet or, to spend on him however she saw fit.

Whenever they dropped by, Sheila's parents treated me like a king, I suppose because their son was in the clear. And even Mike showed his appreciation by keeping me stocked in beer. Lori hadn't shown me her cleavage lately, maybe because the two of them were trying to patch up the marriage. My disappointment eventually passed.

Another favourable turn: my injuries and what happened to Garnet brought Sheila and me closer together. But offsetting that, my decision to rekindle the search for Lake and his associate had the opposite effect, even though she admitted she knew I had to pick up the pieces again. Relationships are like that.

It was while I was sitting at my favourite table beside the picture window at the front of Gert's, looking out on Main Street, that Tiny Cole showed up. He burst through the front door forcing, without a second glance, two customers to step aside.

"Jack Beer!"

I twisted my neck toward the shout. Only it was more like a roar. I braced myself.

Tiny knocked an obstacle course of chairs out of the way in his 'straight as the crow flies' rush to reach me. I stepped back but failed to escape the big man's bear hug. He slapped me hard on the back, yelled some expletives in my ear and informed me he was hungry and that he damn well expected me to buy him lunch. And a candy ass sandwich, tucked in beside a cup of girly soup, would not cut it. He needed steak and fries and garlic bread and beer.

Tiny dropped me, to let me breathe again, and turned on Sheila. She went into a semi-crouch, telling Tiny, "This may seem like just a butter knife in my hand. But, you come anywhere near me, I'm using it on you."

Tiny laughed, eliminated the space between them and lifted her off the ground, kissing my girlfriend long and hard on the lips. Then he let her go.

"You are easily the most disgusting man I have ever known," she said.

Tiny Cole is the former biker boss who may or may not have visited me while I was in the hospital. And whose life I once saved in the course of making the biggest arrest of my police career. Our paths crossed shortly after that when I helped negotiate a job for him as a police informant, working first in the apprehension of the scumbags who murdered his younger brother and later in solving a long list of drug and extortion cases for the RCMP.

Last time I saw Tiny – that is to say, the last time I was certain I saw him, he'd arrived a man transformed, from a full grown wooly mammoth covered in tattoos to a neatly trimmed grizzly bear covered in tattoos. He came to Grand Bend to help me solve a tough murder case involving a developer, a preacher, and the preacher's daughter, who happened to be a former girl-friend. And stuff happened we couldn't have predicted. Together we sorted everything out.

Now, the beard and the salt and pepper shoulder length hair were back. But the excess weight stayed off, meaning he was still tipping the scales at something equivalent to an adolescent mammoth.

"Well?" he shouted. "What about it? You gonna feed me or not?"

I didn't answer right away, still recovering as I was from the shock of seeing the guy after more than half a year.

He turned to Sheila, who again raised the butter knife before his eyes, which broke them both up.

"You can come along too, girly," he said.

Tiny is a sexist and a boor. And he's the only man possessing such traits that I have ever known Sheila to tolerate. Like many hard men, Tiny was a paradox of cussed meanness and soft heart. And he makes Sheila laugh. I guess that's why he's her friend.

I'm less sure what I see in him. Except, he's the strongest, toughest and most loyal friend I have ever known. And I will be forever grateful to the man whose capacity for violence, nearly a year ago, made the difference between a life alone and a life with Sheila.

Ignoring his protests, Sheila retreated to the kitchen and Tiny settled for the sandwiches she made and a pot of strong coffee. We spent the afternoon catching up.

Then, we turned the coffee shop over to the night staff at six o'clock, which was an hour early – Tiny was hungry again - and walked to 'Nick's,' a Greek restaurant that caters more to the locals than to the tourists. Tiny ordered enough food to affect Nick's bottom line. I never even tried to keep up, a situation that prompted a derisive snort from Tiny. Sheila had barely food enough to qualify as a midnight snack by Tiny's standards.

When Tiny finally came up for air, I threw him the question that had been on my mind since he arrived. "What are you doing here?"

To his credit, Tiny didn't toss off a song and dance about wanting to spend quality time with the only former cop he'll ever bend elbows with. Instead, he answered straight up.

"Sheila called me."

They exchanged glances. A conspiracy.

"So it wasn't a dream. You've been here before," I suddenly knew it. "You visited me while I was in the hospital."

"Mostly, I didn't," he said. "Mostly, I sat on a chair in the hall, outside your room."

"You were guarding me?"

Sheila looked sheepish. And maybe a little worried. "Someone tried to kill you, Jack," she said. "Over what you know. And what you were about to find out."

"So, you called Tiny?"

"Hughie spelled me off when I got bored of protecting your sorry ass,"

Tiny said.

"Did I need you?" I asked.

"Late one night, a guy, 240 pounds, maybe 250, 6 foot 5 or 6 shows his 'kiss my ass' face in the hallway. He's wearing green cotton pants and those V necked shirts they all wear, trying to pass himself off."

"As a doctor?"

"No, the Green Hornet."

"You know who it was?"

"When I first got here, Sheila showed me pictures of Lake and Maxwell."

"Well, it wasn't Lake." I went by the size.

"He's the smaller one?"

"So, it was Maxwell?"

"Think so. I didn't get too close."

"He left when he saw you?"

"I chased him down the hall into the stairwell, but then I stopped."

"Risk assessment tell you to?"

"Could have been one of those tricks you see in the movies," he said.

"A diversion?"

"Yeah. So I came back in case the asshole's partner showed up."

"He didn't though?"

"Nah."

"Those guys likely don't catch too many movies," I said.

"Nope."

"Anyone watch Garnet's room?"

"No, it's pretty well known the guy's out for the count. You're the only witness with a mouth that works. Trouble is the bad guys don't know about your brain."

"My brain's fine."

"You say."

"And now?"

"And now, I'm thinking you need help finding the sumsabitches who did the number on you."

"And who took Garnet out," I said.

Sheila looked at me expecting she didn't know what. Usually, I don't appreciate people making decisions on my behalf. But there were more than a few days I was missing in action. How could I be angry at her for bringing Tiny Cole on board? Besides, I did need help in tracking down Peter Lake and in finding Dwayne Hicks' killer, whom I figured were one and the same. And as partners go, Tiny's the best. Garnet was next best, even given the short time I knew him.

I took Sheila's hand and I thanked her, not so Tiny would notice.

Then I started to tell him about the case. Except he stopped me.

"Sheila gave me the plot outline. Otherwise, I like to learn about stuff as we go," he reminded me.

thirty five

"WHERE DO WE START, MAN?"

"With a woman named Honey Olson-Hicks."

"So, let's go find the bitch."

Tiny belched and leaned back into the corner made by the door and the bench seat of my Chevy pick-up. He closed his eyes and all conversation ended by the time I lost Grand Bend in my rear view mirror.

We slowed for Bayfield. Tiny stirred and he wanted to know more. "Remind me. She the widow of the guy was killed?"

"She is."

Not counting my rock compilation CDs, the truck cab went quiet again. This time for the next eighty kilometers.

As I turned right onto Highway 9 at Kincardine, another probing question popped to mind.

"She a suspect?" he said.

"She knows things she won't say."

"About the murder. Or about shooting Garnet and running you off the road."

"Maybe all of that."

"She's someone with information then?"

"Yeah."

Tiny returned to a Zen state until we reached the Hartley House in Walkerton. Over the lunch buffet of cholesterol and cold draught beer, Tiny thought up another question. "With no criminal responsibility?"

"You talking about Honey Olson-Hicks?"

"We been talking about anything else?" he said, ignoring the fact he'd mostly been asleep.

An impatient look went with my answer. "I never said she's not criminally responsible."

"What the fuck's that mean?"

"She's slippery."

Later still, over coffee in Singhampton, he speculated, "This broad – she born with a silver spoon?"

"And all the rest of the cutlery."

Which answer I saw set Tiny to thinking, until he dozed off again.

As I parked in front of Olson Enterprises, Tiny grabbed my arm and said, "She work here?"

"Right after he sacked Peter Lake, Daddy made her the Vice-President of Corporate Affairs."

"And the fricking world too, I'd bet."

"You know the type."

"Remind me about this Peter Lake dude again."

"He's one of the guys I figure shot Garnet."

"And tried to kill you. Sheila told me that much anyway."

"Okay, the guy was a hot shot at Olson Enterprises."

"And now Honey's the one with her fancy title. Ms. Hyphenated This and That gets to throw her weight around?"

"And look pretty."

"And make money for the company?"

"I think that's still Daddy's job," I said.

Tiny released his grip on my arm, indicating he knew all he needed to know and allowing me to get out from behind the wheel.

I straightened my body and twisted left and right. Forward and back. Then side to side. My back was sore. An ache that started in the vicinity of my bullet wound wandered vaguely south from there.

Which may have explained my piss-poor mood. Throw into the mix a gnawing determination - I needed badly to solve the Hicks murder, and worse than that, I needed to find the men who shot Garnet Henderson – and I was ready to spit nails.

I walked through the foyer, ignoring the new plastic secretary. Courtney, probably a Peter Lake hire, was gone. In her place was another runway model type put together from media images, trying to decide what kind of pose was called for as I rumbled by. Over my shoulder, I watched her stand up, face featuring wide eyes and a dropped jaw, hands dramatically perched on skinny hips. Taken together, she was obviously going for her indignant, but still cute as a button look.

Tiny stayed behind to make sure the precious little receptionist girl did as she was told – meaning she was to 'sit her pretty little ass in her chair' and 'act like a mannequin' is how I heard Tiny put it.

I pushed through the door that said, 'Vice-President. Honey Olson.'

Her name plate told me she'd come full circle. Single babe to married babe with two last names to widowed babe to single babe again with one last name. The remnants of her Dwayne Hicks connection were wiped clean before the body had fully settled into the subsoil.

Aside from the fancy furniture and artwork, the office was empty. I went to her desk, looking for clues. The flip calendar was a day behind, telling me she hadn't been to work that day, unless I got my dates mixed up.

I retraced my steps to the first door I'd passed. 'Executive Assistant,' it said. I took the word 'assistant' as an invitation. No-name was in, and I figured he was ready to assist me. But he looked a little startled. I picked up a card from the desk. 'William Rogers. Assistant to the Vice-President,' it said. Wow.

He was fifteen years younger than me, and he would have had a struggle to catch a bus unless he was running downhill and the driver saw him coming. I will never understand a guy who is thirty or under and is supposed to have brains, who lets himself go. It's not rational on my part but still, his fat annoyed me.

In a voice that matched his paisley tie and pin-striped suit, William Rogers tried the executive assistant run-around on me, something about appointments and protocols. All before I had a reasonable chance to tell him what I wanted. That was strike one.

But I was prepared to let him have two more swings.

"You're head gopher around here now," I noted, handing him my own card.

He nodded in the affirmative.

"And how long were you with the company before you got promoted to this lofty position?"

"Three years. I kept minutes, did the books."

"So, you'll be on top of everything."

He shrugged.

"Of course," I encouraged him.

Another shrug.

"So, for starters," I said, "here's a job for you. Get a hold of Honey Olson and tell her Jack Beer needs to talk to her."

"She's not reachable."

"Strike two."

"What happened to strike one?"

"Don't talk back to the ump, boy."

"Well, it's true. Even I can't reach her."

"Where's her Daddy?," I said.

He studied his computer screen and tried to look too important to continue the discussion.

"I'm going to make a wild guess here, William. You're about to tell me that Ted Olson is also unreachable."

He nodded, stealing a glance my way.

"Let's move on to another question. Tell me what you know about the assholes who took out Garnet Henderson. You do that for me and I might not mess up your outfit."

"Who's Garnet Henderson?" But he wouldn't even give me a glance this time.

That was revealing.

I stared at the man, hard.

Then he picked up the phone and said, "I'm calling the police."

Strike three.

I nudged him with my foot, wondering whether my shoe would disappear into the stomach folds along with his belt. "Get your sorry ass off the floor, before I really get pissed off," I told him.

"You hit me," he whined.

"No, I didn't. I prevented you from making a bad mistake. By throwing you to the floor. And tossing your phone in the waste basket."

"What's the difference?"

"Between hitting you and not hitting you?"

"Yeah."

"If I really hit you, there'd be blood." I leaned close. "You bleeding?"

"No."

"And you'd be scared shitless that I might do it again." I leaned closer. "You scared shitless?"

I knew his type, the kind who figured he could lie his way out of any mess he was in, but who got the snot beat out of him figuratively and sometimes literally when he got caught. And his type never learned that holding back never works.

"No," he said.

"So if you haven't at least peed your pants, I didn't really hit you."

"Did so, asshole. You caught me off guard."

"Wouldn't have mattered if I caught you on guard," I said.

"I'd have done something," he said.

The nerve.

"You want a shot? Eh, Mr. Chief Assistant Memo Writer? You want to give me your best shot? Get up. Get up and you got it." I straightened, hands behind my back, chin jutting forward.

I was being a jerk. It happens, especially when I'm annoyed at my own failings.

Rogers' face went all scrunchy, taking on a 'don't hurt me' look.

His shaking embarrassed me, upset me. I had in fact scared the poor guy, so badly he might have been too scared to be any use. Changing tact, I helped him to his feet and smoothed out his jacket. He jerked his arm out of my grasp, asserting himself I guess, despite the fear.

"What happened to Garnet Henderson, William?" I said.

"I told you I don't know."

"Let me jog your memory. For starters, don't tell me you don't know the name. He was working with me and I was working for your boss, Ted Olson."

"I never met you either."

"Even if that's true, you damn well heard of us, William. The attack on Garnet Henderson was in all the papers. It was the main topic of conversation in all the coffee shops. The cops have been nosing around here. Asking questions. This business, especially head office here, isn't that big. So, don't tell me you never heard of Garnet Henderson. Or me."

I waited and he said, "I may have heard the name, now that you mention the incident."

"How about before the 'incident'? The name Garnet Henderson ever come up before that?"

"Maybe, once."

"Let's have it."

"What do you mean?"

"The details surrounding the mention of the name, Henderson. He didn't work here. Had no business with you. Why would his name come up?"

"Mr. Olson and Peter Lake were talking about a man by that name."

"When was this?"

"I don't know. A couple days before Peter and Harry were fired."

"What were they saying?"

"That's all I know. Because they told me to leave."

"Think some more," I said.

"They were both really angry."

"About what?"

"I just don't know."

It wasn't much but it was something. Garnet made Lake and Olson upset. But over what I had no idea, other than a couple of educated guesses.

I left William Rogers to tuck in his shirt and fix his hair. There wasn't a lot he could do about his dignity.

• • • • • •

"Let's go," I said.

"I have to tell you, Jack. This hasn't been any fun for me," Tiny said, "so far."

"You drive." I tossed him the keys.

Tiny started the engine, backed out, shifted to drive and braked at the parking lot exit. "Where the hell we going?"

"Damned if I know," I said, leafing through a pocket phone directory and then punching in a phone number.

"Who you calling?"

"The widow's personal cell."

"Where'd you get the phone book?"

"I found it."

"Where?"

"Suitcoat pocket."

"Which suit?"

"The one belonging to the Executive Assistant to the Vice-President. His suitcoat pocket."

"Figured."

"So why'd you ask?"

After eight rings, the phone stopped. A low sexy voice came on and invited me to leave my number or to call again, because the voice really 'wanted to talk with me'. It was decidedly not a business phone.

I did as instructed and in a low baritone I told Honey Olson I 'really, really' wanted her to call me back.

Tiny sighed or it could have been a groan.

"You hungry?" I said.

He gave me an 'are you an idiot' look.

"Connie's Grill has good pies."

Maddie hustled over to meet her newest customer.

Brushing back her hair, which was beyond help, and smoothing her apron, which made no difference, she smiled at Tiny while talking to me, "Who have we here, Jack?" She winked at the hairy monster sitting across from me.

"Maddie," I said, "Please say 'hello' to Sheldon Cole."

"I go by 'Tiny,'" said Tiny.

"I don't believe that for a minute," she said, laughing and winking again.

Tiny smiled broadly and leaned back to check Maddie out, top to bottom. I swear the little vamp squirmed. And despite the permanently bad hair, Maddie knew how to turn heads.

"What can I do for you?" she said, practically cooing.

Tiny locked eyes with the woman's for a full minute before he said, "Take me home and I'll show you."

"Two coffees and two pieces of your freshest pie," I said, "please Maddie. Unless you two want to find a motel room somewhere."

I detected an extra sway in her tush as she left to fill my order.

"I think maybe she likes me," he said.

"Where'd you get that idea?"

Our food arrived and Maddie managed to keep her clothes on.

When she brought the bill, she gave it to me and turned to Tiny to say, "I usually get off at ten."

"Okay, but what time does your shift end?"

Maddie laughed and dropped her phone number on Tiny's plate.

I had a wisecrack ready to go when my cell went off.

It was Honey Olson. And she was on the warpath. Angry that I hassled her staff, annoyed that I had her personal phone number in my possession, offended that a 'two-bit detective from some backwoods hick town' interrupted her day on the golf course. And that's where I cut her off and let her have it with both barrels.

"You owe me, Babe. I saved your financial ass," I told her, "and your Daddy's too, by outing that deadbeat boyfriend of yours. And my frigging payment for this exemplary service was a bullet in the back and a head injury that nearly killed me. Meanwhile, my partner's payment was …."

The line went dead.

"Honey Olson?" Tiny said.

"Yeah."

"How'd that go?"

"She asked me over for afternoon tea."

We laughed. I dropped a twenty on the table and got up to leave.

"Where?"

"To Honey's."

"Seriously?"

"I may have to kick her goddamn door in but, yeah, I'm going to her place."

"For that cup of tea?"

"And some answers."

"Mind if I skip this one?" he said. "It's not like you need a bodyguard to meet with some broad."

"What are you gonna do?"

"Thought I might pass a little time with Maddie. Traffic's starting to slow here."

I smiled at him, told him to call when he finished working his charms and I left.

thirty six

HONEY'S CAR WAS IN THE driveway.

She wouldn't answer her doorbell but I saw a shadow through the curtain that covered the tall opaque window beside the door. I goddamn needed answers so I returned to my truck for the crowbar I keep beside my old service revolver, in a locked tool box.

"Watch out for broken glass," I yelled, as I raised the crow bar over my head.

The door swung open.

"What the hell are you doing?"

I walked in and tossed the steel bar on a shiny hall table, hoping for an irreparable scratch. "Got any coffee?" I said.

"Get out."

"You hung up on me."

"You were lecturing me. Nobody goddamn lectures me."

"Given your behaviour and your actions, a lecture lets you off the hook way too easy."

"My behaviour? My actions?"

"Uh huh."

"You think you know me? You don't know me." She screamed the words.

I grabbed Honey Olson's blouse in my left hand and pointed the index finger of my right in her face. "I know you better than you think, Honey."

Then, I let her go, because otherwise I might have hit her. "We need to talk," I said.

"Go to hell," she said and she walked into the kitchen, straight ahead.

I followed her.

"I thought I told you to fuck off."

"Not until you answer my questions."

She took a stool. I leaned back on the fridge and took a few deep breaths. Calming down.

"Get this straight, Mr. PI," she said. "You do not know me." Did she think I didn't hear her the first time? The way she said it, through gritted teeth and pronouncing each word carefully, it was as if it was a matter of critical national importance.

I answered the challenge in her tone. "Yes, I do know you," I said. "Here's what I know. And it's all so damned obvious."

She shot me a finger.

I took the gesture as an invitation to continue. "You were born beautiful and as you grew up, you got even more beautiful," I said. "It was partly genes and later it was partly cosmology or cosmetology, or whatever the hell you call it. And for all I know it's partly plastic. And you count your beauty as an accomplishment."

She sneered at me, "Are you through?"

"There's more. You come from wealth and because you don't know any different, you've come to believe you earned it. And with all your beauty and with all your money, people treat you like you're special. So that after a while you believe that you are special. That you're entitled. And therefore that you'll never be held to account."

"You don't know shit."

"Beauty and money gave you power over others. But here's the thing, Honey - none of it's real. Your beauty sours on others because eventually the real you shows up."

"How dare you talk to me this way," she screeched.

"Here's another dose of reality, Honey. Your money can disappear in the blink of a real estate crash.

"And your power – that's superficial, too. Because it's not the kind you take. That kind of power is real. Yours is the kind others let you have. And they can take it back at any time.

"And here's one last little secret Honey - the time's coming. Fast. You're about to be knocked back on your ass. Start counting the days."

"Why are you treating me like this?"

"Part of it, I told you on the phone, if you were listening."

"I listened."

"The other part is you're holding back."

"If you're talking about what Carrie Griffith is saying about that accident, that's both bullshit and ancient history."

"I'm talking about Peter Lake. I think you knew he was going to come after Garnet and me. And if that's true, I'll prove it and you'll pay."

"I never..."

"I will make you pay, Honey," I said again. "Unless and this is your only out...unless you decide to tell me where to find Lake."

"How am I supposed to know that?"

"I'm guessing you're still in touch."

"You're guessing wrong."

"I don't think so."

"You don't think so?" she said, mimicking my voice. "Saying something over and over again won't make it true."

"Oh, I think you know."

"You planning to beat the answer out of me? An answer I can't give, by the way. Because I don't fucking know."

I paused a moment, then changed tactics. She was right - this wasn't getting me anywhere.

"Where's your goddamn father, Honey?"

thirty seven

I FOUND TED OLSON IN the clubhouse bar, attached to Collingwood's most exclusive golf course, sitting with a very classy looking woman.

Olson's date looked more sophisticated, more confident than the buxom brunette he had hanging all over him at the Festival VIP dinner. It may have been her blond hair, cut short, and kind of swirling around a face that shone under perfect makeup.

At the same table were the Mayor and Mrs. Mayor.

Olson had scotch or maybe rye straight up. But the rest of the table's drinks were adorned with umbrellas, cherries and celery sticks. I considered asking for a bright red drink with a tall stirstick of matching colour and with little pieces of fruit perched on the lip of the glass but I'm just a simple man. "Does this place serve beer?" I said, inviting myself to the table by pulling up a chair. I waved to the waitress and gave her my order.

Mayor Watson and his wife looked uncomfortable, which bothered me a little because he seemed like a good guy for a politician.

"How the hell did you get in?" Olson said.

"Guy at the front asked me if I was a member and I told him confidentially that you got my daughter pregnant and I needed to discuss the paternity suit."

The prospective trophy wife at his elbow snorted, likely blowing the audition.

"That you helped me once does not entitle you to…"

"Shut up, Olson," I said.

"I will have you thrown out."

"No you won't, Teddy."

"What do you want, Beer?"

"Straight answers."

I took his scowl as a yes.

"Did you and Peter Lake talk about getting rid of two thorny problems?"

"What's that supposed to mean?"

"Garnet Henderson, being thorny problem one. Number two thorny problem would be yours truly."

"I don't know what you're talking about."

"Let me spell it out for you. While Peter still worked at Olson Enterprises, you and he had a heated discussion about Garnet and me. I'm thinking it was about the direction of our investigation. A few days later, we were both near death. I recovered. Garnet didn't. That's what I'm talking about." I tried to sound dead sure of myself, but the truth was, my accusation was dead guesswork.

Before Olson could answer, the Mayor's wife announced her departure.

The Mayor and Olson's date followed suit.

Olson didn't try to stop them. Instead he watched them go and remaining calm, said, "Yes, Lake and I had a discussion. He told me you were looking into the old hit and run accident that some people think involved my daughter. I wanted to stop that."

"So you authorized the attack on Garnet Henderson and me?"

"No, I told Peter we were going to wait. See if anything else happened."

"You didn't wait long."

"I never told him to do a damned thing to you."

"Or Garnet?"

"Or Garnet."

"Convince me."

"This discussion all took place before you told me Lake was after my money. My accountant proved you were right, by the way. But I admit, before that when I heard you were looking at the hit and run…"

"I wasn't."

"Whatever the case, I thought you were and I got mad. I didn't want anybody opening those old wounds. I was going to talk to you, but then you told me what Lake was up to with my money."

"And the attack happened after that?"

"Yes."

"Proving?"

"If it was Lake and Maxwell who attacked you it's because they had reasons of their own. One possibility – you got them fired," he said.

"This doesn't convince me of anything," I said, although I was wavering.

Olson hesitated, whether to concoct a lie or own up, I wasn't sure.

"You're right. I can't prove a damn thing," he said. "You'll have to take my word for it."

"So, the discussion between you two didn't involve violence?"

"No."

"Even on his part?"

"No."

"You never suspected he was going to take a run at me?"

There was another hesitation. "Was it him?"

"You're asking if Peter is the one who took a shot at me? You tell me," I said.

"I'm sorry about what happened to you and Garnet. But, it had nothing to do with me."

I looked at the man, assessing, thinking and I came to a decision. I believed him. Maybe because there was no way to prove otherwise and I wanted the truth out of him on a more important matter.

"You know where Lake is?" I said.

"I don't."

"No theories?"

He shook his head.

"Wild guesses?"

"Not a clue. He just worked for me. We didn't socialize outside the office. Honey might know."

"She might," I said but I had serious doubts. I'd pushed her hard and got nothing.

He tried to look apologetic. Maybe he was.

"Look," I said, forcing my blood pressure the rest of the way down, "I need to figure out what Lake's doing. He's pretty much disappeared. But he can't hide forever. Unless he leaves the country."

"He once mentioned a place in Mexico."

"Details?"

He shook his head.

"What do you know about his financial situation?"

"I was able to get his assets frozen. First step in a civil suit, to recover what he took from me."

"Okay," I said, "but he should have been able to put his hands on some money, right?"

"Who can't come up with a couple grand?"

"He'd need more than that." The cost of creating a new identity had to be in the neighbourhood of ten or fifteen big ones.

"I don't know what else to say, Jack."

I didn't either so I walked away, just as my beer arrived.

thirty eight

BEFORE I REACHED THE CLUBHOUSE exit, Mayor Watson corralled me.

"I was sorry to hear about your accident."

"Did you say, 'accident'? It wasn't an accident, Chuck."

"But Leonard Boroski told me…"

"Boroski's a fool. He knows damn well Garnet Henderson wasn't the only one who was shot."

"Yours wasn't an accident?"

"I was shot too, Chuck. And run off the frigging road. You want to know the score, forget Boroski. Talk to Bronson. "

"I usually do. Look, that's not what I wanted to talk to you about."

"I can hardly wait."

Watson looked hard at me, admonishing me I suppose. As if I gave a damn.

"What's going on between you and Ted?" he said. "He looks worried."

"Olson's got nothing to worry about. Unless he's lying to me…"

"He's no liar, Jack."

"He damn well better not be."

"If only his wife were still alive, she usually fixed things up."

"His wife?"

"Yes…"

Before he finished his sentence, I was on my way out the door, heading back to Connie's Grill.

The restaurant was mostly empty, except for the cook and a waitress who were playing a lackluster game of gin rummy out front, and an older couple reading the local paper, over empty coffee cups. And Maddie and Tiny too, sitting across from each other in a booth, giggling over one of Tiny's lame jokes. I sat beside Maddie because Tiny made his side a tight squeeze.

"I need to talk something through," I said.

Tiny shrugged.

"Why's Peter in hiding?" I said. "Answer: He had to know that if I survived, I'd have a story to tell."

"And because he wasn't able to finish you off while you were flat out on your back in the hospital," said Tiny.

"So, where's he been hiding?"

"Lots of options in these parts," Maddie said. "Off the beaten track B&B's, a couple hundred mom and pop motels, twice as many abandoned farm buildings."

"But he can't hide out forever."

"So far, we're just talking the obvious," Tiny said.

"I know. Have a little patience."

"Wake me when we get there."

"Okay, here's something. I was wrong to think he'd be knocking on Honey's door. Or that he'd tell her anything."

"Because?" said Maddie.

"Because dirt washes off her backside like manure runs off tractor treads in a thunder storm. Then, she finds a new source of dirt to wallow in."

"What's that mean?"

"To Honey, Peter Lake is yesterday's news. She's looking for the next rising star now and it isn't Lake."

"I thought Honey was a suspect in the Hicks murder," Tiny said.

"She was involved somehow, maybe as an instigator," I said. "But with her, it's always someone else does the dirty work. Then she moves on."

"You're saying if Peter showed up at her door, she'd have turned the bastard away." It was Maddie again.

"If he'd turned up there."

"I don't follow."

"Lake not only knows that she'd turn him away, he also knows she might turn him in to the cops."

"How's this help you find Lake?" she said.

"I'm getting to that. If Lake needs something what is it?"

"What?" said Maddie.

Tiny knew where I was going.

"Money," he said.

"And as I said, I had figured he'd go running to Honey, if not for refuge then for money. But now I know he didn't."

"So where would he go?"

"I was just talking to Chuck Watson."

"And?"

"A man gets in trouble, where does he turn? When everything else fails?"

"Where?"

"The wife," I said. "He's goes to the wife."

"Jody Wilcox," Tiny said.

"Exactly."

"What if he's already been there?"

"If he were, I believe we'd have heard," I said.

"What do you mean?" said Maddie.

"She'd have called me."

"Or what if…"

"I'd rather not talk about that particular 'what if,' " I said.

"I'm missing something here, Jack," Tiny said.

"Join the club," I answered him.

"What's bothering you, Jack?" Maddie asked.

"I should have figured Lake would make a move on Jody Wilcox the day he went on the run."

"While you were on your back, unconscious?" Tiny reminded me.

"Doesn't change the facts. She's vulnerable and I let it ride."

"Maybe you're not too late," said Maddie.

"Sure hope not."

• • • • • •

I dialed her number. Thankfully, Jody Wilcox answered.

"Jack Beer," she said. "Of course I remember you."

"How are you? Any developments at your end?"

"You mean with Peter?"

"Yeah."

"No."

"Have you heard from Harry?"

"Funny thing, that. I thought he'd dropped off the face of the earth. It'd been over a month. Then, yesterday, he called."

"What'd he want?"

"I'm making him lunch."

"When?"

"Tomorrow."

"Jody…"

"What is it, Jack?"

Possibilities and strategies tumbled around in my head. Should I tell the cops? But if I did and they showed up, Lake and Maxwell might catch wind and fly. Should I tell Jody to get the hell out of the house? Maybe. But maybe too, I had time to plan a welcoming party for Jody's visitors. Because one thing I knew for damn sure, Harry wasn't coming alone.

"You still there, Jack?"

"Jody, I have some news. Information really."

"About Peter."

"Yeah."

"What is it?"

"It's better if I tell you about it in person."

"Why can't you tell me now?"

"It's easier to explain face to face. I was hoping to come by tomorrow."

"I guess you can. Maybe mid-morning. Before Harry arrives."

"Done. And Jody, if anything happens, you still have my number?"

"Yeah, why? What could happen?"

"Just call me if you need me."

"Okay," she said, sounding confused.

"Bye."

I turned to Tiny, "You carrying?"

"Always. You?"

"Mostly never."

"Still haven't got your license?"

"Left wing government still believes private investigators don't need handguns."

"Meanwhile the terrorists and loonies are free to build their arsenals, since they don't think the law applies to them. You still got your piece though?"

"Yeah."

"We gonna need it?"

"Maybe."

"This one of the exceptions to 'mostly never'?"

"It's in the truck."

"Where we going?"

"Newmarket."

"When?"

"Now."

"I figured."

thirty nine

JODY'S HOUSE WAS A CENTURY home, two storeys, in the oldest part of Newmarket.

It was an excellent location for a stakeout. The houses were close to the street. Ancient maples jammed the boulevards between driveways. Cars and SUVs and small trucks spilled out of the laneways and filled the spaces along the west-side curb. My old Chev pick-up could easily be mistaken for a teenager fixer-upper project, an acceptable fit for the neighbourhood.

The unobstructed sightlines to Jody's front porch gave me confidence I'd be able to see what might come our way.

Tiny was in the backyard, sitting on a lounge chair he liberated from a house one street over. The night shadows made him invisible, unless you knew where to look.

Nothing happened until quarter to eleven when Eric Clapton nearly made me fill my pants. I picked up.

Tiny said, "Got anything to eat in the truck?"

"You took everything I had with you."

"How well do you know Jody?"

"Not well enough to ask 'what's in the fridge.'"

Tiny hung up.

A black SUV turned the corner from a busier street at the next block to the south. It slowed at Jody's house and then continued on by as I sunk lower into my truck cab. I decided the SUV was worth telling Tiny about.

"You find something?" he said.

"Yeah."

"Chocolate bar?"

"No. I think Peter just made an appearance."

"Harry with him?"

"Couldn't be sure," I said. "You got any idea what Jody's doing?"

"Bathroom light went on. Then off. Then on again. And off again. And maybe it happened all over again. Hard to remember."

"Useful to know."

"You're the detail man," he said.

"Anything happen that might actually interest me?"

"After she turned out the bathroom lights for the last time, she went into her bedroom and did some stretching exercises. She was wearing a nightie. You missed the show."

"I meant something that would interest me as a PI."

"You never said she was 'hot.'"

"You forget Maddie already?"

"She's hot, too."

"Anything else?"

"No. She pulled the drapes."

"When was this?"

"Fifteen minutes ago."

"Lights go out?"

"Just before you called."

"Let's get ready for them," I said.

Tiny and I met in Jody's sideyard. I figured the SUV was coming back and our plan was to ambush the bad guys before they reached the doorbell. We stationed ourselves in the flower beds on the far side of Jody's front porch, where we waited.

And waited.

Eventually, Tiny dozed off, leaning back into the lattice which hid the porch's crawlspace. At two in the morning, we switched. Every two hours after that we had a formal changing of the guard. Tiny took his turn at six and

I never heard a thing until a voice woke me around half past the hour.

It was saying, "Jack? Jack Beer, is that you?"

I looked up to see Jody Wilcox, wrapped in a terrycloth robe leaning over the porch rail, red hair looking frizzy and wild, the morning Toronto Star in one hand, a coffee mug in the other. Tiny was right. She was hot.

"Good Lord Jack, what are you doing in my flower bed?"

I tried to stand but my wonky back conspired to shortcircuit the process.

"You been drinking?"

"Wish that was the case, Jody." I struggled to my feet.

Jody screamed.

I turned my head, which didn't help my back any. Tiny appeared from around the corner of the house, zipping up.

"Holy Shit," she said.

"It's okay, Jody," I said. "He's with me. This is my colleague."

"He's kind of a big fellah."

"Thank you ma'am," he said, extending his hand.

She declined the offer. Instead she smiled, covering a grimace and said, "I'm Jody Wilcox."

"Tiny Cole."

"What are you doing here?"

"Jack seems to feel you're in some kind of danger."

"Danger?"

"Yes ma'am, and we're here to protect you."

She turned back to me, "You slept out here?"

I nodded.

"All night?"

"Most of it."

Tiny interrupted us, "You got any food for us, Ma'am?"

We followed Jody Wilcox into the house. Beyond a vestibule, a jog to the right sent you up an oak and pine staircase. A left turn led to a Victorian living room rich in dark greens and maroons. Straight ahead, at the end of a hallway, Tiny spied a clue.

"I'm guessing that refrigerator's in the kitchen," he said.

Jody laughed and followed my monstrous friend. And I followed her.

I passed a second door off the hallway, on the left. Dining room.

It wasn't until I entered the kitchen that I felt the gun. I flinched. The pain shot to my scar near the middle of my back. With his other hand, the gunman shoved me hard into Jody. Tiny held a coffee pot, ready to pitch it. He stepped off the rubber when he saw the handgun.

Jody looked over her shoulder. "Harry, what the hell are you doing?"

"I decided to drop in early," he said.

"We decided to drop in early." Only it wasn't Harry repeating himself.

Jody completed her turn at the sound of the second voice.

"Hello, Jody."

"Peter?" she said. Shock backed her up two steps.

"Yeah. It's me."

Jody Wilcox was white, white the way Robin Hood flour is white.

"You look so different. My God, what happened to you?" she said, her voice almost a whisper. Then, louder, "Why is Harry pointing a gun at us?"

Good question, but nobody was answering.

Harry ordered us out of the kitchen and into an add-on room, a family room/art studio. It had a rustic feel to it; wide pine-paneled walls painted grey, stone floor, sky lights, wood stove, old, comfortable looking couch, throw rugs thrown around, a painter's easel and paintings stacked here and there. It was a cozy space, in décor not at all compatible with gun violence.

While Tiny and I stood, hands on top of our heads, as directed by the muzzle of Harry's Smith and Wesson semi-automatic 9mm, Peter frisked us.

He found nothing on me. But I pictured my own police issue service revolver, snuggling with my crow bar, both securely locked away in my tool box in the bed of my truck. I felt foolish, until I realized my handgun was a million times better off in the back of my truck, parked on the road, than in the hands of the bad guys.

Peter found Tiny's shoulder harness and followed the leather strapping to the holster under his left arm. Peter tucked Tiny's gun in the back of his waistband. And just like that, Tiny was disarmed. Except the wink he threw my way gave me hope, though I couldn't have said why.

Lake ordered Tiny and me to sit on the couch facing him and he motioned Jody toward an armchair, separated from our couch by her easel. Harry moved into position beside Peter. I thought they both looked dead tired, making me wonder where they'd been hiding out.

Peter cleared his throat like he had an announcement to make.

But Jody beat him out the blocks. "How'd you get in?"

"Woman living alone should learn to be more careful," Harry said, pointing with his gun at the door, at the far end of the room, leading to the backyard. "Cat wants out, you lock the door after. Never know who might just walk in."

I caught Peter giving Jody a sideways look. To his credit, maybe Peter was ashamed of himself, embarrassed. "It wasn't supposed to happen like this," is what he said.

"What wasn't supposed to happen?" Jody said. I sensed emotions building in the woman.

Peter hesitated.

"Tell her, Mr. Lake." I threw a lot of sarcasm into my words.

"Shut up, Beer," he said.

"The thing is, Jody," I said, ignoring Peter, "have you ever heard of the condition called 'multiple personalities'?"

"Peter has schizophrenia?"

"Maybe. But what I mean is this: Peter has a variation of the condition."

"Shut up, Beer." Now Maxwell was giving the orders and the gun hanging loosely at his hip was harder to ignore than Lake's mouth.

Still, for some reason, keeping the conversation alive seemed the right thing to do. "You see," I said, "Peter has a bad case of multiple identities. Peter Wilcox, your husband, is one of those identities. In fact, it may be his true identity."

I looked at Harry and then Peter. So far they hadn't decided to shoot me.

"And then," I continued, "a couple of years ago, Peter Lake is what he started calling himself. And that's the way it stayed until recently, like a few weeks ago."

"And now?" Jody asked.

"And now he needs another identity. Don't you, Peter?" I said, which comment he took as an invitation, picking up a vase and throwing it, grazing my temple. I heard the pot break apart when it met the wall behind me.

Jody shook her head, confused, upset, holding back tears. "Where have you been, Peter? What are you doing? Is Jack telling the truth? What do you want?"

"Originally," I said, "Peter just wanted insurance money. See, when you decided to have Peter declared dead, Harry began using his romantic charms on you. Maybe marriage was in the stars, along with the associated paperwork, like the redrafting of your will. To be honest though, I don't know what you see in the guy."

Jody looked at me and then at Harry, a guy whose face had what amounted to a look of admission. Whether that was an acknowledgement of his deadly plans for Jody or his bad luck with women I couldn't tell.

"Well," I said, "now you know Harry's an asshole."

"Shut up." This time Harry did point the Smith and Wesson at me.

"I don't get it, Peter. What's Jack talking about?" she said.

"Are you listening, girl? They were gonna kill you and split the insurance money you collected on Peter's staged death," Tiny said, prompting Harry to change targets.

"Insurance fraud was just one of a number of schemes," I said. "Peter's quite entrepreneurial."

"Is this true, Peter?"

"No," he managed to say, convincing no one.

"But it is true," I said. "And in case you haven't noticed, people are figuring you out faster than the stock market's rebounding. Let's make a list; fraud, assault, murder, jaywalking."

Jody's jaw dropped. "Murder?"

"And attempted murder. That's why Peter's on the run," I said.

Jody's face changed again. The full impact of the story finally slammed her in the gut. Taking a minute to collect herself, she asked her husband, "What do you want?"

"I need help, Jody."

"No," she said. "Why are you here? Today? Right now? What do you want from me? Exactly what?"

"He needs money," I said. "As much as you can put together."

"What for?" She was asking me now, because I was the only one answering her questions.

"He needs a new name and a passport. And other identity papers, all fool proof, all phony. And all of that stuff requires money, lots of money. The people who make this stuff don't come cheap. And on top of that guess what

- he needs still more money. Cash. Cash for bribes, for contingencies. And I don't think he plans to pay any of it back."

"Where's he going?"

"Mexico. He's got a place down there, And a stash too, money he can't get hands on right now, not from here anyhow."

"What about Harry?"

"Needs money for the same reasons."

"Is Jack right, Peter?" she said.

Peter said, "Yes."

"How much?"

"You'll have to empty your bank accounts. And sell some mutual funds."

"I don't have much."

"It will be enough."

"Then what?"

"He'll kill you," I said. "Or Harry will."

Harry stormed over to where I was sitting and poked me with the barrel of his gun. In the temple. The same temple which a minute ago deflected a vase off to the side. "Shut the fuck up," he said, "or you die now."

"Bullshit. You kill me now, the neighbours will hear, and they'll call the cops. Kill me before you finish conducting your business? Not smart, Harry. Ain't gonna happen." My argument was valid but not valid enough to remove his gun from my head.

Jody's face was red now, with anger.

"Is he telling the truth, Peter? Are you going to kill us?"

He wouldn't look at her. Jody stared alternately at her husband and at Harry.

"Where do you keep your papers? Bank books," Peter said, moving to a small roll top desk. "Still in here?"

"I said, 'are you going to kill me,' you goddamn son of a bitch?"

Harry turned his head toward Peter, maybe wondering what he would say by way of an answer. And he didn't notice Jody picking up the knife, a razor knife, the kind artists use for trimming canvases. Her hand and the knife were not in his peripheral vision. So, he also didn't see Jody thrusting that razor knife from below, like an uppercut, deep into his forearm.

Harry's arm flew up and he shot the skylight dead.

Glass fell all around us.

A split second behind Jody's surprise move, Tiny whipped a stiletto out of a sleeve in his motorcycle boot and in the same motion flung the steel at Harry's head. Blood sprayed me as Harry dropped his gun and reached with both hands for the blade, buried deep in his neck.

Peter made a grab for Tiny's gun, jammed into the back of his waist band. But it was an awkward move and it gave me all the time I needed to dive over a coffee table and drive into his mid-section with my shoulder. We fell into the wood stove. The back of his head met with the cast iron door. The fireplace utensils spilled over. Peter grunted in shock and pain but the small man had a powerful constitution, and a build to match. Out of a tangle of legs and arms, he wrapped me up in a headlock.

I struggled, without success, to slide my head out while I pounded my left fist into his gut, all the while worrying about the whereabouts of the gun. Until I saw it momentarily, as we rolled on the floor. It was resting beside the back left leg of the wood stove

Feeling more hopeful, I switched hands and went for a kidney with my right fist. Lake moaned softly and his arm loosened a little. I squirmed away – it felt like I left my ears in his armpit - and bellyflopped across the floor trying for the fire poker. But Peter had the same idea.

I got there first but I only managed to push it out of reach.

At close quarters again, in a vicious embrace, we traded jabs and gouges and chops. When I elbowed him in the face, he went for my throat. I grabbed his arm with my left hand and swept the floor for a weapon with my right. Finding nothing, I squirmed onto my back, pulling him with me.

Eventually and somehow, my hand found a piece of firewood, which I decided might make a good club. As a test, I wacked him in the ear with it. But our close proximity reduced the force of my swing and the damage was minimal. Still the blow was enough to cause him to abandon his efforts to strangle me.

I scrambled away, got to my feet and readied myself to face off against him again.

But time froze. We stood like two wrestlers, noses twenty four inches apart, each looking for a weakness to exploit. For a takedown.

A guttural groan from Harry across the other side of the room gave me the moment's distraction I was looking for. I threw my best right cross, catching Lake in the mouth. A tooth hit the window and a swelling appeared on his lip before he could get the word 'ouch' out.

Except he didn't say 'ouch,' maybe because he was stunned. Or maybe he was asking, 'where did everything go wrong?' No matter, I followed up the advantage by kicking his balls through the uprights fifty yards down-field.

Peter Lake squeal-groaned, taking to the fetal position. For Garnet's sake, I prayed I killed him. But I knew these kind of prayers are seldom answered. So, not wanting to go another round and in case he wore a hockey cup, I picked up the fire poker and drove the sharp end into his right knee. I heard breaking and sensed tearing. I should have checked on him – I thought he passed out - but I had trouble taking my eyes away from his ruined knee, nearly throwing up.

Three quarters of the fight was over.

Peter Lake was incapacitated and Harry Maxwell's wound was a bad one. Near the back door, an oscillating fountain of blood spewed from Harry's neck, but he wasn't down. Tiny was holding him upright with his left hand and he was thrashing him with his right. He put his shoulder into every punch and each time Harry's head snapped back. And I heard bones in his nose and around his eyes splintering.

"Tiny," I said. "Enough."

Tiny looked at me and then back at Harry Maxwell, his head lolling loosely to one side. Tiny shook the big man and when his head came up, he spit in Harry's face, his head then falling back.

Tiny let him go and watched him crumble to the floor, his head bouncing on the stone tile. He half rolled before gravity caused a reversal and he settled onto his back. His left hand came up and then it flopped back down.

"That fucker's dead," Tiny said.

"Looks like."

"Let's finish the other one."

I thought about Garnet Henderson, confined to a bed. Forever. And I thought of Carrie Griffith. And I damn near said, "Yes."

forty

I COULDN'T FIND JODY. UNTIL I heard a low squeal and looked behind the couch. She was on her haunches, hands squeezing her ears, keeping the madness out. Blood splatter stained her bathrobe and darkened her hair on one side. Panic distorted each breath she took.

"Jody," I said, bent over and inches away, talking directly into her face.

"Is it over?" she asked.

"Yes. You want to come out?"

"No," she said, her heading shaking madly.

"Okay." I said, leaving her to try and steady her heart rate. I told Tiny to dial 911.

He looked at me, still breathing and sweating heavily. "Our story straight?" he asked.

"Self-defense, all the way," I said.

He opened his cell phone.

I felt like collapsing. Instead I checked Peter's pulse. It was strong. Soon, the pain that made him pass out would wake him up and he'd faint again. Or, he'd writhe around on the floor screaming for relief.

Either way it wasn't my problem.

Harry Maxwell was still on his back. He hadn't moved. His forehead was a milky white. Otherwise his face and neck were a bloody pulp. The spreading pool of blood told me our first diagnosis was wrong. He wasn't dead but he only had minutes to go, unless he got help, fast.

My conclusion about his condition resurrected some fundamental belief, nearly forgotten in the carnage. I shrugged off my sweatshirt, tossed it aside and tore my t-shirt off my body. Kneeling, I placed a hand on his chest. Harry's breathing was shallow and it was a bad sign that the fountain from his neck wound had nearly petered out. I pressed my cotton shirt into the area around the stiletto, rejecting the natural urge to pull it out but wondering whether the pressure would do more harm than good.

Whatever the answer, I sensed, no matter what, Harry Maxwell wasn't going to make it.

Tiny knew it too. "Forget it, Jack," he said. "The man's no more."

"Gotta try," I said, as I tested his weakening pulse again.

Fifteen minutes later the police arrived, guns drawn. Six of them.

For the second time that day, Tiny and I found ourselves standing, our hands reaching for the ceiling. I tried to convey our self-defense argument as we were being cuffed. Tiny kept his mouth shut because he knew nobody was listening.

They collected the two handguns, Harry's nearly overlooked among a dozen or so paint brushes and paint tubes, beside a knocked down easel. They found Tiny's where I last saw it, under the wood stove.

Then like a jack in the box, Jody stood up in the middle of all this activity and let go a wail, spooking our captors and me too, even though I knew she was there. Thankfully, no one tasered her.

Once the scene was secured, one of the cops went back for the paramedics. Another radioed for a senior officer.

A female attendant rushed over to Peter. Following a two minute assessment she said, "Vitals are stable. Serious leg wound. We're not going to extract the goddamn poker someone stabbed him with. Not here. But it's going to be very awkward moving this guy. I need to immobilize the leg," she said.

"Don't you be complaining, girlie. The idea was to immobilize more than his frigging leg," Tiny said.

"Shut up," the cop nearest told him.

The male half of the medical team was still bent over Harry, when all of a sudden, he started pounding Harry's chest. "I lost him. Get the AED in here."

The defibrillator did him not a lick of good. Because he was almost done even before the cops arrived. The guy just bled out.

Jody, Tiny and I were taken away in separate squad cars. At the station, we each dictated statements. The cops let Jody go. But they kept Tiny and me for tougher questioning. Still, our stories must have compared favorably, because in three hours we were released too.

forty one

TWO DAYS LATER FROM A hospital bed, still in excruciating pain, Peter Lake-Wilcox learned the Newmarket detachment of the York Regional Police laid a dozen charges, which distilled down, amounted to kidnapping of Jody Wilcox and assault on Tiny and me.

Back in Collingwood, Peter was charged with fraud, which was given more attention than his other crimes. Sheila was miffed that there was a debate on whether to pin him with attempted murder for his attacks on Garnet Henderson and me. While he was dragging his feet on that one, Boroski hit me with a summons to appear before a magistrate, alleging I obstructed the police in the performance of their duties. Apparently, I was in violation of the Criminal Code for not revealing my suspicions sooner that the driver and passenger in the SUV that ran me over the edge of the Niagara Escarpment were Lake and Harry Maxwell. Hughie said that it was a bluff and that my temporary amnesia defense would prevail.

Speaking of poor Harry, he escaped all charges, which according to Tiny, only seemed right as he was too busy being prepped for burial.

Meanwhile, Bronson, the only cop willing to have a decent conversation with me, told me his colleagues were reviewing the file, re-interviewing witnesses and meeting with the Crown Attorney. The consensus was that the murder of Dwayne Curtis Hicks should be added to the long list of infractions otherwise known as the Peter Lake crime wave. All that was missing was the slam dunk proof.

A week later, Lake was carted off from the hospital bed to jail and that same day, Jody Wilcox phoned to thank Tiny and me for saving her life. And then, another week after that, Jody and I paid a visit to Mrs. O'Connor, Lake's one-time foster mother. We broke the news her one-time foster son was in jail.

"Maybe he'll get the help he needs there," she said, ever the optimist.

As we left the old dear, Jody promised she'd stay in touch which as much as anything else in the case, left me with the sense that my efforts may have resulted in some good, however small, for someone deserving.

Tiny stayed around for nearly a month, until one day he announced it was time for him to get out of our hair.

For our farewell party, Sheila cooked up a pan of her world famous lasagna, a dish which always tastes better the second night, not that I ever mention anything of the sort. But thanks to Tiny, there were no leftovers for me to confirm my theory the next night. After dinner, over Tiny's seventh, my third and Sheila's second beer, we rehashed the case.

"If there's a God, he faces hard time for what he did to Garnet," I said.

"And to you," said Sheila.

"They got enough to convict?" Tiny asked.

"They're damn slow getting around to it, but I hear ballistics show it was Lake's gun that shot Garnet," I said.

"What about the bullet hit you?"

"It's somewhere north of that crossroads…"

"Kemble?"

"Yeah, it's lodged in a tree or it's under a rock at the bottom of the escarpment. Doubt it'll turn up. But they're assuming I was wounded with the same gun."

"They know who the shooter was?"

"I know," I said. "It was Harry. He was using the Smith and Wesson."

"You saw his face?"

"The smaller one was driving."

"That helps Lake?" Tiny said.

"Doesn't matter who the shooter was. Legally, they were equally responsible. And even though he didn't pull the trigger, don't go feeling sorry for the bastard. Lake's guilty of plenty of crimes," I said. "He stole big bucks from Olson Enterprises and he clearly planned to off his wife for the insurance. As a kid, I don't doubt he tortured kittens and as a teenager, he likely killed his own brother for his parents' estate."

Sheila said she was glad it was over. We drank to that and to each other. And then we drank to Garnet and to the Tigers. When we ran out of things to drink to, I asked one of the questions that nagged at me. "So, anybody want to tell me exactly why Lake killed Hicks."

"He did it," Tiny said. "And after that, who the fuck cares about anything else?"

"Me."

"Why?"

"Can't help myself sometimes, man. Stuff gets under my skin. And I need to dig it out or it festers."

"You want goddamn motive? How about this: he wanted Honey or, he wanted Daddy's money, or both. Just pick one of the three of 'em. And then, move on."

"Just getting reflective."

"Find a new frigging case to reflect on," Tiny said, belching again to mark the end of the conversation.

forty two

THE NEXT MORNING, SHEILA AND I waved Tiny away.

Sheila got busy with the coffee shop.

And I should have been busy too, passing time with customers, making coffee, cleaning the kitchen, running errands. But I was unsettled, edgy. The case was closed but there was no satisfaction. And Hughie had sent no new cases my way to fill the void.

"Take the bike. Go somewhere," Sheila told me, one day over breakfast. Only she said it with a big sigh.

"Where?"

"Just get out of my hair for a while."

"I'd be doing you a favour?"

She just smiled. So, I fired up my motorcycle.

Deciding to poke along through Huron County and the Bruce, I drove to Exeter first where I turned north to a crossroads named Kippen. From there, I followed the dead country roads that go through Seaforth and Walton. And then, I pulled over at Cinnamon Jim's in the Village of Brussels, for soup and a sandwich, which I followed-up with a massage, two doors uptown.

Thankfully, as the boomers age, decent coffee shops along with physiotherapy clinics can be found in the sleepiest corners of the world. On the downside, country taverns are gradually disappearing. You take the good with the bad.

From Brussels, I entered Bruce County and found still other ways to soothe my troubled soul, visiting hidden gems called Chepstow, Cargill and Pinkerton, old mill towns on the tributaries of the Saugeen River.

In the early afternoon I took another break, this time on the back porch of a tiny restaurant in the village of Paisley, in the middle of a downtown that looked like a postcard from 1914.

I dug out my binoculars and spent an hour testing my bladder capacity with a half dozen coffee refills while trying to pin down the flycatchers in the thick tree cover between me and the river. Eventually I disqualified the Alder and Willow and settled on the Least Flycatcher. The conclusion brought me a measure of the satisfaction that I'd been missing of late.

When the server expressed surprise I was still hanging around, I decided I'd eaten up more than enough time and resumed my journey up the spine of the Southern Bruce. I turned east at Burgoyne, eventually making my way via Tara and Inglis Falls until my route became a gravel run, reminding me of the outing Garnet and I never got around to. I returned to civilization at Thornbury, a short jaunt from Collingwood.

As I approached the front door of the nursing home, new digs for Garnet, a place that I hoped beat the hospital all to hell, I had to work hard to hold onto the buoyant mood that came from biking cross-country. But my spirit took a body blow at the sounds of an institutional kitchen on my left and the sight of a dozen women 'lounging' on my right, their eyes distant and their heads nodding forward. Three or four men, bodies worn out, slouched over as well, in the same common room. The smell of bodily fluids and antiseptic cleansers filled the spaces my eyes and ears missed.

My only hope for recovery from the letdown was to find Garnet sitting up in bed, with a beer in his hand, and another waiting for me, in a cooler beside his bed. At the very least, I needed him to be off the ventilator.

I knocked and Carrie Griffith opened the door.

"Jack," she said.

"How is he?"

"Same."

"Damn."

"Yeah, I know."

"How's Rob?"

"Same."

"Damn."

"No kidding."

The bathroom door swung open and Penny Sue Stanfield walked out.

"Jack," she said.

"You two come together?"

"Carrie's old Plymouth needs brakes," Penny Sue said.

Carrie sat beside Garnet at the top of the bed. And before I could move, Penny Sue took the only other chair at the foot, like she had a prior claim. She looked at me, trying, I thought, to make me feel like an intruder. Carrie's smile was a stew of resignation, sadness and relief. The resignation and sadness I was familiar with. I guessed the relief was in having someone else in the room besides a comatose father and a woman who was borderline nuts. I hoped as well there was a coffee spoon of gladness in her heart at my arrival.

"I'll sit on the bed. You take my chair," Carrie said. As we jockeyed by each other she pecked my cheek and squeezed my hand. An emotional charge brought a lump to my throat and mist to my eyes.

Before I got comfortable, Penny Sue cleared her throat, like an announcement was on the way. And it was. "I want to say something to you, Jack Beer," she said, redundantly.

"What is it?"

"If it weren't for you…"

"Penny Sue, don't you dare," Carrie said.

"I'm only saying, Garnet would still be …"

"Damn it, if it weren't for Jack, Dad would have kept spiraling."

"I never saw much difference."

"He was finding himself again, working with Jack, and you damn well know it, Penny Sue."

I got the feeling this was an old argument, one that likely started the day after Garnet was shot. And until now, I would have agreed a hundred percent with Penny Sue. Garnet Henderson would be whole, if not for me. But now, I had another point of view to consider and I was thankful to Carrie for it.

"How's the case going against Lake?" Carrie asked me.

"He's going down for the assault on Garnet."

"What about Hicks?"

"I don't know."

"Bronson says they have good circumstantial evidence," Penny Sue said.

"Good," I said.

"Damn right it's good."

I looked at Penny Sue.

"You don't play poker do you?" I said.

"What's that supposed to mean?"

"Your face, Penny Sue," said Carrie.

"What about my face?"

"You're happy, it's in your face," Carrie said. "You're upset, everyone can tell. You're angry, that's the easiest one."

"So, we're head to head on the last draw and you fill an inside straight," I said, "and I'd know. I'd read it." Although at other times I couldn't even begin to figure the woman out.

"You'd read it in my face?"

"Right."

"And you can tell by looking at me, I'm mad at Peter Lake?"

"You're mad about something and the subject came up. Two plus two." I decided against mentioning she looked ready to decapitate someone.

"Well, goddamn it, he put Garnet here. He deserves to rot in hell."

And here I thought she only blamed me.

"And he probably killed Hicks," I said.

"Who gives a damn about that jerk?"

"Hicks? What'd you have against him?" I asked her, though I looked Carrie's way when I posed the question.

"I'm not crazy about any of the pretenders," Penny Sue said.

"He sang all right."

"There were better."

"But?"

"He was stealing from Elvis."

"Stealing?"

"Yes. Stealing. They all steal from Elvis; his voice, his songs, his hair, his clothes. None of it works. They're all phonies."

I looked at Carrie who was shaking her head.

"Hell," said Penny Sue. "Hicks couldn't even die authentically."

"Right," I said. "Elvis died of an allergic reaction to his prescription. Isn't that what you told me?"

"Or, he was a junkie and just overdosed," Carrie threw into the mix.

"Elvis wasn't stabbed to death in all events." Penny Sue glared at Carrie.

All conversation ended on that happy note.

I lasted five more minutes. Then I stood and took Garnet's hand and squeezed gently, praying for a response. There was none.

I kissed the top of Carrie's head and her arms encircled me as I stood over her.

When she let me go, I eased by Penny Sue. She looked away, like there was a picture of Elvis, wearing boxer shorts, taped to the wall that she couldn't take her eyes off. At least she didn't stick her foot out and trip me.

forty three

OCTOBER ARRIVED ON A THURSDAY and Grand Bend's Main Street was as dead as the decomposing corpse of Collingwood Elvis. In a month the village would be even deader. The PI business was dead, too. I guess there weren't any new insurance scammers walking around with the idea they're too smart to be caught. I was okay with that. At the coffee shop, the cash register drawer rusted away in the closed position.

Sheila and I fell into our comfortable routines. The snail's pace gave us time for dinners at Nick's Greek Restaurant, for movies in London and for books on our beat-up couch. And I found extra running time in the shelter of Southcott Pines, a beautiful neighborhood built into Lake Huron's sand dunes.

A week after the doctors warned me for the tenth time not to expect any progress, Carrie phoned to report Garnet started to breathe on his own. Occasionally, she said, he opened his eyes, too. But while his lips moved and sounds came out, he said nothing and, as far we knew, his eyes saw nothing whenever they happened to be open.

Still, his daughter spoke in hopeful phrases, with an optimism that was just what she needed. Even with that, there was no escaping her burdens.

I was a lot luckier. I had my escapes. And Sheila, she never needed any. We were back in Grand Bend, home.

Standing back from it, I should have been as content as Sheila. And for the most part I was, aside from the dull ache I felt in my lower back on cold damp mornings and the nagging sense of unease that came with it, like I'd missed something.

Of course, something usually is missing. In my experience, no case ends perfectly.

Sure, I'd plucked Sheila's brother from the deep end. And Harry Maxwell had been 'dispatched', while Peter Lake faced major prison time. Two very bad guys were no longer a threat to decent people. Lake stood to be thoroughly punished for what he did to Garnet and to Jody Wilcox and, I hoped, for killing Curtis Dwayne Hicks. I didn't care as much about the damage Lake did to Ted Olson's bottom line.

The case was closed. But that wasn't enough.

Distilling down all the psycho-analytical musings Sheila threw at me, I realized I needed to take another run at the file…. if I only knew how to go at it. But I didn't. It was like stalking a warbler in the spring foliage. You hear it. You almost see it. But it's too small and too far away and the shadows are too deep. And it won't stay still except for a split second, but not so you can zero in with your binoculars. By the time you close in, it's gone.

I'd been so damned close to finding that pesky little clue, the one on which the whole case pivots. Then, the last elusive piece to the puzzle flies off. Gone forever.

That's how it was, until one day a missing piece turned up, that final, pivotal clue. Or maybe it wasn't. Maybe it was just a common yellowthroat, interesting but not newsworthy. At the least, it was something to consider, to study, to see where it fit and if it fit. Or to learn it wasn't even worth a journal entry.

It was a particularly slow morning at the coffee shop, a Tuesday, and I was planted by the front window when a car pulled up to the curb, interrupting my view of the street and the stores opposite. A man got out the driver's side.

"Fat Elvis," I said, loud enough to let Sheila know what we were in for.

"Jack, you promised."

"Is that your brother?" I said, real quick, remembering my pledge to discard the nickname. "And is that his wife?"

"You know damn well it is," she said, shaking her head at me.

"That Lori. She better not try prancing around my coffee shop, showing off her cleavage. What will the customers say?"

Sheila made a fist and went to the door for the obligatory hugs.

The exchange of niceties out of the way, they descended on me, the consolation being the fresh butter tarts and coffee Sheila brought out for them. Lori was dressed like a librarian and Mike looked like an accountant on a day off - their version of a makeover.

Two tarts and half a coffee later, Mike Mackie got down to business.

"I never did thank you properly," he said.

"For?"

"For pulling my ass out of the fire."

"I like to think I rescued you from the trash heap."

"Your cliché's stupid," he said. Sheila sided with her brother.

"They charge Peter with the murder?" I asked, for the sake of conversation. I already knew the answer.

"They're heading that way. But the main thing is this, Jack - Boroski told me he doesn't believe it was me. He said the Crown wants to drop the investigation."

"The investigation of you," I said, feeling a need to clarify.

"Yeah," Mike said, as if that's all that mattered.

"If that's what Boroski said, better put Hughie back on the clock," I cracked, sneaking a look at Lori, wondering if she planned to remove her high necked cardigan. The weather hadn't deteriorated enough yet to warrant putting tank tops into winter storage. Or to fasten so many buttons.

"Anyway," Mike said, "if it wasn't for you…"

"Sheila made me do it," I said.

"I know. Still," Mike said, "here." And he handed me an envelope.

There was a cheque inside. I peeked and saw a four followed by three zeroes.

"I understand you didn't really have a paying client."

It seemed like the wrong time to mention the bonus Olson paid me.

"You don't have to do that, Mike," Sheila said. "We're family."

I put the cheque in my wallet.

"Give it back, Jack," Sheila said.

"No," Mike said. Lori didn't seem to have an opinion.

"I agree with Mike," I said. And that settled it.

After Sheila politely asked her brother and sister-in-law to stay for dinner and after they politely declined, our guests made fidgeting movements that suggested they wanted to leave. Lori went off to 'freshen up.' I thought of turning the thermostat up, hopeful she'd change into something lighter than a sweater.

As I was busy picturing his wife's new outfit, Mike wrestled his bouncing foot into submission and came to a decision. He leaned close, "I have a question, Jack."

"No, you can't have the money back," I said.

"I'm serious."

"Me too."

"What did the cops do with Collingwood Elvis' sash?"

"What sash?"

"The one wrapped around his neck."

I looked at him and said, "I thought you were putting all this stuff behind you."

"Just curious."

"Well," I said, "it's likely still in the evidence room."

"At the Collingwood police station?"

"That's right."

"Do you think Penny Sue's been asking for it?"

I looked hard at the guy to be sure I understood the question. Meanwhile, Lori came back, disappointing me. In fact, now her buttons were fastened all the way to the top.

"What?" I said.

"You heard me," Mike said. "Has Penny Sue Stanfield been trying to get her hands on the sash?"

"I wouldn't know. More important, why do you care?"

"Just wondering."

"Nah Mike, there's more to it than that."

He hesitated and then confiding in me, "It's valuable."

"The sash is valuable?" I stifled a laugh. "Why's that?"

"It's like the holy grail."

"What?'

"Maybe I'm exaggerating a little but it is an original."

"Original? What's that mean?"

"It belonged to Elvis."

"You mean Elvis Presley?"

"The king himself."

'No way."

"It's true."

"How do you know?'

"The provenance was impeccable. When Hicks and I were on speaking terms he showed me the paperwork. In fact, Elvis had his initials embroidered into it."

"Maybe it belonged to Eddie Penfold."

"Who's Eddie Penfold?"

"Guy I went to high school with."

Sheila laughed at that one. Lori didn't and Mike looked at me like I'd lost my marbles.

"Well, I'm just saying," he said, "it's a shame if it's just sitting there in the police station."

"And you think Penny Sue's been asking for it?"

"If she knows it's there, I'm thinking she'd try to get a hold of it. She's obsessive."

"You're right about that."

forty four

I COULDN'T SHAKE MIKE'S QUESTIONS about the Elvis sash. Was it a clue, a TSN turning-point kind of clue that would lead to resolution? Or was it the warbler conundrum all over again? You know the darn thing's there but you can't see it. The little bird won't sit still and the leaves are too dense. So it teases you, singing a song that you can't identify. But because you know it's there, somewhere, you don't give up. You keep looking.

I knew that's what I had to do, look again. But harder this time, more carefully. I had to figure out what the sash meant. Mike and Penny Sue were both interested in its disposition. Should I be surprised? They were both Elvis obsessed. But my gut told me it wasn't so simple. And I knew this: there was more to Hicks' murder than the police knew. They missed something and it had to do with the sash. For Garnet's sake - Carrie's too - I had to find out.

On the lonely autumn highways between Grand Bend and Collingwood, I went over my conversation with Mike, knocking his words around. Until the frustration spilled over and I told myself to let the answers come to me. So, before seeing Garnet I pulled into Connie's, hoping Maddie would know something, say something, anything that might blow the analytical embers to life. Except the first face I saw was one I'd rather have dodged. The man dipped a French fry in a pool of ketchup.

"The fuck you looking at?" he said. His attitude toward me hadn't changed much from the day I watched Carrie Griffith knock him on his backside at the Heart Breakers tavern.

"Hey J.D., can I have a fry?"

"Get stuffed."

"Just one."

He gave me the finger. Then he mumbled something into his plate. It may have been, "Thought you left for good."

"And I thought you might have found the money for a personality transplant."

He snarled, picked up the vinegar bottle from beside his plate and cocked his arm. I grabbed a ketchup bottle. Trouble was mine was plastic.

"Boys!" It was Maddie. She held out her phone, at arm's length. She was pressing buttons.

I stopped in mid wind-up. So did J.D.

"911?" she said. "I'm calling from Connie's."

"Piss on it," J.D. growled. He tossed his vinegar bottle onto his fries, picked up his hat and walked out the door.

"Did you pay?" I called after him.

"Forget it," Maddie said. I hoped her words were meant for the dispatcher.

She put the phone down, shaking her head. Then she grinned, came around the counter, gave me a hug and asked how Tiny was doing, leaving me with the feeling the hug wasn't really for me.

"Tiny's fine."

"That's good."

"You two in touch?"

"He calls."

"Often?"

"Yeah. Says he wants me to come up to Ottawa and visit."

"You should."

Maddie looked into my eyes like she was searching for answers. "I can't leave the restaurant," she said.

"It'll still be here when you get back."

"What if I don't come back?" Her forehead creased but she looked happy, expectant.

"Maybe that'll be a good thing for both of you."

"Thanks, Jack." This time the hug was for me.

"You're welcome."

"Coffee?"

"And pie."

"How's cranberry, apple, raisin sound?"

"Is that one pie or three?"

"One."

"It needs a simpler name."

"It's too good to change one damn thing about it."

"With ice cream?"

She smiled and nodded.

I knew she'd cure me.

When I finished, Maddie poured me a refill and sat down. She asked after Sheila, mentioning that I was a lucky man. I mentioned Sheila was a lucky woman. She laughed like I wasn't serious. Then we talked about Garnet and we compared notes on his condition. We worried over Carrie's emotional state and we grimaced over Penny Sue's weird behaviour.

Then I asked her if J.D. had been giving Carrie any grief.

"No," she said. "But how'd you happen to know J.D. Morgan?"

"I'd prefer we never met. I didn't even know his last name until just this minute."

"Well, remember it, Jack. In case you want to look him up. He knows something."

Another damn warbler.

"What's that supposed to mean? Even Sheila's brother, Fat Elvis, knows something."

"About the murder?"

"Yeah, Mike knows something but he doesn't realize it."

"Well, J.D. knows something and I think he knows he does."

"We are talking about the Hicks murder, right?"

"No one calls him that anymore."

"Collingwood Elvis?"

"Yeah. It's all about the town's image."

"Calling a dead guy Collingwood Elvis is good for the town image?"

"Yeah."

"What about the murder? What's J.D. know?"

"I don't know."

"Then I'll tell you. He knows squat."

"Maybe."

I thought about it for a while. Then I said, "Any details?"

"Just that I heard he was blowing a lot of hot air one night at a bar."

"And?"

"He was bragging he knew how it went down."

"What do you think?"

"Drunks I know talk too much."

"And two thirds of it is bullshit."

"But the other third isn't," she said. And that was the truth.

I left Maddie's and went looking for J.D. at his favourite bar. The Heart Breakers was half full. Other than Garth, the bartender, I recognized nobody. So I quizzed Garth, but he hadn't seen the guy in a couple days.

I looked him up in the book and dialed his home. A woman with a husky voice said he'd gone for lunch and then he was leaving with a full load of hogs for a meat packer down Toronto way. Wouldn't be back for a couple of days.

Used to loose threads that unravel all the way and fall to the floor, I gave Honey Hicks a call. Something Penny Sue said during one of my visits with Garnet put together with Mike's strange comments about the woman and the Elvis sash tweaked a renegade brain cell.

"Honey?"

"Who's this?"

Expecting a hang up, I hesitated to say, 'Jack Beer.'

"Who is this?" she repeated.

"Inspector Boroski," I said, finding an inspiration.

"What is it? Aren't you finished the investigation yet?"

"Just a small matter, Ms. Hicks."

"It's Ms. Olson now, inspector."

"Right, easier without the hyphen."

"What's the question?"

"Was your husband allergic to any of the medications he was taking?"

"Medications?"

"Okay, the drugs." I guessed the cops knew Hicks used a wide range of pharmaceuticals. "Was he allergic to any of them?"

"If he had allergies, I never noticed."

Damn, I thought. My batting average keeps getting worse and worse.

It was almost as an after-thought I asked her, "Were there any medical conditions?"

"No."

"Thanks," I said.

"Oh wait," she said.

"What?"

"He had high blood pressure."

I hung up and made my way to the nursing home. I needed somewhere quiet. I needed someone to talk to. Someone like Garnet Henderson.

<u>forty five</u>

I TALKED MY HEAD OFF BUT Garnet still wasn't saying much. So I went home, to Grand Bend, for a more thorough consult.

Over stifado with fried potatoes and Greek salad on the side, I confessed, "Sheila, I made a mistake."

"You'll get over it. You always do. Comes from practice."

"This is a big one."

"How big?"

"First, answer me a question. Why would Peter Lake attack me and Garnet?"

"This is old territory."

"Indulge me, Babe."

"Okay. The way I see it, he had to take you out. You had him in your sights for the murder of Hicks."

"Okay. Put that to the side for the moment."

"Why?"

"As I said, humour me. Any other reason?"

"Come on Jack, let it go."

"Was it because I exposed him as a fraud?"

"And you found out about the scam he was pulling on Jody Wilcox. And for all he knew, you uncovered something about his role in his brother's death. Maybe even in the fire that killed his parents."

"That's what I thought too but those explanations are too easy."

"How so?"

"There's no way he knew I was talking to Jody. Same with whatever I found out on his brother. Or the fire. He couldn't have known I knew one damn thing. Not at the time he took at run at me."

"We're back to the Hicks murder then. You were about to expose him as the killer."

"That makes sense...."

"But?"

"But, that's the mistake."

"The mistake?"

"I was off target," I said. "Way off."

"I don't see it."

"Okay, here's another question: what was his motive for offing Hicks?"

"To get to Olson's money through Honey," Sheila said.

"That's what Tiny said. And I thought so too. But it doesn't stand up. At best, it's a weak theory."

"But Lake had a clear path to Honey and her daddy's money with the husband out of the way."

"Maybe, but he was getting there anyway."

"Meaning?"

"He was smooth. I'm thinking Honey would have left Dwayne for Peter Lake. No fuss or muss."

"At least not the kind that goes with murder."

"That's my point."

"So there was some motive we didn't know," Sheila said. "Something to do with their affair. Something to do with jealousy and revenge."

"Unlikely. They all slept around."

"What are you telling me?"

"Lake didn't have any reason to kill the guy."

"Come on, Jack. Of course he did."

"No, listen. There's something else that doesn't fit. Look at how Hicks was killed."

"What do you mean?"

"Peter Lake's smart. A planner. He always covered his tracks."

"And he wasn't smart the way he killed Hicks?" Sheila said.

"No, he wasn't. Sure, he was capable of it. And as you said, Hicks' death served his purpose. Maybe that's what threw me off. But the fact he benefited doesn't mean he did it. We tied Hicks' murder and the shootings of Garnet and me together. But that was a coincidence."

"He didn't kill Hicks?"

"I don't believe he did."

"What changed your mind?"

"Why would he throw caution to the wind and kill him when he was making good progress with Honey and her father? Besides…"

"Oh yeah. You're thinking even if he saw an advantage in killing Hicks, there were smarter ways to do it? And because it was a dumb way to do it, he couldn't have?"

"When he planned everything else so well, why choose to kill a local celebrity in a place where there are hundreds of people coming and going?"

"Peter Lake was known to all the festival insiders," she said.

"So he chooses a place where he was bound to be seen by people who can identify him? It doesn't add up. Why didn't he wait until the festival was over? He could have done it when there was no one around. He could have made it look like an accident."

Sheila stared into her empty plate.

"So Sheila, I have to ask myself why the son of bitch suddenly got stupid."

"Okay, if he didn't kill Hicks, because he was too smart to do it that way, you have to explain why he took a run at you and Garnet. You're investigating the Hicks murder and even though you think at the time Lake was the murderer, isn't it a bit excessive to go after you? I mean, if he was innocent."

"Because he thought we were closing in on Honey and she was his meal ticket."

"What? You're kidding. Now you think Honey killed her husband?"

"She was in the vicinity and she may have played some part. But no, I don't think she killed him, " I said. "On the other hand, it's possible Lake believed she did it."

"And he didn't want you to prove that."

"It's also possible he thought we were on the verge of pinning the old hit and run case on Honey."

"So you think he attacked you and Garnet to protect Honey."

"To protect his interests, yeah."

"But you said he was smart. Attacking you and Garnet wasn't a 'smart move'."

"Only because I happened to live. Remember there were no witnesses to either assault. More Lake's style, don't you think?"

"Maybe."

"You see my problem?"

"Yeah."

"If Lake didn't kill Hicks and his wife didn't do it either…"

"Then who did?"

"I don't know," I said.

"Jack, can't you just do what Tiny said?"

"What was that?"

"Move on."

I'd been back in Grand Bend for less than a day and Sheila already wanted to kick me out of the house, a sign I had to stop being a major annoyance. By way of apology, I asked her to join me for a run on the beach. I even wore the Spandex running shorts Sheila bought me months, or maybe it was years, ago.

"What's with the olive branch?" she said.

"What do you mean?"

"You're not wearing your checkered Bermuda shorts. Or the beige ones with a million pockets."

"I'm trying to prove I'm not such a big pain in the ass."

"Find something useful to do, like another case to solve, and you're half way there."

"How do I achieve the other half?"

"Take me out for dinner tonight."

"That all?"

"Later you can finish taking care of the other half."

But I ruined the second half of the remedy during dessert when I asked Sheila whether her friend, Dianne McLeod, could get me a copy of the Hicks autopsy report.

forty six

DETECTIVE SERGEANT DIANNE MCLEOD WORKS for the Ontario Provincial Police, the Western Region Crime Unit, located in London, and although Collingwood is outside her jurisdiction, I knew she'd have contacts. I phoned her, at home, but not before Sheila greased the wheels. Even though I like to believe Dianne and I get along fine.

"I nearly let it go to message," she said to me, by way of hello.

Sometimes, I really hate call display. "Didn't Sheila talk with you?"

"It's why I picked up, Jack."

"How's Melissa?" I said.

Melissa is Dianne's six year old. A real sweetheart, she lets me push her on the swings in the backyard and we play 'hockey ding-ball,' as she calls it, in the kitchen. We have something called 'rapport.'

Truth? whenever there's a get together and Dianne tells Sheila it's okay to bring me, I seek out the kids. Otherwise, I'm stuck with the adults whose topics of conversation range from the price of real estate to the state of the stock market and then back again.

"Sheila tells me you want the autopsy on this guy, Dwayne Curtis Hicks."

"Did you get it?"

"Yeah."

"Man, that was fast."

"Ever hear of a fax machine?"

"I think there's one in my computer."

"But I'm guessing you haven't found it. Am I right?"

"I haven't really looked very hard yet."

"And people hire you."

"So, can you fax the fax to me?"

"Not even if you could actually tell me your fax number, Jack."

"Why not?"

"I'm sticking my neck out, you moron, way out. I don't want you having a hard copy to leave lying around the coffee shop."

"So, I should drop by?"

"Not without Sheila."

Sheila was happy to take an afternoon off to drive to London, although she's never thrilled with the prospect of another brouhaha breaking out between her friend and me.

Dianne opened the door, hugged Sheila and ignored me, not counting the complaint about breaking one of her favourite tea cups the last time Melissa and I played hockey ding-ball. This time Dianne's china set faced no real danger. Melissa was visiting her father's house, leaving me with no one to play with.

While Sheila and Dianne had coffee and cookies in the family room, I took the autopsy report into the dining room. And in no time flat, I learned that Hicks did not die of natural causes. Seemed a straightforward conclusion to have reached. Because apparently, a knife slicing through the aorta is a trauma that falls outside of the norm, something that is prone to cause cardiac arrest.

The report described the victim as a six foot one inch, medium-build male who outwardly appeared to be healthy but who inwardly showed a) the beginnings of liver damage and b) an enlarged heart, the latter point fitting with a notion that had been nagging away at me.

I read more details about the damage a knife in the chest causes. But then, the autopsy got confusing over the matter of 'toxicological tests.'

As a former Chief of Police for a pinprick on the map called Grand Bend, I didn't often have occasion to read technical reports. And when I did, I usually had a translator.

Luckily, Dianne was on hand.

"What's the 'Dillie-Koppanyi' test for?" I shouted into the living room.

"Barbiturates."

"Not a smart thing to mix with alcohol," I said more to myself than to the women in the other room, because I noticed, as I was saying the words, that the result was negative. And the next few test results were negative too.

Just when I thought I'd been wasting my time, I came to a section with a lot more words, put into sentences and paragraphs. That caught my eye. The title told me an 'ultraviolet spectroscopy' was performed. Fortunately, I didn't have to pronounce the term because the last line revealed what I needed to know – blood analysis showed the presence of amphetamines.

I read through the rest of the autopsy report. There was no further mention of the positive test for 'uppers,' the little magic pills which prompt the fight or flight response, increase your energy and produce a high. There were no details, no observations connecting back to the results of the ultraviolet spectroscopy, no implications and no speculations. 'Amphetamines present,' that was all. Everything else left up in the air.

"This report's kind of sketchy isn't it?" I shouted.

"I doubt it," Dianne shouted back.

I went into the family room and took a spot beside Sheila on the couch, out of Dianne's striking range.

"Who asked you to join us?" she said.

Sheila chuckled.

"They found amphetamines but they don't say how much," I said.

"So?"

"So, why not? Why not say it was a trace amount? Or, the stuff was spilling out of his ears?"

"That's all that test does. Tells you the amphetamines are there. Or they aren't."

"Are there other tests to tell you how much?"

"Quantity depends how much he took and how long they were in the system. No way to know that. Besides, when the cause of death is so obvious – and last time I checked a knife in the heart is pretty suggestive of cause - they just do a screening for drugs and toxins."

"And what," I said, "the presence of uppers isn't worth following up?"

"I heard the guy was a doper."

"So, you guys hear he's a user, you see no reason to look deeper. To ask questions."

"What questions?"

"My information is he stopped using, and if that's true, why were the drugs present?"

"Who says he stopped?"

"His wife."

"Wives never lie?"

"I never saw any reason for her to lie about that. I think he really did quit."

"So he quit. He slipped back."

"Speculation."

Dianne paused, maybe to let out some of the steam.

"Got any beer in the fridge?" I said, thinking we could all use a break.

Dianne didn't agree. "I have plenty of beer but you can't have any."

"I can't?"

"No. Because you're pissing me off with all the frigging questions. And the implied criticisms. Shit Jack, it wasn't even my case."

"I know," I said. "It was that jackass, Smith. It was his case."

"He is a jackass," she said, the first time we'd agreed on anything since the day we met.

I blew her a kiss.

She gave me the finger.

forty seven

ON OUR RETURN TRIP TO the Bend, Sheila said, "You're going to Collingwood, again, aren't you? And not just to visit Garnet."

When I didn't answer she said, "Can't you just call Smith?"

"I could but it's the kind of thing you do in person."

"What kind of thing?"

"Ask him why he didn't know about Hicks' heart condition."

"What?"

"And why he didn't know about his high blood pressure."

"I don't understand."

"And how he explains why Hicks would risk taking amphetamines when he knew the strain they put on his heart."

"Jack, Hicks was stabbed. All this health and drug stuff. What's the relevance?"

"I won't know until I find out," I said.

"And Smith should have found out?"

"Damn right."

At 2:30 in the afternoon the next day, I put my questions to the Detective Constable. As luck would have it, his boss happened to be at the station. So my meeting with Smith turned into a pissing match between Boroski and me. And in the middle of all the shouting, Smith broke into the fight long enough to say, his onion-breath mouth three inches from my face, that he intended to do nothing to correct 'the oversights.' Because there weren't any 'goddamn oversights.'

I figured he came to his decision quicker than he might have were it just him and me. But the decision wouldn't have been any different.

And my next steps were no different than they would have been if we'd never had our little meeting. I needed to find J.D. Morgan, hoping to God he'd refute the loose theory that was jingling around in my brain. I tried the trucking firm where he worked. I checked the bars and coffee shops. I phoned his house. There was no answer anywhere. Not until later that evening. The same husky voice I spoke with the last time I went looking for Morgan gave me the clue I needed.

I picked the guy out the second I entered the Heart Breakers tavern. He was drunk and belligerently getting nowhere with a tipsy black haired bar hopper in a denim mini and tight, black, lace-frilled tank top. Giving up, he scanned the rest of the playing field.

"Hello, handsome," I said, blowing him a kiss.

"There you are, you son of a bitch." It was like he was expecting me and I'd arrived two hours late.

Unlike our first encounter, this time I didn't need a minder. This time, I was stone sober. But J.D. surprised me anyway. He was a fast drunk, giving the other patrons barely enough time to clear a path as he eliminated the twenty feet that separated us. But he moved too fast for his own good. And it gave me the advantage you need against a bigger opponent. I took half a step to the right and leaned the same way, while catching his front foot with my left. I reached out for him, planning to facilitate his fall, but he was already by me. And he flew out the door, head first.

I followed him out double time and watched him fly off the low ramp, which hugged the outside wall, and he skidded face down across the gravel. As I reached him, he was still sprawled out but making like he meant to get up. I dived onto his back, my forearm driving him further into the stones, trying to trench a ditch with his forehead.

His low groan told me it was over.

I let him catch his breath, grabbed two handfuls of flannel and pulled him to a sitting position. It wasn't easy. Morgan was thick and wide and none of it was fat.

"Buy you a beer, J.D.?" I said.

He looked at me and called me a son of a bitch again. But then he nodded his head. We walked back into the bar and I was careful to make him go first.

A waitress brought a wet towel, a pitcher of draught and two glasses. I filled his.

He used the towel to clean the dirt and blood from his face and informed me, "You don't fight fair." He extracted a small sharp stone from his lower lip.

"What's fair? Standing toe to toe? Giving you the chance to pound the crap out of me? What's fair to you isn't going to be fair to the other guy."

He spit a mouthful of bloody saliva onto the floor and downed his glass in one swallow. Mine sat empty.

"I have some questions," I said.

"'Bout what?"

"About the night Dwayne Hicks was killed."

"Why you asking me?"

"There's a rumour you know something."

"Who you been talking to?"

"Didn't need to go far. You've been shooting your mouth off all over the place." I saw no reason to bring Maddie's name into it.

"Bullshit."

Given his attitude, I came at him through a side door. "You been staying clear of Carrie?"

"Screw you."

"Because if I find out you've been harassing her…"

"The bitch doesn't want anything to do with me."

"True, but you followed her that night anyway, didn't you J.D.," I said, hoping for denial. Still wanting him to prove my theory wrong.

He didn't.

"I just went to the hotel to party. Along with everyone else."

"Carrie was there too though, wasn't she?"

"Yeah. So what?"

"She with Rob?" I said, still hoping for an answer I liked.

"No," he said, disappointing me again.

"She was sitting at the bar with that asshole Hicks."

"Liar," I said.

"Fuck you."

"If you're telling me just the two of them were having a drink, I don't believe it. She couldn't stand Hicks. Why'd she be having a drink with him?"

"Wasn't just Carrie. Another woman, too."

"Who?"

"The one with big hair, all the time squeezes her big ass into tight pants."

"Leopard skin?"

"I guess."

"Penny Sue Stanfield?"

"Yeah. Her."

"Where was Garnet?"

"Probably sleeping it off somewhere."

"What'd you see, J.D.? A couple of women sitting down for a drink with a guy. No big deal in that. What'd you see?"

"Hicks and fat ass left together. He had trouble staying upright."

"You see where they went?"

"Took the elevator."

"You could see the elevator from where you sat?"

"Uh huh."

"What time was this?"

"Fuck if I know."

"What'd Carrie do after Penny Sue and Hicks left?"

"Finished her drink."

"Then what?"

"Hell, I don't know, man."

"J.D., you've been stalking the woman. And there was no other reason for an Elvis-hating, Kenny Chesney fan to be in that place. So goddamn it, tell me, where did Carrie go when she finished her drink."

"She left."

"Where'd she go? You followed her into the lobby, didn't you?"

"She told me to get lost."

"She's been telling you the same thing for years. You just don't listen."

"No one tells me where to go."

"Then what?"

"What do you mean?"

"I mean you're in the lobby watching her. Or, maybe you're standing right beside her and she's trying to get rid of you. I don't care about the details. What I want to know is this - where did Carrie go?"

"She got on the elevator."

"What floor did she go to?"

Needing a drink, I filled my glass, took a long pull and waited, knowing what he was going to say. But hoping he wouldn't.

"Five."

"The fifth floor? You sure?"

Hicks' room was on the fifth floor.

Hicks was murdered on the fifth floor.

forty eight

EARLY THE NEXT MORNING, CARRIE LOOKED up and jumped. She'd been beside Garnet, half dozing in a chair at the head of the bed.

"How's he doing?" I said.

"Hard to tell."

That he was off the ventilator was major but there were no signs he was getting ready to come out of his coma. I sat in the other chair, on the opposite side of the bed.

We watched Garnet for a few minutes.

Then Carrie said, "Penny Sue's paying some of Garnet's bills."

"Good."

"And she's been selling off her Elvis Collection."

"She tell you that?" I said.

Her eyes questioned my tone of voice.

We fell silent again.

That lasted until I got up the nerve.

"Was it your knife?" I said, looking into her face.

"What?"

"Was it your knife?"

She turned her head from my glare and looked at her father, searching for help and finding none.

I didn't like her reaction.

Carrie looked out the window behind me and to my left, allowing me to read the real answers in her face.

"Did you spike his drink?" I said.

"I don't know what you're talking about."

I wanted to believe her but she wasn't doing a very good job of convincing me.

"Why were you having a drink with Hicks?" I asked, turning the clock on that evening back a couple of hours from the moment of death.

"Who told you that?"

"It was a public place."

Carrie's pursed lips and wandering eyes searched for the right phrases.

"Penny Sue was the one having a drink," she said. "I just sat down to find out what the hell she was doing with that bastard."

"What'd you find out?"

"Nothing much. The woman's nuts. Does crazy things. You want the honest truth?"

"Yeah."

"I think she wanted his sash. She kept looking at it. Feeling the material. And Hicks let her. Which was strange. In fact, it wasn't just the situation that was strange. He was strange."

"How so? Was he drunk? Stoned?"

"Maybe both."

"Why'd you follow them?"

"What do you mean?"

"Penny Sue and Hicks left together. And you followed them."

"Why are you doing this, Jack?"

"Doing what?"

"Saying these things."

"You didn't follow them?"

"I didn't."

"You were seen getting on the elevator and going to the fifth floor."

"So?"

"So, Hicks' room was on the fifth floor."

"So was Penny Sue's. I was going up to see my Dad."

"Did you?"

"Yeah."

"You saw Garnet. Why?"

"Why what?"

"Why did you want to see him?"

"We were slowly patching things up. I just wanted to see him."

"But he was drunk?"

"Yeah. Passed out."

"Then what?"

"I left."

forty nine

I RETREATED TO MADDIE'S GRILL, arriving well after the early risers and just before the coffee break crowd. The restaurant had a different feel to it but it was a full minute before I figured it out.

Leona, Connie's number two server after Maddie, sidled over with a fresh pot.

"Hello Jack," she said.

"Where's Maddie?"

"Don't worry, dearie. I know how to pour coffee."

I grinned an apology. I decided months ago, Leona was not someone to be trifled with.

"Bless her heart," she said. "Maddie's gone."

"Gone?" I didn't like the sounds of that.

"Yeah. Just up and announced she's taking an extended vacation on the back of a Harley Davidson motor bike. At least that's what she called it – an extended vacation. Southwest U.S. of A."

"With the big guy, covered in tattoos and hair?"

"Yeah. Name's Tiny," she said. "Oh wait, you know him don't you?"

"Not as well as I thought," I said.

"Never figured on Maddie running off, either."

"And with Tiny Cole."

Leona and I had a good laugh.

The coffee cleared my head.

I pulled out my cell.

"Congratulations," I said, "You just won two free tickets to Nassau in the Bahamas."

"No thank you," the voice said, ruining my sales pitch by disconnecting the line. Penny Sue Stanfield was home.

Even though it was damaged, I had decided to give her Collingwood Elvis' belt buckle, the one that deflected the gunshot that was meant to kill me. I figured it would serve as a collector's piece, with an interesting footnote attached. Besides, I needed to get rid of it. Sheila found it upsetting whenever she looked at the thing sitting on my desk in my office.

She opened the door and I handed the damaged keepsake over.

Unlike the last time we met, Penny Sue acted happy to see me, inviting me in for a drink, throwing her arms around me and squashing her impressive chest against me. Must have been the gift.

She pointed me to a chair and we talked about past events. But at the mention of Garnet's name, Penny Sue's mood broke. And she burst into tears. I'm no good at the comforting thing, and I didn't feel like trying, especially not with her. I gave her a couple minutes but it wasn't enough. She left the room to compose herself.

That gave me the chance to snoop and I soon found what I was looking for.

When she returned, I held up the red sash and said, "I'm surprised the police let you have this, what with the murder trial just getting started."

She ambled over to the couch, like her mind was working as she went. She sat down, wiped her eyes and said, "Well, they did. They let me have it. And now hand it back to me."

I ignored her demand. "Strange," I said.

"What do you mean?"

"That the cops gave up the sash."

"They said there was no trace evidence."

"No tell-tale hairs. Or fibers,"

"That's right. They said there was no need for it. Or something along those lines. They said I may as well have it." Her voice was an octave higher and her tone was defensive.

"No, they didn't," I said.

Penny Sue Stanfield stiffened and just stared at me.

"The police said no such thing," I said again.

"Oh yes they did."

"No Penny Sue, they didn't. You know how I know that?"

Though she turned red in the face and she still wasn't answering, I decided she might be curious nonetheless. So I told her. "I know because I talked to the cop in charge of the evidence room. According to him, you never came into the station to talk to him, or to anybody else."

"What are you talking about?"

"I'm telling you, Penny Sue, you never asked the cops for the sash."

"Then you talked to the wrong cops."

"Doesn't matter who I talked to. I know you didn't go there."

"What makes you so damn sure?"

"You've had this authentic Elvis scarf ..."

"It's a sash."

"Whatever. You've had it all along."

"You don't know what you're talking about."

"Yeah, I do. This sash is real. And you took it off the body."

"I did not."

"You did. After you killed him, you wrapped a replica sash around Hicks' neck."

"You're a liar."

"I've asked myself why. Strangulation wasn't the cause of death. Drugs slowed him up. Maybe caused his weak ticker to speed up, act erratically. But it was the knife wound that stopped his heart. So, if you wanted to switch the sash I wondered why not tie the thing around his waist? Just like the original?"

Penny Sue went bug-eyed.

"Then it hit me," I said, answering the question. "It's easy enough to slip a sash off a dead body. But not so easy tying the replacement back on. Dead people are heavy and they usually don't cooperate when you're trying to dress them. When you're trying to make the sash look right, look even. That's hard to do with a dead man. Isn't that right, Penny Sue?"

"I wasn't even there."

"You told me you looked in. You saw Mike over the body."

"You're mixing me up."

"You poisoned him, Penny Sue," I said, holding onto the hope she acted alone. Praying Carrie Griffith told the truth, that she was not involved. "But why stab him?"

"I...I..."

"Why couldn't you wait? You told me once you were a nurse. You know all about drugs and their side effects."

"No."

"You fed him a good dose of amphetamines, didn't you? Enough to cause a bad heart to flat-line? But not so much to make a medical examiner suspicious."

"No."

"You drugged him. And then you left him. But you didn't wait long enough for the drugs to take their course, did you?" You wanted that sash. So you went back for it. But he wasn't dead, was he? Maybe he was on the road to cardiac arrest, but he wasn't quite ready yet, was he? Not for an authentic death, anyway. Not like Elvis."

"Don't you dare bring his name into it," she said referring to her idol.

"What was it Penny Sue? Hicks wasn't gone far enough?" I went at her again. "Did you miscalculate? The amphetamines and booze weren't doing the job? Were you afraid he'd call the cops? Implicating you?"

"You don't know what you're talking about."

She looked around and I wondered if she was looking for something she could use as a weapon. Then her eyes stopped searching and she looked down and shook her head. Like she just gave up.

"You know what this means, Penny Sue?"

"What?"

"It was premeditated. You planned to kill him and you did. For a frigging piece of fabric."

"That wasn't why I did it."

"So, tell me."

"I did it for Garnet."

"I know," I said.

"You do?"

"Tell me about it anyway."

"It wasn't about the sash. Sure, the sash was there. I knew about it. I never thought anybody would ever notice the difference. But..."

"The main thing was killing Hicks, right?"

"Garnet couldn't do it. He couldn't bring himself to kill the man. As much as he wanted to. He could never kill anyone in cold blood. Even the piece of dirt who ruined his life. Who ruined my life."

"Your life?"

"Yeah, after Garnet's wife died, he took up with me. We were going to be married."

"And then the accident happened?"

"It wasn't an accident. Maiming someone with your car while you're under the influence is no goddamn accident."

"No argument here."

"After that, everything fell apart for Garnet and me. He took to drinking more heavily than ever before. He lost his job. And Carrie got mad at him. And I..."

"And you were alone again. With your collection."

"Yes."

I paused to think through my next question.

"Tell me Penny Sue, why did you implicate Sheila's brother?"

"What do you mean?"

"The phone call. You called and said you were Honey Hicks. And you invited Mike up to the room. Only it was Dwayne's room. Not hers."

"Bull."

"It stands to reason - if you killed Hicks then the caller had to be you. You were convincing, too. Mike was sure it was Honey Hicks who called."

"I never called him. But I did see him there."

Her statement struck a cord. After confessing to murder why would she lie about a phone call? I could see no reason.

Well, he got the goddamn phone call, I was sure of that, And it was a pretty safe bet Mike would have been doing his listening with his dick.

"Okay, let's pretend I believe you. You didn't call him."

She looked off.

"If you didn't call him," I said next, "why'd you tell me about seeing him there?"

"Just acting on opportunity. Shifting the attention elsewhere. I never thought he'd get charged."

"Bullshit, Penny Sue. You wanted him to take the fall for the murder."

"It was convenient, yeah."

"And the dumb bugger managed to help your cause considerably. Leaving fingerprints. Wiping Hicks blood on his own shirt."

"Yes."

"Tell me - what did Mike ever do to you?"

"He's just another hack impersonator."

"Offensive to true fans?"

"Something like that."

"You need help," I told her.

"A lawyer."

"I was thinking of a head doctor."

She gave me a blank look.

"Hicks did it, you know," she said.

"You mean he ran Carrie and Rob over?"

"I have proof."

"What kind of proof?"

"One time when he was drunk. I overheard him crying in his beer."

"You and Hicks don't travel in the same crowd."

"It was at last year's festival. In the hotel bar. Late. He'd been drinking the whole day. Honey tried to shut him up but I heard."

"He confessed?"

"He said enough."

"I understand there's a possibility Honey was the driver."

"No."

"Garnet figured she was there."

"She was. Which means she's as much to blame as he was."

"So, you decided to do what Garnet wanted to do but couldn't."

"Yes," she said. "And when the cops arrested Mike Mackie and you and Garnet started chasing down Peter Lake for the murder, I thought 'this is good'."

"All kinds of suspects to divert attention?

"Yes. I thought I was home free."

"You were. Until the bastards shot Garnet."

"And that was my fault."

"Garnet's shooting? I thought you blamed me for that. How do you figure it's your fault now?"

"If I hadn't killed Hicks…"

"Sure. A lot of crappy things wouldn't have happened. But…"

That's when she pulled the gun from between the cushions.

"Part of the Elvis collection?" I asked, knowing the answer. The king was almost as hooked on guns as he was on drugs.

"Cost me plenty."

"Authentic?"

"Of course."

"Good working condition?"

"It works fine," she said.

I rose to my feet.

"Where do you think you're going?"

"I'm leaving, Penny Sue."

"I'll shoot, you son of a bitch."

When I reached the door, I heard the revolver's hammer click. Once. A second time. And a third.

"Jack! Stop. What are you going to do?"

"I'll think on it," I said, stuffing the sash into the left front pocket of my Bermuda shorts and the bullets from her revolver into the right, and walking out the door.

fifty

IT WAS PENNY SUE'S WORD against mine. But I told Smith and Boroski about our conversation anyhow, leaving out the part where she pulled a gun on me and squeezed the trigger three times.

A couple days later, Boroski was decent enough to phone and let me know Penny Sue Stanfield signed a confession, the Readers' Digest version of which said she drugged and then stabbed Dwayne Curtis Hicks to death. But he didn't have enough decency left over to thank me for my role in the collar.

I closed the file but I bookmarked the last page, thinking I would like to have been there to hear the confession first hand. Not that Boroski's version of Penny Sue's confession didn't have the ring of truth to it. She admitted her guilt to me. It's just that, at the time, she was a little vague about parts of it.

And I kept thinking about J.D.'s story. But as Maddie said, you can't rely on two thirds of what a drunk tells you. Except in my head, the murder scene as I imagined it got confused by all the traffic, all the people going to and coming from Hicks' room.

I moped around the coffee shop and Sheila never once mentioned my mood.

Not until a week passed.

We'd just finished a fast 10K run and a shower. Sheila sat me down in my favourite chair, in front of my favourite window, with a coffee and butter tarts. And I knew a serious discussion was due to start any minute.

"You're not talking," she said.

"I don't talk most of the time."

"You're not talking more often than you used to."

"Lot on my mind."

"Like what?"

"I tell you about Tiny and Maddie?" I said, hoping it was a topic that would satisfy.

"She ran off with him to go on a big bike tour. You already told me."

"Now Tiny's talking about making it long term."

"Maddie and Tiny, married? No way."

"Not sure how they're defining 'long term.'"

"Does Maddie know what she's doing?"

"Yeah. She thinks Tiny Cole is the sexiest son of a bitch she's ever known."

"She tell you that?"

"More or less."

"And after having met you, too."

"World's a crazy place."

"What else you got on your mind, Jack?"

"Guy I know - his bitch just had a litter," I said.

"What kind?"

"Yellow lab."

"I love labs."

"I came into some new money," I said.

"How so?"

"In a way, it's from Penny Sue."

"What?"

"She had a real, authentic Elvis sash."

"No kidding."

"Yup."

"And?"

"And, I took it from her."

"What?"

"The sash. It wasn't really hers, anyway. She took the thing from Hicks' dead body in the first place. And who knows how Hicks really got it."

"You stole the sash?"

"Actually, I confiscated it."

"Why?"

"It's valuable."

"And?"

"I sold it on EBay. While I was in Collingwood."

"You don't know how to sell stuff on-line."

"Roy Orbison's double and his buddies helped me. Somehow, they were able to drive the price up."

"How much did you get?"

"Five thousand and change."

"What'd you do with the money."

"I kept the change."

"How much?"

"About three hundred."

"What'd you do with it?"

"Nothing yet but I could use it to buy one of the pups. How's that sound?"

"Good," she said.

"I think so, too."

"What about the five grand?"

"I'm going to give it to Garnet's daughter and his son-in-law."

"That's good, too."

"Thanks."

"Your welcome. But it didn't work, Jack."

"Huh?"

"As happy as I am for Tiny and Maddie. And for us, getting a dog. And for Carrie, getting the sash money….That stuff's not really what's on your mind."

"What's on my mind?"

"The case isn't closed."

I may have grunted. Sarcastically.

"Hughie says he's going to argue diminished capacity," I said. Now that Mike was off the hook, I convinced my longtime lawyer friend to represent Penny Sue Stanfield.

"That going to work?"

"I think she's crazy enough to fit the criteria," I said.

"Good. She needs help."

"It's for the best."

Sheila sipped her coffee and leaned back. Two regular customers came in and she smiled at them as they approached the counter. Apparently, she concluded our teenaged staffers could handle their orders without interference from the old folks. Sheila joined me in gazing out the window. Two poker players, waiting for the other to tip his hand.

"Nice try, Jack," she said, playing what she may have thought was a pair of aces.

"Huh?"

"Five minutes ago, I said the case isn't closed yet."

"It wasn't anywhere near five minutes."

"Am I right?"

"Not really."

"I am right."

"No."

"What is it then? What's on your mind?"

"Just a few loose ends."

"So I was right. The case isn't closed."

"No. Really, it's closed," I said, though I was no longer sure of that. "As I just said – loose ends. That's all."

"Loose ends? Like, who called Mike?"

"And convinced the guy to show up at a murder scene…"

"Was it Penny Sue?"

"Her answers were evasive."

"Who then?"

"I usually don't believe in coincidences but I think in this case it's the only sensible explanation."

"I'm not following, Jack."

"You talked to your sister-in-law."

"It wasn't Lori, for God's sake."

"No, but she played a part."

"Meaning…"

"She was having an affair with Hicks."

"How's that play into it?" she said, adding, "the little tramp."

"And your brother's an innocent?"

"Keep to the topic."

"Okay… Lori and Hicks. I figure Lori was meeting him that night."

"No way. She was at the hotel?"

"Yeah."

"You could be mistaken. She could have been looking for Mike," she said, but there was no conviction left in her words.

"No. She went there to meet up with Hicks. And I believe somehow Honey found out."

"About the meeting?"

"Yeah."

"So?"

"So, she tried to arrange a confrontation. She wanted Mike to find Lori and Hicks together."

"You think Honey asked Mike to meet her and gave him Hicks' room number."

"Yeah. But the timing was off. By minutes but it may as well have been an eternity."

"Was Lori the witness at the door?"

"She may have been. Maybe she saw Mike leaning over Hicks and then she disappeared in the chaos. Or more likely it really was Penny Sue at the door. And Lori arrived after the excitement started and snuck away before anyone saw her. The place was busier than Union Station at rush hour. In either case, the outcome's the same. Hicks was murdered and neither Honey nor Lori did that."

"No, it was Penny Sue."

I hesitated to think through what to say next but Sheila jumped ahead on the script.

"Wait a minute. You don't think it was Penny Sue? I don't believe this Jack! Is that the other loose end? After all this time, you don't think Penny Sue was the murderer?"

"Don't put words in my mouth. Penny Sue's a killer. But…"

"You're not sure."

"As I said, there's a loose end. One final question."

"Just say it, Jack."

"It's Carrie. She's the loose end."

"Pardon?"

"I'm sure Carrie knows more than she's saying."

"How are you sure?"

"I know." Although there are varying degrees of knowing.

"Talk to her, then."

Which was the right thing to do, of course. But sometimes it's hard.

"Do you feel sorry for Carrie?" I said.

The question puzzled her.

But she answered anyway. "Yeah, she's had it rough."

"Which brings us to my problem. One of them in any case."

"What do you mean?"

"She won't give up," I said.

"She wants Honey Hicks held accountable for the hit and run accident?"

"Something like that."

"You going to help her?"

"Should I?"

"Yeah, you should."

"Hmm."

"Will you?"

"Depends."

It was something I would decide after I got the truth out of her.

fifty one

SHE WAS ALONE WITH GARNET. And she didn't invite me to stay, even though I just handed her a cheque for five thousand dollars.

"I talked to Penny Sue," I said.

"When?"

"Just before she confessed."

"So?"

"Confused woman."

"What'd she tell you?"

"As I said, she's confused."

Her shoulders lost some of the tension.

I took a seat and asked my question across the prone body of her father, "Why didn't you tell me the whole story?"

"What do you mean?"

"What really happened that night, on the fifth floor?"

"I told you."

"You said you went up to see your Dad but he wasn't in good enough shape for visitors. I want to know what happened after you left Garnet's room."

"What about it?"

"You passed an open door."

"No."

"Yes. Hicks' door was open, wasn't it?"

"No, Jack."

"Maybe Penny Sue had already left. You looked in, to see whether the drugs worked."

"No."

"Except Penny Sue didn't know what she was doing, did she Carrie? What did she tell you when she left Hicks' room? That he was unconscious and near death?"

"She told me nothing."

"Sure she did."

"You can't trust anything Penny Sue says."

"It's not about what she says. It's about what makes sense."

Carrie shook her head and looked down at her father's quilt-covered legs.

"And then," I said, "maybe you looked in. You couldn't see anything. So you couldn't resist pushing the door the rest of the way open. To go in, to see if he expired."

"You're way out of line, Jack."

"Or maybe Penny Sue was still there?"

Carrie stood and went to the window. I joined her. A raptor soared high over the field behind the rest home. It circled and then it plummeted, focused on the kill.

Then she looked at me. "No," she said. "You were right the first time. She'd gone."

It wasn't the answer I hoped for. It was the answer I expected.

"Where was Hicks?"

"He was there. And he wasn't there."

"What do you mean?"

"His eyes were all glossed over. He couldn't stand up, not without swaying. And shaking. Never seen him so drunk. At least I thought he was drunk."

"He wasn't drunk." I didn't say he was suffering from a drug overdose because I wanted to hear what Carrie had to say next.

"Well, I thought he was drunk."

"Then what?"

"I shouldn't have, but just like you said - I walked in. I planned to ask him point blank, was he the driver? Did he run Rob and me down?"

"Then what happened?"

"He saw me."

"I thought he was already facing your way."

"He was. But I don't think I registered at first."

"And when you did register?"

"I never even got the chance to say a single word to him. He just started screaming."

"Screaming what?"

"He said, 'Where the fuck is Penny Sue.?' Then he said something about her poisoning him."

"But you knew all about that."

"Actually Jack, I didn't."

I looked into her face. It didn't seem like a lie. But I'd been wrong so often. While I was trying to read through the defiance, Carrie picked up the story, "That's when I saw the knife."

"You picked it up?"

"No. It was in his hand."

"Hicks had the knife? Did he come at you?"

She didn't answer my question.

Instead, she said, "Then, he starts accusing me."

"Of what?"

"Of trying to kill him."

"He thought you and Penny Sue…"

"I don't know, Jack."

"That's all he said?"

"That's all that made sense."

I knew what to ask next, except I didn't want to say it. But Carrie saved me the trouble.

"That's when it happened."

"What happened?"

"I killed him."

"Tell me."

"He took a step my way."

"Threatening you?"

"That's what I keep telling myself."

"How'd it go down, Carrie?"

"I moved away, circled the couch. He followed. I waited."

"You waited?"

"Yeah. Then he took a swipe at me."

"And you took his knife away?"

"It wasn't hard."

"You could have run away. He was all doped up, wasn't he?"

"I don't know, Jack."

"And then what?"

"I stabbed the bastard."

"You wipe the handle clean?"

"I don't remember."

"And you left the room?"

"Yeah."

"Anybody see you?"

"No." But there was a hesitation.

"You saw Penny Sue as you ran away, didn't you? She was coming back wasn't she Carrie, to check on Hicks," I said. And to get the sash, I thought.

Ignoring my speculations, she said, "I killed him, Jack."

I moved away from the window and so did Carrie. Then I turned my eyes to Garnet and then back to Carrie again.

I wasn't lost anymore. I knew what to do.

I opened my back pack, retrieved a CD and slid it into the player on Garnet's bedside table.

"What's that?"

"Your dad and I liked the same music."

Tears filled her eyes.

"And I made a promise."

"To make him a CD?"

"To make one for both of us."

She read the label I wrote on the cover, "Fakeouts?"

"He knows what I'm talking about."

I pressed the play button and walked out of the room.

"Jack?" she called to me from the doorway.

I was already at the end of the hallway but I looked back and I thought about the question in her eyes. I retraced my last ten steps. The question was still there begging for an answer. And then I told her, "He was dying anyway."

She mouthed her thanks.

I didn't want her gratitude. At least not then.

So I left Carrie to beat back her own demons.

For my part, I needed to find Sheila, even though I knew what she would say. But still needing to hear her say it: "Jack, you did the right thing."

Collingwood Fakeout

Copyright © 2009 by Rick Hundey

rickhundey.fauxpop.tv